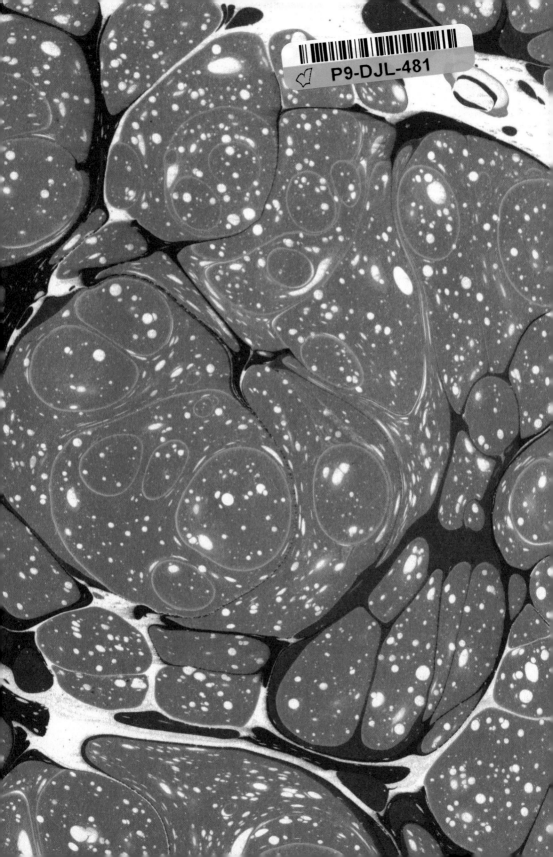

A BRIGHT MOON FOR FOOLS

A BRIGHT MOON FOR FOOLS

JASPER GIBSON

A Herman Graf Book
Skyhorse Publishing

First North American edition published in 2015 by Skyhorse Publishing

First published in Great Britain by Inside The Dog Press, 2013
Paperback edition published in Great Britain by Simon & Schuster UK Ltd, 2014

"Sobremesa" by Eugenio Montejo, original Spanish version reprinted by kind permission, appears in Fábula del escriba (Editorial Pre-Textos, 2006)

"Sobremesa" by Eugenio Montejo, the English translation reprinted by kind permission, appears in In The Trees (Salt Publishing, 2004)

The author/editor and publisher gratefully acknowledge the permission granted to reproduce the copyright material in this book. Every effort has been made to trace copyright holders and to obtain their permission for the use of copyright material. The publisher apologizes for any errors or omissions in the above list and would be grateful if notified of any corrections that should be incorporated in future reprints or editions of this book.

Skyhorse Publishing books may be purchased in bulk at special discounts for sales promotion, corporate gifts, fund-raising, or educational purposes. Special editions can also be created to specifications. For details, contact the Special Sales Department, Skyhorse Publishing, 307 West 36th Street, 11th Floor, New York, NY 10018 or info@skyhorsepublishing.com.

Skyhorse® and Skyhorse Publishing® are registered trademarks of Skyhorse Publishing, Inc.®, a Delaware corporation.

Visit our website at www.skyhorsepublishing.com.

10 9 8 7 6 5 4 3 2 1

Library of Congress Cataloging-in-Publication Data is available on file.

Cover design by Lewis Heriz

Print ISBN: 978-1-63450-609-0
Ebook ISBN: 978-1-5107-0047-5

Printed and bound in the United States of America

For my mother, my father and my sisters

Sobremesa

Hesitantly, surrounded
by the mist that falls from days long gone,
we once more sit down to talk
and can't see each other.
Hesitantly, cut off in the depths of the mist.

On the table the breeze stirs slowly.
As we dream those who are absent draw close.
Loaves where bleak moss has passed long winters
now waken on the table-cloth.

Steam from the coffee cups drifts around us
and in the aroma we see old faces,
once more alive, float past
clouding the mirrors.

Empty chairs set straight
wait for those who, from far off,
will return later on.
We start talking
without seeing each other, without thought of time.

Hesitantly, in the mist
that grows and surrounds us,
we talk for hours without knowing
who is still alive and who is dead.

Eugenio Montejo
Muerte y Memoria (1972)

Sobremesa

A tientas, al fondo de la niebla
que cae de los remotos días
volvemos a sentarnos
y hablamos ya sin vernos.
A tientas, al fondo de la niebla

Sobre la mesa vuelve el aire
y el sueño atrae a los ausentes.
Panes donde invernaron musgos fríos
en el mantel ahora se despiertan.

Yerran vapores de café
y en el aroma, reavivados,
vemos flotar antiguos rostros
que empañan los espejos.

Rectas sillas vacías
aguardan a quienes, desde lejos,
retornarán más tarde.
Comenzamos a hablar
sin vernos y sin tiempo.

A tientas, en ha vaharada
que crece y no se envuelve,
charlamos horas sin saber
quién vive todavía, quién está muerto.

Eugenio Montejo
Muerte y Memoria (1972)

Caracas, Venezuela
2008

Caracas, Venezuela
2008

1

Harry Christmas strode out of Caracas airport with little more than a wallet full of stolen money and the dried-up brain of a long-haul drinker. Beyond the terminal building lay the sea. Beyond the car park there were mountains. The sunset was coronary.

Christmas bowed to an imaginary welcoming party and then turned to examine himself in one of the building's glass panels. Fifty-eight years old, fat, moustachioed, sporting a Panama hat, red trousers and a cream jacket, Harry Christmas flared his nostrils and sucked in his cheeks. He thought he looked *terrific*.

"*Señor?*" said the taxi driver, watching his fare with amazement. Christmas bared his teeth with a smile, then swept an arm forward, bidding him lead the way. It had been an eventful journey. Now Christmas was ready to gorge on the fatty pleasures of an international business hotel.

The two men arrived at a white Toyota. The driver held open a rear door, but Christmas headed for the front seat. They drove off towards the city in silence. The taxi driver looked at Christmas. Christmas looked at the taxi driver. They both looked at the road.

"Your trousers, *Señor* – they are on the wrong way round." Christmas looked down.

"Correct," he said. A further silence ensued. Night fell.

"So," said the taxi driver, trying again, "for how many days will you be here in Venezuela?"

"As long as it takes."

"What will you do here?"

"I'm on a mission."

"With no bags?"

"It's a pilgrimage."

"I'm sorry?"

"I'm here to see the sights," sighed Christmas. A truck rolled by, leaking smoke like a stricken Spitfire. "Breathe the air."

"My name is Pepito," said the taxi driver, offering one hand from the wheel. He had large, alarmed eyes, freckles and gelled hair. "Pepito Rodriguez Silvas."

"Harry Christmas," he replied with a shake, "*mucho gusto*."

"Are you a business man?"

"I want a drink."

The road, cutting through mountains, suddenly opened out to reveal hills rippled with lights. "Oh, how charming," said Christmas.

"That is the *barrio*," nodded Pepito. "You can go in there and they kill you."

As the traffic clogged and unclogged they shifted into Caracas, stacks of matchbox houses stuffed up against the El Ávila mountain range. The air was warm, the moon struggling through cloud. The city greeted Christmas blindly, feeling his face through the windscreen while Pepito swore at other motorists. It began to rain. Beggars flowed between the moving cars and crowded around the

2

bins. A pregnant woman selling packets of fried banana jumped to avoid a motorbike. Revolutionary murals covered every wall. Christmas noticed the driver was looking at his trousers again.

"How far to the hotel?"

"*No sé,*" he shrugged, "the traffic is a problem. But Gran Melía hotel is a very nice hotel. So what kind of business will you do here in Venezuela?"

"Freelance diplomat."

On through the streets they choked, past unfinished construction projects jutting out from shadow, past people running for shelter with jackets and newspapers held over their heads. "You want to go to a nightclub, *Señor*?" said Pepito, as they pulled up outside the hotel. "I can pick you up later. Nice place. Good show, live girls ..." He was bouncing his eyebrows.

"No, thank you. Here you go – keep the change."

"So I pick you up *mañana*?"

"No, thank you."

"In the morning?"

"I said 'no'. Thank you."

"You want, maybe, nine o'clock?"

"Oh well, in that case, perfect," huffed Christmas, intending never to see this man again. He hauled himself out of the taxi and squared up to the hotel. Pepito drove off. Christmas adjusted his hat and flexed his moustache. He was still drunk.

Like other hotels of its ilk, Gran Melía liked to punctuate its relentless shininess with hysterical flower arrangements and excessively polite staff. Staying here was an extravagance but, if Christmas hoped to make any progress in this town, impressions would be all-important. He identified and marched towards the reception desk, holding the receptionist's gaze so that she might not notice his trousers.

"Buenas noches, Señor."

"Harry Christmas," he beamed, "checking in." Christmas handed over a credit card and his passport. The receptionist busied herself at the computer. Everything was in order. His room key was in her hand.

"It's room 4422 – your luggage, *Señor?*" she queried, examining the empty space around his feet.

"I don't have any."

"No luggage?"

"Do you have any luggage?" Christmas demanded.

"Me, *Señor?*"

"Well, now that we've found some common ground, perhaps you could send two large glasses of Laphroaig up to my room." On the verge of replying, the receptionist hesitated. This guest had his trousers on the wrong way round.

"Thank you so much," he concluded, sliding the key from her fingers.

"*Señor*, if you can please ask to the room service—" but Christmas was off, giving the lobby a cursory sweep for lonely women before marching into the lift.

His room was large. Royal blue furnishings. Dark wood. He found the mini bar and inspected its contents. He checked the bathroom, acknowledging the shower with disdain. Showers symbolised everything that was wrong with the modern world: quick, loud, stupid. He caught sight of himself in the mirror and straightened up.

Christmas had been handsome in his youth, and though the strong face remained, his many vices had left him corpulent, with disgruntled skin and mottled teeth. Even his nose had grown fat, but Christmas saw only beauty. His cheekbones were bold, his eyes a furious blue. He admired his own moustache. He admired his head in his Panama, making imperceptible adjustments to its angle. He sat down on the bed, took off his shoes and trousers, stood up, and admired himself again.

A knock on the door. "What the devil is it now?" he barked. Outside was a man with two large glasses of single malt. "Bravo!" Christmas signed the bill with an indecipherable glyph. He took the drinks, kicked the door shut and downed one immediately. Gasping with satisfaction, he put the other on the bedside table and took off his hat and his socks. He examined his feet. He had always considered them to be rather fine – proportioned, elegant – and was pleased once again to confirm his own opinion. He took the remote control from its holder and turned on the television.

President Chávez, dressed in the colours of state, was making a speech to the assembly about proposed reforms to the constitution. He spoke like a boxing ring announcer, great undulations of pitch and rollings of the 'r'.

"*R-r-r-r-r-evolución*!" practised Christmas, turning it off. He drained the second scotch, undressed fully, and flopped back into bed. He yawned at the ceiling and felt fatigue grind into a deeper gear. Air travel be damned! There would be several palm-fanned evenings of tropical enterprise before he subjected himself again to that kind of institutionalised maltreatment. Christmas smiled. Yet here he was. He had escaped.

He reached over and turned off the light. His eyes adjusted to the dark.

He stopped smiling.

2

William Slade finished his exercises and lay on the floor of his living room, breathing heavily. He closed his eyes for a moment then rolled to his feet as if from a judo mat. He went to the window. He looked up the street and out into East Grinstead, making eye contact with his elderly neighbour who was getting out of her car. She looked away. Slade closed his curtains. He checked his watch.

In the middle of the room a rowing machine faced an enormous plasma screen television. On the opposite wall there was a set of barbells next to an IKEA bookshelf rigid with military history, biographies of war leaders, weapons manuals and books about the Dark Ages. On the floor, a kitbag lay beside neat piles of clothes. A large black leather armchair sat beneath the window and behind it, in the corner, a yucca plant was slowly dying.

The walls were white and bare except for two framed photographs. One was of fifty men dressed as *thegns* – Anglo-Saxon knights – wearing decorated woollen tunics, leg bindings, leather turnshoes and cloaks pinned to the shoulder with circular broaches. Some had broadswords, others battle-axes or maces. Slade stood in the middle next to the society's leader, the *eorlderman*, a retired West Sussex police chief. Under the photograph the caption read 'Battle of Hastings 2007 – *sle cowere feondas*', Old English for 'smite your enemies'. The second was of his father, Andrew Slade, and his stepmother Diana, taken at their old house in Crawley. His father sat behind his desk while Diana leant against it. Slade always thought she looked elegant in this photograph – her hair pulled back tight, her head high, the way she was standing with her arms folded, the long fingers of one hand not quite touching the elbow. His father was smiling and stroking his cat, The General. Beneath the desk, a young William sat cross-legged, hiding something behind him.

Kneeling on the floor beside his packing, Slade carefully pushed his clothes into his kitbag, followed by a travel wallet that could be strapped to his waist, a wash bag, his passport, a photograph in an envelope, one thousand pounds in cash, a credit card, sleeping pills, an iPod, leads, a charger, a plug adaptor and travel speakers all neatly wound together.

He was a bulky, cumbrous man with sacks of flesh saddled to his frame and a belly from all the pints, takeaways and Tesco meals for one. Thick black hair mossed his scalp above small eyes that withdrew into the permanent squint he'd been affecting since he was a teenager. He checked his watch again, straightened his back and rotated his shoulders.

Slade inspected the rest of the house, turning off light switches and plugs. Whenever he left a room he said, "Clear". Finally he came to the broom cupboard under the stairs and opened the door. Hanging from brackets on the wall there was a crossbow, a baseball bat, a double-headed war axe, a broadsword and twenty-three different knives. He took down an Austrian hunting knife with a seven-inch folding blade and a hilt made of antler. He selected this one because he had inherited it from his father. Slade shut the cupboard door, locked it and hid the key under the carpet. He went back into the living room and tucked the knife deep inside the kitbag.

3

Christmas lay in the dark trying to get comfortable. He felt too hot and stuck a leg out. Then he felt too cold and wrapped himself with the duvet. He rolled over and tried to ignore the steady disappearance of feeling in his right arm while reliving his escape: his arrival at Gatwick airport like a man in need of the toilet; his panicked purchase of a return ticket to Venezuela; the sensation of being hunted. There was a school sports team idling in front of the check-in desks. "Out of the way, you little shitters," he muttered, picking his way through the haircuts. Their extremely tall teacher said something to him in French – one of Christmas' favourite reasons to ignore someone – and he proffered his passport to the easyJet representative. With his mouth hung open in a smile and his mind fixed on a drink, he watched with satisfaction as she looked several times between photograph and subject. Yes, the new moustache made all the difference.

"Anything to check in, sir?"

"No, young lady, I have only my—"

"Did you pack these bags yourself, sir?"

"I don't have any luggage."

"Oh yeah!" she giggled, "Sorry. Mind's gone to pieces. Has anyone given you anything to carry?"

"No."

"Could anyone have interfered with your luggage?"

"I've told you I don't have any luggage."

"Oh yeah! Oi, Lisa, you'll never guess what I've just done ..." Christmas looked behind him. No one was in pursuit. There was, however, the lofty Frenchman with his arms folded, staring straight at him, trying to make some sort of physical point. Christmas pulled a face as if he'd just opened a fridge full of rotting food and then turned back to the desk. The girl and her colleague were weeping with laughter. An elderly couple looked on blankly. Christmas felt as if he were queuing for execution.

"Dear me, sorry, sir," the check-in girl said, bringing herself under control, "now then, here's your boarding pass. Seating code B, watch the departure board for times, gate number twelve. Have a good flight." Christmas tried to take the pass, but she held onto the end of it. "Aren't we going to say 'thank you'?"

"What?"

"That's it," she said, letting go. "And cheer up – it might never happen!" Had he not been so eager to get to the other side of customs, Christmas would have visited a swingeing verbal punishment on this brassy servant of The Rot. "Nice 'tache," she added, waving at him like a schoolgirl until the giant Frenchman stepped up to her counter. "Hello, sir. Right – security question: is it raining up there?"

No sooner had Christmas picked up some speed than he hit a queue. Teenagers in yellow jumpers were ordering people to join different lines. "Got any gels?" said one, "Creams? Hairsprays?"

"What do you think I am?" grunted Christmas, "An extremely ugly woman?"

Security always infuriated Christmas. Why should he have to prove he existed, the devil take them! He was real. The state on the other hand was pure construct. It should have to prove *its* existence to *him*. Christmas quelled the urge to ask the officer for his passport in return.

Shuffling. Undressing. Dressing. Shoes, belt, arms raised wide. Christmas breathed heavily through the indignity. However, once he was past the last gum-chewing staff member, his considerable frame was shot through with exhilaration. He looked back at the queue: the polished, empty faces of Europe. He'd made it. He had deliberately bought an indirect and open-ended ticket to Venezuela. Even if he were tracked to the airport, there was no way anyone could know his ultimate destination.

Gatwick airport departure lounge – an amphitheatre of tat. Christmas headed straight for Yates Wine Lodge for a remedial double scotch, trying to block out the conversations around him.

"... Don't watch it at all anymore."

"Oh God, me neither."

"I mean I don't think I've watched it in weeks."

"Did you see that whatsername yesterday? The one from whatsit?"

"God she looked fat!"

"What about those kids being forced to examine what was in their own poo?"

"... in Bangkok, he gets completely wasted and ends up fucking two prostitutes. Un-fucking-believable."

"But that's Bangkok, mate. Standard fucking practice."

"Not when you're on your honeymoon."

Christmas stood up in despair, deciding he should eat. He sat down again in Garfunkel's.

"And how do you want your steak, sir?"

"Right through the heart. And bring me a large scotch, would you? Laphroaig, no ice." Christmas watched the crowds and remarked to himself with no small sense of wonder how everyone seemed to be dressed for an amateur sporting event. Were Muslim women the only smart people left in England? A cheerless steak was plonked in front of him by his cheerless waitress. He ate it cheerlessly, consumed several glasses of scotch and asked for the bill.

"Is the tip included?"

"'Sh'd'no," she replied.

"*What?*" but she just shrugged and ambled off. Who were these people? Why the devil did they behave in this way? But Christmas was a man of temporary passions. No sooner had the hedgehog of disquiet bristled its spines than it was run over by the spirit of adventure. Caracas. No more looking over his shoulder. In Caracas things would be different. In Caracas, perhaps, The Rot had not taken hold. He might be temporarily potholed in Gatwick airport departure lounge, but soon he'd be riding horseback with dusky-eyed girls from the reef. Christmas enjoyed a long outward breath until he saw a youth with an Adidas tattoo on his arm. He went insane with fury.

"Are they paying you for that?" he asked, prodding the offence. "Are. They. Paying. You?" After a brief conference of the eyes, the youth fled. "The devil take the lot of you!" Christmas cursed after him. Moments later, back in Yates Wine Lodge and facing a conspiracy of drinks, he stirred his agitators to a pitch and then dispensed them to the cause. Damn these children. God damn them all.

From his position Christmas overlooked a couple sitting at one of the tables for McDonald's. The man had his computer open. The woman was wearing a headset. She was crying, attempting to look away from everybody but failing as they were sat right in the middle, her body and neck twisted over the seat. "Oh Lesley," she sobbed into the mouthpiece, holding it close, "I'm so sorry, love,

I'm so sorry, oh that bastard, that bastard – how could he do that? Honestly, Lesley, you're such a lovely person –" *Rubbish*, thought Christmas, *Lesley's an absolute bitch.* "– yeah, yep, that's right ... You're always thinking about other people ... so what I'm saying, love, what I'm saying is let other people look after you a bit too, OK? ... yeah ... when you're back at work, bit more steady on your pins kind of thing ... yes, yes of course ... and Gary sends his love." Her husband had a hand on her knee, but the other was tapping away at the keyboard, his face an expressionless mask. Christmas took out a slim volume of poetry from his inside jacket pocket and began to read.

"Mind if we ...?" Christmas looked up. Another couple were hoping for the two free seats that other travellers had wisely avoided. In an airport full of people secretly trying to kill themselves, Yates Wine Lodge had become rather full. Christmas spread the air with the back of his hand and carried on with his poetry book and his Laphroaig. Something in the silence caused him to look at his guests. They wanted to talk.

"Cheers," said the man, holding up his drink. Christmas, who was already holding up his drink, bared his teeth with a smile.

"Off anywhere nice?"

"No," said Christmas. "Paris."

"We're going to Spain. To Alicante."

"We've moved there," said the woman. *Oh have you*, thought Christmas, closing the book, his inner voice already starting to slosh about, *have you really? Oh have you, have you really? You've moved to Spain. Have you really? Spain? Really?*

"Just back from visiting our son."

"He's a psychologist."

"He's a child psychologist."

"And they give him the time off school?"

"Pardon me?"

13

Psychologists. Absolute blackguards. Passed themselves off as scientists when they were little more than witch-burners.

"Our daughter's at university in London," continued the woman, "studying theology."

"Really," said Christmas. A family of witch-burners. Why were they telling him this stuff? Did he look like the fucking taxman?

"We try to come back as often as we can but – well, London just seems to get worse and worse and worse." And why oh why did people like this always moan about London? It had improved considerably since they got a handle on the plague, and at least these days you required a license for the distillation of gin. "All the bombs and everything – and do you know what happened at my granddaughter's school?" she continued, "They've closed the pool! She absolutely loves swimming and they've gone and closed the pool because," she lowered her voice, "the Muslim children don't do it, do they?"

"I have no idea," said Christmas, wearily sensing the direction of the conversation.

"I mean I'm all for civil liberties, but the police have got to be allowed to do their job."

"In the swimming pool?"

"Excuse us?"

"There are police operating in your granddaughter's swimming pool?"

"Not police, Muslim girls."

"I thought you said they didn't care much for swimming?"

"They don't."

"Well I hardly think that merits police action."

"We're not talking about the pool."

"Yes, you were."

"We're just saying, you know, I mean no one feels safe, do they?"

14

"From police frogmen?"

"From the bombs."

"I'm sorry," said Christmas, pulling a face, "'bombs'?"

"The bombs. Exactly."

"There are bombs being planted in school swimming pools?"

"No, but I mean, where *is* it all heading?"

"Where the devil is *what* all heading?' said Christmas, down-right confused.

"I mean there's got to be a limit, hasn't there?" agreed the woman.

"Look here," said Christmas with a huff, "I didn't like swimming much when I was a child – verrucae and so forth – drowning – so I rather take umbrage at your suggestion that one should be forced to do it because of one's religion."

"I didn't say that."

"Yes, you did. And as for bombs – well ..." Christmas forgot what he was talking about for a moment. Then he had an idea. "A lead box. That's the thing. With you in it. And besides that, a lead box for *Monsieur* here, and beside that, rows and rows of lead boxes with us all in them, feeding tubes up our backsides, and they'd say 'yes but you're all safe, that's the main thing', that's what they'd have to do to make life safe, and who, madam, wants a safe life? Are we chickens? No, madam, we are not, we are the fox, and if we have to fight some dogs then we'll fight some bloody dogs!" Christmas accepted the deafening applause of an imaginary rally. *I stand before you all as a man who has just survived nothing less than an assassination attempt and—*

"You're not one of those hunting lot, are you?"

"I beg your pardon?"

"You're not one of those toffs on a horse, are you? Because, I'm sorry, that is just plain sick."

"No madam, I am not on a horse."

"Mm ..." she replied, disqualifying Christmas because he was

15

obviously posh. Then she saw a family coming up the escalator all wearing the same football shirts. She let out a small 'hmph' noise and immediately lost interest in the conversation. Christmas saw the self-satisfied look on her face, followed her line of sight, saw the family and immediately fingered her as the type of middle class person who, while celebrating their gritty roots, is an exacting snob when it came to modern members of the working class. As he ground his teeth through this judgement, Christmas noticed her husband settle an empty look upon him.

"You know I think the point is ..." the husband started, "I mean we were saying just the other day –"

Christmas made a firm decision to attack. He didn't sit down with these galoots, damn it, they sat down with him, and it was they who would be standing up again. He gave the husband a broad, cheerful smile.

"– well, these friends of ours were saying, and I do see their point, if you know what I mean, that there's nowhere to be English any more. The North's out and so's the Midlands and the Southeast. There's Devon and Cornwall and bits of Kent – basically that's what's left and it costs a fortune to live down there."

"So," Christmas nodded enthusiastically, "scandalized by immigration, you've emigrated."

"We—"

"And of course, Devon and Cornwall, they're full of yokels."

"Ha, ha. Well, I—"

"Big-breasted, scrumpy-swilling, hay-chewing yokels that prowl about in the woods planting maypoles and smearing each other with cream." The woman returned her attention. "There's packs of them," Christmas continued, "stuffed either side of the bridle paths, waiting for retirees on tandems that they can kidnap at Cornetto-point and subject to Cornish grammar seminars by the light of the horrible moon." The couple exchanged looks.

16

Christmas leant forward, "and they'll force you, yes, force you, madam, and you, sir, force to your knees, your *kneeeeees*, naked! Facing holy Exeter, shrieking God of Barley, God of Corn, take these supplicants that they might reject the false idols, the lord of frozen cakes, of industrialized fishing, of tarty news readers that sit on the edge of their desks because evidently genocide requires a casual delivery!" He slammed his glass down on the table, closed his eyes and began to breathe heavily. When he opened them again the couple had left. Christmas burped with satisfaction and picked up his book.

4

Flight EZ116 to Paris. Christmas leant his head against the glass. The sun slipped down onto the horizon and the clouds became one territory, endless bodies lying side by side. Jolting and shaking the aircraft lowered into this battlefield until finally the sky cleared and he was able to see the tiling of the earth.

Christmas closed his eyes, imagining himself twenty years younger. He wasn't running away to Caracas. He was flying to Paris for a trade show. At the trade show he was going to meet Emily. She was here, next to him. Christmas opened his eyes, but there was only a child's face rising above the seat in front. Higher and higher he went, with a widening smile until his upper body bent over into what was incontrovertibly Christmas' zone. Christmas searched his drink for a last drop and crunched on an ice cube. The boy burst into a grin. Christmas looked out of the window.

Parisians respect rudeness. This normally gave an advantage to a man like Christmas. When shopping in Paris his technique for commanding their guarded attention was to approach their most expensive item and ask for it 'in crocodile'. Once they had to admit that it didn't actually come in crocodile, a certain superiority of extravagance was conferred on Christmas and they would start to kowtow accordingly. Powered by scotch, and with two hours to wait in Charles De Gaulle airport, Christmas summoned a variant of this approach in order to gain access to the business class lounge.

"Now look here," he broadcast to the receptionists, swinging his frame through the doors, "one of your colleagues promised to fetch the manager and I am still waiting!"

"I'm sorry, *Monsieur*, if I could just—"

"Waiting, I said!" interrupted Christmas as a party of business travellers entered behind him, "I'll be waiting in here." And off he walked, unchallenged, into the exclusivity of free coffee and marginally larger seating. There were two glamorous couples laughing and talking about Milan, otherwise it was full of the usual harried men and women unable to figure out their BlackBerrys and reading the *Financial Times* at incredible speed. Christmas went to the buffet, filled a bowl full of chocolate croissants and sat down with a triple espresso.

"So I bought a book for the journey," a businessman opposite was saying to his colleague, "called 'How To Improve Your Memory', and guess what?" *You forgot it*, thought Christmas. "I forgot it!" said the man. Christmas frowned. He had, of late, become concerned about his own memory. He used to be rather proud of it, but now he found himself forgetting names, which lies he had told to whom and historical facts and personages that had once been at his fingertips. These days if he didn't write the thing down, it vanished from his mind just as completely as those infuriating objects left for only a moment vanished from sight.

Christmas spied the manager picking his way through the tables. "*Monsieur*, you—"

"Why haven't you got the *Asian Daily News*?"

"Excuse me?"

"The *Asian Daily News* – why don't you have it, man? Or at least the *Hong Kong Gazette*. Many of your guests I see here are undoubtedly destined for the East, and yet I notice a woeful lack of provision in your newspaper range. Messrs ADN and HKG are, in particular, noticeable by their absence." The manager relaxed. There was no earwig in the milk. There was no stolen bag, no mouse, no insult from a staff member. There was no crisis. He took out a pad of paper and slowly pretended to write down the newspapers' names. In fact he was writing the French for 'fat English cunt'.

"Mmm ..." he said, "We do get these in from time to time, but I am afraid that in the past they haven't proved very popular. However, I will take this up at our next meeting, and hope to rectify the situation before your next visit. Would that be OK, *Monsieur*?"

"That would be adequate."

"Now if you will excu—"

"Too bloody right," said Christmas, biting into a croissant. The manager departed. Munching and wiping his hands, Christmas walked over to the internet consoles and typed 'best hotel in Caracas' into Google. He made a note of Gran Melía's phone number. He took his mobile out of his pocket and switched it on for the first time in two days. There were thirty-eight voicemail messages. He called the hotel, booked a room for a week with a secured credit card – the last type of card he was allowed – and then tossed the phone into the bin.

5

The Paris–Madrid leg of his journey was notable only for the peanut that refused to be scooped out of his scotch and the struggle over the armrest that his elbow conducted with his neighbour's. Both travellers submitted to the unwritten lore of this ancient combat: combatants do not acknowledge the combat; combatants do not acknowledge each other. In the end, Christmas settled for his arm lying over the front of the armrest while his neighbour's elbow was squashed against the seat, both suffering the kind of pressurised proximity that pride alone could deem acceptable. Only Christmas, however, could deem it enjoyable.

Once in Madrid there were yet more security checks. Everyone sighed and tutted. If the few were to die for the increased convenience of the many, then surely that was a price worth paying? It was certainly paid in other contexts, but Christmas suspected that the multiplication of such procedures – this taking off and on of one's belt, shoes and coat, the delving for coins and keys – had nothing to do with 'the war on terror'. It was plain humiliation, a public stripping to cow you into accepting the delays and the food and the modern scandal of in-flight alcohol rationing. Shaken and observed, they wanted you to stare into the plastic tray of your life, examine its pittance, and then be grateful for seven per cent off five hundred fags.

Christmas walked onto a travelator and stood with everything crossed until it delivered him to a bar. Here he consumed a slice of tortilla, a glass of beer and two large Dewar's – the only available alternative to that well-known whisky for children, Jack Daniel's.

"So where you headed?" asked the barman.

"My wife's grandmother is Venezuelan," he munched. "We're going to track down where the old woman grew up. Guiria – heard of it?"

"No."

"Any more of that tortilla left?"

"So you've left your wife with the bags?"

"She's reading. Always bloody reading." The barman cut him another slice. "Beautiful woman, my wife," added Christmas. "Doesn't take any shit. Have you ever met a woman from Stoke-on-Trent?"

"I don't think so."

"Well, you'd know it if you had."

The Dewar's was disgusting and with every sip he vowed never to touch the stuff again, taking this time to concentrate on his drinking strategy for the next nine hours. The trick with drinking on planes was to pick the right stewardess early on and make her laugh. Then start with single orders, nothing too shocking, engaging her in an anecdote about one's fear of flying. Getting her to laugh at the expense of some other passenger was always profitable, making the two of you part of an ill-defined gang. Without such groundwork one could attempt to order from different hostesses

22

and hope they were unaware of the overall tally, but that was risky. One could be refused.

As in all aspects of life The Rot had corrupted the natural order of things. Christmas let out a fond sigh, remembering the era when you could smoke on planes and everyone drank like hell because they weren't used to flying and no one gave a damn about how many you'd had and people were swapping seats and having fun. Back then you could get a stewardess to sit down with you and share a gin. These days they were more like nurses condescending the aisles of some outpatient day trip; *could you turn that off, please? Could you turn that on, please?* Who has the right to tell a grown man he's had one too many miniatures? Not some used-looking ex-dancer with an orange face, that's for sure.

Christmas felt drunk and spiteful. He attempted to walk to his gate but fell in behind a woman who was leading a suitcase on wheels. He stumbled over it, regained his footing and booted it sideways. The woman spun round.

"Did you just kick my bag?" she cried out in Spanish.

"I thought," replied Christmas in English, "it was your dog. *Do*, I mean to say, *please* pass on my apologies to your valise, that is to say, to whit and so forth—" he paused to flurry his hand like a composer with something on the end of his baton "—in said action the court finds in favour of the plaintiff, if it pleases your honour, humble regards, deep, prodigious bows and bowels. Case!" he stiffened like a drill sergeant, "Dis-missed!" and off he marched.

Christmas strode past the vast windows and took in the planes taxiing into position. This was the first time he had been in Spain since he and his wife Emily had given up their house in Benhavis. They had spent their holidays there, driving out from Malaga airport, bleach green golf courses slicking through the burnt hills, rows of spotless time-shares staring out to sea. Their place looked down into the village and they would lie in bed getting pissed, a breeze coming in from the balcony carrying sounds of children and their neighbours arguing. Scottish couple. What were they called? Tarrant? Tavish? Tavistock? Emily fell out with the wife. Something to do with the free English class they both used to give the kids there. Always helping someone, old Emmy. *Except me*, thought Christmas with a smile, *always telling me to get off my arse*.

He remembered her standing at the foot of their bed, trying to decide what to wear for a dinner with the neighbours to try and patch things up.

"I'm getting fat, Pops," said Emily. "Look at this dress. It used to be sexy. Now it looks bloody ridiculous."

"Oh come on, Em," he said, shifting himself down the bed towards her. She was twisting in front of the mirror, and getting upset. "You look beautiful."

"I do not."

"Yes you do." He grabbed her waist and toppled her back onto the bed while she protested and fought.

"I'm getting old," she mumbled as he kissed her, "old and fat. It's not fair. It's all right for you – you're a man."

He pulled up her dress and kissed her belly and said, "If you get an inch thinner or lose a single grey hair I will divorce you, because you are the most perfect woman on earth and I love you more than life itself."

Emily looked at him and said, "What fucking grey hair?"

6

Christmas arrived at the gate to find his flight delayed. There was a coffee bar nearby. He bought a large cappuccino and, trying to wriggle between two chairs, spilt it on a blond business-man. "For God's sake!" Christmas exclaimed, as if he were the one whose testicles felt as if they had just been dipped in a fondue. The man jumped up, face ablaze. "I mean what's the point?" agreed Christmas. The man swore in some Nordic language. Christmas nodded thoughtfully, noticing that the seat he was going for was now taken. "Chin up, old man," he said, sitting down at his victim's table, "helps get the noose over."

"Will you apologise?" bayed the man in crisp, sturdy English. Christmas never apologised. It was always an invitation to trouble.

"Do you know, I've never met a Nordic who couldn't speak perfect English," he said. "What age do they start you off? Two? Three?" The man stared down at Christmas for a long moment and then dismissed him with a wave of his hand. He gave a gruff curse and then sat back down at his computer, dabbing his crotch with a paper napkin. Christmas, alive with whisky, started to find him funny.

"You know the best thing to do if you don't want that stain is to throw your trousers away."

"I do not wish to talk to you."

"Perfectly understandable, perfectly understandable, and I'll say again, perfectly understandable. Now if I were to—"

"With," seethed the man, "respect, please just—"

"Oh dear!" exclaimed Christmas, "If you are going to insult me, don't say 'with respect'. It's without respect! Surely that's the point. Now, without respect, I'm a ...?"

"..."

"A bastard?"

"..."

"And you wish I'd just go away?"

"You—"

"There, you see! OK, so now I know how you feel, we can have a conversation. Fuck off."

"How—!"

"You just called me a bastard, so I'm saying 'fuck off'."

"I did no—"

"We all heard you!" declared Christmas, motioning to the passengers grazing around them, "and I said, 'Fuck off!'. We're trading insults, man, wake up!"

"Will you—Leave this table right now, will you, please."

"That's the spirit!" cheered Christmas.

"I am giving you warning."

"Fantastic!"

"I shall not be responsible for the consequences."

"Oh come on," booed Christmas, "you were doing so well, but that 'responsible for the consequences' stuff is really—" The man stood up and cuffed Christmas about the face the way some people

26

hit their dogs. Then he slammed his computer shut and stormed off.

Christmas held his face, absorbing what had just happened. "Snow Nazi!" he called after the man. Satisfied that both he and his public had drawn a line under the incident, Christmas decided he should inspect for damage.

Once facing the toilet's mirrors, he exercised his jaw, advancing and retreating from his reflection. There was no mark. He shrugged the drunken shrug of a drunken shrugger, then arched his top lip as far down toward his chin as it would go. This new moustache really was dapper.

7

" *This is your Iberian Airways flight IB412 to Caracas ...*"
At least here in his seat he should be spared any more unpleasantness from all the travelling Neanderthals who seemed bent on ruining his passage. The Rot was everywhere.

The last seven years had seen a grave acceleration in England's decline. The Rot, that corroding plasma of infantilisation that Christmas could see smeared over everything, was now filling the country's lungs. Christmas couldn't breathe. More enslavement to the little screens, more uniformity, fewer individuals. The culture was mewling and puking and soiling itself and all its adults were dead. Yes, he thought again, examining the runway, the William Slade situation had brought a rather sharp focus to his plans, but this trip to Venezuela had been decided long ago. There was nothing left for him in England. He would stay at least a month or two, but if some opportunity arose, some chance of company or profit, then he would certainly stay longer, and at that boozy moment he felt good fortune to be inevitable. Christmas closed his eyes. Latin America ... Dust and passion and blood and poetry. Floppy-hatted peasants playing guitar and drinking rum while you spirited away their feisty daughters. Now what was it that Emily's grandmother used to bang on about? *Em-pan-adas*: delicious fried pastries on every street. Sunsets that could move you to tears. Salsa. The friendliest people on earth. Surely an adventurer like himself could flourish in a land like that. *Ca-ra-cas*. Wasn't it a fine word? Did not the very timbre of its capital promise a city he could no longer find in Europe, one whose 'historic centre' had not been embalmed for tourists, one where The Rot's flag was not fluttering from every miserable corner?

The plane pulled away from the earth. Once the seat belt signs were off, Christmas pressed the call button. He had already spent several minutes trying to work out whether this particular stewardess was pretty or not and now she was approaching ... Was she or wasn't she? Those slender legs, yes. Her shoulders, somewhat rounded, no. Her face, on balance, no, but now she was pulling her hair back, yes, though as she was about to speak he noticed a cluster of spots on her forehead ...

"Yes?"

"No."

"*Perdona?*"

"But yes to a drink! Do you have any decent scotch?"

"Yes, *Señor*. If you could wait a moment we will be—"

"I am sorry to bother you," he said in Spanish, "but flying makes me very nervous."

"Oh really?"

"Very nervous I'm afraid, I ... we ... I mean to say my wife Emily and I, we ... had a bad experience a long time ago. When she was still alive." He looked into the stewardess' eyes as deeply as he could. They were light brown. *Trading on your dead wife's memory for a drink. You're in hell, Christmas. You are in a bar in hell.*

29

"Well, why not," he muttered. "Why shouldn't it do some fucking good? I've bloody well survived a near-murder today, for fuck's sake!" He felt the eyes of the couple next to him. The stewardess brought him a scotch. He downed it. The stewardess brought him another. Then he had two bottles of red wine with the meal. He watched a movie about people who evidently detested themselves treating each other terribly yet being somehow happy with the outcome. Then he had two more scotches. Then he had a beer.

A man listening to his iPod began thrapping out a drumbeat on his fold-down table. It was annoying everybody. Christmas swung out of his seat. He lurched over to the man and thrapped out a quick rhythm on his head. The man pulled out his earphones in astonishment.

"Do hope you enjoyed my drumming as much as we're enjoying yours."

"What – who – who the hell do you think you are?"

Christmas paused to consider his response. "Harold Agapanthius Christmas," he decided, "at your bloody disservice. I don't hope you do have a pleasant flight," and with that he returned to his seat. Another passenger gave him a secret thumbs-up. Christmas gave a sarcastic thumbs-up back. He drank another whisky. One of the stewardesses asked him if everything was all right. The iPod man had made a complaint.

"I mistook his skull for the overhead locker," he replied. The stewardess gave him a weak smile. Christmas got the sense that something was unravelling.

The progress map appeared on the overhead screen. They were above St Lucia. He saw the word 'CARACAS'. Christmas felt a swell of enthusiasm dampened only by heartburn. *Good heavens*, he said to himself, *I am* roaring *drunk*.

"Roaring drunk!" he repeated out loud and found it so funny that he let out a roar, such as a lion might make. If it were drunk.

30

More people came to ask him if he was all right. Someone offered him water. He batted them away like flies. He examined the people sitting next to him. He suddenly felt as if he wanted to talk to them, to find out about their lives. He felt a warmth for them, and that warmth started in his stomach. They were a young couple. The man was spindly, with glasses and rather bad skin about the nose. The woman was plump, in an ill-fitting top that allowed a girdle of flesh to hang over her jeans. They were holding hands and looking out the window, stiff with hope that he wouldn't talk to them. Christmas thought this a pleasant scene.

"I say," he began, "terrific." The couple turned to him as he nodded to the window, "Mountains. Cloudy. Terrific. Mountains, aren't they?" *Jesus*, he thought, *I really am pissed.* The couple smiled awkwardly and looked back at the terrific cloudy mountains wishing they were stranded on one, or indeed anywhere but next to this ageing beast.

"Going to Caracas?" asked Christmas.

"This is a plane to Caracas, yes," replied the boyfriend with a heavy accent that Christmas couldn't place.

"Been there before?"

"No."

"Is it easy to get a taxi at the airport?"

"I don't know. We've never been there."

"You know I remember once when I was your age, down near Malaga with my wife, there was this taxi chap down there – what was his name? Kamal? Was it Kamal? Kermit? Anyway – had a terrific drug problem. Sold everything in his flat except this huge old fridge. Hid in the bloody thing for two weeks. Absolutely paranoid. Was convinced that the police surveillance X-ray mind reading frequencies or what have you couldn't penetrate through the metal lining in the fridge ..." and he was off. He talked and drank and drank and talked "... and then did you hear about that chap from Oxford? Invited four hundred people from the phone book whose last name ended in 'bottom' and then didn't show up so they all had to introduce themselves, 'I'm Mrs Higginsbottom. I'm Mr Ramsbottom. We're the Bottoms ...'" Christmas was guffawing loudly. The stewardess asked him to lower his voice. Then she refused to serve him another drink and told him he should try to sleep. He told her to go away. The terrific cloudy mountains seeped into his brain. At one point he could remember telling the girl next to him not to slouch. He tried to put a hand on her shoulder to help her with this correction when the boyfriend knocked it away.

"Hey, just chill out, OK? Relax." It was a bad thing to say to Christmas. Nothing infuriated him more than being told to 'chill out' or 'relax' by someone other than a doctor holding a defibrillator.

"Oh, I see ... dreadfully ... I should relax, should I? I should 'chill out', should I? That's what I should do, is it? That's your professional opinion, is it?"

"Look," started the girl, "why don't you just—"

"And what *is* your profession, young lady?"

"I'm a sports therapist."

"And what's this then?" laughed Christmas. He had two inches of her flab between thumb and finger. "Eh? What the devil is all this?"

Threats ensued. His stewardess appeared with back-up and Christmas noted with surprise that she had completely lost her friendly demeanour. There was some admonishment, some arrangement he was dimly aware of. The alcohol began to rub him out. Another interaction with more senior members of the crew came next, but Christmas would always remain unsure of what exactly transpired. He did have a memory of being in the toilet and laughing. When he awoke they were one hour away from Caracas and his trousers were on the wrong way round. The seats next to him were empty. He passed out again. When he came to the whole plane was empty. They were on the ground.

He took his Panama from the overhead locker and gathered his things while being watched by the crew. "*Adios*," he smiled to his stewardess on the way out. She didn't reply. So, with head high and breath bad, Christmas walked through the airport, past the U-bend of passengers nervous for their luggage, towards the taxi drivers and moneychangers. He showed his passport, nodded to the soldiers and strode out into Venezuela.

8

Christmas awoke with a start. He had been dreaming that a clown lover was trying to run him over in her tiny car. *Where the devil am I?* he thought. *Bloody hell. Caracas.* Christmas pulled his tongue off the pillow, pushed his eyes to the front and swung out of bed. He opened the curtains. There were the El Ávila Mountains, a cable car plotting its way to the top. He drank all the bottled water in the room. He went back to bed, his belly uncomfortably stretched, battling an old feeling of dread that was always worse with the hangovers. He closed his eyes and rummaged through other thoughts. He found some that were pinned to the future and dressed his mind in their confidence. Venezuela. Everything would be better here.

He got up again. He went into the bathroom. "Morning, Christmas," he said to a group of Christmases all standing off at an angle from one another. Christmas made a slight bow to them. They all bowed back. Christmas let out an oddly high-pitched fart. Everyone found it funny.

Down by the outdoor pool on the first floor, white and green striped awning covered the breakfasters. Skyscrapers rose up beside them. Women read magazines on sun-loungers and trailed their hands in the water. Inside, Christmas violated the buffet. Scrambled eggs, streaky bacon, hash browns, waffles, syrup, fruit salad, orange juice. He sat down with a copy of the *International Herald Tribune* as his guest. Once he had grown tired of the newspaper he amused himself by observing the business people in relaxed mode – bare white ankles sticking out of yachting shoes, knowing laughter, rigidly pressed shirts and shorts. They all looked desperate.

He was disappointed with the coffee – far too bitter – but he drank a vaseful anyway, beckoning refill after refill until he could feel it hot-wiring his subterranean ignitions. Christmas decided to explore the hotel. He walked its corridors and discovered restaurants. He went into the business centre. He found conference rooms being prepared and came out into a shopping arcade. From a walkway he saw a man living under the flyover opposite fixing his roof with a new cardboard box. He re-entered the hotel. He went into the gym. He inspected the Jacuzzi.

"Feel like a work-out, sir?" said the receptionist.

"Don't be ridiculous," he scoffed.

Once the first coffee of the morning had worn off, he'd usually had enough of being alive. Today was different. Today he was in a new city. Yes, he breathed deeply to himself, marching along the corridor to his room, here he would triumph. He got to his door and realised he'd lost his key.

Like most logical people, when Christmas lost something he assumed it had been stolen by supernatural forces bent on sabotaging his life. After several furious seconds he found it again. Once inside, he took a bath, dressed, and counted his money ready to go shopping. He spent several minutes getting the angle of his Panama right. Then he lost his room key again. He finally found it in his back pocket. "It's the mischief of the devil himself," he muttered in bewilderment. Christmas returned to the mirror for final approval and then set off into Caracas.

Outside the hotel's force field of wealth lay the Sabana Grande district. There was something about its shops that reminded him of Derby in the 1980s; a kind of tropical Eagle Centre, with a similar mix of jewellery, hi-fis and bargain shoes. The air was close, clouds struggling to keep off the ground. Beggars watched old men play chess. People stood by food stands eating corn *arepas* stuffed with ham and cheese, while Chávez looked down from the billboards, his impressive face balancing on a bright red shirt: *POR NUESTRO FUTURO, POR NUESTRA REPÚBLICA!*

Christmas sat down in a café. He drank an espresso and settled down to watch the Venezuelans. They were of every hue, from morning pink to oak black. They talked and laughed. Hands were grabbed, cheeks kissed, backs slapped. Christmas congratulated himself. This city was full of beautiful women, and if they were not beautiful, they were sexy, and if they were not sexy they looked like fun. "Tonight I shall take to the bars," he declared to himself as a passing woman raised her eyebrows. Christmas tipped his hat. A man with part of his ear missing sat down next to him. Several moments passed before Christmas realised this man was offering to shine his shoes. Christmas declined. The bill arrived. An old woman came to his table selling pens and bamboo mugs. Then a man selling lottery tickets. Then another man selling children's posters, lighters and packets of nuts.

Christmas left the café, wandering between the stalls and malls. He changed some money. He bought two suits, pills for gout, gastric reflux and his blood sugar levels, underwear, shirts, socks, another pair of shoes, toothbrush, shaving equipment and finally a suitcase, making him one of the few people to have packed for a foreign country after their arrival.

Looking for somewhere to lunch, Christmas was stopped by a policeman. He was a fat-necked teenager with acne. He had been sitting alone on a plastic chair at a police check-point and stood in front of Christmas with the usual, brutish comportment of bored authority. Christmas looked at his uniform. It said '*Metropolitana*'. The police officer went through his shopping. Then he searched Christmas, paying particular attention to his genitals.

"I shall start charging in a minute, young man," Christmas said in English.

"*Pasaporte!*"

Christmas handed it over and the adolescent flicked through it forwards and back while looking at the people walking by. Christmas understood that this was about money. They talked in Spanish.

"Where are you going?"

"I don't know. I haven't got there yet."

"Where are you going?"

"I don't know. I am looking for somewhere to eat, and I don't know where I am going because I haven't found it yet. Perhaps you can recommend somewhere?"

"Why are you here?"

"I'm a tourist."

"Do you have any family here?"

"No."

"Do you have friends here?"

"No."

"Why are you here?"

"I'm a tourist."

"Where are you going?"

"I don't know."

"Where is your health certificate?"

"I don't have one."

"Where is your health certificate?"

"I don't have one. You have my passport right there. I've never heard of a health certificate."

"You need a health certificate."

"I asked your embassy in London," Christmas lied, "and they told me that all I needed to be in Venezuela was a valid passport, which I have here, in your hands."

"You need a health certificate."

"No, I don't."

"Do you have family here?"

"No."

"Where is your health certificate?" Christmas was dumbfounded. The officer was a simpleton.

"What is your favourite colour?" he replied in English and then started to point at random objects, enunciating like a parent. "C-ar. Shop-ping Cen-tre. Big el-ec-tric cl-ock." The policeyouth was dumbfounded. The tourist was a simpleton.

"Be careful," he advised Christmas, returning his passport and deciding against extortion. "Many things happen here."

"Do give Watson my regards," replied Christmas.

Christmas settled on a large restaurant themed like a 1950s American diner. The waiters wore bow ties and waistcoats. A panpipe version of Hotel California floated along the wallpaper. Christmas took a table by the window and sat his new suitcase on the seat opposite.

"What do you recommend?" he asked his waiter, whose impressive moustache evinced wisdom and good character. "Do you have any of these *em-pan-adas*?"

"I'm afraid not, but we do serve typical Venezuelan *criolla* food here, *Señor*. I can recommend a classic *criolla* dish that wonderfully reflects the mix and tastes of the Venezuelan people. Is this your first time in Caracas?"

"Yes."

"You speak excellent Spanish."

"Thank you."

"You have lived in Spain? I can tell by your accent."

"That's correct."

"But you are Dutch?"

"Good God, no!" countered Christmas. Despite the moustache, the man was an idiot. "I am an Englishman." The waiter's face brightened.

"Manchester United!" Christmas' face dimmed.

"London Divided." Christmas had strong opinions on sport, predicated on never doing it. Football and golf were particular party games of The Rot, but he abhorred it all; personally, because people always felt they had to do some before they could come to the pub, and generally because it boiled down to running after little balls. It turned men into dogs. Chess, on the other hand, he considered the pastime of heroes, as was backgammon, Go, Canasta, bar billiards, Tac, snooker, pool, boxing, Shithead, Connect Four and darts.

"So what's in a *criolla* dish?" he asked, wishing to change the subject.

"The beans are from the indigenous people, the cheese is from Europe, the rice is from Asia, the banana is from Africa, the fish is from the sea, the egg is from the chicken."

"Wonderful," acknowledged Christmas flatly. "And a cold beer, please. Large one. Biggest you've got." Drink had started its daily queue-barge to the front of Christmas' mind. Christmas took out his wallet and inspected his dollars and his bolívares. He separated out his bolívares, counted them, folded them and put them in his trouser pocket. His wallet he put in his inside jacket pocket.

Put it in the room safe, Pops, he heard Emily say, *you'll only get shitfaced and lose it like in Italy*. Christmas chuckled to himself, remembering their honeymoon in Amalfi, staying in a hotel on the cliffs that had once been a convent. He'd lost his wallet and all their money and she'd watched him, giggling from behind her

39

champagne glass, as he charmed the hotel manager so much that the man ended up lending them some of his own cash so that they could enjoy the town. Once their replacement credit card had arrived, they had taken the manager out for a gargantuan meal that ended with them all dancing in the dawn at a local policeman's retirement party. When they got back to the hotel, Emily realised she'd lost their replacement card and they had to do it all over again.

Christmas could remember the moon over the sea from their hotel balcony. He could remember them making love. He inhaled, trying yet again to recall Emily's smell, but he could not. The beer arrived and Christmas took a deep slug.

The meal was excellent, and he left such an audacious tip that the waiters cheered his departure. Outside the restaurant, he saw Pepito the taxi driver leaning on his car talking to someone.

"Hey! *Señor Christmas*!" he shouted, "*Hola*! It's me, Pepito!" Conversation was unavoidable. "I was at your hotel but you did not come."

"My watch was still on English time. When I woke up I thought it was time to go to bed."

"I wait for you many hours." The man was a liar and a scoundrel. No doubt about it. "But don't worry – you want that I show to you Caracas?"

"Well, actually, yes, there is something you could help me with ... Yes, I do believe there is. Pick me up from the hotel tonight at ten?"

"And you going to be there, right? I no wanna wait, you know, please."

"Ten *a punto*," said Christmas, "On my honour."

9

"*Señor* Christmas!" He had just entered the lobby of the Gran Melía carrying his new suitcase. "*Señor* Christmas!" It was the lady from reception.

"Good God," Christmas grumbled to the ceiling, "can't I go anywhere without being recognised?"

"I see you have recovered your luggage, *Señor.*"

"What?"

"Your luggage, *Señor.* It has arrived from the airport?"

"No." There was an uneasy silence.

"*Señor,* there seems to be a problem with your credit card. Could I ask you for—"

"May I just go to my room? I am expecting an extremely important phone call. I'll just go up to my room and I'll be straight down to answer any questions you may have."

"Of course, *Señor,* but—"

"Too kind," he said, and walked off.

Once in a change of clothes, Christmas returned to the ground floor and, avoiding reception, made for the piano bar. The hotel suddenly seemed very full. He found a seat next to a nervous-looking man and ordered a Laphroaig and a beer. Striking clumsily for the plate of bar snacks, he sent some salty shrapnel spinning onto the man's papers.

"Oh – don't worry," said the man, brushing them off. "Are you here for the conference?" *Worry?* thought Christmas. *What the devil is he talking about?*

"Excuse me?"

"The youth marketing conference?"

"Someone is actually going to *sell* the little buggers? Who are they going to flog 'em to – the Chinese, is it?"

"I'm sorry?"

"The Russians?" Christmas considered enquiring about job opportunities then decided against it. The man's phone rang. He looked at the number and immediately shrank.

"Sorry – excuse me – Hello, sir? ... Right ... yes ... sorry, yes," he bobbed his head like a mandarin. "I realise that, sir ... yes, I'm very sorry ... yes ... of course, yes. Thank you, sir, thank you. Goodbye, sir." *Up on two legs, man*, thought Christmas as loudly as he could. *Up on two legs!*

"The boss," the man laughed weakly, putting his phone away.

"Bully, is he? If there's one thing I can't stand, it's a bully."

"Well, he does ask a lot – but you get out what you put in, right?"

"When the odds are even," Christmas muttered darkly. "Harry Christmas," he said, offering his hand in brotherly consolation.

"David Dubois." Christmas immediately withdrew his hand.

"Dubois? French? You don't sound French."

"Quarter French, actually."

"Mmmn ..." replied Christmas, reflecting on how garlic always overpowers the rest of the dish. "So what irks the *Dauphin*?"

"What? Oh – well, err, not irks really, just, well, I meant to – stupid, really – meant to co-ordinate with some of the other delegates—"

"You know what gets me is that you French are always grateful to the Yanks for the Second World War but you never mention the English. Why is that?"

"Um ..."

"You were saying?"

"Well, err, I work for a human rights organization here – we organise 'reality tours' of the barrios and ..." The man simulated the quote marks with his fingers. Christmas' face tightened.

Christmas had so many pet hates he had a zoo – a zoo of hate – filled with some quite ordinary creatures, such as the French, men who called people 'guys', the internet, scatter cushions and so on, as well as more exotic types such as women who said the word 'coffee' as if they wanted a cuddle, and cold remedies that did not make you feel drowsy. Miming quote marks with one's fingers was in the infuriating animals section, a hairy-arsed fiend that swung hooting from its bars, flinging its four-fingered filth at the public. Why did people emphasize their refusal to take responsibility for the words in their own mouths with a couple of bunny ears? He longed to seize those twitching fingers, to twist them. So he did.

"Ow!" cried the man. "W-w-w-what are you doing?"

"I am not a child! I do not need a puppet show!"

"What?" The man was horrified.

"Oh, forget it," Christmas downed his drinks and left. He felt bad about what he'd done for a moment and then he felt good. He felt very good. *I 'think' I'll have a 'drink' somewhere 'else'*, he said to himself, quote fingers pumping.

After a dinner of swordfish, potatoes, rice, avocado and cole-slaw, washed down with two bottles of Chilean Montes Alpha M and followed by vanilla ice cream covered in hot caramel sauce,

Pepito picked him up in front of the hotel as arranged. Christmas'
logic was this: if this man was a rascal, he should know the best
place for a drink. He explained the kind of bar he wanted to go
to: somewhere with a band, somewhere with Venezuelan women,
somewhere without teenagers.

During the drive Pepito tried to sell him a gold watch. Then he
tried to sell him a camera. Then he tried to sell him marijuana, and
finally cocaine. Christmas said no to everything.

"Why do you say no to everything?"

"Because I don't bloody want any of it – the devil take you! Is
this a taxi or a Turkish bazaar?"

"You want take a bath?"

"No, blast you, I do not want a bath, I want a drink! Why don't
you try and sell me one of those."

"Sell you drink? But *Señor*, this is not a bar. I am not a barman."

"More's the pity, Pepito, more is the pity."

They turned into a street with a group of oily-clothed men
huddling around some steps.

"Look," said Pepito, "*craqueros*. Crack-heads. *Hola!*" he shouted,
tooting his horn, "*Hola*, crack-mans! *Hola, amigos!*" The men
turned round. Christmas could see the flame and the pipe. "*Buenas
noches, amigos, hola!*" The men scattered in fear. "*Recogelatas*. They
spend all day picking up cans. When they get one kilo of aluminium, they get five bolívares, and with five bolívares they can to buy
one crack rock. All day, every day, picking up cans."

"Do they know you?"

"Of course. I am a policeman."

"What!"

"I am a policeman."

"You just tried to sell me drugs!"

"Policeman in Caracas only get minimum wage. We must buy
our own uniforms; we must buy our own bullets. Everyone has

number two job. Sometimes number three job. I drive the taxi. Lucky for you my friend," Pepito started to laugh and slapped him on the knee, "you don't buy the drugs. Don't worry. I like you."

They pulled up outside a bar called *El Mani Es Asi* – 'The Peanut Is Like This'. It was packed, a central bar with the door on one side and a dance floor on the other. A band of lively old men were playing salsa hard and fast.

"This is a typical Venezuelan bar. This is a place for salsa."

"I can hear that."

"I like this place when I like to dance with the women. When I like to drink with a woman, for *más romantico*, I go this other place, El Barco," Pepito handed Christmas a business card, "It's my brother's place, very near your hotel. You take this card and maybe you go and visit, OK?"

"Is it full of policemen?"

"You dance salsa?"

"Not so far."

"Salsa come from Puerto Rico, you know. It come from the prisons."

"They have trumpets in prison?"

"They made search of prisons here last week and they find machine guns and grenades. If you want a trumpet," he shrugged "you can get a trumpet."

Couples were pressed against each other. The air was heavy with smoke and rum. Pepito knew everyone. Christmas shook countless hands, half-heard conversations thrown against the music. They drank and drank and drank. Christmas told Pepito and his friends stories about English women. Everybody laughed and refused to let him buy a round. "You are my friend," said Pepito. "My English friend!"

"So," said Christmas, his arm around the man's shoulder. "Your brother owns a bar. Now I'm thinking of starting a business here, you know, that kind of thing. And what with you being a copper and so forth, what's the process, what's the procedure, the red tape? I mean what's standing between a man like me, a foreigner and day one – bingo – the cocktails start jumping over the bar, you follow?"

"You want to open a bar in Caracas?"

"Why not?" Pepito began to answer but Christmas' attention had wandered over to a woman. He smiled at her. She smiled back. He raised his glass to her. She smiled even wider.

It was rare to see gringos in this place, much less such an interesting-looking one her own age, and this man looked like he was fun. He had a cheeky smile, a rugged face and mischievous eyes. They had the same build. Lola Rosa distrusted skinny men. Her mother had always told her that skinny men were liars.

Harry Christmas, shining with charm, went over and introduced himself. "Do you think you could teach an old gringo salsa?"

"I doubt it," she replied, "but we can try." She gave him a wink and stood up. Christmas was smitten. Her lips and eyes shimmered with make-up. She had green eyes, an enormous bottom in tight jeans, and titanic breasts crammed into a small yellow top. He told her he was a movie producer.

When the salsa proved to be beyond him, he insisted on exaggerated foxtrots and waltzes. He made her laugh. They took breaks at the bar and drank rum and coke. She was staying with family in Caracas for a few days before going back to her village, San Cristóbal.

"Where's that?"

"In Sucre. On the Caribbean side. Opposite Trinidad and Tobago."

"Is that anywhere near Guiria?"

"Guiria is not far, yes."

"Well I never," beamed Christmas. "That's why I have come to Venezuela. To visit exactly that part of the country."

"You going to make a movie there?"

"A final scene."

"So maybe," she said, patting his face, "you can come visit." Her hands were rough and calloused. Christmas leant closer. Yes, there was something of Emily about her.

"You are funny," she said. "I like you." Two men stood up, grabbed at each other, then one smashed a glass into the side of the other's face. Everyone stopped to watch the fight. People scurried clear, or waded in. Christmas stepped in front of Lola.

"*Verga!* What are you doing?"

"I'm protecting you."

"I can't see."

"I am a human shield," he boomed, raising his arms wide. "No harm can come to you!" She gave him such a dimpled smile it triggered the shining of a gold tooth in the back of her mouth. The fighters were dragged away. The music started up again.

10

"You fuck like my husband," she said, smoking at him from her bed. Christmas adjusted his hat in the mirror. It was early next morning.

"Where is your husband?"

"He's dead."

"My dear woman, are you implying I don't move around enough?" Christmas gave her a hearty laugh. She was obviously astounded by his performance. They often were. "How do I look?"

"You look old."

"Everyone looks older in the morning."

"Especially old people," she said, stubbing out her cigarette with force. He turned around, marvelling at this woman folding her arms before him. Christmas assumed he'd been masterful. In fact, sprawling with rum, he'd barely managed to get his clothes off. It had been a long time since Lola had liked a man enough to sleep with him. This one had really let her down.

"Why don't we have dinner tonight?"

"I don't want to have dinner with you."

Ah, the spirit, he chuckled to himself, *of these Latin women!* Putting his hands in his pockets, his fingers came across the business card for Pepito's brother's bar. "Do you know this place in Sabana Grande – El Barco?"

"Yes. I know it."

"See you there at eight?"

"*Verga*! I told you. I don't want to see you for dinner. I don't want to see you again."

"Wonderful," said Christmas, granting his hat-angle final approval, "eight it is."

He showed himself out through an apartment full of pictures ringed with lace and children watching television. Two old women gave him toothy grins. It was raining. He caught a cab back to the hotel, easily avoiding the receptionist in the vast lobby. He went back to his room. He counted his money. He decided to spend the day exploring Caracas and work on his plan of action for the weeks ahead. He could travel to Guiria with Lola! Perhaps he would open a bar there. Or work as some kind of consultant for people wishing to trade with Europe.

After a nap, he breakfasted on *cachapas* – corn pancakes – stuffed with ham and cheese, *guyaba* fruit, and several slices of buttered toast and marmalade. Then Christmas went wandering through the city. He walked through Sabana Grande, Los Caobos and Pinto Salinas, regularly stopping for beers. He crossed streets that ended in clouds and mountains. He found decaying squares and market stalls. Artisans lay beside their bracelets. A man with a white beard guarded trolleys full of books.

Christmas took the metro to Bellas Artes and walked into Parque Los Caobos, wandering beneath its trees, noting joggers, a practising saxophonist, school groups all in red. Junkies queued for food and treatment at one of the Chávez *misións*. Lovers by the fountain watched a man sing. Outside, Christmas found a restaurant covered with patterned tiles. Here he ate his first *empanada*. Emily's grandmother was right – they were delicious: fried corn pastries stuffed with meat or fish, onion and spices. He left Emily the last bite on his plate and ordered coffee. It was weaker than he was used to, and bitter, but serving it in these little plastic cups really was a stupid idea. How was a man meant to pick it up without burning his fingers? It trembled and sloshed about. Christmas let it go cold then downed it in one. He patted at his brow with paper towels and stared out into the street. A man wheeled a safe down the pavement. Christmas paid up and followed behind, past the soldiers, the music and stalls and phone cards and lottery tickets and cheap underwear and pirate videos and food and graffiti and the Chávez government is your government. His feet began to hurt but his eyes grew younger, dazzled by the beauty of Venezuelan women. "In Caracas a man can fall in love twenty times a day," he proclaimed to an invisible audience, "and twice, seriously."

"Lo-la Ro-sa!" he sang at a bemused luggage porter while approaching the entrance of his hotel, "Lola Rosa. Lola Rosa. Lola," he gave her last name a Chávez roll of the 'r's, "R-r-r-rosa!" and skipped into the lobby.

"Mister Christmas?" A tall, thin hotel manager appeared in front of him. He had a strong American accent, and seemed to have been taught English by the internet.

"Yes, my good man! How the very devil may I be of service?"

"Mister Christmas, in regard to your residency and payments due thereof, certain questions have been raised vis-à-vis your—"

"Credit card? Must have handed over an old one when I got here. I'll go straight up to my room, have a shower and be back with another one in two ticks. OK, young man?" He patted the manager on the arm, then smiled at him like a proud father.

Christmas returned to his room and ordered a lunch of scallops and then Argentine steak along with a bottle of extremely expensive burgundy. Then he enjoyed an extended siesta. Then an extended bath. Then an extended period of dressing and self-examination. "Well, damnation seize my soul!" he exclaimed cheerfully to the mirror, identifying the lightly agitated sensation in his stomach as nerves. Nerves indeed. Harry Christmas didn't feel nervous about women! He checked himself again and then his watch. It was time to meet Lola Rosa.

Out in Caracas, the evening was under way. Transsexual hookers on Avenida del Libertador were already recommending themselves to passing cars underneath a huge banner that said: '*SOCIALISMO*'. Almost seven feet tall in their heels, one had an Adam's apple so pronounced she looked as if she'd swallowed a cricket ball. Christmas marvelled at those wonderful breasts, solid as helmets and far from the only amplified bosom on display. Indeed, Christmas had become convinced that Caracas was the breast enhancement capital of the world. Everyone, it seemed, was in training for the Miss Venezuela competition, but if one thing was for certain, it was the rapid technological progress of vanity. Christmas couldn't help feeling that in ten years time all these stiff tits would look terribly out of date.

He entered the bar at exactly eight o'clock. It was a wooden submarine, with a low curved roof and a vaguely naval feel to the doors and uniforms. He took a seat. They were playing a salsa version of 'Hotel California'. In the middle of the spirit shelves a 'Polar' beer sign hummed below the music. A weathered-looking couple folded over each other gave him a brief look. Otherwise the place was empty.

Christmas had once owned a bar. The son of a Streatham dentist and his former assistant, the young Harry realised in his late teens that there were easier ways to get on in life than further education, so he left grammar school, poshed up his accent, and got a job at an auction house. The antiques game had given him a taste for embellishment – and so began a career of running doomed and dodgy businesses, including a bar, a drinks delivery firm, a company that imported glassware from the Far East and a curtain fitters.

"*Si, Señor?*" The barman was in front of him. He scanned the rows. City of London Gin – an obvious fake. Dewar's, Grant's, Chivas Regal and other revolting whiskies shamelessly parading as the cream of Scotland. Blended filth. The only blended filth that Christmas had affection for was Whyte and Mackay to which he said 'och aye' on the frequent occasions when he didn't have twenty-five pounds to spend on a bottle of scotch, or he did have twenty-five pounds, but needed two. He decided to test the available rums and ordered a Superior. It was predictably inferior. Ten minutes passed. Lola Rosa still hadn't arrived. He tried a Gran Reserva. Passable. Twenty five past eight. He tried a Cacique. That was better. More time passed. The Cacique was rather good. At nine o'clock, he officially knighted the brand as his rum of choice by touching the glass on each side with a cocktail stick and then bidding it rise to his lips. The bar was filling up. Lola Rosa wasn't coming. After a few more drinks, he stopped looking up when someone came in. Lola Rosa. Lola Rosa. Why the devil hadn't she come?

"So where are you from?" asked the barman in English. It was midnight. Christmas was drunk.

"England."

"England? So which is your team – Manchester United?"

"I detest football."

"English and you hate football? Seriously? Wow. I haven't met an English before who doesn't like football."

52

Christmas looked into his rum.

"How much does it cost to start up a bar in this town?"

"Really I don't know. You want that I ask my boss?"

"No. Don't bother. Thanks anyway."

"So, why you come to Venezuela?" Christmas shook his drink. Then he put his finger in it, stirred it some more, took his finger out, licked it and downed what was left. *OK, OK*, thought Christmas loudly to himself, *Why am I here? Ran off with my fiancée's money. Wasn't my high point. Bit short on high points of late. Bit fucking scarce. Bit fucking thin-on-the-ground, the old 'high points'* …

"Awful."

"*Que?*"

"I did something awful. Shameful. Ran out like a coward. Ran here. Caracas. Tell me, young man, what's the worst thing you've ever done to a woman?" The barman laughed uncomfortably and filled his customer's glass.

"I try not to do bad things to anyone."

"This isn't a fucking job interview. We're here, two men, and I'm asking you – have you ever betrayed a woman?"

"Sure," the barman shrugged, "I have fooled around."

"Not just cheated on, *betrayed*. Are you following?" Christmas downed his drink and gestured for another. "Do you know what Whites is?"

"Whites?"

"It's a gentlemen's club in London."

"I have never been to London."

"I am probably not the first man to have completely fucked himself up by accepting a dinner invitation to that contemptible place."

"And there was a woman there?"

"No women allowed, matey! I wish there had been. Atmosphere was like a funeral."

"Somebody died?"

"Government was about to bring in their bloody Nazi smoking ban. Old Harry here finds himself at their final cigar dinner. Champagne, cigar, soup, cigar, white wine, cigar, main course with several different reds, cigar, pudding, cigar, dessert wine, cigar, port, more port and another bloody cigar." The barman took an order, nodding to Christmas that he was still listening. "So there we were, drunk as priests in this old panelled dining room stared at by endless portraits of droopy-eyed toffs and I had the misfortune to be sat next to some old boy who had long forgotten how to use consonants. Couldn't understand a bloody word. He joined in the toasts all right, but beyond that – ooo-uuu-aaa-ooo-aaa – completely incomprehensible. Anyway for some reason the old bugger took a shine to me and after we left the dining room I couldn't shake him, mumbling into my ear about Tony-bloody-Blair or something – anyway I tended to nod and say yes and he seemed so over the moon that somebody was finally agreeing with him he insisted I come back to his house in Pimlico and crack open a special reserve '59 he'd been saving—"

"One minute, please." The barman served some more customers, then returned to Christmas.

"Now then, due to circumstances I shan't go into, I didn't actually own my own place any more, so I thought, 'Why not? – do the old bugger a favour.' Of course he hadn't said 'Pimlico', he'd said 'my place in Plymouth, shall we go?' but without most of the bloody consonants – well, suffice it to say he had a Daimler outside with his chauffeur. I got in, passed out, woke up near bloody Plymouth! Quite a shock I can tell you, and by the time I'd worked out what had gone on, there we were, pootling up the drive to this bloody great pile, dogs, staff, the whole caboodle. I'm shown to an extremely comfortable guest room, the old boy insists I stay the weekend, won't take no for an answer, and so I say to myself, why the devil not, eh Christmas, why the devil not?

Anyway, turns out I'm not the only guest. He's got his god-daughter staying there – Diana, about my age, not bad looking in a country sort of way. Sand bags and glad rags. Lots of teeth – you know the type. Well, you probably don't, but anyway I could tell she took a shine to old Harry right from the off. So I told her I was a widower – true – and a big shot in the media – not so true. Didn't take much to convince – just acted like a complete cunt and made a couple of loud phone calls to no one about 'the project' and how 'Woody and I' were going to 'hump the money pig' – you know, all that bollocks. Well, you probably don't, but it worked a treat. Kept the old boy happy of course, agreed with every damn thing he was saying even though he could have been reciting Eskimo poetry for all I know, and pretty soon I could tell he was telling her what a fine chap I was, in fact I wouldn't be surprised if the crafty bugger hadn't brought me down with his goddaughter in mind. Hubby had popped his clogs a few years back and as far as I could tell she was rather fond of the good life and was sick of waiting around for the old man to do the decent thing and croak. Bottom line: she was on the look-out for a man with the readies to take care of her, i.e. yours truly." Christmas finished his drink and tapped it on the side for another. The barman filled his glass.

"A weekend became a week, the weeks became months and pretty soon we were back in London living at hers. I'd kept up the bollocks about my glittering career, how I didn't have a house because I'd just sold mine to George Michael etcetera, arranged a couple of people I know to drop by, or bump into us in the street, talk business and what have you, drop a few names to get her excited, and then after she'd been sending out the hints, dived in there with the old, 'We're not getting any younger, let's just do it right now' speech, 'Got Cannes coming up' blah-di-blah. Well of course she jumped at it. So then—" Christmas sighed. "So then, we open an account together, she sticks in a big wodge and I take the lot out in cash and leg it, which, I may say, was pretty much what she was planning to do to me, though perhaps more of a slow march towards the grave than the old hit-and-run ..." The barman began to have a conversation with one of his colleagues, but Christmas kept going. "Needless to say of course Diana screamed blue bloody murder. I mean I – can't blame, I mean – look I've done some – but I'd never done anything like that before – don't feel especially terrific about it, but I was in a hole, *am* in a hole, and when you're in a hole, well, you don't know what you'll do, until you're in one ... anyway ... well, anyway, like I said, it's just what she was planning to do to me, exactly the bloody the same if you really look at it. She wouldn't have given old Christmas a second look if she knew he was up to his eyeballs in debt and without a pot to piss in ..." Christmas took a swig and crunched down on an ice cube. "Besides, she was hardly Snow White. Hadn't even told me she had a son. In fact, she explicitly told me she didn't have any children. Technically true, I suppose. Stepson. One of her friends let it slip in the end. Total nutter. Does all that battle recreation stuff at the weekends, you know, well, you probably don't, but anyway Hubby had this kid from a previous marriage. First wife died in mysterious circumstances. Topped herself, by the sounds of it because Hubby was a first class bastard. Used to knock Diana about, and the kid. He gets thrown out of the navy or something, becomes a history teacher, drops dead.

"The stepson, William – absolutely mad about his new mother. Followed her everywhere apparently, like a puppy, but once Hubby had keeled over he goes from bad to worse. Chip off the old block. Kicked out of school for bullying. Pretty much raped a girl at a party once. Girl was sparked out from the booze and she woke up with Junior on top of her. Well, that was it as far as Diana was concerned. Didn't want to have anything else to do with him, but he kept turning up drunk in her garden in the middle of the night, that sort of thing. Totally obsessed with her. She got a restraining order in the end. Yes, she kept shtum about Mummy's little cherub, didn't she, until she started threatening me with him ... Christ. He turned up at my place. Like I said, not really my place any more according to the bank, but that's another story. Fucking great knife! Nearly fucking killed me!—Escaped by a whisker young man, by a *whisker*. Scared the fucking bejesus out of me, I can tell you." Christmas looked down. His hands were trembling.

The barman walked away to serve another customer. Christmas downed his drink. He closed his eyes against the memory: parking outside his flat in Streatham. The 'For Sale' signs were back up, and he was just about to pull them down again when he heard someone shout his name. The next thing he knew, William Slade was running up the pavement towards him, a knife in his hand. Christmas only just got back into his car in time, accelerating up the road with Slade in the rear-view mirror. He had driven straight to the airport and bought a ticket to Caracas.

Christmas ordered another Cacique. Then another. The rum was taking over. He rotated his knuckles against his eyes until they stung, stirring the last few drinks into the cauldron of feeling that was bubbling up through his veins.

What the devil had he taken Diana's money for in any case? Twenty-six thousand pounds. It certainly wasn't enough to reverse his fortunes. What was it then? Just a needless prolonging of the inevitable. What did he really think he was going to do here? Discover oil?

He took out the poetry book from his jacket pocket, *Muerte y Memoria* by Eugenio Montejo. It was Emily's favourite book, the red jacket still clinging to the cover, always beside the lamp on her side of the bed. He used to read it to her when she was ill or when she couldn't get to sleep. It had been a present from her beloved Venezuelan grandmother and Christmas hadn't let go of it since the day of Emily's funeral. She had always wanted to visit Guiria, her grandmother's port town on the Caribbean side of the country. He'd promised that one day he would take her. Now he was going to take what he had left, this book. He would sit on the beach she'd dreamt of, read to her one last time and push the book into the sand. Christmas gave the book a kiss and put it back in his pocket. He sighed.

So this was the plan? He was just going to bury Emily again, spend all the money, go back to England, and then what – back to penury and disgrace? The bar was crowded and loud. He was alone. Was he to become one of those pensioners checking the coin tray of every public phone, shivering in his slippers, alone in a bedsit somewhere with nothing to keep him company but complaints? No, no, no – there was no going back. Better off adrift in foreign waters, playing his own tune even if the ship were going down. He was better here, unhindered, the sovereign of his own decline. Death and the banks had taken everything he ever had, but even they could not—

Oh stop it, Pops, for God's sake, he heard Emily say, *listen to yourself. Honestly – you're like a child. A great big pissed fat child.*

"Typical bloody woman!" Christmas announced to the bar, cocking his head to the roof. "You're dead. Leave me alone!"

Shut up, Pops. You're making a fool of yourself. Look – you're annoying everyone.

"And why shouldn't I make a fool of myself, Emmy, eh?" he thundered.

"Please, Señor—" said the barman.

"Who fucking cares?"

"*Señor*, your voice, please. Lower." Christmas looked at the barman. He blinked and returned to his rum. A glut of tears rose in his throat. He drank it down.

Alcohol cloaked his mind. He would never remember Pepito coming into the bar, also drunk, embracing him noisily. He asked Christmas lewd questions about Lola Rosa and then ushered his brother, the owner, into the bar from a back office. The three men drank shot after shot of a clear, sweet liquid that Christmas could not pronounce.

At some point, Christmas left. Staggering under the weight of the booze, he wandered down the street. People approached him, whispering and propositioning. He waved and grunted them away. He stepped over a man asleep in the street. He walked on a few paces, stopped, took out twenty bolívares, went back, and stuffed it deep into the man's grimy pocket. Somehow he made it back to the hotel. With assistance from the night porters, Christmas finally crashed into his room and collapsed onto the bed. The ceiling fan was on. He took off a shoe and then fell backwards again. He threw the shoe at the fan. It caught a blade, bounced off the wall and hit him in the face.

11

Slade stood in the doorway of the hotel room. He imagined various scenarios all at once: fights with assailants who had tried to catch him sleeping; hooded men counter-ambushed and disabled with devastating efficiency. There wasn't enough room for exercises. The mattress looked thin. He shook his head and pushed past the concierge. With his kitbag on his shoulder, Slade walked through the lobby and out into the Chacaito district of central Caracas. He was in unfamiliar territory. The air smelt of damp trees, gasoline and fried corn. Salsa music swung in and out of hearing. Businesswomen trailed hair and cigarette smoke. He had not slept during the flight.

Slade was trying to decide whether he was bigger than most Venezuelans. The only other time he had been out of Europe was a trip to Thailand to have sex with prostitutes, and he'd enjoyed the sensation of being taller than the local people.

Two soldiers walked past, teenage recruits. Slade had tried to enlist in the army when he was eighteen but had walked out of the induction as soon as he realised it was full of men tougher than he was. He lied to everyone that he was kicked out because he had failed the psychological examination. *Unable to accept authority*, he told them. *Too much of a lone wolf.*

He sized up the two soldiers now stopping to chat with a woman and imagined how he would attack them: a blizzard of punches and kicks, balletic moves executed with a serene face.

Slade walked past a school belching children and saw a hotel. It was full. He walked further down the road. *'Explosion del Poder Communal'* said the billboard. *'Nadie detiene La Revolución!'* There were more hotels, but they were either full or too expensive or failed his strategic assessment. Light rain began to fall. Slade fell back into the familiar reverie about defeating Harry Christmas. He imagined calling Diana, saying the words 'it is done', then hanging up. She would stare at the phone, weeping tears of gratitude, desperate to be reunited. No one would ever dare to hurt her again. He could be summoned at an instant: her protector, a Saxon warrior, a vengeful ghost. Slade saw distant neon and followed a long wall covered in graffiti. 'This is for Diana' he imagined himself saying as he held Christmas' body by its neck before administering the final crackling twist. As he realized that the neon lights were not a hotel but a bar, three men crossed the street, coming towards him in a hurry.

One of the men said something in Spanish. Another pulled out a screwdriver and pointed it at Slade. They surrounded him.

They were shouting, pushing him. One was tugging at the kitbag. *They are robbing me*, thought Slade, several seconds after it had begun.

Something heavy slammed into the side of his head. He let go of his bag as his hands went to his face. He felt blood. He was punched again in the neck and jaw. He went down and covered his head. 'No! Please!' he cried, begging them to stop, to leave him alone, as they kicked and stomped him. A shoe crushed his face against the pavement. They were still shouting and hissing in Spanish. One of them spat in his face. They ran off.

Slade lay there for several moments. Someone approached and asked him if he was OK. Slade rolled over and looked at the sky, at the young man trying to help and the unfamiliar buildings. He blinked and exhaled, then got up. Once on his feet he realised that he was shaking and the young man was holding his arm. Slade pushed him away and ran off up the street, gripping the side of his head. He was wearing the travel wallet around his waist. He still had his passport. He still had his money, his credit card and the photograph of Harry Christmas. But he had lost his father's knife.

Slade was in a side street. He stopped running and crouched against a wall. He pressed his knuckles into his eyes and made a sharp, guttural noise as if this could clear away what had just happened. Slade stood up, wiping away tears. He went out onto the main road, trying to control his breathing and met eyes with a frail junkie sitting on the curb. The man had no shoes on, his clothes and body smeared with dirt and the constant breath of traffic. He had the physique of a child, eyes black with poverty and craving. Scuttling to his feet, he followed Slade, jabbering pleas with pinched fingers bobbing at his mouth. He tugged on Slade's shirt. Slade told him to go away and turned down an alley. It smelt of burnt sweets. The man followed, begging and tapping his arm.

Slade suddenly turned, pushing the man against the wall. "Where's my father's knife?" Slade cried. The man looked at him in disbelief. He began to whimper. Slade headbutted him in the face, breaking his nose. The man was silent. He touched his nose and looked at his hand and saw the blood. Slade stepped back. He tried to give the man a roundhouse kick to the head. He only got as high as his waist but it still sent him flying into rubbish on the floor.

"*Yes*," hissed Slade. Then he ran off.

12

Christmas woke with a hangover. The outer shell of his body recognised the comfort of pillow and sheets, yet inside there was turmoil; unnamed forces raced about like frightened animals. His heart hammered at its cage.

He thought about beer, a cold, cold beer to slake his thirst. He imagined it fresh from an icebox, dripping lasciviously, erupting on his tongue with fountains of refreshment. He looked about him and spied a bottle of water. It was empty.

Christmas was so hung-over his head was a different shape. His eyes were smaller, his skull swollen. When he pulled on his hat and looked in the mirror it didn't suit him any more. He went into the lobby but it was too shiny, too full of sheen. Everyone seemed to be staring at him.

"Mister Christmas," said the junior manager, suddenly appearing before him. "Could you come with me please?" Christmas let out a deep sigh.

"How do I look to you?"

"Excuse me?"

"I said," he repeated, holding his forehead, "how do I look to you? Do I look like a man who wants to have a conversation about mistakes that some credit card company has made, which don't even matter, as I have plenty of cash, or do I look like a man who needs some remedial assistance of a liquid or deep fried nature, should he be denied which, may result in some unfortunate effluence all over your nice clean floor? Do I make myself clear?"

"Mister Christmas, while trying to make every effort—"

"This is an outrage!" bellowed Christmas, "Do you mean to hold me to ransom?" and with that he strode away from the startled manager.

Christmas hurried to the restaurant serving breakfast. He asked for a beer. He was given a Solera. He downed the thing and then looked at the bottle incredulously. How could they be allowed to get away with this? It wasn't beer – it was some horrific soft drink, thin, weak, but yes – cold. He asked for another and ate a quail egg *arepa*, followed by a croissant, four fried eggs on toast, a bowl of honey porridge, a plate of potatoes fried with onion, a bowl of fruit salad and two double espressos. He signed his bill and returned to the reception desk.

"Now then," Christmas started, "apparently there's some problem with— " He put his hand in his pocket for his wallet. It wasn't there. He tried his other pocket. He tried all his pockets. "Sorry," he said. "Just a minute." He went up to his room.

Christmas strode through the door expecting his wallet to be on the sideboard. It wasn't. It wasn't on the bedside table. It wasn't on the desk. It wasn't by the sink.

He undressed the room, checking every drawer, every fold, every corner, every gap. He manhandled himself. He shouted and swore. He had felt it this morning in his jacket pocket, or had that been his passport? He went through his clothes. When had he taken it out? Where had he put it down? This morning? Last night? He checked the toilet. He checked the safe. He stood on the bed. He leant out the window. He sat down. He leapt up again. He checked the room again and again, whispering, "This is not happening, this cannot be happening ..." Panic swept through his system. He emptied his pockets, checking through his remaining bolívares, as if it could somehow contain a wallet between the paper notes. All together he had 263 bolívares in cash. His wallet contained four thousand dollars. He looked under the bed. He kicked the bed.

Christmas went down to reception, sought out the junior manager, asked where the nearest ATM machine was located and informed him that he was withdrawing the necessary funds right away.

Without dark glasses to act in his defence, Christmas was interrogated by daylight, the sun sitting in judgement while an unfamiliar, feverish city whispered and accused. He went back to El Barco. It was barely open. There was a different man behind the bar and someone else cleaning the floor. They looked at him blankly and shook their heads.

He went back to the hotel and made it to his room without being stopped. He searched it again. He went into the bathroom. He checked under the towels, in the bin, under the sink, inside the cistern. Then he sat down on the toilet and closed his eyes, seething black spells of hatred against the world. How could this be happening? He went and sat down on the bed. He took out Emily's book and held it against his face, groaning. Why hadn't he listened to her? Why hadn't he put it in the room safe?

His secured credit card was undoubtedly out of funds. Apart from an emergency thousand pounds hidden away in London, the rest of Diana's money he had already spent or gambled. He paced around his room until lunchtime. There was neither a friend nor a bank left in the world that would lend him a penny more. He was stranded. "Up on two legs, man!" he shouted at himself. "Pull yourself together!" Most of his money was gone. That was no longer the point. The point was: what was he going to do next?

Christmas rang room service. He ordered a large vodka and tonic, a bottle of carbonated water, cream of tomato soup, roast chicken with fried rice and vegetables and a cocktail glass stuffed with balls of sorbet. He consumed the lot, summoning energy for his next move. Then, as he had anticipated, the phone rang.

13

"I'm sorry to keep you waiting, sir," said the duty manager as he hung up the receiver. "Actually Mister Christmas said he's on his way down.

"Remember," said Slade, "it's a surprise." The duty manager gave him a professional smile. The side of Slade's face was bruised. He smelt of alcohol.

Slade sat beside a table fanned with magazines that faced the elevator doors. He took in the luxury that Christmas was buying with his stepmother's money.

Once Slade had found a hotel room he had cleaned the blood from the cut above his ear and ordered a bottle of whisky. It was a wretched room that stank of cigarettes but he had taken it anyway, desperate for Caracas to be on the other side of a locked door. He sat on the bed staring at a television he couldn't understand with toilet paper in one hand and a glass of fake scotch in the other, patting his head for new blood, hands starting to steady as he got drunk and retold himself what had just happened: how he had sprung to his feet as soon as the bandits holstered their guns and fled; how he chased them; how they disappeared into their own city like the rats they were; how if they had fought like men, he would have walked away from a pile of bodies with his kitbag still on his shoulder; how it was Harry Christmas' fault. They were his men, sent to deliver another insult, another humiliation, another theft. Slade thought back to his first encounter with Christmas and cursed the fat man's escape.

Diana had freely opened an account with her fiancé so the police were not interested when Christmas disappeared with her money. Slade had no idea she even had a boyfriend. He hadn't talked to Diana in almost two years, though he often drove past her house and wrote letters and emails that were never answered.

When she called, she was so raving drunk he could hardly understand what she was saying. He went over to her house and she was crawling around the kitchen floor as if newly blind, empty bottles of wine everywhere, screeching and sobbing out the story of how Harry Christmas had betrayed her; how she wanted his legs broken; how she wanted him dead. Finally, he had a mission.

Diana started to droop and he gathered her up and carried her to bed and watched her sleep as he used to when he was a child, curling up on the end with the bedroom door locked against his father, her eyes swollen, his hands in hers.

The next day Slade started his own investigation. He found a tracking company on the internet and spent fifty pounds to find out where Christmas lived. He ignored the phone messages from Diana, apologising, saying she had changed her mind, ordering him not to do anything, and drove to a quiet residential street in Streatham, South London. He couldn't find anywhere to park but drove around and around for more than an hour until he found a space from where he could still make out the front door of

Number 14, Holly Avenue. He got out, walked over and rang the bell. No answer. He went back to his car and waited.

Slade was on a stakeout. For the first time in his life he felt a craving for doughnuts. He left the car and jogged up the road onto the high street, nervous that he might miss Christmas. He found a Greggs bakery but they didn't have any doughnuts left so he bought a tuna sandwich, a large bottle of Coca-Cola, a coffee, and a gingerbread man. Slade went back to the car, put the food inside, then rang the doorbell. No answer.

Listening to the car's radio he ate the food and drank the coffee. He needed to piss. When there was no one around he urinated as fast as he could between two vans on the other side of the road. He went back to his car and waited.

In the glove compartment there was a Bowie knife and Slade practised getting it out and springing from the car. It got dark. He needed a shit. For an hour he fought the sensation as it grew ever more merciless, receding, coming back with greater urgency until, just as he was ready to shit between the two vans, one of them drove away. He was tormented by the certainty that the moment he took his eyes off the street, Christmas would appear. There was a pharmacy on the corner so he hobbled there and bought two packets of Imodium and some ProPlus. He went back to the car, nearly shitting himself. After swallowing half a pack of the antidiarrhoeals, the urge subsided, but his stomach hurt. He was sweating. He glared at the people who walked past and peered at him in his car going nowhere. It was the middle of the night. He had been there for more than ten hours. To stop himself falling asleep he took the caffeine pills and stayed awake all night until the dawn spread over the street.

When London woke up, vehicles sometimes blocked his view and he would curse and get out until they moved on. Another day of the shooting pains in his stomach, sticky clothes, the radio.

He took more Imodium, more ProPlus. When he could no longer ignore the hunger Slade risked another trip to Greggs and bought bags of doughnuts and cookies and crisps so that he wouldn't have to go again, but as he ate the urge to shit came back. He took a handful of Imodium. He was increasingly disturbed by the idea that Christmas might have already left town. He thought about breaking into Christmas' house but he didn't really know how to disable an alarm system.

Through the whole of the next night, Slade waited, joining in with the radio discussion programmes, insulting everyone who spoke, taking more caffeine pills, his stomach swelling and twisting. He saw in another dawn, staring through his windscreen at the blue front door, until late that morning Harry Christmas drove past him in an old beige Mercedes and parked right at the other end of the street.

Slade, his hand shaking from caffeine and exhaustion, grabbed the knife, wrapped it in his jacket, and crossed the road onto the pavement. There wasn't anyone about. His prey locked the Mercedes and Slade yelled, "Christmas!" Slade saw him turn, straighten, and then bluster himself back into the car. Slade started to run. The jacket fell, the knife exposed. He sprinted towards the Mercedes but he had given himself away too early. Christmas pulled out into the road and tore off, leaving Slade running after him until he collapsed on the bonnet of a parked car, heaving out his breaths, the knife still in his hand. People were staring and pointing. Slade panicked. He ran back to his own car and drove off in the opposite direction, back to Sussex, driving right up behind people on the motorway until they moved, beeping his horn and shouting at everyone to fuck off.

Slade might have lost the trail there, but he went to see his *eorlderman*, the leader of his Dark Ages re-enactment group. Peter Dunstone, a retired West Sussex police chief in his late seventies, was a living history enthusiast so lost in his favoured period that he plaited his beard. When Slade, one of his best *thegns*, told him that Harry Christmas had dishonoured his mother and the memory of his father – the great Saxon sin – he was only too happy to reward his loyal subject by abusing powers meant for the prevention of terrorism. With a few phone calls to his old friends, he obtained details of Christmas' passport use and credit card purchases. Slade rang the outdoor pursuits company where he was working as a paintball marshal and told them he had a family emergency. He booked himself on the next flight to Caracas. Once installed in the hotel room he called his *eorlderman* who told him that a secured credit card registered to Christmas had been used to book a room at the Gran Melía. Slade went straight there in a taxi.

The elevator doors pinged open. A wealthy family. They pinged open again. A group of businessmen and a child. Something caught Slade's eye to his right, across the lobby floor. He thought he saw a cat rush behind a chair. He looked again – the man on the chair – his hair, his suit, the way his head tilted back as he read – the man on the chair was his father. Slade stood up. He was in trouble for losing the hunting knife. The man closed his newspaper. Slade refocused. The man stood up. It wasn't his father. Now he was coming closer, he didn't even look that much like him. *Ping*. More businessmen. Again and again the elevator doors opened, offering everyone but Harry Christmas. After several minutes he had another conversation with the duty manager who sent up a porter. The porter returned with an empty suitcase.

"This is very bad, *Señor* – your friend – we are waiting for—"

Slade ran off into the hotel. He ran around the pool. He went into all the restaurants and bars, up the emergency staircase and along the corridors, into the business centre and even the conference rooms. He ran outside. He ran around the hotel. He ran back in and went downstairs and into the gym, the sauna and then the jacuzzi.

The air was heavy with mist. There was a thin, elderly Venezuelan man, hairy as a bear, in red goggles and blue swimming cap. He was bobbing up and down playfully in the water. He waved at Slade.

Slade returned to the concierge desk. "I need to see his room."

14

Christmas put down the receiver and then put on two pairs of trousers. He tightly folded as many of his clothes as possible into a plastic bag. His new suitcase would have to stay.

He put on his Panama hat and left the room. Instead of taking the guest lift, he took the service elevator to the ground floor and headed in search of the staff entrance, his heart full of remorse that there were at least two restaurants on the lower ground floor that must remain unassailed. Christmas walked as far as Avenida del Libertador before he realised that he'd left Emily's book on the bedside table.

"What the fuck is wrong with you!" he cried out. He cursed and shook his head and studied the sky. He had no choice.

Outside the staff entrance, he ducked behind some bins and stuffed the plastic bag and his hat out of sight. He smoothed down his hair and strolled confidently back into the staff entrance, playing the part of the idiot tourist. "This way? Sorry, what? Thank you, thank you ..."

He took the service elevator back up to his floor.

He stepped out. It looked clear. At the far end of the corridor he could see trolleys outside the rooms being cleaned and restocked. He still had his room key.

Christmas walked briskly to the door. It was ajar. He entered the room to find two men looking at him. At the foot of the bed, only a step away, was a hotel porter holding Emily's book. William Slade was by the window.

A strange moment elapsed as they all looked at each other. Christmas thought he was going to collapse. The shock of seeing Slade had emptied his body of all its strength but for the mad thudding of his heart.

"Get out," Slade told the hotel porter but the man didn't move.

"How—" Christmas started, but Slade cut him off.

"I followed the stink of shit," he grinned.

"*¿Qué está pasando aquí, Señores?*"

"Nice room. How much was it?"

"*Señores?*"

"Where's the rest of the money?"

"Now look—"

"Thieving CUNT!" Slade lunged toward Christmas, but the porter caught and rammed him against the wall, shouting for help. Emily's book was sticking out from the porter's hand by Slade's chin. Christmas snatched it and fled, stuffing it into his jacket pocket.

He ran back towards the service elevator. He hit the button but it didn't open and he dared not wait. Slade was howling out and he was too scared to check if he was being chased so Christmas crashed through the next door, not realizing it was the emergency stairs, charging into empty space, his right leg buckling with its mistake. He fell down a flight of ten concrete steps.

The first impact was on his right shoulder. His scalp gashed open on the edge of a step. He bounced, hitting his back, his hip, his knees, slamming against the wall.

Dazed, blood already streaming down his face, the miracle of fear had his vast bulk up and then down the stairs with only half a glance above him to see if Slade was following. Moments later Christmas found himself on the ground floor in a corridor full of laundry. He grabbed some hand towels from a pile and held them to his head. Blood was running down his neck, his heart rioted in his chest. He staggered past the kitchens, waiters and cleaners calling out to him. His lungs were clutching at breath; he couldn't run anymore; his legs were starting to seize up.

Christmas heard a shout. He looked behind but Slade wasn't there. A cook was in front of him. Christmas took away the towels. The man saw his injury and, wide-eyed, let him pass. Out of the staff entrance he made it to the bins, grabbed his plastic bag and his hat and stumbled out into the street. He stopped a cab, checking behind him. No Slade.

Christmas thought he was going to vomit. The taxi driver was asking him where he wanted to go. "Forward," he crowed, "Just go, keep going, go!" He took the towel down from his head and looked at the blood. He passed out for a second.

"*Qué pasa? Qué pasa?*" the taxi driver was asking him. Christmas came to.

"Fell – down the stairs," he managed. Pain was booming across his skull.

"*Qué?*"

"*Abajo las escaleras – me caí.*" They turned a corner and Gran Melía disappeared. He was trembling. He gripped Emily's book in his jacket. He eked out tiny breaths against the crushing of his chest, towel against head, great flows of sweat pouring all over his body. Slade was in Venezuela! How could it be? How could it be?

Christmas tried to calm himself, to manage his breathing. The taxi driver was watching him in the rear view mirror. "Take me to a hotel," he said. "Cheap hotel."

The Jolly Frankfurt Hotel was an uneasy dollop of bricks between two apartment blocks, off Avenue Lecuna in the Teatros district. Rooms were sixty bolívares per night, fifteen per hour. Christmas heaved himself up a steep and filthy staircase holding on to his hat and plastic bag, still patting his head with the gory towel. His right arm was surely broken. His shoulder was agony. He arrived at reception. An ancient man in spectacles and a cowboy hat smoked as he watched a dubbed episode of *Friends*. Wheezing and drenched, Christmas collapsed against the bell. The old man unfastened the cigarette from his lips and turned to inspect his latest victim.

"*Si?*" He looked over a hundred years old. His face had died, but somewhere at the back two lights had been left on. They talked in Spanish.

"Do you have a room?" whispered Christmas heavily.

"What happened to your head?"

"I fell down some stairs."

"These stairs?"

"No."

"Oh. Good."

"Do you have a room?"

"Yes." There was a pause.

"Can I see it?"

"Yes." There was a longer pause.

"Are you going to show me?"

"No."

"Why not?"

"It's open. Take a look yourself."

"What number is it?"

"Two."

"Where is it?"

"Next to one, *cabrón*."

76

"Well, where's one?"

"I don't know. I don't work here."

"Well, who the hell does, man? For the love of God, I am not in the mood!"

"They've gone out."

"Then how do you know two is open?"

"I've just been in there."

"Why?"

"It's my room."

"Well, what do I want with your room! Jesus Christ!"

"I don't know. You asked me if I have a room, I said yes. My room."

"Listen to me – are there any free rooms in this hotel, yes or no?"

"Number four is free."

"You *do* work here, don't you?" said Christmas leaning over the counter. There was a pause.

"Yes."

"Give me the key." The man unhooked the key for number four from a nail and handed it over. He whistled at his feet and a hound stood up.

"My dog will show you the room. Number four," he said to it. The animal went under the counter, pushed past Christmas' legs and plodded up the stairs. The old man returned to the television. Christmas followed the dog. At the top it turned left and went to the end of the corridor. It pushed Room Four's door open with its nose, barked, and then went back downstairs.

The kindest thing to be said about Room Four was that it was basic. The bed was wedged between two walls, so Christmas would have to climb onto it from the bottom. *Probably enough genetic information in that mattress to restart the fucking human race.* The minuscule bathroom had a pubic hair on the wall by the toilet, no bath, a basin, and a shower head bent in shame. Christmas inspected his head in the mirror and washed his face. There was a gash an inch or so long on top of a tender, swollen lump. His hair was matted with blood. *At least my face is all right*, he thought, examining his neck. He wriggled his moustache.

He took off his jacket and his shirt. It was agony. The bruising had come up quickly, huge patches covering his forearms, his back, the right side of his upper body, arm and shoulder. He took off both pairs of trousers he was wearing. His buttocks and thighs were also badly bruised. His right hip ached. He emptied his belongings from the plastic bag onto the mattress with his left hand. He turned on the ceiling fan. It ground slowly into life and then whirred so fast it threatened to fly off its attachment. He lay down painfully.

Slade was in Venezuela. Christmas tried to make sense of it. How had he found him? First Streatham and now this? He must have discovered which flights he'd taken – but the hotel? Perhaps he had people working for him, people who hacked into computers, that kind of thing – people could do that these days, couldn't they, if they knew how? *Jesus fucking Christ, this is not worth twenty-six thousand pounds.* Had to be the computers. Slade was following him through the computers somehow. He had to use just cash from now on – but what cash? He hardly had any left ...

Christmas battled despair. "No!" he shouted at himself, "Up on two legs, man!" After all, this wasn't the first kicking he'd received. Far from it. He needed to get a grip! Sort himself out! He needed to think, to formulate a plan. He needed stitches in his head, and by the devil and all his works he needed a drink.

After lying there for a long while, Christmas got dressed again, wincing at every move. The headache was astonishing in its power. He still felt dizzy on the stairs. He paid sixty bolívares for the room and prised the location of the nearest medical centre out of the old man. He then headed out onto the street, walking slowly towards

La Clínica Popular *El Paraíso*, checking around himself all the time, his heart full of fear.

He crossed the Autopista Francisco Fajardo and entered the hospital, part of Chávez's *Misión Barrio Adentro* offering free care. He queued for three hours in a room that smelt of lemons, seated between old couples, mothers and boys with bandaged knees. He told the doctor he had fallen down the stairs. The doctor evidently did not believe him. He gave Christmas twelve stitches in his head and implied that the patient had escaped broken bones only by virtue of natural padding. Christmas was given pills for pain and antiseptic cream for the wound, with instructions to keep it clean and to return in a few days.

Patched up, Christmas put on his Panama and went back into the streets to find a *licorería*. Standing away from the sunshine with a Solera in his hand, scanning the passersby, he took stock of his circumstances. *Your circumstances are that you need to stop checking around every five seconds like a rabbit!* Christmas snapped at himself. *Slade got to the hotel, that's it. He's not here, he doesn't know where you are.*

Yet Slade was in this city and evidently meant to kill him. He counted the fold of notes in his pocket – 190 bolívares. Three nights in that shitpit of a room. He drank another beer and thought of Emily and was ashamed. Christmas bought a quarter bottle of rum and made for the metro station, resolving to go back to Parque Oeste and sit beneath the trees until he had come up with a plan.

Once there, he found a stone bench under a *jabillo* tree. He sat down. He tried to concentrate, sipping on rum and feeling his lump. "*El futuro? El futuro?*" A woman was waving a Tarot pack in front of his face. She had short grey hair, her arms covered in bangles, her nose full of rings, and was in a raggedy black dress. "Five bolívares," she said in Spanish. Christmas waved her away.

"Very cheap."

"No, thank you."

"Are you OK?"

"No. Thank you."

"You look very sad," she said. Christmas gave a deep sigh. "I read your cards for free, OK?."

"Oh, why not," he relented. "Might give me some ideas." The woman settled on the other end of the bench. He split the pack for her and then she set about arranging the cards. Her face began to drop.

"Many troubles. Many problems."

"You're the one begging in a park."

"The cards say you are alone. Much travel, much restlessness, much moving from place to place. No time for love. Only time for self. Self, self, self, self, self—"

"OK, that's enough thank—"

"The cards say you face great danger, but also great opportunity. You are at a crossroads. This is why destiny has led you here, to Caracas. Many things happen here."

"That's what the policeman said."

"Policeman read your cards? They take everything! I have spent years—"

"Do you mind?"

"OK, OK, relax ..."

"Don't tell me to relax, woman! I've just had the shit kicked out of me. I am being pursued by a maniac, and I will not be told to relax!"

"I didn't tell you to relax."

"What?"

"The cards tell you to relax."

"Oh, for pity's sake ..."

"The cards say you are at an important moment in your life. Destiny has brought you to this place."

"It was the metro."

"On your right is happiness. On your left is—"

"Dog shit."

"Yes," she agreed, looking at the hardened faeces, "dog shit. You must climb the mountain of your soul. Only then may you fight the demon of your ego."

"Are you recommending the cable car?"

"There is a lovely view."

"Look," huffed Christmas, "this is all a bit vague. That's always the problem with you people – can't you give me something a bit more exact? Look, here's five bolívares. Take it." The woman took the money and returned her gaze to the cards. She turned over two more, nodding her head with interest.

"You will live until the age of ninety-four."

"Ninety-four? That's not bad."

"I didn't say you'd be healthy."

Slade was in Venezuela. Christmas still couldn't believe it. For the rest of the day he stayed in his hotel room, not wanting to risk being outside. All his lines of credit were closed. How could he have been so stupid as to lose his wallet? Why hadn't he left it in the safe? Perhaps it wasn't his fault. Perhaps he had been robbed but just couldn't remember it. For a moment he considered going back to England – he had a flexible return ticket – but he was here to take Emily to Guiria. He squeezed the book in his jacket pocket. He must not let himself be defeated. He must find a way to get some money. He must get out of Caracas.

Eventually he left the hotel to go to El Barco, and was assured again by different staff that his wallet was not there. Lost in thought, he walked for an hour or maybe more without concentrating on where he was going, until he found himself in a leafy residential area, with large white houses behind security fences. He came across a smart café. He went in, sat down with a gasp of pain and ordered an espresso. *Just money*, he was still telling himself, *just a bit of bloody money*. He was used to losing money. "But damn it!" he said out loud. Everyone looked at him. How had Slade found him? And if he had just remembered to take Emily's book! ... The espresso arrived. He took a sip and burnt his lips. "The devil!" He closed his eyes. He felt under his hat for the lump, breathed deeply and counted to ten. Harry Christmas was still alive. He opened his eyes.

The lady he saw in front of him was so unmistakably British you could have spotted it from the moon. She was wearing a flowery summer dress, sandals and a straw hat. She had a large forehead with hooded drooping eyes that made her look as if she were falling asleep and paying attention at the same time. She seemed to be interested in some dreadful pottery that was on display in the window, and, with her business concluded, she was shown to a table. Christmas noticed she wasn't wearing a wedding ring. Then he noticed her large purple feet.

The woman delved into her handbag and pulled out a book. She put on her glasses and began to read, sipping a juice and tapping one foot against the air. Christmas strained to see what she was reading. The author's name was also Harry – *THE NAA TREE POSTAL SERVICE* by Harry Strong. This, surely, was a sign.

She put the book down for a moment and Christmas stood up. He stepped past her table, purposefully knocking the book onto the floor.

"So sorry," he said in Spanish, wincing, picking it up for a quick check. He was in luck – no author's photo. He began to laugh. "Oh dear," he said in English, adjusting his accent up a notch, "Oh dear, oh dear, oh dear. That is funny!"

"What's funny?"

"Do you mind me asking – are you enjoying this?"

82

"Yes, thank you, just finished it. Why do you ask?"

"Well, this is rather embarrassing ... Allow me to introduce myself. My name is Harry – Harry Strong."

15

"You mean you—"
            "That's right."
"No!"
"Yes."
"No!"
"I'm afraid so."
"Judith," she said hurriedly, "Judith Lamb. This is extraordinary!"
"Well, sorry to disturb you—"
"Oh, no, please ..."
"And to knock your book, well, my book, well, *our* book, on the floor."
"Our book ...!"
"Hope it held your interest."
"Oh, it's marvellous, but Mr Strong—"
"Harry, please."
"But Harry – Venezuela – Caracas – I mean what are you doing here? Are you an ex-pat?"

"No," replied Christmas, "my name has always been Harry."

"Pardon me?"

"Actually I'm on a sort of sabbatical. I came here to – I'm afraid it's rather a long and boring story. I'm sure you're much too—"

"Oh no, I would *love* to hear it! Won't you sit down? Can I get you a juice or something or are you off somewhere important?"

"Not at all."

"Will you join me then?"

"Well ..." smiled Christmas, "why not?"

"Marvellous!" said Judith in a deep voice. "Tea with the author straight after the last page! How *vital*. Now hang on and I'll get Juan Carlos on the job. He does a wonderful mixed fruit thingamajig – how about one of those?" Christmas gave Judith a grateful smile and she tore off to the counter. He grabbed the book, turned to the back and read the bumph:

THE NAA TREE POSTAL SERVICE. When University Professor Steven Trafford finds out that his star pupil is in fact his illegitimate son from a forgotten affair, memory and fate compete as the story dips between contemporary Bristol and 1970s Sri Lanka. As conflict with the Tamil Tigers rages, a young teacher and his new wife begin their first term at Colombo's newly-built School of Excellence, run by the beautiful and mysterious Mrs Amarikidivada ...

'Warm and compelling. A tour de force. Sweet and sour and then sweet again.' – EVENING STANDARD

'I thought it was a wonderful book. I really, really did.' – THE GUARDIAN

'Blisteringly urgent. Wistfully timeless.' – TIME

'Three letters, one word, one sound: f**king WOW.' –
GORDON RAMSAY

How dreary, thought Christmas, turning to the inside cover.
The real Harry Strong was married with two children, lived in
Canterbury and was the author of *GHOSTS OF AMARILLO* and
PEABODY'S BOAT.

"So!" said Judith sitting down with his juice, "how did you
think of that ending?"

"I didn't really think of it," he replied, "it sort of ... thought of
me." He knew how these people talked.

"What do you mean?"

"Well, one often feels like one is taking dictation, you know,
and wherever these stories come from, one's just glad that it picked
one to be the mouthpiece."

"But that woman ... when she ... incredible. Is it based on
anyone you know? Oh, I am sorry – listen to me firing all these
questions at you."

"Not at all, Judith. You're spot on. She's based on my wife."

"Your wife killed herself with a snake!"

"Character, I mean. Only partially, you understand, but yes,
definite touches of my wife. My ex-wife now, I should say."

"Ex? Oh you poor thing. Have you just ...?"

"Well, it's all to do with why I'm here, actually. I'm sure you
don't want to ..."

"Oh please," said Judith, leaning forward, "do tell." Christmas
sighed and, looking as deeply into her eyes as he could, set about
creating his new life.

He was recently divorced. No one was to blame, they had
simply grown apart. Rocked yet liberated by the separation he
had decided to come to Venezuela, a country about which he
knew little, in search of inspiration for his next book. The

emotional trauma had been giving him writer's block and he hoped that by throwing himself open to experience his creativity would bounce back. Unfortunately, he had been violently robbed by a taxi driver called Pepito, so he was stranded, all possessions gone, waiting for the credit card company to send over a replacement and for the embassy to arrange a passport. It should have taken a week, but there had been a mix-up, everything was sent to the wrong hotel and sent back again, and now he was stuck in Caracas for he didn't know how long.

"Robbed?" inhaled Judith. "Were you hurt?" Christmas solemnly took off his hat and showed her the stitched lump. Then he pushed up his sleeve to reveal his blackened arms. She clasped her face and shook her head.

So here he was with these plans for escape, for change, for putting his divorce behind him, and he was beginning to regret ever coming here.

"Oh, but Harry, Venezuela is exactly what you need. I got divorced myself not long ago—"

"Oh God! And there I was yabbering on about myself. Judith, forgive me."

"No, no, no. It's fine. It was my choice really. We certainly weren't in love any more, but even so, when you're just so used to someone ... Anyway the point is that's why I didn't go back to England. Creatively, the energy, the light ... it's so *vital*. And the key thing is you've got to move forward. Even if things get a little rough, you've just got to stick it out, haven't you?"

Judith suddenly looked so sad Christmas had to cough before speaking. "Now, please, you've been patiently listening to me, can I get you anything? A coffee or something?"

"Oh, I never touch the stuff. Body is a temple and all that."

"Free to get in?"

"What?" The sadness evaporated. "Oh, I get it! Oh – ha ha ha!" She began to laugh. It was an incredible, ear-splitting sound, like someone practising scales on a rape alarm. "You know I have masses of questions to ask you about your book. I mean for instance when she—"

"If you don't mind Judith, I'm trying to put that book out of my mind. My wife, you see ..."

"Oh, of course, of course, I'm so sorry."

"Plus I have got this silly superstition never to talk about a book once it's finished. I'm convinced it will bring bad luck."

"Really? How interesting."

"Let's talk about you. So how's your boyfriend? Everything working out all right?"

"I beg your pardon?"

"Actually," whispered Christmas, as he leant in close, "what I really wanted to say is 'will you come for lunch with me?'. I was just checking you were still single." Then he winked and pulling back, assumed his previous voice and position. "Did I say boyfriend? I meant your Spanish. How's that coming on?" Judith blushed.

Christmas took Judith out for lunch in an upmarket restaurant, gambling eighty-one bolívares of his remaining 170. They ate tapas, drank a bottle of white Rioja, and talked about art, books and antiques.

"So you live out of town?" asked Christmas.

"Oh yes. I live in Estado Sucre, over in the Caribbean part of the country, *el Oriente*. Have you ever been?"

"The Caribbean part. Really." Things were getting better and better. "Do you know, I have always wanted to go there."

"The colours, the landscape ... Really, it's just what you need. You'll go completely mad cooped up in Caracas for another month. When Columbus arrived, I think it was on his third expedition – he landed in Estado Sucre and do you know he really believed he had found the literal Garden of Eden? Everybody naked. Whopping great fruit everywhere!" Judith began to laugh again. It truly was a painful noise.

"Columbus?"

"Avocados and mangos and coconuts and coffee and bananas and – oh, Harry, the most amazing chocolate rum – you've never tasted anything like it – and well, it's just amazing."

"Are you anywhere near Guiria?"

"Other side of the peninsula. It's on the south coast and I'm on the north – so it's not next door, but not a million miles away either – why?"

"Oh, no reason. It was recommended to me."

"Well, that whole part of the country is so ... I don't know – *vital*."

"It sounds like heaven."

"You must come and visit." Christmas sat forward in his chair, clenching his teeth against the pain.

"Oh Judith, do you really mean that?"

"Yes – yes of I course I mean it." Judith was blushing again. "God, I can't tell you how nice it is just to talk to someone with the same – you know, someone English. I know it sounds awful, and don't get me wrong, I love the people here, but there's not much in the way of chat about Ruskin and Turner."

"You must get lonely."

"Oh no," she gulped at her glass. "Far too busy."

"Far too tough, you mean."

"Well, it's all about moving forward, isn't it? Shall we have some more wine?"

After the meal Christmas took her back to her hotel in Alta Mira. He suggested a nightcap at the bar.

"I'd better not."

"Oh, come on, Judith. Where's the harm?"

"No. I've had a lovely evening, thank you, but I really must go off to bed now, I think." They stood for a moment in silence. Christmas took her hand. She was rather startled. He kissed her on the cheek. She pulled her hand away.

"Goodnight," she peeped, and scuttled off. Christmas turned round and went out of the hotel. He looked up at night sky. He was running out of money. He was running out of time.

The next day he called for her at her hotel but she was out. The day after he tried again. He now owed the Jolly Frankfurter for two nights. If Judith didn't come through with an offer of help he was done for. Another runner from a hotel. Bus to the airport. Failure.

Just as he was heading through the door, checking all around him for Slade, he saw her chatting with the concierge.

"Harry!"

"Judith. I hope you don't mind me dropping in to see you ..." Judith let out a theatrical breath then marched over to him and pecked him on the cheek.

"I got upstairs to my bedroom the other night and realised I didn't have your phone number or anything—"

"Me too, so I thought—"

"Anyway—"

"So I came back. God, it's nice to see you again." They smiled at each other for a moment.

"Do you have any plans today?" asked Judith.

"None whatsoever."

"Then I'm taking you to lunch and I'm paying this time and that's that." Christmas opened his mouth in protest, closed it again, and gave her a deep bow.

The waiter filled their glasses, wiped the neck of the wine bottle and ground it back into the ice bucket. They were in a corner booth of a *tasca* restaurant, just around the corner from the Hotel Continental. Christmas had one hand in his pocket, fingering a fifty bolívar note. It was all he had left.

"Have you ever worked as a waiter, Harry? Or in a kitchen or anything?"

"I have as a matter of fact. Judith—"

"I remember when I was young and waitressing in this Italian place in Bath and a customer came and said he wanted his coffee right away and then went in to the loo, so when his espresso was ready I took it in there and pushed it under the door. Got the bloody sack!" Judith laughed hysterically. Other diners looked over. He downed his glass. He looked down at her purple feet. He had to make his move.

Christmas stopped eating, sighed and looked into the middle distance.

"Harry? Are you OK?"

"God. It's so stupid," he said, refilling his glass.

"What? What's stupid?"

"Look at me. I'm drinking like a fish. I mean I know I'm never going to see that psycho taxi driver again but I can't shake this feeling that he's going to appear around the next corner, or in here, and attack me again. It's ridiculous, I know, but – but – every time I see a taxi. I just—" He covered his eyes.

"Oh Harry, you poor darling ..."

"I was on the phone to the credit card people again this morning. Can't get a word of sense out of them so here I am, stranded, trapped, all I want to do is get out of Caracas and they can't bloody well give me my own money to do so – it's insane. It's a nightmare. The whole thing has been a nightmare except ..." He gave her his most soulful look. "... except for meeting you, of course."

"Harry—"

"Well, I'm just going to have to suffer it, aren't I?"

"But—"

"Grin and bear it, I suppose."

"Harry, look – I know we've only just met but – well – I'm heading back to my place in Estado Sucre. Why don't you come and stay? Get yourself out of here?" Christmas sighed. His ribs were agony. This was a triumph.

"Judith, that really is so kind of you but, well, I haven't two farthings to rub together at the moment."

"Harry, darling – please – forget all about that. After what you've been through – look – you need some R+R and you'll be staying at my house so you won't need any money and the hotel can ring through when your cards arrive. Besides I'm sure we can find a way for you to earn your keep."

"Oh Judith. I don't know what to say."

"It's an eight hour drive at the least from Caracas, five hundred kilometres, and the fact is, I could really do with the company. The roads are quite dangerous, especially if it rains, so you see, really it would be you doing me the favour. But listen to me charging on – you've probably got lots to do here."

"Not at all. Like I told you, I'm completely stuck."

"Then why don't you let me try and unstick you?" She patted his knee.

"Chocolate rum, you say?"

"Our very own writer-in-residence! And there is a town nearby, so if we want to strangle each other after a couple of days you can easily escape. I know we've only just met, but I do trust my instincts. I think we might just have a whale of a time. What do you say – how about a little adventure?"

"When are we off?"

"Oh, how marvellous!" she clapped her hands together. "In about a week." Christmas sat back. This was a disaster.

"A week?"

"Week – week and a half. I've got to buy some bits and bobs for the house, then there's this terrible set of old curtains I've got to collect and—"

"Judith. I've got an idea."

"Yes?"

"Why don't we go today?"

"Today?"

"Or tomorrow – why don't we just do it? Just get out of here?"

"But Harry I can't possibly—"

"Can't you feel it, Judith? Spontaneity! Do you know ... I think I can feel those creative juices flowing again already."

"If I didn't have all these chores then I'd love to but—"

"May I tell you something?" said Christmas, putting his hand in his pocket and tightly scrunching his last note into a ball. "The truth is, since getting so viciously beaten up and everything, well, I really am pretty jumpy here as I said – stupid, I know – I mean I'm sure I won't see this man again, of course ..."

"Oh, Harry ..."

"So you know, I promised myself – I mean I absolutely swore to myself – that I would leave town tomorrow whatever happens, because I don't really feel safe here at all and I'm sick to the back teeth of feeling like this and tomorrow – well – OK, I'll just come out with it – tomorrow is my birthday."

16

Slade had seen it from every angle of the city – from Altamira, Palos Grandes, Chacao, Las Mercedes, La Campiña, Parque Carabobo, Campo Alegre, Bello Monte, El Rosal. He had seen it when leaving the Hilton, or the Four Seasons, or the Continental with a photograph of Harry Christmas in his hand and the chalk of dead ends in his throat: the cable car.

Slade was visiting every luxury hotel in Caracas, every day squashed into the streets, heat fermenting his clothes, rain insulting his efforts. Each morning he rang his *eorlderman*; each morning he was told there was no passport or credit card activity. Christmas was still in Venezuela.

Slade paid five hundred dollars to the police and fifty dollars to each hotel staff member he had fought with while trying to chase Christmas. He gave both the police and hotel management all the information he had about Harry Christmas. They let him go, but only after he'd been waiting all day and half the night, in the hotel, in a police car, outside the police station where they wrote up their report on a table in the sun, back to his own hotel so they could

94

search his room, back to the police station, standing in the police courtyard, perspiring, unable to work out if they had forgotten about him, following the guns in their holsters as the officers came in and out of the station. Did they know what he could do if he wanted to?

He took out some more cash with his credit card and bought a dive knife with a rubber handle and scabbard that he could attach to his belt. He bought a new rucksack and new clothes: shirts and T-shirts that were big enough to cover the weapon. He stayed in the areas the guidebook said were safe, but kept his hand on the knife handle whenever people or cars approached too quickly, or too slowly. He wanted someone to try to rob him again. He wanted the world to witness what happened when a Saxon warrior was ready.

He bought hot dogs at roadside stands to conserve his money. The slightest exchange was difficult, every question and answer a wrestle of repetition, incomprehension, confusion and delay. Slade often looked up suddenly, and imagined catching Christmas at a window with a long-lens camera. He questioned well-groomed concierges in glistening halls: "No. This man. In the photograph. I am looking for this man."

"You want I take you photograph?" Slade was sure they all spoke English. He was sure they had been bribed to confound him.

In the evenings he returned to his den on the tenth floor of the Hotel Lux. It was a cubed room with tinted windows, white walls, white bed, white bathroom, white floor. He lay on his bed and drank whisky, staring at the photograph of Harry Christmas he had tacked to the wall, talking to it, promising. He threw the dive knife at it but it never stuck.

Slade barely slept, and when he did he always dreamt of The General, his father's cat. He had hated that animal when he was a boy. He hated all cats; self-satisfied, scrawny vermin that belonged outside the house but had somehow gained protection from the world of men and languished there, pampered and plotting, servile and haughty. After he had been found tormenting The General, he was not allowed to touch the creature. He dreamt it was lounging on his father's desk, licking itself. "Let the fat man escape twice," said the cat, "Boo-hoo." Slade woke up. Christmas' face was being kindled by the city at night. From his bed Slade could see the lights of the cable car snaking up the El Ávila mountains. Christmas would go there, he decided. He imagined him surveying Caracas from above, laughing, spading expensive delicacies into his doughy mouth. That's where he would pick up the trail.

It was late afternoon. The taxi dropped him off in the car park. He stood in the grey light and noticed a police station adjacent to the cable car's entrance. He stared at it for long moments, trying to decide if and how he could enlist their help. Finally he returned to the sales booth and bought his ticket for the *teleférico*. No, she did not recognise the photograph. He walked through the empty turnstiles and into the passenger dock. He showed the photograph of Christmas to the attendants. They shrugged and shook their heads. He showed them again.

The cabins descended noisily, shunting and rattling into place. He was about to have a pod for himself, but just as its doors were closing a mother, father and their little girl stepped in. The parents each held one of their daughter's hands. She was smiling. The cabin lurched. They left the dock.

It was going to rain. Soon they were surrounded by cloud. The child twisted in her seat, desperate for something to see. The father said something. Slade examined him, then his wife, then his daughter.

"English," he announced. The little girl stared, kicking her legs. He produced the photograph. "Have you seen this man?" The family inspected it, then shook their heads, asking him questions he couldn't understand. Slade put the photograph away. Rain pattered the windows. The lights and structure of a tower yawned out from the mist as they passed it, receding just as quickly. The ground was steepening. Again they were enveloped.

Slade felt unbearably heavy. He rubbed his face and looked out into the mist and remembered being in the Peak District with his father. They were walking across the dales. They were lost. His father was getting angry because he had misjudged the route. It grew dark. William was cold. He was panting and sweating and nursing the back of his head where his father had clipped him for complaining. They came to a stone wall. His father was shouting at him to hurry up and get over the stile. The next field was full of horses. They were agitated. William was frightened. His father grabbed him by the arm and dragged him over. A horse came out of the mist, whinnying with curiosity and his father whacked it across the mouth with his walking stick. It reared and fled and William cried out. His father turned round cursing and hit him with the stick and William fell over and then ran off into the mist and he was alone. He could hear the shouts of his father and the braying of the horses and he clutched his head and prayed for Diana to come and get him.

After almost an hour the cable car arrived at the top of the mountain. It was cold. The family hugged and shivered. They said goodbye to him. Outside the cable car station rows of fast food stalls were closing. He went into a fondue restaurant built from dark, heavy wood. He sat at the bar and showed round the photograph. He drank whisky and then left, following the path past a playground and an ice rink to one of the many observation points. There was no mist here, only Caracas, a glittering hell of light. Slade gripped the handrail.

He turned to find the family beside him, the parents lifting their daughter so that she might see through one of the old coin-operated telescopes. Beyond Caracas, the dark giants of the Valles Del Tuy slept on to the south, rolling towards the Amazon, towards Brazil. He was sure Christmas could not survive in such territory. He must be down there. He must still be in the city.

The family was having a problem with the telescope. "What's the matter?" he called to the father.

"No work," said the man, "We put the money. No work." Slade went over. He looked through the telescope but it was blank. He began examining the machine. "No problem, no problem," said the father.

"I can fix this," said Slade. He put in some change. He looked again. It still didn't work. He rattled it.

"No problem, no problem," repeated the father. His wife said something in Spanish. Slade hit the telescope with the butt of his hand. He looked. He hit it again a few inches further up. He looked again. He went round the other end and looked into it. The family was talking to him. He hit the telescope harder. Nothing. He shook it and kicked it and cursed.

The family was walking away.

He watched them go. He put another coin in. He looked. Nothing. He hammered it with his fist. He looked. Nothing.

There was nothing.

17

Christmas arrived at Judith's hotel with his second new suitcase. He had not paid his bill at the Jolly Frankfurter. Despite the painkillers, his headache was still acute, his body ringing out with distress. They had breakfast. Judith was in a very good mood. She sang 'Happy Birthday' and had the waiter bring him a croissant with a candle stuck in it. Her own birthday was in three weeks. "That means we're both Geminis, Harry. Isn't that funny?"

"Spooky," he smiled. His real birthday wasn't for months.

They were in the car before nine, shunting through Caracas before joining the highway going east. They drove along the northern coast of South America, from one traffic jam to the next, threading between mountains and the sea. The potholes cracked pain through his hip and up his arm. They shifted alongside fields of sugar cane and roadside stalls, beneath gannets and cormorants, past weirs and patchwork shelters and cars that were becoming part of the ground. Chávez appeared on billboard after billboard embracing diminutive state governors: 'POR AMOR A VENEZUELA!'

"So you're a potter. What sort of things do you pot? Pots and so on?"

"It's more like … I create thoughts. I mould ideas, objects, forms – I really try not to put a label on them." Christmas saw her knuckles twitching. Had she not been holding the wheel there would have been quote fingers pumping all over the dashboard. "I just let my hands communicate with the clay. Try and find where our energies meet. And once I've found that place I just let the energies take over." *Ah*, thought Christmas, *so they're shit*. "I have my wheel right at the edge of the garden. It used to be in the most wonderful gazebo but the insects munched it to death so now I've got an open-sided tent. We're quite high up so you can look straight out over the sea. Oh, it's a wonderful place for creativity, Harry. So *vital*. I'm sure it's just what you need to get your juices going, though I'm afraid we don't have a computer or anything like that. We've been waiting to get the internet connected for months and months."

"Wonderful news. I'm a paper and pen man."

"But for the typing process – are you Mac or PC? I simply can't decide which way to go."

"I use a typewriter."

"Isn't that rather slow?"

"It comes with a secretary."

"You've got a secretary that uses a typewriter?"

"It's historical fiction, this next one. I'm trying a kind of method acting-writing thing. Stanislavsky. Drive myself up the fourth wall."

"But I thought you didn't know what you were going to write?"

"Have you read my other books?"

"Not yet."

"Oh good."

"Good?"

"They're almost as dreary as the Noo-Naa whotsit. Anyway, fed up with my own dreariness, I decided to take my work in a radical new direction, experimental, you might say."

"Interweaving narratives?"

"Victorians with removable vaginas." Christmas eyed her, wondering whether he had pushed it too far.

"I beg your pardon?"

"A gothic experiment conducted on insane women by a gynaecological Dr Frankenstein."

"Oh Harry, be *serious*. Are you serious?"

"It's a work in progress that's currently out of progress. Thought myself into a cul-de-sac. Probably going to abandon it."

"And what are its, you know, *themes* and so on?"

"Multiculturalism."

"But insane women with removable minnies ...? I mean aren't you objectifying ... I mean won't people, the critics and so on ... won't people think that's kind of anti-women?"

"It is anti-women! It's anti-men. It's anti-children. It's anti-blacks and it's anti-whites. It's anti-God and it's anti-the unbelievers."

"Well, what's it pro?"

"It's not pro anything. What the devil is there to be pro about?" Then Judith started to ask him all sorts of odd questions. His head, his neck, his backside, his upper body clamoured with injury, yet this woman refused to shut up. Did he like beetroot? What was his favourite type of jacket?

"Oh, how funny!" she laughed, "How funny you are!" *What is this bloody woman on about?* he thought, unable to find humour in anything that had been said in the last hour. He shifted in his seat. His breakfast had taken a wrong turn in his guts and he needed to force a re-direction.

"There," he said, spotting a roadside restaurant. "Why don't we pull over and stretch our legs a bit. I'll take a turn with the driving."

"Oh, don't be silly," she said, going straight past it and continuing with anecdotes about her ex-husband.

"There!" said Christmas, spotting another, "Judith, you must let me take a turn at the wheel. Let's stop at this place here."

"Really, Harry, don't worry. I'm enjoying it."

"Well, I'm afraid we need to stop anyway. I need to use their conveniences."

"Why didn't you say so?" she said, shuddering to a halt. They were on the side of the road. "Out you pop."

"Judith, the restaurant is just up there."

"Oh, don't worry," she said, squeezing his leg. "I won't peek."

"Judith, I require a cubicle."

"A number two? Why didn't you say? Oh, how funny!" Judith started laughing. She started the car up again.

As with all roadside restaurants in Venezuela there was rubbish everywhere and a three-legged dog. Uniformed waiters stood behind a counter that announced a vast array of *arepas*, and Christmas left Judith admiring the choice as he went off to find to the toilets. They bore no sign, were completely hidden from view, and by the time he had located them Christmas was desperate.

A filthy shed housed a couple of buckets and a contingent of insects straight from the Old Testament. He barged into the only cubicle to find a toilet bowl in the middle of some profound alchemical transformation. With trousers down and actual contact out of the question, Christmas assumed the Johnny Wilkinson position, his podgy discoloured thighs shaking with strain and disagreement. Then a cockroach crawled up his ankle at exactly the wrong moment. A flurry of batting, squeezing and shouting ensured that Christmas left the toilet more agitated than when he'd entered it.

"Harry," said Judith as he rejoined her at the food counter. "Whatever is the matter? You look awful."

"I saw a ghost. What have you ordered?"

"Bits and bobs, Harry, darling, but a ghost? What was it doing in the toilet?"

"I think it had quite understandably mistaken it for a portal back to hell." He scanned the board overhead. As long as you wanted an *arepa*, anything was possible.

"Give me an *arepa* with bacon," he asked in Spanish.

"We don't have bacon today."

"With prawns?"

"No."

"With quail eggs?"

"No."

"With beef? With chicken?"

"No and no."

"With sausage? With fish? There are fifty options here, man, are you telling me you don't have a single one of them?"

"Cheese. We have cheese. Don't you like cheese?"

Judith refused to let him drive. "Don't be ridiculous, Harry. You're completely black and blue, you're in a state of shock, it's your birthday and you're my patient now. I'm taking care of you." Back on the road, they drove on through Barcelona and Puerto La Cruz, through mud flats and beaches of salt. They saw flamingos, the sky in sudden blossom. They drove past painted stones announcing the revolution while roadside Santa Maria's prayed in their boxes. A refinery shone and flared. It began to rain. They entered a desert of rusting hills and hit another traffic jam. It dragged them past a crowd standing over a body on the road next to an upturned car emitting black smoke. Then the rain stopped and the sun came out. The rocks and scrub became fields of corn and *ocumo*. The hills rolled with jungle. Christmas thought of Emily.

It was late afternoon. They stopped and bought fish *empanadas* and cold beer from a child. The road overlooked a bay, overgrowth and flowers sweeping down to a fingernail of sand.

"We're in Estado Sucre, darling. Not long now." Christmas nodded. He couldn't take his eyes from the coastline. He felt for the poetry book in his jacket pocket. *We're here, Ems*, he thought, giving it a squeeze. *See how beautiful it is?*

Two hours later, the traffic stopped dead between Carúpano and Rio Caribe. Drivers hung from their windows, shouting ahead to find out what was happening. Another accident. No one was going anywhere. As soon as the news broke, all the car doors opened, everybody spilling out onto the road. Salsa music burst into the air. Boots were popped open and people began to mix drinks. "Come on!" said, Judith, jumping out.

Christmas leant against the car and propped up his Panama hat with a cowboy finger. He smelt the sun and the sea salt. A man leant beside him. He gave Christmas a plastic cup filled with rum, ice and lime juice. The two men toasted each other. Barefoot strangers were dancing to invisible pianos and trumpets and drums, and there was Judith, in the middle of it all, laughing and swirling. A teenager in nothing more than shorts and a bra took his hand and he twirled her round once before he had to give up. His shoulder was too painful. Someone new filled up his glass. They all wanted to know him. Where was he from? Where was he going? What did he think of Venezuela? Judith swayed past and patted his cheek. Cars came up the other lane beeping and whooping as they rolled slowly by, drinks poured into the passing mouths. *These people*, Christmas thought to himself, *are magnificent*. Then, as suddenly as it had begun, it stopped. Doors shut, the cars began to move. The jam moved on.

"Wasn't that fun!" said Judith, breathless as she jumped back into the car. "Rio Caribe just coming up. Then we're onto the Paria peninsula proper. My place isn't far." A blackened chassis appeared on the side of the road.

"Not another accident?" asked Christmas.

"Nope. Some fellow from Caracas came down here for the weekend and got so drunk he had a\ fight with one of the locals, pulled out a gun and shot the man in the leg, so they all beat him to within an inch and set his car on fire."

Pelicans perched on beached fishing boats. Families sat in front of their doors drinking beer. Every house was a different colour and men with big bellies strode around in shorts.

Once through Rio Caribe, they headed inland, meandering between hills and villages, carried up for a view of the lumpy valleys before dipping back to follow the coast. They passed huts selling balls of cacao and bottles of chocolate rum, bowls of avocados for sale on the road, donkeys grazing, old men sitting outside, bright flowers and groves of short *cambur* bananas. After an hour or so they turned up a track into the hills, the car bouncing between potholes until they went through a gate and began to wend up a steep slope. "And here we are!" she said as white walls became visible through the trees. "*Casa mía.*" It was completely isolated. Harry Christmas felt a thunderous urge for a drink.

18

A hacienda in the colonial style, Judith's house sat high on a plateau burly with jungle. The house itself was rectangular, built around an inner courtyard, the first floor balustrade pausing at one end to deliver a staircase down onto mosaic floor tiles, frayed wicker chairs and piles of old magazines. Outside, her carefully tended flower beds followed a colonnade around the house to the portico and main door. Here two hammocks swung between the columns and steps led down to the lawn. Sprinklers fought the heat. Trees and bushes, flowers and fruit dotted towards the sea, the tropical forest sloping sharply away on either side into the sound of crickets.

Judith pulled up to the side of the house. They got out of the car and a mosquito bit Christmas on the neck. It was a rich, pink evening. Two cats trotted out of the bushes and Judith crouched down to meet them.

"Hello, darlings, we've got a guest! This is Harry. Harry this is Alexei and Gregory."

"The Orlov brothers?"

"Oh, how clever of you!"

"Catherine the Great's henchmen who helped her get rid of her husband."

"Digby was allergic to cats, which was a great problem for him. He was also allergic to bonking, which was a great problem for me. Now then, let me show you around the house."

"It's been rather a long drive, Judith, I'm sure you'd just rather go to be—"

"Nonsense! It's your birthday! Let me fetch a couple of gins and a sandwich or something and we'll do a quick tour. It's the perfect time. The evenings here are so ..." she gave a little shudder, "*vital.*"

"And this is the dining room," she announced, pushing open some double doors at one end of the courtyard. Christmas was nearing the end of a gin so stiff it could join the army. He felt much better. The woman might be a loony, but what a house! The drinks cabinet was well stocked and there were plenty of comfortable spots where a man could snooze away the afternoons and think about important stuff.

"Do you recognise the colour?"

"Green?" Christmas surveyed the room. It was covered in British hunting scenes. Every piece of furniture was a grumpy antique.

"Harrods green. Took me bloody ages to get it right. Digby insisted, the toffee-nosed prat."

"That's an impressive hunting horn you've got on the wall there."

"I got it from my father."

"Your father gave you the horn?" Christmas swilled down the last of his gin and made a trumpet noise into his glass. "And how long have you had the horn for?"

"I can see I'm going to have to watch you," she said, giving him a poke in the ribs. "You're one of those naughty men, aren't you? How about a refill?"

"Those orange flowers, that's a *trompeta*, a little blue plumbago over there, and that rather shocking red thing is a *passiflora coccinea*. Unbelievable colour, isn't it?" They were wandering through her garden towards the sea.

"Don't you ever get lonely up here on your own?"

"Oh, look – here we are," she said. They had come to the edge of the lawn. A molten sun was half in the waves. There was a wheel, a stool and piles of materials under the cover of a Bedouin tent. Her creations were laid out on the grass. *Looks like a sale at a garden centre*, thought Christmas.

"What do you think?" she said, holding up a ceramic phallus with what looked like an angel shimmying up the side.

"A charming prospect."

"Not the view, silly, my *Eroi*."

"*Eroi*?"

"Well, I don't really know what to call them." Christmas realised that amongst the figurines and other indeterminate shapes, there were lots of these clay penises popping out all over the place.

"'Phallus' is so vulgar, don't you think? So I plumped for Eros. *Eroi*. This is one of my latest *Eroi*." She passed Christmas the object and started dusting the rest with a rag. Christmas looked at Judith. He looked at the sea. The indigenous population, he mused, could have well done with Judith being on hand when Columbus arrived. Might have saved them a few hundred years of plunder and genocide.

"Fourth of August," Christmas muttered to himself, "Year of Our Lord fourteen hundred and ninety eight. We arrived off the coast of the unknown continent and hoped to claim it for the glory of God and King. Unfortunately the whole atmos of the place has been ruined by a randy old bint with a taste for shit pottery, so we've decided to call the whole thing off."

"Sorry, darling, did you say something?"

"Might pop back to the house for another drink," he replied, handing back the *Eroi*. "What about you?"

19

"So, when the BP job came to an end, Digby went back and I stayed. He's a sweet man really, a sweet, harmless man ... but dear me, what a bore. Used to sit in that chair and read the *Times* back to front and out loud, even if there was no one else there. What about you, Harry, will you miss your wife?" They were in the courtyard on a couple of wicker chairs beneath the night sky. Christmas scratched the insect bites on his ankles.

"Yes." They had drunk almost a whole bottle of gin.

"Was it rotten for a while?"

"Rotten?"

"Your marriage. Before the divorce."

"I was rotten to her. And she was rotten to me. I mean that's what happens, isn't it, when two old fruit sit together for too long. Best keep yourself in the fridge."

"But the children, darling – you can't be in cold storage for the children. Even when it was non-speaks with Digby and I, we always pulled our fingers out for the children. Oh, my daughter Bridget is such a wonderful, wonderful, young lady. So ..."

"Vital?"

"Exactly! That's it exactly. You know, even if I hadn't read a single line of yours, I could tell, I would know, that you, darling, are a writer." Christmas bared his teeth with a smile. "But Benjamin, my eldest – I don't know where we went wrong with him."

"The name, perhaps?"

"Benjamin?"

"Sounds like a type of pyjama."

"Well, whatever it was, he's been an utter terror ever since he was young. Do you know he once did a poo in the ice cream tub?" Christmas had to put the emergency brakes on some gin, which then reversed through his nose.

"It's not funny," said Judith. "He took it out, did a poo in it and put it back in the freezer." Christmas gave out a belly laugh to the stars.

"And – ho, dear me – what does he do now?"

"Stop it. It's not funny!"

"Sorry, sorry, Judith I – the ice cream tub? Oh, that is good, ha, yes, oh dear me ..."

"He doesn't do anything now. Nothing in the noggin, that's his trouble. Complete wastrel. Sixty hour labour more or less – always was a lazy bugger. I remember I was in the middle of cooking spag bol when my waters broke, all over the bloody floor, and I shouted to Digby. 'Digby,' I said, 'the baby's coming.' 'Oh good,' he said, 'make sure it's a large one.' '*Baby's*, you idiot, not *Baileys*.' But that was old Digby through and through. Didn't have a bloody clue. How I got pregnant in the first place I'll never know. I mean Benji isn't a bad boy deep down. I just wish he was a bit ... nicer. What do you think makes people nicer?"

"In my experience?"

"In your experience."

"The medical establishment giving them news of a terminal illness."

"Oh Harry, you are terrible."

"It's true."

"And what about your brood? You've got two, right? Boys or girls."

"Boys."

"What are they called?"

"They're called …"

"Can't you remember?"

"Harry Junior …"

"And the other one?"

"Xerxes."

"Xerxes!"

"The wife is very keen on the Persians."

"Still it's a bit – anyway, none of my business. Are your parents still alive?"

"Not last time I checked."

"Oh, be serious, Harry," she growled, "I'm trying to find out about you. What was your father like?"

"Mine?"

"Yes, yours! Were you close?"

"No. My room was downstairs."

"I mean *emotionally*."

"I have no idea. We only spoke at Christmastime."

"Oh, you poor thing."

"Well, festive port can do that to a man."

"And your mother?" Judith shifted her chair closer.

"My mother?"

"I know, I know," agreed Judith, swinging her head.

"You know what?"

"Oh, you poor thing …" Judith had her hand on his thigh. "No one in the world … on your birthday …"

"I'm sorry, what—"

"You poor, poor, *poor* thing ..."

"Err ..."

"You poor, poor, poor, thing, thingy, thing—"

Moments later they were in Judith's bedroom and Christmas felt as if he was being undressed by a crazy nurse. She seemed to have forgotten he was injured. She threw off his hat and thrust him onto the mattress. She stripped him like a banana, pausing only to gasp when his shirt came off and she saw the full extent of his bruising. Christmas looked across at himself. There was a storm under his skin.

"Oh you poor man," she said, "but Judith's going to take care of you." He tried to speak. She closed his mouth with her own, yanking and rubbing his hair. She rubbed the lump. He cried out. "Whoops," she said, sitting up. She tore off her dress in one motion. She wasn't wearing any underwear. Christmas put his arms out to hold her but she pinned him to the bed and went to work. Some minutes later Christmas found himself having sex while biting back the pain with his teeth. Judith was still on top, her hands roughly massaging his chest while her hips ground against him. Her eyes were closed. Her head swayed from side to side. She started to hum.

It was a low, wandering tone at first, but it soon began to ascend. He couldn't quite make out the tune. Her nostrils flared. Her eyebrows furrowed and unfurrowed. Her hips moved faster. Then she began to sing. It was a tremulous, wordless, warbling song and despite the torture of his bruises, and his wound rubbing roughly against the sheets, Christmas got the giggles.

He closed his eyes. He opened his eyes. She seemed to be conducting. He laughed so violently through his teeth he had to disguise it as a gasp of passion. She was hitting operatic form now, higher and louder, hips moving faster, Christmas' head bouncing off the pillow. He was so red in the face with the giggles he thought he was going to have a heart attack. Her nails were digging into his chest, the note surging up the scales until ... finally ... she hit a high note and came.

"Bravo!" Christmas exploded. Judith slumped onto his face.

"*Amore* ..." she whispered.

"Bravo!" he exclaimed, cheering away the laughter, "Bravissimo!"

By the end of the second session, Christmas wasn't finding it so funny. Covered in sweat and scratches, he lay star-shaped on the bed, pulverized, his chest hair standing on end. His back, legs and arms formed a single cartel of punishment.

"Do you mind if I have the light on, *amore*? I want to read."

"Of course not," he creaked. Christmas rolled the other way, pulling the sheet over him, flinching as he tried to find a position that didn't hurt. Sleep. All he wanted was sleep. He closed his eyes and was drifting off when a great ripping noise gave him a start.

"Sorry, darling, but with these big heavy books I always rip a page out once I've read it. Otherwise old Ken Follet here would break my bloody arms off!" She gave a quick burst of her jack-hammer laugh and then kissed him on the forehead. Christmas turned back to the wall. His shoulder screamed. He closed his eyes. He shifted. He drifted ... *riiiiiiip*! It was going to be a long night.

20

Christmas woke to the sound of a dog barking. He went to the window. It was dawn. A raging tide of acidity washed up and down his throat. He found some tablets in Judith's bathroom and sat down to piss. Tiny ants were conducting a biblical exodus across the tiling. The sight of them made his bites itch.

He inspected his stitches in the mirror, testing the lump. He examined his bruises. He examined his face. He swallowed some painkillers and got back into bed. The world was slowly diluting itself into morning. He turned to look at Judith. Her mouth was open, her tongue hanging out over her teeth. It was a ghastly sight. Christmas rolled towards the ceiling.

He fell asleep. When he woke again the bed was empty. He dressed. He found his hat and jacket and went downstairs. He made himself some toast. There was hot coffee on the cooker. It had a post-it note stuck on the side that said: 'For you, *amore*'. He poured himself several cups. From the window he could see Judith at the potter's wheel. He decided to explore.

Christmas went outside. It was too hot for a jacket. He took it off and folded it over one arm, taking care that Emily's book was secure. Following a path down to a beach bordered by coconut trees and dotted with pelicans, he went to the water's edge and sat against a tree trunk in the sand. His jacket folded beside him, listening to the sea turn itself over and over, Christmas inhaled the salt and the sludge, grey mountainous shapes in the distance, trees decapitated by the wind. There was no one. *Cotera* birds circled high above, pterodactyl-like in outline. He took out Montejo and read a few lines. He laid the book on his jacket and dug into the sand beside him, searching for Emily's hand.

Christmas looked up the shoreline. "It's not quite right, is it, Em," he whispered. "Not the right beach." He looked up at the sun and pictured his wife, eleven years younger than him, a small, square woman with dark hair and freckles.

When they first met at a house and garden tradeshow in Paris he was the subject of four separate legal proceedings and was receiving treatment for gout. She had quickly defined his bad behaviour as in two categories: what was fun and what was stupid. The fun part she delighted in. The stupidity she outlawed. She had a Stoke accent and always called him 'Pops', unless she was in a bad mood and then it was 'Harry' or 'the Prat', as in 'does the Prat need me to repeat myself?' What he would give to be scolded like that again, but the world had eaten her, this rotten world she was always so keen on defending.

He looked down at the red book. Emily's grandmother married her grandfather while he was working as an English teacher in Caracas. They returned to Stoke in 1932 so he could take his place in the family firm, and Emily was raised on stories of life in her grandmother's Caribbean village. It had already disappeared by the time of her grandmother's death, consumed by the growing port of Guiria, but still Emily wanted to go and see the area for herself.

They had an old map of Latin America on their kitchen wall. She used to tap Venezuela with a wooden spoon while she was cooking. *One day we'll be there on a beach, Pops*, she used to say, *and we'll have a drink in our hands and there'll be this amazing sunset and it will be perfection. It'll be magic.*

Christmas was going to find Guiria. He was going to find the right beach with the right sunset and read to her one final time. Why hadn't he done this sooner? He had planned this trip since her funeral, but time had been performing strange acts. It didn't feel like seven years since she died. It didn't feel like one year. She died this morning, a lifetime ago. What had he been doing since? *Acting the cunt*, he thought. *Doing one bloody fool thing after another.*

Once they were married he took a job working for her father's ceramics company and they settled in Staffordshire. He stopped drinking so much, stopped getting into trouble. For the first time in his life he threw himself into work. He couldn't bear to let her down.

Christmas pulled his hand out from the sand. There was one black cloud in the distance. *That is death*, he thought. A black cloud, coming ever closer, until you are lost in it, calling out, then you turn round and you're gone. It was just there, an ever-present sensation, mimicking his movements with glee. No, this wasn't the right place for Emily's last poem. He got to his feet and walked back up the path to the hacienda, nodding to a couple of gardeners along the way.

Judith was still at her wheel. "*Amore!*" she trilled as she saw him approach. "Oh, *amore*! What a wonderful day!" She stood up and gave him a kiss. He felt her hand clasp his crotch. "And how's Mr Willykins this morning?" Christmas looked out to the ocean. He needed a cocktail.

21

The days passed and life at Judith's settled into a steady routine: Christmas drank. He read the available books. He avoided the sun. He kept his passport hidden behind the wardrobe and the book of Montejo's poetry always in his inside jacket pocket, hung up beside Digby's old clothes that he was encouraged to borrow – short-sleeved shirts, espadrilles, baggy Moroccan trousers.

With Judith in full song and his head being rattled off its shoulders neither he nor Mr Willykins were sure how much more they could take, but during the days she was either busy in the garden or at the wheel. She refused to let him borrow the car, citing the drink in his hand, but despite being confined to the premises he could, for the first time in years, relax. No one knew where he was, no bailiffs, no debtors, no Slade. He was safe here. His bruises were turning green.

Yet he had to get to Guiria, and for that he needed money. He tried to concentrate, to come up with a plan, but he just couldn't get his mind straight. He felt tired in some deep, distant way. His thoughts drifted from Emily to Lola Rosa, then Judith would appear smiling, asking if he was all right and he couldn't help agreeing that he was. As long as the gin was going down he could convince himself that she wasn't another Diana, that he wasn't preying on her affections, that pretending to be someone else was just a game, just a pause on reality while he gathered his strength.

It was sunset, the moment when yellow turns to gold. Christmas sat on the viewing bench, hidden by a clump of *noni* trees at the edge of the lawn, reading Montejo.

"*Amore! Amore!*" Christmas let out a sigh. He hid the book under his leg. "Where are you?"

"Over here ..." Judith appeared. Christmas bared his teeth in a smile.

"There you are! And how's my handsome writer this evening?"

"He is ... splendiferous."

"Splendiferous!" she clapped her hands in delight. "And the writer's block? Still a bit ... blocky?"

"'Fraid so."

"Oh, don't worry, *amore*. I am sure it's all going to start flooding out any minute."

"I'm sure you're right."

"I'm going to make fish and mango curry tonight with some *picante* from the garden. Perhaps that will turn the old switch on."

"*Ojala ...*"

"Here, *amore*, I just read this article in Cosmo. And did you know—" she said, marvelling at the front cover, "—that apparently the latest fashion is to have an ugly girlfriend?"

"What is it?"

"It's the competition. Interview with Ethan Stone – the one that's invented a new way of writing."

"Really? Where does he stick the pen?"

"No, silly, a form – it's called – it says here – 'the disinterested narrator.'" Judith passed Christmas the opened magazine. A profound contempt for the man and his entire generation swept over him.

C: So how did the idea for the disinterested narrator come to you? Were you consciously looking to break new ground, or was it more organic?

Stone: Well, no, what happened was, I was thinking of writing a novel, and then I couldn't be bothered, and then I thought, hang on a moment, there's something in this.

"Ha!" laughed Christmas, "I really should shoot myself."

"So the man just rang up about the internet." Christmas stopped laughing. "Should be here in a few days, isn't that wonderful? I can read all your interviews! Have you done many?"

"Oh, you know …"

"With some of those dashing author photos, the ones where they're looking over their shoulders a bit, as if the photographer has just interrupted them while they were saying something terribly important. Have you got some of those on the internet?"

"I don't know if—"

"Oh, the internet! How *vital*! And all your reviews! I'm going to ferret away at you, Harry Strong!" she said, pinching her fingers together and raining ferret heads all over him. "I'm going to find out all about you …" She slowed down her attack, sat on his lap and began to kiss him.

The internet. Christmas had strong opinions on the internet predicated on hating all the people he had ever met who were enthusiastic about it. The internet was an electric Gulag, a network of lonely children indulging in communities of self-surveillance.

Particularly loathsome were the people of his generation who made out that it had changed their lives when all they were expressing was the fear of being left out. If you want anonymous sex with strangers, join the navy. Everything else was available at the library. And in some libraries you could get that too. He refused to welcome its terminology into the lexicon. 'Going online' was a suicide attempt; a 'blog' surely some kind of woodcutter's privy. On top of it all here it was, the robot supergrass, about to parachute into the jungle and blow his cover.

"*Amore?*" she said, stroking his hair, and nuzzling his ear.

"Yes, darling?"

"*Amore*, if I asked you to do something, a little favour, something that required you to do literally nothing, you wouldn't refuse me, would you, darling?"

22

"Is it really necessary to do this naked?" The following morning Christmas found himself without clothes, sitting on an uncomfortable arrangement of stones and ordered into the pose of Rodin's 'The Thinker'. He was in front of Judith's pottery tent where she was working at reducing his sizeable bulk to a foot-high figurine. She wore special half-moon glasses for this type of detailed work, her flowery dress protected by a clay-splattered apron.

"I said—"

"Sssh, *amore*, please. I'm trying to concentrate. I told you, I can't do clothes yet. You'd come out looking like a Mr Man. Juan Carlos in Caracas insists I send him figurines. 'Figurines!' he says, 'Figurines!'"

At first he thought she wanted to model his penis. He was so relieved when she said his whole figure he immediately gave his assent.

"Any chance of letting the blood back into my legs?"

"Patience, *amore*, patience is a virtue."

"Patience is a virtue I haven't got time for. Oh God!"

"What is it *amore* – oh ..."

"The devil take you, woman! You said it was their day off!" The two gardeners were watching from a distance, swigging from a bottle of rum and laughing. Judith started to giggle.

"Hang on, *amore*, I'll go and see what they want."

"Well, Mona Lisa here wants a bloody drink. A bloody stiff bloody drink!"

Christmas extracted himself from his pedestal and put on a dressing gown. He flicked a V-sign at the gardeners. They waved back. He went over to look at what she'd done. He was horrified. It looked just like him. *Am I really that fat?* he thought. He was frowning so much his face looked oriental; in fact the whole thing looked like a sumo wrestler with a Wild West moustache failing to touch his own toes.

Christmas let out a deep huff of despair. He looked down to the cove below, down to where he had stood alone before dinner the previous night and witnessed carnage in the evening sky, a battle of swarming souls, the heavens tormented with colour. When it had all turned into night, he had climbed the path back to the house, able only to pick out the shapes of the mountains – a caravan of misshapen beasts – his hands feeling his way along tree bark with Emily somewhere beside him. He had entered the kitchen as if from another world. The sensation was still with him.

"They just wanted to borrow some tools, *amore*. OK, you have a break. I'll go and get you a drink. Can you hear—? Oh it's the phone!" Judith hurried off. When she came back she had nothing in her hand. She was sobbing.

"Oh my God, darling!" said Christmas as he stood up, "Have we run out?" Judith stood before him, her hands covering her mouth.

"It's so awful ..."

"But there's a little scotch, isn't there? I'm sure I saw two bottles of scotch."

"It's not the … it's the – the—"

"What's the matter? Judith, what is it?"

"My friend Fiona."

"Fiona?"

"Fi's had a stroke!"

A great wave of relief rushed through his system. "Your friend has had a stroke."

"She's going to be paralysed for life! Oh God!" Judith threw her hands around his neck.

"Poor thing," said Christmas, "Makes you wonder where the phrase 'stroke of luck' comes from, doesn't it? Perhaps if you get away with just a wonky face."

"What?"

"Come on, let's sit you down." He walked her along the edge of the lawn and over to the viewing bench.

"And the worst thing is her bloody daughter was only home for a couple of days and has buggered off to some party! The friend that rang is going over there right now. I mean can you imagine it! A party! What an absolute bitch! Oh Harry, it's too awful, it's too awful!" Judith began to sob. Christmas wasn't quite sure what to do. So he patted her head.

"There, there …"

"That poor woman, such a tough life … and that bloody daughter … I can't believe it …"

"Well, look, it is understandable, running off to some party to drown your sorrows." Christmas noticed the increase in noise coming from Judith and decided to leave it there. He adjusted his dressing gown and was about to suggest a restorative when the faint noise of the telephone started up from the house again.

"Fi!" cried Judith as she tore off to answer it. When she returned she seemed somewhat recovered.

"False alarm?"

124

"No, oh, Harry, that was my daughter Bridget. Great news, *amore*, she's coming tomorrow!"

For the rest of the day, Judith chattered excitedly about Bridget. Even though it quickly began to annoy him, Christmas tried to keep her on that subject and away from the unfortunate friend or any attempt to get him back on the stones. Bridget was modern. Bridget was *vital*. Bridget had done that, Bridget had won this – Christmas was full of loathing for the achiever. He had a profound distrust of people who enjoyed honours from institutions as fake and as dedicated to anti-learning as schools. All he had ever won at school was a bet.

"Oh, I do hope Bridget meets a nice man," she sighed. "All her boyfriends have been a bit ... drippy. They don't stand up to her and she ends up pushing them around and then she gets bored. That's the main thing, don't you think? Looks and everything have their place but the main thing is to find someone that doesn't bore you."

"Quite," said Christmas, thinking about the time Emily got so cross with him she took the handbrake off and let his car roll into a river. "Quite," he said again, laughing down at his feet.

23

The following afternoon Christmas was drinking on the viewing bench, savouring the smell of jasmine, when voices reached him from the other side of the *noni* trees.

"What is it, mummy?"

"My surprise, darling, my wonderful surprise!"

"Do you mind if I sit down for half a minute before you show me your latest clay penis?"

"It's not ceramics, darling."

"Orchid from the South Pole?"

"It's not a flower ..."

"Then what is it?"

"It's ..." The two women rounded the trees. Christmas stood up, gin in hand. "... a lover!" Bridget and Christmas took each other in. Bridget had a piercing little face. She had crystal eyes, slender arms, almost no breasts and a beauty spot above her lips. She was extremely pretty, in a fierce, starved kind of way. Bridget's conclusions about Christmas were rather less favourable.

"And he's famous!"

"How do you do," she said flatly. They shook hands. His were sweaty.

"Harry, Bridget, Bridget, Harry. Oh this is exciting. Who wants a cup of tea?"

"I've just been in Brazil visiting a friend so I thought I'd drop up to see mummy." All three were sat round a table in the shade of the house.

"How is Amy, darling?"

"I don't know. She's still in such a mess. It's her birthday in a couple of weeks. I've got to send her a good present to cheer her up. What do you think?"

"Something smelly? All girls like that."

"I know, I know, but it's not very original is it? Not very surprising."

"Surprising … smelly …" offered Christmas, "Stink bombs?"

"Thanks, Harry. Very useful. Anyway you can't buy stink bombs any more. Not in England anyway."

"What?"

"Most borough councils have banned them."

"Banned them?"

"Because they stink. Itching powder, stink bombs, the lot." Christmas sank back in his chair, absorbing yet another jab-cross combination from The Rot.

"Itching powder …?"

"It's abusive." Christmas looked to the sky.

"Anyway," Bridget continued, "she's doing far too much yoga. She's starting to look like a boy."

"I knew a woman once," said Christmas, coming back to earth, "who did so much yoga she could put her trousers on with her feet."

"But darling, is she really not feeling any better?"

"A bit. I mean I think she's got to the stage where she's treating the whole thing like some horrible dream."

"Terrible story. Why don't you fill Harry in while I get the ginger cake?" Judith went into the house.

"It's nothing really," started Bridget, feeling uneasy in Christmas' company. "Just my friend Amy got married and the whole thing was a disaster. Turned out he was a nasty piece of work so she divorced him after five months and ran away to Brazil. I think she just can't quite believe she made such a bad judgement of character."

"And is she pretty?"

"Amy?"

"This friend of yours, yes – is she pretty?"

"Yes, she is as a matter of fact. What's that got to do with anything?"

"Then she'll be all right, won't she."

"Excuse me?"

"I said, you know, she'll be all right."

"To find another man, you mean."

"That kind of thing."

"So her happiness, her life, depends on whether a man will accept her – is that it?"

Whoops, thought Christmas. "I'm sorry," he said, "I didn't realise you were a ..."

"A what?"

"You know. A squeezy lemon."

"What?"

"A high-heeled farmer."

"What are you talking about?"

"Look, I didn't know – and neither does your mother, by the way."

"What—"

128

"Sundown on the hairy prairie? Two seats by the window at the Oyster café?"

"Are you trying to say you think I am a lesbian?"

"If you want to put it crudely."

"God!"

Judith appeared with the cake. "Everything all right? Oh bugger, I've forgotten the slicer."

"I'll get it," offered Christmas cheerfully, sliding out from the table.

"Thanks, *amore*. So ..." she whispered, "... what do you think?"

"He's a total shit."

"Bridget!"

"What's he doing here?"

"He is a famous writer and he's just been through a terrible divorce and a vicious robbery and he's got writer's block and I'm helping him through it all. He's under a lot of pressure. He's in a very pressurized environment."

"Like a shit."

"Bridget, please ..."

"He just told me he thought I was a lesbian."

"Well, your hair is rather short."

"Mother!"

"Oh, I know he hasn't got much in the way of airs and graces but that's why he's rather fun."

"Where did you find him?"

"Fate, darling, fate brought us together."

"What *do* you sound like?"

"Oh please do try and make an effort. You know how I've been lately and he is making me, well, you know, happy ..."

"Urrgh, mother, please, I do not want to know. And that moustache ..."

"I know he looks eccentric."

"He looks fat."

"Bridget, don't be horrid. Harry may be a pompous old sod but he's got a good heart and I happen to like him, so if you wouldn't mind, just this once – I mean here I am, completely on my own, the only news I get is dear friends having strokes, and you—"

"OK, OK, I'm sorry."

"—I mean, it's not as if—"

"Mummy, don't start, I said I'm—"

"OK, there, *amore?*" Christmas had reappeared on the lawn brandishing the cake slicer. He'd had a couple of vodka shots in the kitchen and was feeling—

"Rambunctious."

"Now listen you two – I know you are both punchy characters, but I want you to promise to be nice to each other, right?" Christmas clacked his heels together and bowed his head. Bridget sniffed.

24

Dinner was over. They sat in the dining room drinking coffee, surrounded by Harrods green and hunting scenes. There were candles on the table and a blue insect killer in one corner that cast a strange blue shadow on the proceedings. It buzzed with short funerals.

"So, Mr Strong—"

"Please, Bridget, *Harry*."

"—whereabouts in England are you from?"

"Oh, nowhere special. South-east corner. Back when there were still a few scraps of countryside left. It was what you might call a typical, old-fashioned rural community."

"Cricket and the church spire, *amore*?"

"Inbreeding."

"I beg your pardon?"

"Absolutely rife. The spastics' bus was a double-decker."

"Oh, Harry!"

"Whole bloody village shared the same nose." Bridget was shooting him a venomous look.

"You cannot say 'spastics' any more."

"Well, that seems a bit cruel."

"Excuse me?"

"I mean the poor devils have got to eat."

"I said 'say' not 'pay'."

"Harr-eee," said Judith, trying to head off the impending scene with her daughter, "why don't you tell us about the new book idea you were talking about the other day?"

"Part of it's set now, part of it four hundred years ago and part of it in a Victorian brothel with space aliens that have removable—"

"Not that one, *amore*. The other one. The other night. The other space aliens."

"A UFO armada swoops over the earth and everyone feels put out because they've come for the whales."

"Are you a science fiction writer?"

"No." Silence fell on the room. Everyone sipped politely. The insect killer sparked.

"You used to work with whales, didn't you Bridget, darling?"

"Turtles."

"Oh yes. Turtles." Several more moments passed.

"Well," announced Judith, "It's my birthday in a couple of weeks' time."

"Two weeks' time? Really?" Christmas finished his coffee, then topped up his wine glass, still wincing from the shoulder injury. "And what is the traditional birthday celebration in these parts?"

"Oh, just one of our little evenings. But this time, as we have a special guest, *amore*, I thought I might spread the net a bit wider, you know, a few more bums on seats. Perhaps you'd give a talk or something."

"A talk? About what?"

"Anything. Books. Writing. Something to peg the evening on. You wouldn't mind would you?"

"Do you have to turn the house into a Rotary Club meeting every time I'm here?"

"It's my birthday, Bridget, and I shall do whatsoever I like."

"Here, here," said Christmas, raising his glass.

"But who will you invite, mummy?"

"The Richardsons."

"You hate the Richardsons."

"That's not the point. Then there's that Italian chap with the nice wife from Merida who runs the *posada*. Alejandro Gomez, our neighbour from a couple of miles down the road—"

"Gomez is a fascist."

"Oh shush, Bridget. Then there's Dr. Puig – Oh Bridget, stop looking at me like that! We are going to have a party – why don't you organise it, darling? You know, Harry, Bridget's got terribly good organizational skills. She spent all last year on a reforestation project in Aragua. It was Aragua wasn't it, Bridget?"

"What's happened there can only be described as wholesale environmental slaughter. What with disaster just round the corner – I mean it's just so irresponsible."

"Around the corner?" asked Christmas. "When is that exactly?"

"Well, of course no one knows for sure. The Mayans predicted the end of the world in December 2012."

"Oh good. Just after the Olympics," noted Christmas. "Nothing gets me in the mood for annihilation better than Gary Lineker and the long jump."

"The point," continued Bridget, ignoring him, "is that this sort of behaviour is no longer sustainable. The world needs to reinvent its approach. We need to change ourselves." She looked straight at Christmas. He met her stare with a quizzical look and a mouthful of Pinot Grigio. She continued, unfazed. "You should cut down all the flying you do, mummy, for a start."

133

"I'd love to travel by train if it weren't for my back. Dr. Puig's been an absolute tyrant – no sitting down for long periods at a time."

"You could stand. You could walk up and down the train."

"Don't be ridiculous, darling. I am not a ticket inspector. More coffee anyone?"

"Coffee is not going to solve it, mother. If we keep on at current impact levels, if we don't modify our behaviour, then millions of people are going to die in floods, droughts and wars over resources. Don't you think so, Harry?"

"Sorry?" He was thinking of the previous night and Judith on top of him, singing like a porno Julie Andrews. "Come again?"

"We're talking about the environmental movement. I said what do you think?"

"Well, I suppose it's given the children of the wealthy something to do."

"*What?*" Christmas didn't reply. "Perhaps," continued Bridget, "some of us here think they can ignore what's happening to the world around them, but climate change is not ..."

Christmas turned to the window and began to drift off. *Emily would have made short shrift of this girl. She would have got along fine with Judith, but it'd be scruff of the neck time for Miss Bridget: 'I'll stop you right there, young madam. Being lectured at by a snotty little teenager who's nicked all her ideas off the internet is not on the menu tonight!'* Suddenly Christmas felt a sharp pain in his chest. He inhaled. He looked about the table, but no one was watching. Judith was leaning her hand on her chin, pretending to listen to her daughter. He gripped himself, then the table. It was as if someone was trying to strangle his heart.

"... like the banks and the arms industry," Bridge was declaiming, "who get all sorts of subsidies and bail outs ..."

Was this a heart attack? His mouth wouldn't work. He tried to breath but it was agony. A patina of sweat appeared over his face.

"... Thatcher said the mines had to close because they were inefficient, but government expenditure remained the same, the money just went into arms to sell to Saddam Hussein instead ..."

Was he dying? Was this it? He tried a breath and got a little further out. The pain began to ease.

"... and I'm sure we all agree that the Iraq war was a disaster ..."

He wasn't going to die. He took long, exploratory breaths and massaged his chest.

"OK there, *amore?*" Christmas nodded vigorously. She had caught the scent of distress and he was anxious to prevent any fussing. "You've gone a dreadful colour." Bridget paused for a moment then rattled on a little louder, making sure the fat man in the corner didn't derail her gospel. "... which is how the crisis is related to the war machine. The economic road map follows the military road map. Even Gaza – and I don't mean just securing the middle east oil reserves. There are massive natural gas reserves just off the coast. The Palestinians own them and the Israelis want to ..." Christmas wiped his face then took a drink.

Death. If only he could believe that he might meet Emily again, but he knew that was a lie. Emily and their raw baby girl were extinct. Trodden on like insects. Scraped off and slid into the ground. That pain in his chest was the weight of the same awful foot, testing, pressing, readying for the stamp. "... they tried it first in Chile, then Thatcher did it with the Falklands, then Iraq and Afghanistan, all so they could keep our minds on disaster while they deregulated the markets and robbed people's savings, the 'real' economy ..." Bridget mimed the grammar with the dreaded quote fingers.

"Oh, good God!" cursed Christmas.

"*Amore?*" They both stared at him. He wanted to lecture them about the quote fingers malaise, but he paused instead, and in that pause there was a flash of Slade running at him with a knife. He willed the image away and forgot what he was talking about. When he remembered, the length of the intervening pause had somehow made such instruction unsuitable. He decided to improvise. "It's about ... whether ... God's good. Don't you think?" He did it rather badly.

"Oh, not religion," groaned Bridget biting into a mango slice.

"You were talking about the environment?"

"Well, yes, kind of."

"What I meant was ... if you believe that God is good ... then when it comes to an impending ecological apocalypse, then couldn't you say, I mean, couldn't you, you know, *saaaay* ... that it was a good thing?"

"A good thing?" spluttered Bridget. *Bingo.* He was going to enjoy this. He was going to annoy her.

"I mean let's face it – we could probably do with another ice age."

"We?"

"The human project. The rascal multitude!"

"So you believe that a benevolent God would want to wipe us all out?"

"If he had his head screwed on."

"Do you believe in God?"

"Not in the religious sense."

"Then why bring him up?"

"Oh no, it's very interesting," said Judith, relieved that she could finally join in. "What do you believe in, *amore*? Life after death?"

"Well, if it does exist, I bet it's like life: unfair. There's no life after death for the elderly. Something like that. I think we can assume that death is more than a little ageist."

"No heaven, no hell?"

"Perhaps a hell, but only for people who believe in it. And perhaps the hellish bit would be the disappointment, you know,

136

you'd fall through the hole or whatever and land expecting to find adamantine chains, lakes of sulphur, harpies and so on, but actually you'd be on some boy scout's field trip being bullied by an omnipotent Akela – an eternity of wet socks and Kendal mint cake."

"And no gin, *amore*. How will you cope?"

"So, are we to understand, Harry, that the famous writer's position on the bleak future facing the world if we don't take radical action and completely overhaul our paradigms is, in fact, utter resignation. We could do with another ice age. My, how profound."

"Well, everyone can see how keen you are on profundity, Bridget dearest, but look," he said, shifting onto his elbows, "let's say here it comes, ecological disaster and floods and population displacement and the rise of tyranny and chaos and looting and rape and murder. Sounds like an average day on planet earth to me. Or let's say it's swifter than that. Let's say a chunk of the Greenland ice shelf slips into the ocean overnight, knocks out the Gulf Stream – bang – it's woolly mammoths and spears before breakfast. I'm afraid I can't help driving along the travelator of South East England, repeating backdrop after repeating backdrop, and thinking that an ice age is exactly what's required." Christmas took a drink. "Does not our hubristic nation deserve its Arctic punishment? Indeed if everything is going to go underwater, then the only sensible way to face what's coming is ... probably ... become a better swimmer. And get a gun."

"So that's your answer? Guns and swimming?"

"Sounds like the navy, *amore*. Were you in the navy?"

"Well, I think it's pathetic! You've just turned the most serious issue ever to face mankind into some kind of boys' adventure holiday."

"And spears before breakfast? Not an activity I would have thought on the roster for a portly English gent."

"My dearest Judith, the only activities fit for an English gentleman these days are drinking and cultivated opprobrium."

"So ignore everything and just go down the pub. Well, if that's what life's about, Mr Strong, it's all just great, isn't it?"

"No, it is not!" bellowed Christmas. He was getting rather drunk. "Hardly any decent pubs left! Red bloody squirrels in hiding from the bloody grey squirrel of these bloody office pubs, these idiot stables with televisions in the corner and nowhere to sit. I tell you both, it won't be long before they've invented a vertical toilet so you can vomit while standing up, right by the bar. Give me a Breezer. Bluurrrgh. Give me another Breezer. Bluurrggh. They'll stop selling beer altogether and it'll just be vicious wines and coloured syrup still sold to the medical industry under its original name. No, young lady, the character of English drinking is by no means a given." Christmas emptied his glass.

"And how would you define the English character these days, *amore*? Do you think it will be able to withstand all these horrors Bridget is talking about? In its swimming trunks? With its gun?"

"Judith, I'm sure it will flourish. Being English has always been about a mix of good manners with utter sadism. It's what allowed us to cut the throats of half the world, build an Empire, come home and still apologise to the person who has trodden on your foot. I think it's the perfect character set to deal with the four horsemen of the whatywhat. Or what have you." Christmas noted the quickening of inebriation.

"Guns and swimming," repeated Bridget with disgust.

"Right then," said Judith wiping her mouth. "Glass of pudding wine anyone?" She wanted to check herself in the mirror. "Back in a tick."

Bridget and Christmas were left alone. Hunched over the table, Bridget glared at her plate, then darted her eyes at him. She snorted. Christmas put his glass down. Her face was so screwed up it was like looking into a wastepaper basket.

"For the love of Christ!" he said, "Will you stop slouching!"

"Excuse me?" she gasped.

"Young women shouldn't slouch like that. You look completely fucking disabled."

"Oh. My. God."

"There. That's better."

"You know, for my mother's sake, I've been trying to change my opinion of you, but—"

"And what is that?"

"That you are a selfish, self-satisfied, wholly unlikeable *wanker*."

"Well, my opinion of your opinions, young lady, is that the gallows, arsenic and the firing squad would all be preferable to tasting any more of the tripe that drips from your stillborn sensibilities."

For several moments, Bridget could do nothing but blink. "What the fuck are you doing in my house?"

"I'm writing a book. About a murderer who can't drive. I shall call it, 'Drop me off at the corner of hell, just opposite the bookies'."

"You're sponging off my mother."

"Well, that makes two of us. I, on the other hand, am an invited guest. And what are you doing, may I ask, other than swanning around South American yoga retreats and whingeing about men? In fact it's pretty clear that underneath the armour you're just a normal little girl who wants to find a nice little boy, only you'll reject a string of men who you'll deem not clever enough and you'll end up the wrong side of forty, bitter but *right* – you'll be so *right* about everything you'll be *wrong*. You'll be a wrong person."

Bridget folded her arms. "I'm sorry it didn't work out for you, Harry."

"Me?"

"You're obviously speaking from experience and just dressing up your failures as some kind of priceless and hard-won wisdom. Well – newsflash – I don't want a string of men, and besides, which way do you think you're headed, Mr Strong? Because wherever it is, I'd say you've run out of time. We all know you've run out of ideas. You're what, seventy or something? Obviously you think you were too good for your marriage, too good for a real job, probably too good for any real friends. You've certainly lost all your looks if you had any in the first place, and calling me bitter is the kind of rank hypocrisy that could only come from a man whose self-image is so very far away from reality. You are a fat, beaten-up old alcoholic. What's making it all worth it, Harry? Got a secret?"

"Yes," said Christmas, "Find someone to love you."

Bridget opened her mouth then closed it again. After a moment she said, "You know, Harry—" but Christmas roared at her, leaping a little way across the table. It was so loud, so unexpected, that it genuinely frightened her.

"Now if I may beg your leave to pursue my libations ..." he said, settling back into his seat, "I would be so very grateful." He downed his glass and bared his teeth with a smile. Bridget stormed out of the room.

"Where's Bridget?" said Judith re-entering a moment later with a bottle of Sancerre and rearranged hair. "What was that noise?"

"She's gone to bed. I was trying to cheer her up with some animal impressions."

"Really, Harry, she's not a baby."

"Isn't she?"

"Oh, look, *amore* ..." Judith put the bottle on the table and slipped onto his lap. "... we're alone ..." She caressed his face with a drunken hand, poking him slowly in the eye. It was time to succumb to the inevitable.

25

That night Christmas dreamed he was with Emily. They were on the balcony in their house in Malaga. Slade came out of nowhere and cut her throat.

He woke gripping the bed. Judith was already up and gone. He turned to the window. A trail of insect bites registered themselves across his back and arms.

Christmas stood beneath the shower, the gash on his head tender under the heat. He rested his forehead against the tiles and replayed his argument with Bridget. He had to leave. He had to find Guiria. Expanding his torso, he thought about the chest pain of the previous evening. There was no tightness, only a belly hot from drink. Christmas rotated his arm, pinched the top of his nose and cleared it towards the plug.

Walking downstairs to breakfast, Christmas spied Bridget already in the kitchen reading a newspaper.

"Hullo," he said, sitting down, ready for round two.

"Oh, hello," she said brightly. "Do you want my egg?"

"Egg?"

"Here you go. I don't want it," and with that she put her boiled egg on his plate, flicked him a smile and continued reading the newspaper. Christmas was surprised, but quickly recognised the phenomenon of women, used to endless supplication on account of their beauty, enjoying nothing more than being violently disagreed with. Indeed they could develop a strong affection for anyone who treated them normally. In Bridget's case this was compounded by the small embarrassments of a hangover. She hadn't meant to call him a fat old alcoholic in quite such forthright terms. She'd had time to reflect on how happy her mother was. This man had roared at her like a lion. Perhaps he was quite interesting.

"Listen to this," she said, reading aloud, "'Armed Pirates Loot French Lawyer's Yacht: The attack came just a few miles out of Puerto La Cruz where the family were in the middle of a two-week fishing holiday. Anchored for the night, the thirteen-metre steel-hulled ketch was approached at dusk by a six-metre open fishing boat that contained five men carrying pistols and machetes. The family was bound head and foot, and a shotgun held to their heads while the boat was ransacked for electronic instruments, sail clothing and other effects.' God, how frightening."

"Could've been worse."

"Worse?"

"They could've outraged the women. Pressed the lads into service."

"I bet you fancy yourself as a bit of pirate, don't you, Harry? Bet you think you would've fitted right in."

"A gentleman of fortune? An ambassador for the Republic of the Sea? Never thought about it."

"Of course you haven't."

"Well, m'lady, perhaps you wouldn't be so slow to sign the articles and step under the Black Flag yourself."

"A female pirate?"

"Ever heard the story of Mary Read?" he said, de-shelling his eggs.

"Nope."

"Seventeenth-century daughter of a sea captain. Brought up as a boy so the mother could ensure her husband's inheritance for her 'son' after his death. The young Mary gets a job as a footman but then runs away and finds work on a Man O' War. Big mistake. Not fun."

Christmas smeared the eggs onto a piece of toast. "Mary jumps ship, joins the military – all still as a boy, mind – is promoted to the Horse Regiment after displaying bravery at the Battle of Flanders, falls in love with a soldier, confesses her sex, the two get decommissioned, marry, scandalize the military and open a pub." He added a layer of marmalade over the eggs. "Hubby dies, she gets bored, gets a ship to the West Indies which is captured by the notorious pirate Calico Jack and his mistress Anne Bonny. Bonny takes a shine to her, discovers her secret, Jack gets jealous, draws his cutlass, and so they let him in on the secret too. Mary joins the crew and off they go a-pirating."

He squeezed out a flourish of tomato sauce on top of the marmalade. "A few adventures later, Mary, still a man as far as the rest of the crew are concerned, falls in love with a sailor from a captured vessel. This sailor falls foul of one of the other pirates who challenges him to a duel. Now, Mary knows her sweetheart hasn't a chance against the seadog, so she challenges the rogue herself."

"Are you really going to eat that?"

Christmas added salt and pepper. "In accordance with pirate law," he continued, "the two get rowed ashore for the fight. She is about to get overpowered by the big brute when she rips open her shirt and shows him her breasts. The ruffian is so shocked to find out that his crewmember is a woman that he stands gawping for a fateful second – enough time for Mary to swing at his head—"

Christmas picked up the toast, "—and kill him dead." He bit into it. Bridget wrinkled her face. "No one messed with Mary after that," he said through his mouthful.

"That is disgusting."

"Why? She had no choice. Anyway, the whole crew were caught and sentenced to be hanged, but as she was pregnant with the sailor's child, she got a stay of execution, which didn't matter much in the end as she died in prison from the fever. She is famed for saying that hanging wasn't such a bad thing, because without it 'every cowardly fellow would turn pirate, and so unfit the sea that men of courage must starve.'"

"Well, you learn something every day."

"And forget," chewed Christmas, "a little bit more. Perhaps I should go down to Puerto la Cruz and get my own band of pirates together."

"And do what?"

"Mount a raid."

"Where?"

"Here."

"I'm sure you've outraged my mother quite enough."

"But her legendary bounty, the famed and priceless *Eroi* ..."

"Oh god – don't start with those things."

"I shall sell them to Dutch traders in return for gold and furs."

"You'll be lucky if you get the sideburns off a rabbit. She started doing them when Daddy was still here. I think it started off as some kind of horrible hint."

"Oh look," said Judith, coming in from the garden with a basket full of tools, "everyone's getting along! How fabulous."

"Mummy, Harry's going to be a pirate."

"Isn't that nice. Now who's going to help me with the lunch?" Bridget slipped off her chair and gave him a wink. OK, yes, Christmas reflected, he was in a cage of sorts, but a gilded one,

144

and if these were his two feisty guards then why shouldn't he enjoy himself? If he couldn't find his way out, at least Slade would never find his way in.

26

"Oh, *sí, Señor*," said the concierge, "I know this man."

"Is he here?" Slade threw a look around the lobby.

"Here, *Señor*?"

"You said you knew this man."

"Yes. I see all his films. I like the best the one – the actress with the red hair? They in Japan—" Slade snatched back the photo and quit the hotel. He opened his guidebook and crossed out another name. It was growing dark. Slade took a metro train back to Chacaito and his room at the Hotel Lux.

A mirror overlooked his bed. He inspected himself. He had lost weight and grown a beard. He was hardly eating. There were dark prints underneath his eyes. Slade took off his T-shirt and flexed his muscles. He started doing sit-ups but suddenly he just lay down on the floor and covered his face with his hands. "No!" he cried. He carried on with the sit-ups, faster this time, until he gave up and rolled onto his side, breathing heavily. Scrambling to his feet, he sat down by the bedside table and took the phone. He made a call. The ring seemed long and distant and endless until it cracked open and there was Diana's voice.

"Hello?"

"It's me."

"William? Oh God, William, what's this number? Where are you? I've been going out of my fucking mind!"

"He's here."

"Where? Where are you?"

"I've followed him. I've tracked him down. I've—"

"I told you I didn't want you to do anything. I don't want you to hurt anybody, do you understand? I was very upset then. I was drunk – where are you?'"

"Venezuela."

"Oh God..."

"He's here. He's here in Caracas. I found out—"

"Just fucking leave it, William, OK? I don't want you to do anything! Just leave it and come home!"

"Home?"

"You know what I mean."

"But now – can't we—"

"Not all that again, William. We shouldn't even be talking. You know what the situation is between us – Oh God, what a mess ..."

"He's not going to hurt you any more."

"He's dead, William."

"I meant Harry Christmas."

"Harry Christmas isn't going to hurt anyone. Not like that. Harry Christmas is just a – he's just a scumbag. Stop whatever you're doing, do you understand? Just stay out of my life!"

Slade listened to the noise of her voice for a few seconds longer then put the phone down. He put his T-shirt back on and opened the door. He checked the corridor left and right whilst replaying Diana's words of gratitude.

147

He took the elevator down and went out into Caracas, walking through the Chacaito district, along Avenida del Libertador. He looked up at the skyscrapers. One had a Pepsi ball on top of it, another a giant red Nescafé cup. He stood beneath government billboards, *'UH! AH! CHÁVEZ NO SE VA!'*, *'LA NUEVA GEOMETRÍA DEL PODER'*, *'PATRIA, SOCIALISMO O MUERTE'*. He registered every face that walked by, monitored every movement. He saw a cat sniffing at an empty burger box and tried to kick it.

Across the other side of the *autopista*, bodies skulked alongside the barriers and climbed down towards the river and the makeshift tents and shelters that clawed onto the embankment. Beyond the streetlights he could see the dark trees of the Jardín Botánico and Parque Los Caobos. He walked up Avenida Quito and Las Palmas, past rowdy kids playing baseball with a rock and a stick. Strong winds surprised the rubbish, pulled at skirts and hair. The rain began. Citizens began to run.

Slade followed some men into a corner Chinese restaurant. Inside, drinkers sat in high-backed chairs across tables covered in paper cloths and beer bottles. The Chinese waiters looked pale and bedraggled. Everyone was smoking. There was a television showing baseball, one man sitting below the screen, his fingers and wrists covered in gold. He talked into his phone as he ate, spraying food. Slade took a seat. He ordered whisky. He had no appetite.

A mix of Venezuelans and foreigners sat at the table next to him. He kept his eyes on the baseball and homed in on their conversation, picking out an Australian accent.

"... fucken gorgeous she was, mate, fucken gorgeous, great fucken tits – and she's going at it, then she stops and says why don't I bring a mate, two's a company, three's a fucken party type thing, so first I'm thinking 'whatever' and giving her head the old cafetiere, y'know, get back down there and fucken get on with it, but I'm thinking to myself, why not give it a go, right? So she calls up her mate, the doorbell goes and it's some fucken bitch with a huge fucken knife! Just fucken comes in with her fucken knife fucken ties me up and fucken robs me! The fucken two of them! Fucken ransack the place! So I am so fucken distraught I spend all the next day with the door fucken double-locked, curtains drawn, smoking fucken Mary Jane to fucken calm me down, right? And fucken someone, right, some fucken neighbour or something, fucken smells it in the corridor, calls the police, me fucken doorbell goes – two fucken cops! And guess what they fucken do! Fucken tie me up and rob the place!"

Slade was studying each of them. He saw himself smash bottles over their skulls, driving the broken ends into the faces of other diners who tried to stop him. He imagined fighting every single person in the restaurant – kicks, punches, reverse elbows – until it was strewn with groaning bodies. Slade finished his drink and went back to the Hotel Lux. The storm was over. The streets were wet. At every turning he expected to bump into Harry Christmas or the three men that had robbed him.

Once in front of the Lux he rang the bell. There was a different receptionist, a badly-shaven man with white hair. He released the security door and greeted Slade with a smile. "*Buenas noches, Señor. Todo bien?*" Slade assessed him. He walked into the lift. The man skipped out from behind his desk and held the door. "American?"

"Where's the other one? The woman?"

"Are you an American?"

"Who are you working for?" said Slade after examining him for a moment.

"*Que?*"

"Are you working for Christmas?"

"You are not an American?" Slade didn't reply. "*Chicas?*" the man whispered. "Girls? Nice one. Young one. You want?" Slade stared at him. "OK, you want, you ring to reception, *vale?*" The man pointed at his phone. "OK, *Señor?*" he winked. "No problem!" he slapped Slade on the arm and slid back to his seat. The doors of the lift closed. Slade travelled upwards through the floors, thinking back to the last time he'd had sex.

Kimberly Canning was coming out of a pub in the centre of East Grinstead late on Friday night when she bumped into Slade. She had just decided that she hated her husband and was out drinking to celebrate. She had one arm round a friend. They were in heels and short skirts and were laughing at almost everyone that passed them.

"Ooooh, look at you," she said, pulling up in front of him. She knew her husband was wary of Slade and that made her want to fuck him.

"Kim," he nodded.

"And this is Fran," she said. "You off somewhere nice?"

"Not really. You?"

"We're off up Dreamers," she said, "Want to come?"

He took the two women to Dreamers nightclub. After an hour, the friend went home and Kimberly, a small woman with big breasts, had her hand on Slade's leg. She was drunk. "I'm a passionate woman," she slurred into his ear against the bass, "and he doesn't even make love to me any more! I mean, can you believe that? I'm pretty, don't you reckon? Don't you reckon I'm still pretty?" Slade was watching a group of men he had taken a dislike to.

"Yeah," he said. "You're still pretty."

Slade took her to his flat. They started kissing in the hallway. They went into his bedroom. Once most of their clothes were off and his penis was hard, he positioned her on the small sofa so she was kneeling against it with her face to the wall. She was drunk. She wouldn't stay still. He moved in behind and started fucking her. She was giggling.

He banged her head against the wall. She cried out. Clapping his hand over her mouth, Slade took his penis out of her vagina and forced it into her anus. She couldn't move. He held her head, front and back, muffling and controlling her. Then he fucked her as quickly and as powerfully as he was able. He came.

He let go and stepped back from her. She was weeping and shaking and holding her face. She grabbed her clothes and fled.

Slade lay on his hotel bed. He turned on the television. There was no movie in English. He turned off the television. He picked up the phone and called down to reception.

When the doorbell rang, Slade was wearing a towel. "*Hola, Papi*," she said, "*Wow. Eres un macho, Papi, eres un macho de verdad.*" She was tall, with a thick mane of straight black hair and heavy black make-up around her eyes. She was wearing white boots that went up to her thighs and a tight black dress. Slade let her in, checking the corridor outside.

She prowled around the bed, saying things he didn't understand. She rubbed her fingers together and shook her Hello Kitty purse. He gave her the sixty dollars he had ready on the bedside table. Once she had it in her hands she gave him a big smile and turned on the television. She found a channel playing music videos and turned up the volume, bending down to see herself in the mirror above the bed, mouthing the words of the song, dancing, flirting with herself. She beckoned Slade over and laid him down on the bed. She ran her hands across his chest and then flopped her hair in his face, straddling him, swaying and singing. Once she had peeled off her dress over her head, Slade put his hands on her breasts. They were fake. She smiled and carried on looking at herself in the mirror as he ran his hands over her and she ground against him, lap-dancing to herself.

The song ended. She sat back on his ankles and pulled open his towel. Slade had an erection. His penis was long and thin. She slipped from the bed and started giving him a blowjob. Slade rolled his head back to see if he could see his reflection. He could not. He looked forward. The prostitute was flicking her hair from one side to another, making noises and staring at herself in the mirror while she sucked his cock.

Slade put his hands on her shoulders, motioning that they change position. He got out from beneath her and kneeled on the mattress, putting on a condom she gave him from her purse. She slipped off her knickers and, with her boots still on, got on all fours, reversing her backside towards him. She curved her back and offered up her rump. Slade clenched it, round and firm and brown, the spots of a shaving rash visible either side of her vagina, then he watched himself in the mirror, his penis moving in and out. He glimpsed a cat in the corner of the room. He turned. The cat was gone. He looked down at her backside.

She shuffled backwards, edging him out of the mirror so she could see herself, "*Sí, Papi,*" she squeaked at her reflection, "*me gusta como me coges Papi, qué rico, Papi, qué rico ...*" She was occupying the whole mirror. He couldn't see a thing. He looked down at his penis sliding in and out and didn't recognise it. He stopped thrusting. He took his penis out but she kept rocking and groaning as if he was still fucking her. "*Sí, Papi así,*" she continued, "*Sí, Papi así,*" she continued, "*exactamente así, Papi, oh Papi baby, sí, qué rico.*" She frowned. She stopped. She looked round. "*Papi?*" she said, "*Hay algún problema?*"

27

The days passed. His bruises were turning yellow. He could brush red dust off the scab on his head. With Bridget in the next door room, Christmas assumed that Judith would cut out her nocturnal arias. He was wrong. A couple of times, sex had bought on the chest pains. Once he got cramp, bellowing out, but even though she had been indulging the roof beam with her own music she shushed him with a finger and pointed at the wall. This did nothing for the cramp. He chopped out some yelps. She took it for passion and put a pillow over his face. Suffocating as well as cramping, Christmas grabbed at the pillow and then bucked her right off, flipping both of them onto the floor. Christmas looked up. Judith was holding her head. She was crying. "Are you—?" She wasn't crying. She was laughing.

The cramp re-asserted itself, yanking his thigh. Christmas struggled onto his feet and hopped round the room. Judith was in hysterics. Bridget, roused by the noise, rushed into the room. She saw Harry Christmas naked and rushed out again, mock-retching in the corridor. "Whatever you two are doing–" she shouted,

"–I mean, for fuck's sake!" Christmas rubbed his thigh back and forth.

"Oh, darling," Judith sighed, "we do have fun, don't we?"

He kept asking Judith if he could borrow the car, but she would say things like, "Oh, you are funny," and carry on with the pruning. The town was too far to walk, the weather too hot or too rainy. Whenever they did need something, she always seemed to drive off while he was napping.

"I'd just like to go for a drive," he said as firmly as he could, "just drive around." He'd studied a map of the peninsula. Guiria was on the other side. If he could borrow the car he could just disappear for a day or two and find Emily's beach.

"You can't do that," she replied, "you're drunk." Judith was right. Christmas was always drunk – in fact he was caught in an endless cycle of meals and drinks. He was either stuffed or drunk or asleep or all three. Then there were his duties as a model. He had put his foot down when it came to nakedness but he was still forced to sit there for hours while she carved his bust or his head. Sometimes in bed he caught her examining his penis with her glasses on. Her most recent *Eroi* looked alarmingly familiar.

He tried to enlist Bridget with ideas for excursions, but she only shrugged her golden shoulders and said, "Ask mummy. It's her car." So while Judith sculpted or did the gardening, Christmas and Bridget were left to joust with each other.

"Yes, yes, Bridget but this is 'real life' as well, you know." Christmas was nestled in the hammock. He pushed himself off with a foot and slurped his cocktail. "You don't have to be in a refugee camp for things to count. I agree that generally speaking life is not a bed of roses but—"

"Life undoubtedly *is* a bed of roses," she retorted. "You stay exactly where you're put and then every so often someone

154

comes along and dumps a load of shit on you. Now shut up. I'm reading." Christmas watched her go back to her magazine. Would his own daughter have turned out like Bridget? So brazen? So beautiful? With a smile he thought back to when Emily was pregnant, how he had started to delight in housework, in performing small errands for her. He remembered how protective he was when they were in public places, how he'd been overwhelmed with kindly feeling, making sure that she was always comfortable, that all her needs were met. He remembered being beside Emily on the gurney while they had a third scan and learnt their baby was a girl: the outline of his daughter's face, the way the image stretched and flickered while he held Emily's hand.

"She's got your nose, Em," he said, "Thank God."

"All babies have got my nose. Basically I look like a foetus." Christmas kissed her. "*We're having a little girl,*" Emily whispered, turning back to the monitor as they watched their child dreaming up a life.

"I hope she's brave," said Emily, once the nurse had left, "like you are."

"I hope she's not like me at all."

"Don't say that, Pops. Stop putting yourself down all the time. You've really started doing that a lot lately."

"I'm just worried I won't be good enough for her."

"You are a stupid old fool sometimes, you know that? Nobody expects you to be perfect."

"There's hardly any threat of perfection."

"Stop it now. Seriously. I'm going to get cross in a minute."

"I've just made a mess of so many things—"

"But that's all in the past, isn't it? Look at you now. You haven't made a mess of us, have you?"

"Do you think we'll have more than one?"

"Let's get this one out first, shall we? I've a feeling we'll have plenty on our hands with madam here."

Christmas cried out. Bridget had given the hammock a huge push and now he was swinging from side to side, his drink going everywhere. "Bitch!" he declared.

"You were making weird noises," she giggled, "I thought babies liked being rocked."

Hovering above it all was the imminent arrival of the internet. Judith kept trying to get through to the phone company; they were coming in a few days. Then they were coming in two weeks. Then they were coming at the end of the week – so the gallows wobbled.

Christmas was sat on the viewing bench. There was a storm at sea. The rain was still some miles away but the wind bawled and swore, thrashing the trees around him as distant lightning photographed the horizon. He felt a peck on his cheek. Judith was beside him, holding down her hair and her skirt. "How can you be reading?"

"Oh, I wasn't really" said Christmas, putting the Montejo book away in his jacket. "Fantastic, isn't it?" They watched the storm together for a while until he felt her eyes on him. She put her hand on his neck.

"God, I've been lonely," she said quickly.

"Judith?"

"I just – I should've gone back to England, but I can't, I was too scared that I wouldn't belong there any more and then I'd have left here and the garden would've – the garden. Too scared to leave the garden. Doesn't that just –" she sighed, "– sound so stupid? Oh, look at me ..."

"No, sweetheart," he began, "please—"

"But then you came and, well, it's been fun, hasn't it? Sorry, Harry, I don't want to—"

"Judith—" and he took her hand as she stood up.

"I sent some figurines to Juan Carlos in Caracas," she said in a different voice. "A couple of you, actually. He's just called to say he

156

loved them. Going to put them on display. Dinner's ready anyway. Think we better ..." and her voice was lost in the wind as she turned round and walked back to the kitchen.

Christmas followed her in. Bridget was sat at the table with a magazine open in front of her. "'What kind of man is the man in your life?'" she read out as he came in, "'and how long will he last?' Well, seeing as you're the only one here, that's you. Are you ready?" Keeping his eye on Judith, Christmas shrugged.

"'One. If you had to choose his best quality, would you say: A) He's good B) He's kind C) He's sexy D) He's funny E) He's loyal.' What do you think your best quality is?"

"Unreliability."

"Your *best* quality?"

"It gives other people the edge."

"Out of these four."

"Sexy. Obviously." Bridget laughed for a full minute. Christmas watched Judith as she spooned out home-made gazpacho. It didn't matter if he wasn't going to raid her bank account. Judith was already another Diana. Christmas wrapped his fist over a chair. The only thing he could do was limit the damage, leave before she fell any deeper. He saw it now – he must simply ask to borrow some money. He'd pay her back when he got to London. He couldn't wait any longer for some magical money-making scheme to appear. There were no schemes here. Bridget gave a theatrical cough of recovery.

"I don't think the 'sexy' option is available to the over-hundreds, sorry, Harry. What about good? Don't you want to be good? Mummy, don't you think Harry should try to be a bit less rotten? Mummy – are you all right?"

"Oh yes," said Judith sitting down and smiling, "bloody garlic on my finger when I rubbed my eye." Christmas poured out the wine.

"You mean good, as in 'Do unto others as you would have done unto you?'"

"If you like," said Bridget, passing round the toast.

"Because as Christ was an obvious masochist, I'd say that was the only honest thumbs-up to violence the church has ever made."

"I'm not talking about the church, Harry. Stop hiding behind these quips. Don't you want to be good? Don't you want to make the world a better place?"

"That usually leads to genocide."

"Harry Strong you are beyond redemption. Hopeless. Mummy, he's hopeless."

"Yes," she said softly, "yes he is."

"Look, here's my theory," started Christmas, clearing his throat, "the whole problem is people wanting to do good. They get so caught up in the higher good, they're so keen to make it happen they'll kill anyone. What the world needs is some evil. We need some people so hell bent on evil they're willing to do horrific amounts of good to get there."

"And that's it, is it? That's what you would like to have on your gravestone: 'Here lies Harry Strong – he wished there was more evil.'"

"No. What I'd like to have on my gravestone is 'Here lies Harry Strong – he came, he saw, he went home again, he went to bed, he got up twice in the middle of the night to pee, he barely managed to get to sleep again, he woke up at four in the morning with no feeling in his right arm.'"

"Isn't there anything in life that's important to you?" He thought for a moment.

"A good hat," he replied, through a mouthful of soup.

"A hat?"

"Judith, the gazpacho is sublime. Bridget dearest, turn your nose up now, but when you start losing your hair, you'll learn to take the noble hat a damn sight more seriously."

158

"So your only values are hats?" Christmas was watching Judith. "You know," Bridget said after a moment, "I can't exactly work out which bits are you and which bits are just a front, but I think basically you're suffering from a psychological complex that everyone is as rotten as you are."

"And I'd say you are suffering from a psychological complex about how flat-chested you are. Two Freud eggs, that's your problem." Bridget gasped. Christmas cheered his own joke.

"If there's anyone with a tit issue round here," said Bridget "it's you. Look at those man boobs – they're obscene."

"Man boobs?" Christmas looked down.

"Have you been having hormone therapy?"

"Bridget, really—"

"He started it! And you know it's true ..."

The two women were both giggling. Christmas grabbed himself by the breasts and pushed them together like a glamour girl. "Do you refer to *these* magnificent things?"

"Urrrgh! Put them away!"

Everyone was laughing. Here was his wife and here was his daughter and this was a family dinner, the storm rain beginning to drum down on the roof. Something surged through him and faded. This wasn't his family. He wasn't even Harry Strong. Perhaps in that café in Caracas he could have approached Judith as himself, just been himself, not caught in the lies, not fearing the arrival of the internet as if it were some giant spider about to walk over the hills. Could he just tell them the truth? No. He was trapped. He should leave tonight. He had to get to Guiria.

"Oh – and did you both hear the phone this morning?" said Judith recovering her composure. "Bloody internet people! They've cancelled again."

"What?"

"Wouldn't even give me a date when they can come. Could be weeks and weeks. Kept giving me a load of technical waffle about the phone lines and the hills interfering with the satellites and whatnot."

"Hooray!" Christmas lifted his glass.

"I don't see what's so *hooray* about it."

"Bridget, as you keep pointing out, I am a man of mature years, and it's not often that the relentless stampede of modernity, in this example the internet, is halted by forces as ancient as geography. So I say – hooray! I toast the past –"

"Furrrrreak."

"– now pass the toast."

28

Slade paced the roof terrace of the café. Church bells rang out above the moans of the city. He had been walking its streets all day and perspiration had made butterfly patterns across the back of his T-shirt. His face was pink and peeling. He took off the sunglasses he had bought from a market stall and examined them. They were cheap and thin and they irritated his ears. He snapped them in two, then twisted the lenses off and threw all the bits over the side of the roof. He sat down beside his beer. He had not eaten. The roof terrace was empty.

Slade was still touring the hotels of Caracas with a photograph of Harry Christmas. He still rang his *eorlderman* every morning but old Peter Dunstone had got fed up and told Slade not to ring anymore, that he would call if there was any news. Now when Slade rang there was no answer. He took out the photograph. He wanted to rip it into pieces. Slade was almost out of hotels to check and had started on the expensive restaurants and bars. He had asked policemen, shoeshine boys and station staff at the metro stops, always with his knife beneath his shirt, assessing everyone around him.

Slade opened his guidebook and turned to the map. He didn't know where he was. He had wandered into a residential area with wide empty streets and uniformed security guards outside gated apartment blocks. He took out his phone. He called Diana. It went onto voicemail. He called again. He had been doing the same thing all day. Harry Christmas was going to walk onto this terrace at any moment, he decided. He just needed to talk to Diana and fate would produce the perfect moment. *Wait*, he'd say. *He's right in front of me.*

Slade went downstairs. It was an upmarket, busy café with art on the walls and counters full of pastries. He walked through the tables towards the door. There was a pottery display in the window. What was that figurine? He stepped closer, disbelieving his eyes. Slade turned, seeing people drinking coffee. Were they laughing at him? Had they put it there? Slade went outside. He pressed his face to the window and peered through, whispering to himself. He went back inside and asked to look at it properly and the owner smiled and told him it was for sale, lifting it out from the window and onto the counter. There it was, unmistakably: a statue of Harry Christmas naked, sitting on some stones.

Slade took out the photograph. Yes, said Juan Carlos, it was indeed a sculpture of the man in the photograph, Harry Strong, the famous English writer. Yes, he knew where he was. *Señor* Strong had met the sculptress in this very café and they were now in Estado Sucre together, near a town called Rio Caribe. Did he want to buy the statue?

"Can you give me the address?"

"He is a friend of yours?" enquired Juan Carlos. Slade grinned.

"He's like a father to me."

Slade rented a car and drove east. When he had got out of Caracas, the road straightened and the traffic thinned. He followed the coastline. There were fields of salt and flamingos. In the rear-view mirror he glimpsed the swish of a cat's tail on the backseat. He turned round but there was nothing there.

He got as far as Carúpano where he spent yet another bad night. Right before he woke he had a dream with nothing in it, just a feeling of unutterable sadness. He phoned Diana. His number had been blocked.

That day he drove into Rio Caribe. He pulled up at a cheap guesthouse on the corner of a wide avenue. The pavement stood tall from the road. Two old men sat in its shade facing the gutter. Slade got out of his car, smelling the ocean. His back was soaked with sweat. A truck full of cacao rolled past. The heat was white.

Inside the guesthouse, Slade took a room. He pointed at Judith's name and address. The owner, a lazy-eyed woman with braids, shook her head. Other women appeared. They all took it in turns to examine the paper. They gave it back, looking at him and muttering. Slade went into his room and lay down. His belly was tight. His eyelids swarmed with patterns. His organs felt as if they were floating.

After a few minutes, Slade left the guesthouse. There were few people around. The town smelt of sea-salt and petrol. He found an internet café full of boys playing war games. He walked across the *malecon* and confronted the ocean. A fat man offered him some fried chicken.

He walked around, asking people, jabbing impatiently at the address, across Plaza Sucre, up and down Avenida Bolivar and Avenida Bermudez while the sun settled into the baths of the Caribbean, staining its waters and mocking his failure. Everyone smirked and shook their heads. No one spoke English.

Heading down a backstreet he heard noise and music coming from behind a tin door. Someone staggering out revealed a cantina inside. Loud *Vallenato* music blared over tables full of fishermen and farmers picking at meat and drinking bottles of Cacique. A drunken cheer greeted his arrival and a fourteen-year old girl showed him to his table. He tried to ask her about the address but she looked at him shyly and said something that made the room laugh. Everyone was watching him. He began to size up the men. There was a shelf with two metal candlesticks amongst the bric-a-brac. He visualised wielding them as weapons.

A huge woman with a slight moustache waddled out from the kitchen with a laminated menu. She said things in Spanish he couldn't understand. "Judith," he said, "Ju-dith Lamb." Then he took out the photo of Harry Christmas. This was passed around the room. Slade stayed on the edge of his seat, observing fingers dripping with animal grease manhandle the image. Everyone was laughing now. Some chicken and *arepas* were placed in front of him. They glistened with oil. He started to pick at the food. Various people were calling things out to him. The music was deafening. A stout man in red shorts and a battered T-shirt had snatched the photo from someone else and was standing up, gesticulating at it and laughing. He grabbed a bottle of beer and made an obscene gesture. The man sat down at Slade's table. He was pointing at Christmas and then pointing at himself. He was one of Judith's gardeners.

"English?" said the man, "English womans? *Ju-dit?*" Slade nodded, "Where does she live?" he tapped the address. "Where is this?" The man understood and, calling for a pen, he drew a shaky map on a paper napkin. It was outside the town, then. The route seemed simple enough. Slade watched the lines being drawn. He flexed his back.

With the napkin in his hand Slade put some money on the table and stood up. There was an explosion of laughter. He took the photograph and shoved it into his back pocket. The man was asking him if he was another model for the English woman's clay penises. He waggled a Cacique bottle against his crotch again. Slade was sure he was being insulted. He scanned the faces surrounding him while he thought about punching this man in the face. In one corner there were two young men, watching him in silence. Slade decided to leave.

The man in red shorts poured a glass of rum. He offered it to the foreigner but Slade pushed past him out of the door, slamming it behind him. "*¿Pero qué clase de coño eres?*" exclaimed the man in astonishment.

Slade headed to his car, his neck stiff with hatred for this country. He turned a corner into the main street and saw Harry Christmas standing in front of the *licorería*.

29

Earlier that afternoon, Judith was wiping her hands on her apron and shaking her head. "But Harry can't go," she said. "He's wounded."

"I am *fine*, Judith."

"It's your birthday party tonight," said Bridget, ignoring him. "We need to get loads of stuff from Rio Caribe, you're up to your eyeballs and I need some help."

"But—"

"Thanks," said Bridget, spying the car keys on the sideboard. She swiped them and trotted out into the garden. Christmas felt a surge of elation and began to hum the theme from *The Great Escape*.

"Do you have to go?" Judith pleaded.

"I haven't left the house in—"

"Don't be long!" She hugged his chest. She smelt of onions. "Promise?"

"Judith, we're just nipping to the shops."

"Yes," she mumbled, "yes, yes."

Christmas looked down at her. He must leave. He must ask to borrow some money, but how much? Fifty dollars? One hundred?

"Judith?"

"Yes?"

"I – listen – oh, look, nothing. We'll talk about it later."

"About what?"

"After the party. It can wait."

"OK," she said, soft-eyed and smiling. She kissed him. "You better take your jacket in case it rains. And be careful on the roads. And don't be long?"

"I'll drive," said Bridget as they walked towards the car. "You're pissed. As per usual."

"You say it as if it were a bad thing."

"You don't think drinking every day is a bad thing?"

"Not if you like it. Why should it be?"

"Sure you're not drinking to forget?"

"Forget what?" asked Christmas.

"I don't know."

"Have you forgotten?"

"Oh, shut up."

"Perhaps you need a drink –"

"Get in."

"– help you remember."

They bounced down the driveway onto the main road and then headed along the coast towards the town. The sun was sharp. Christmas balanced his consciousness between the sea and Bridget's knees. He thought about Lola Rosa, how she had looked that night in the club. How was it possible that she'd stood him up? Bridget gave him a smile. *Oh the devil take you, Harry Christmas*, he thought to himself, *I just want to tell this girl the truth*!

They drove through a village where a long line of children were helping untangle a fishing line.

"That's something you don't see at home," said Bridget.

"Kids? There's a bloody plague of them."

"No, I mean, helping, you know, everyone helping out. Our sense of community has just gone. We're so atomized."

"Bridget, have you ever lived in place with lots of community feeling? It's a fucking nightmare."

"Oh God, Harry, just forget it."

"No, no, no – this is important; ever since your caveman was trying to find his own little corner of the cave where he could chew on a nice bit of mammoth rib without interruption, man has been desperately trying to live on his own."

"Here we go ..."

"Modern man has spent five hundred years trying to get his own flat, and people like you, who've never lived in a community the likes of which you're so keen on imagining, are determined to send him back to live with his parents. An atomized society is a marvellous, wonderful bloody thing. The summit of human achievement. The less I have to talk to my neighbours – especially *my* neighbours – the better. Civilization, if it has any meaning, is the ability to choose one's friends along lines of greater value than the relative proximity of kitchens."

"Have you finished?"

"Not sure."

"So what are you going to do your talk about?"

"Talk?"

"Your speech. For her birthday dinner, remember? You said you'd do a talk."

"I think I'll improvise."

"On what theme?"

"On the theme of improvisation."

"And what about a present?"

"Dunno. Perhaps a nice bottle of rum."

"Rum?"

"What's wrong with that?"

"Why don't you just get her a gun? Or a rock."

"Whatever do you mean?"

"I mean a bottle of rum – it's not very touchy-feely, is it?"

"If it's touchy-feely she wants, Bridget," Christmas sighed, "she should be sleeping with a blind man."

As soon as they parked the car, Christmas went into the *locutorio*, pretending to make a call that would tell him his credit card had not yet arrived in Caracas. When he came out Bridget had disappeared. He walked down the main street, Avenida Bermudez, wide and empty with pavements raised high for the floods and cars dozing in the shade. He saw a *licorería*. It was painted yellow and covered with old posters. Men sat on the steps beneath the counter. He bought a Polar Ice and started chatting to them in Spanish.

"So," said a man in plastic sandals and shorts, "you staying here in Rio Caribe?"

"No. About an hour or so that way. Up on the hills."

"The English woman's place?"

"That's right." The men looked at each other and started laughing.

"The English woman, the one who makes the—?" The man put an empty beer bottle against his groin.

"That's her."

"She make one of yours? Hey!" A couple more friends were sauntering by. "This man stay with the English woman who makes the—" he masturbated his bottle and slapped Harry on the back. Everybody was laughing. "So she make one of yours?"

"She doesn't have enough clay."

"Ha ha ha! Not enough clay! *Que coño!*"

The man offered to buy Christmas another beer, but he saw Bridget coming up the road carrying bags of food. "Another time, gentlemen, another time, excuse me, *adios*." Harry stepped out of the laughter into the sun.

"Made some new friends?" said Bridget.

"We've got similar tastes in art."

"OK. I'm going to the car with this lot; you get the booze?" She held the bags with one hand and dug out her wallet.

"As soon as the money comes through—" said Christmas as she gave it to him.

"Yeah, yeah," said Bridget, "I know."

"Well, it's embarrassing."

"Borrowing some cash after you were beaten up and robbed is not embarrassing. Those breasticles on the other hand ..."

"Oh, very funny."

"You know, Harry," Bridget pouted at him then took in a long breath, "my mum is really happy at the moment."

"Bridget—"

"Shut up. She's the happiest I've seen her, like, forever, and you might be an old pisshead and everything but, well," she shifted her weight onto the other foot, "I'm glad you're here."

"Really?"

"Yes, really."

"Thank you, Bridget. I—"

"Back in a minute then, OK?" Bridget flashed him a smile and walked off into town. He watched her go. She disappeared around a corner. He looked at her wallet. He looked at the *licorería*. He looked down towards the sea and saw William Slade running towards him.

30

S^{*lade.*}

"Oh God."

Christmas pulled off his hat and erupted up Avenida Bermudez. Within seconds he was out of breath. He swung into an alley and then veered right, behind the *licorería*. There were pallets stacked beside fencing. He hid behind them, pale, wheezing, stuffing Bridget's wallet into his pocket. *How the fuck...?*

He saw Slade stop at the corner, look around, then continue down the alley. Christmas ran across the backyard into the *licorería*.

The owner spun round as Christmas came out from the back saying in Spanish, "Stop that other gringo! He's trying to kill me! Stop him!" He dipped under the wooden bar and past the drinkers. Slade heard the shouts.

Christmas crossed Avenida Bermudez. Puffing out short, high, breaths, his heart was pounding so fast he thought it might split. He ran through the door of the Caribana, a luxury posada, as Slade reappeared on the other side of the street.

Christmas skittered past two cleaning girls, his belly bouncing, legs quivering, arms paddling, around the central courtyard, down a corridor, past an office and careered out through a restaurant and into its garden. He heard Slade yell. At the other end there was a high wall with a rickety wooden door. It was locked. He charged at the door with his injured shoulder and busted it from its hinges. Whimpering with pain, he hopped over the broken door, stumbling right and left down back alleys, his lungs sawing for breath. Hunchbacked with exertion, Christmas came out onto Calle Zea, a long straight street. He burst into an internet café.

It was cold, air-conditioned, full of boys playing video games. The man behind the counter said something to him. Christmas hid beside the window, dizzy, gripping his hat. He thought he was going to vomit. Slade ran past.

Christmas couldn't check his breathing. He was gulping, grimacing, his chest felt snagged on barbed wire. He glanced around the room. It had a concrete floor and white walls. The only other door was to the toilet. He wiped back the sweat that was flooding his face and neck, looking out onto the street to see Judith's car turn into Calle Zea, heading his way. Bridget was looking for him.

Christmas lay trembling fingers on the door handle. Slade was still running up Calle Zea in the other direction, into town, though he had slowed to a jog. Another few seconds and Bridget would be level. He could flee from the door, across the street, into her car and away. The owner of the internet café was in front of him, firing questions. Ignoring the man, Christmas craned his head, watching Slade turn around, studying the car. Bridget stopped.

"No, no, no!" Christmas cried.

She parked, got out and went into a vegetable shop. Slade was heading back towards him, past the car. Christmas let go of the door handle. Slade was checking the shops on either side of the street. Christmas stepped around the owner and ran for the toilet, praying that it wasn't a dead end.

Slade stepped into a pharmacist's, a hairdresser's, a general store. Their atmospheres were undisturbed. He got to the internet café and opened the door. By the expression on the owner's face he knew Christmas was in there. Some of the boys had stopped playing their games moments before. They were all looking at him.

In the far corner there was a maroon door marked '*lavabo*'. Slade pointed to it. "Is he in there?" The owner replied, but he didn't understand. He went into the toilet and found that on the other side of the cubicles the room was not yet built. He was standing in a yard. Christmas was gone.

Slade ran through it into an alley. He could go left or right. He chose right. He sprinted. He found himself back in Plaza Sucre. He looked down Avenida Bermudez, ran the other way and looked down Calle Zea. Nothing. Slade ran to his car.

He drove through Rio Caribe as night fell, up and down the streets. After he had criss-crossed the part of town near the sea he headed inland, past the police station, the hospital, the town hall, past banks and taxis and trucks. Rio Caribe was busier here, more bodies and cars to scan, headlights and shadows. He drove past a white church. He found himself in Plaza Bolivar.

Slade stopped. He got out. He stood in the middle of the plaza, cursing. A bus chugged loudly into life. It tooted its horn. It said 'Caracas' on the front. Slade watched it pull away. Many of the curtains were shut but he could still see passengers arranging themselves for the overnight journey. One of the pairs of curtains opened at the back and out peered the hollow face of Harry Christmas, checking to see if he was in the clear. The two men locked eyes.

Christmas, absorbing his mistake, sat back in his seat, winded by self-loathing. He put his head in his hands.

"Oh dear God," he whispered.

31

Christmas bit at his knuckle, watching the other passengers wrap themselves in blankets and heavy coats. The air-conditioning was freezing. The man next to him was already asleep. This was the night bus to Caracas.

They moved slowly through Rio Caribe. Christmas stared out between the curtains, trying to see behind. He saw carefree pedestrians. How could Slade have tracked him here? How had it come to this? Were these the last moments of his life?

The bus leaned out onto Avenida Romulo Gallegos. They were heading along the coast, out of town. His heart was boxing with his chest. A car pulled alongside the bus, but didn't overtake. It was Slade. Christmas looked down. Slade looked up. He grinned. Christmas shut the curtains.

Christmas tried to control the panic. He swept the sweat from his face and hair. He stood up, hauling and squeezing himself over the sleeping man, out into the corridor. He went up to the bus driver and asked when the next stop was. Carúpano. Half an hour away. He looked through the windscreen. They were in countryside now, sea on one side, mountainous rock on the other, the road dark and winding. There were no lights save those of oncoming cars. He was travelling in the executioner's cart. His reflection hovered above the driver's. Already a ghost.

Christmas went to the back of the bus. A single set of headlights was trailing them. The headlights flashed. Slade. Christmas dropped his head. He clambered over the sleeping man and got back into his seat. He opened his curtains. Slade, beside the bus now, looking up. Slade revved his engine. Christmas shut the curtains, took off his hat and held it with both hands on his knees.

Slade saw the curtains shut and moved back behind the bus. He opened the glove compartment and took out the dive knife. He left it on the seat. They swept along the dark road, around sharp corners, up and over headlands, past cars heading to Rio Caribe.

He looked out to the black ocean. He turned on the radio. It was playing salsa. He turned the dial until he heard music he recognised. Christmas appeared again in the rear window. The bus went round a bend. The radio played 'If you're going to San Francisco'. The bus reappeared. Slade waved. Christmas stepped away from the window. In his rear view mirror Slade saw The General sitting on the back seat. He turned around but the cat was gone. He drove along watching the mirror. He pulled alongside the bus. The curtains were open. He could see Christmas.

After twenty minutes they approached a town. They passed a small, illuminated dock, a hotel, a twenty-four hour *arepa* restaurant surrounded by mopeds. Slade drove alongside the bus. There was Christmas. Slade dropped back. The road became tree-lined. It rose to a rough park on a cliff. There were street lights. Another hotel, graffiti that said '*EXXXON MOBIL ... HIJOS DE PUTA!*', a Masonic temple, boarded up and rotting. Then they were in the town and slowing beside a long white wall. Slade could see the tops of buses. It was a terminal. The bus indicated left. It turned in and Slade followed. The bus drew into a bay. He parked up, took the knife, put his jacket over it and ran across the forecourt. He got there before the bus had come to a stop. There were travellers milling about, people selling street food, men with whistles.

The bus doors opened. Slade looked up at the driver who said something to him. Some passengers came down the steps. Slade let them pass. Then he got on the bus. People were standing up, taking bags down from the rack, leaning over seats, talking to each other, looking at him. Slade saw Christmas at the back, still in his seat. He headed down the corridor, pushing past people who were trying to get out.

Harry Christmas.

The fat man was trying to hide behind his hat.

"Peek-a-boo," said Slade, picking the Panama off his face, but it wasn't Christmas. It was a Venezuelan man. He was asleep.

32

Sitting there as the bus had swooped around the bends, Christmas pushed the butt of his hands into his eyes. *Up on two legs, man! Think – you have to bloody breathe and bloody think!*

He clambered out of his seat, half-waking the man next to him and went back to talk to the bus driver. He took out Bridget's wallet. He opened it. There was picture of Judith and Bridget with their arms around each other. He took out fifty dollars and offered it to the bus driver in exchange for opening the door when they went around the next corner.

"Are you crazy?"

"You don't want fifty dollars?"

"You want to jump off my bus?"

"You see that car? The one that has been following us since Rio Caribe? The man in that car is trying to kill me."

"What?"

"Look at me. I swear to God it's the truth." The bus driver glanced at his eyes.

"Why?"

"Because – because he just came out of prison for killing some-one and he went to prison because I saw him kill that person and I told the police and now he's tracked me down to Venezuela and he's trying to kill me!"

"He's a gringo?"

"He's a gringo, he's a murderer, and please, for the love of God I'm begging you, I have a wife and child – look at them, this is their picture – and you're the only hope I have left and all you have to do is open the doors at the next bend. You slow down, he goes out of sight for a second, I jump, that's it. Here, please, in the name of God, fifty dollars, take it!"

"*Señor*, I—"

"One hundred. One hundred dollars!"

Christmas went to the back of the bus. He could see Slade waving. He stayed there until they turned a corner. Slade's car disappeared for three countable seconds. Then it was back. He went to his seat. He crouched in the corridor beside the sleeping man, shook him awake and offered him his hat if they could swap places. Christmas handed the man his Panama. Still half-asleep the man took it, examined it, shrugged, moved next to the window, pulled the hat onto his head and promptly fell back to sleep. Christmas carefully opened the curtain.

He went to the front of the bus. He gave the driver one hundred dollars. That left him twenty dollars and 260 bolívares.

"You're going to hurt yourself," the driver said. "You're crazy."

"I am alive," said Christmas. He went down the steps to the door. The verge was changing width, sometimes down to no more than a yard before a steep drop into nothingness. The doors gassed open.

"Next one," said the driver, watching Slade in the rear view mirror. The verge widened. Christmas felt the rush of wind, the smells of sea and fumes and vegetation. He saw the long grass rushing past.

"Ready," said the driver. They swung round the bend, the driver watching the mirror. "Now!" and a fifty-eight year old, overweight, injured man with fear in his guts and a memory that you had to try and stay loose in a fall, leapt from the bus into the dark.

Crunch.

Grass and branches. Spinning and crashing through undergrowth, his mind empty but for the prayer that he would not fall off a cliff. Christmas came to a stop.

He looked up into the night and heard the fading engines. Panting, Christmas moved his limbs, anticipating pain. His ribs stabbed him. His shoulder felt dislocated. Christmas turned over and pushed himself up a little so he could see beyond the grass. There were no cars within sight. Clearing twigs from his neck, he lay down again, listening to crickets and wiping his face. He heard a noise and lay flat, but it was nothing. Christmas slowly got to his feet, keeping his eyes on the road, wincing and cursing until he caught sight of tail lights curving over the next headland.

Scratched, broken and hobbling, he tried to walk along the verge but the grass was too thick. He went onto the tarmac. Headlights came over the brow, heading back towards Rio Caribe, so he hopped back into the grass and lay down, muffling himself against the pain. It was a truck. Once it had passed he got back onto the road again. Another set of headlights approached. He resisted the impulse to hide. He couldn't be sure that it wasn't Slade, but he had to risk it, telling himself that if Slade had seen him jump he would have stopped immediately. Christmas whispered another prayer and stuck out his thumb. Rio Caribe was too far to walk. He had to get off the roadside before the bus arrived in Carúpano.

The car slowed to a stop. Christmas covered his eyes and squinted. It was an elderly couple. They had never seen a hitch-hiking gringo before.

Christmas eased into the back, biting his lip against the pain. He smiled. The relief overtook him. He started laughing. It hurt, but he couldn't stop.

"You OK?" said the man.

"I'm just very happy," said Christmas, "that you stopped. I got lost."

"Where are you from?"

"England," he said, laughing and the couple were laughing now too, though with bemusement.

"Where are you headed?" said the woman.

"Guiria," Christmas laughed.

"We are going as far as Chacaracuar, OK?"

"That's great," he said, rubbing his eyes, "Wherever." He felt for Emily's book. What if Judith hadn't told him to take his jacket? "Thank you," he sighed, chuckling. "Oh, Jesus Christ, thank you, thank you."

33

Slade checked every face on the bus, every face outside it, underneath the bus, in the luggage compartment. No Christmas.

"Fat," he interrogated the driver, forcing the photograph into his face. "English – that hat there – that one—" louder, over and over again, but the driver refused to talk to him. He shook his head. "No English," he said. The other passengers wouldn't talk to Slade either. The driver had told everyone that he was a gringo murderer, just released from prison. Slade went back to the driver. His coat slipped. The driver saw the dive knife and started yelling for help. Slade left the bus. Men approached. They began to encircle him. They were shouting. His coat fell away. He held the knife in front of him and backed towards his car.

He got in and shut the door. Some of the men tried to block his path. He drove into them. They got out of the way, kicking the car. Slade sped out onto the road. Another car had to emergency brake, horn blaring; more voices swearing, but Slade was on the other side of the road, heading back to Rio Caribe.

The vehicle slid along the dark coast. Inside, Slade punched the dashboard, again and again. He roared and yanked at the steering wheel and punched the roof and took the knife with his free hand and stabbed the passenger seat in the legs and chest. Then he pulled his arm right back and stabbed it through the face and left the knife sticking out. He panted. He dug his hand into his pocket for the map drawn on the napkin. He stretched it over the steering wheel with both hands, examining it, accelerating.

Judith and Bridget were in the kitchen. Bridget had driven around and around Rio Caribe, getting increasingly cross until she decided that the only possibilities were that he was getting drunk somewhere or had already made his own way back.

"What do you mean you lost him, you stupid girl?" Judith was gulping from a glass of wine. "Look at this bloody dinner! The guests are going to be here any minute and they've all come to meet him and – oh God, it's a disaster! How could you?"

"Have you listened to a single word I've said? I told him to wait by the *licorería* and when I got there he'd gone and that, Mother, is not my fucking fault!"

"Don't you swear at me!"

"Well, stop shouting then!"

Judith downed her glass and crossed her arms. "I mean what's he going to do? He hasn't got any money."

"I gave him my wallet. He's got plenty of money."

"You did what?"

"I said, 'Take my wallet, buy the booze, I'll meet you back here.' I told you."

"Oh."

"Look, Mummy, I think we both know what's happened, OK?"

"Whatever do you mean?"

"He's an alcoholic. He's in a back room in Rio Caribe some-where pissed out of his mind, probably passed out by now. Tomorrow he'll wake up and—"

"Shut up!"

"Mummy—"

"He wouldn't do that to me!" She began to sob, "… it's my birthday." Bridget took a deep breath. There was a knock at the door. "Oh Christ!" said Judith, wiping her face. "They're early. Perfect. Just perfect. Haven't even put my face on and everything's ruined and Harry and—"

"Mummy," said Bridget, taking her by the shoulders. "Calm down, OK? I'll take care of the guests. You go and get ready. I'm sure Harry's going to turn up any minute. I'm sure he'll realise the time and he's probably on his way right now in a taxi or something, OK? All right?" Judith exhaled and nodded. Bridget gave her a hug, and then walked through the house to the front door shouting, "Just a second!"

She pulled open the door to meet the boiling eyes of a large white man with a burnt, unshaven face. He looked deranged, as if he had just walked out of a train crash. Bridget stepped back.

"Is he here?" Slade demanded.

"Excuse me?"

"Fucking Christmas! Harry fucking Christmas!"

"What?"

"Is he here?" Slade pushed past her and stepped inside.

"Hey!" she said, "HEY!" He went into the courtyard. He looked up at the doors. "Hey, I'm talking to you! What the fuck do you think you're doing? Mummy! Call the police!" Judith came out of her bedroom.

"What's going on? Who are you?"

"Harry Christmas. Where is he? Is he up there?" Slade ran upstairs and Judith backed away.

184

"What the hell are you doing?" shouted Bridget. Slade was on the landing, pushing open doors. "Mummy, where's the phone?"

"What the bloody hell is going on here? You! Young man, I'm talking to you!" bellowed Judith, following him around. "How dare you go barging around my house like this? Get out! Immediately!" Slade ran downstairs. Judith ran down behind him and over to her daughter, pulling her close.

"He was here though, wasn't he?"

"Get out of my house this instant!" yelled Judith, "This instant!" Slade pulled the photograph of Christmas from his back pocket.

"Who's this?"

"Oh my God! Harry! Why have you got Harry's picture?"

"So you do know him."

"What is going on here?" demanded Bridget.

"Don't fuck me about!" threatened Slade, "Where is Harry Christmas?"

"Harry *what?*"

"He's called Harry Christmas. He's a thieving piece of shit and I'm looking for him and I know he was here and want to know where the fuck he is *now*, understand?"

"What are you talking about?"

"You've been conned. He's a conman, his name's not Strong, it's Christmas, and I want to know where the fuck he is right the fuck now!"

"A conman?" stammered Judith. "What on earth are you talking about? Right, that's it! Now get out! Get out and leave us alone!" Slade wasn't listening. He was running his eyes over the daughter. She had an inquisitive, feline face with cunning little shoulders. She was wearing a miniskirt and a bikini and she knew he was telling the truth.

"Mummy," she said, "where's the phone?"

"It's over there. Call the police."

"I'm going to – just a second. We need to – just wait a second." Bridget went over to a side table. She picked up the phone. She got through to a friend in England whom she told to put 'Harry Strong, novelist' into a search engine and pull up some photos.

"What does he look like …?" Bridget's face began to fall. She turned away. "So he's not fat? At all?" She looked back at her mother. "How old? … Right. Shit. No moustache? No, OK … Look, I'll call you later and explain. No, everything's fine … Thanks – OK – Bye." Bridget cocked her head to the side and sighed deeply. "Mummy …"

Judith sank to the floor. "No, no, it's not true, it's not true, no, Harry, please, no, it can't be true …" She exploded into tears, weeping from her lungs and her gut.

"Now where is he?" said Slade

"Look, dickhead, can't you see she's upset?" snapped Bridget. "Fuck's sake!" Bridget pulled her mother to her feet. "Come on, Mummy, let's get you upstairs, let's lie down, come on, shush, it's going to be OK, shhh …"

He watched Bridget guide her mother up the stairs. He could see her ribs moving beneath her skin. They went into Judith's bedroom and shut the door. After a moment, Bridget reappeared at the top of the stairs. She hovered, swore, and then trotted down.

"So he's like a professional? A professional conman? This is, like, what he does? All the time?"

"When did you see him last?"

"This afternoon, in Rio Caribe. He just … disappeared."

"He hasn't been back?"

"No."

"Do you know where he's gone?"

"Do I know where he was planning to go once he'd conned us, ruined my mother's life and stolen my wallet? No, funnily enough,

I do not – excuse me ..." She went past him into the kitchen. "How did you know he was here?" Slade didn't reply. "Jesus ..." Bridget was rifling through kitchen drawers. "Where are those pills? I mean what a – a bastard ... God, I feel sick—" She stopped. Slade was examining her.

"What are you—" Slade moved towards her.

She backed up against the cupboards.

"Hey, what—" Slade grabbed her face with one hand, squeezing her cheeks together, trapping the noise. With his other hand he grabbed her hair, yanking back her neck, and pushed her against the sink.

"Call me a *dickhead*?" He took her throat, choking her. "Friend of yours, is he?" Bridget could only see over his shoulder. She would never forget what she saw there: a dark window filled with insects.

"Bridget?" Judith called from upstairs, "Where are you?" He spun her round and pushed her head down into the sink, crushing it against the metal, gripping her neck. With his other hand he searched between her legs and ripped down her bikini bottoms. She was struggling, bucking, trying to scream, but when he got his penis out and forced it into her she froze.

He raped her, squeezing at her body, smothering her face, while her mother called out her name and The General stared in through the window.

When he'd come in her, he threw her onto the floor. He thought she looked like a fish, eyes wide, gaping for breath.

He pulled up his jeans and went into the courtyard.

He left the house. The crickets were loud. The forest was vibrating.

He got into his car and was about to start the engine when a jeep came up the drive. He pulled the knife out of the headrest. He stayed in the dark until the new arrivals had got out, chatting and clutching bottles of rum. When he was sure Christmas wasn't among them he put the knife down. He switched on his headlights. They turned round. Slade drove away.

34

Christmas' elation at having escaped Slade was short-lived. As the old couple drove him through the night, he lapsed into confusion and regret. Nothing made sense. How had that maniac found him? Was he some kind of expert? A tracker? A detective? No, he was a thug. What was it then? Luck? Just plain old rotten luck? Now that Christmas could believe in. Sod's law. The exact opposite of what you wanted materialising in front of your face every bloody time. His quarry having disappeared, Slade decides to go to the beach – *What's the nicest bit of beach?* he asks someone – *Sucre*, they say, *the Paria Peninsula, Rio Caribe, it's where Columbus went blah blah blah* and – bingo – there's old Christmas, right bang slap in the middle of the street. Yes, that was the kind of luck he was used to.

And what of Judith? It was the old girl's birthday party, for God's sake. He'd ruined that for her. She'd be worried sick until she realised he'd legged it and then she'd be devastated. Well, it was better than leading William Slade to their door. And Bridget? She'd always think he nicked her wallet on purpose. Christmas let out a profound sigh. There was no helping it. He couldn't go back now. They'd figure out he wasn't Harry Strong sooner or later and then they'd both hate him anyway, so what difference did it make? He deserved to be hated. He was breaking Judith's heart. Yes, she was a bit bats, but she was a game old bird really, a game old thing when all was said and done ...

They drove through Rio Caribe, then took the road south towards Yaguaraparo and Guiria. Christmas tried to reassure himself. If it was luck then – just a case of one-in-a-million, bad bloody luck – then surely it could not happen again. This random car, taking him somewhere only he and Emily knew about – how could Slade possibly follow him there?

A mile before Chacaracuar, the old couple let him out at a posada. Breathing against his pains, he eased himself out of the car, thanking them over and over. Holding his ribs and shoulder, he watched their car disappear and walked up a short drive of rhododendrons and into Hacienda Macuro. The man at the reception desk asked for his passport. Christmas gripped his trouser pockets, then his jacket. His passport. It was hidden behind the wardrobe in Judith's bedroom.

Biting down on a curse, Christmas recited his passport number. The man seemed satisfied, logging it in his guest book while Christmas stood there, furious. His passport was still at Judith's. The man asked for payment, 150 bolívares. Christmas opened the wallet. There were Judith and Bridget, their arms round each other.

Christmas was led up green wooden stairs that he took one step at a time, the man offering help. Christmas waved him on, the pain in his ribs and shoulder jabbing at his temper. They went along a green wooden balustrade to one of the green wooden doors, overlooking a courtyard and a pool ringed with plants. The man opened the door and turned on the light. Christmas turned off the light and shut it again. He had more pressing business.

Next to reception, the green wooden bar was full of murmuring people and the plucking of a four-stringed *quarto* on the radio. A woman behind the bar wiped down the cutlery, dropping it into a tray. It was a tall room with lights covered in ribbons hanging from the roof. Painted driftwood, ceramic animals, flags and rattan baskets all climbed the walls. Christmas stood in the doorway and eyed the rows of spirits. Beethoven's head kept watch above them; electric lights in his eyes simulating fiery talent. He ordered a bottle of Cacique and inspected the patrons.

There was a table of shaggy-haired Germans. They ate at a table while consigning their Venezuelan guide to eat at the bar. This man and Christmas exchanged a nod – in agreement, Christmas assumed, about the turpitude of his party. In another corner there was a family from Caracas, Spanish-looking and fashionable, while next to him an American couple in their thirties were fondling each other's noses. The man was squarely-built, the woman blonde.

Christmas sat down. He took out the wallet. He looked at the photograph of Judith and Bridget. He put the wallet away. The American woman caught his eye.

"Hi there!" she said, "Just got into town?"

"Correct," he said.

"British?"

"That's two out of two so far."

"On your own?" Christmas was outraged by the question. *Yes, I am on my own, the devil take you! What of it?*

"You can come and join us if you want to," she nodded to her boyfriend, who also began to nod, though rather more slowly. Christmas was flabbergasted. Was there no limit to their effrontery?

"You are inviting me to join you at your table."

"That's right." Christmas didn't move. Strange moments passed as he assembled his poisoned, angry energies. Then, barking an impatient

"Rum!" towards the bar, he rose, straining and grunting and grating the table against the floor as he launched himself into their world.

"Chris," he smiled, "Akabusi."

"Linda Craven, and this is Steven."

"Steven Da—"

"I said 'rum'!" Christmas interrupted, sending the order sideways through his face without turning round.

"Hey," laughed the man awkwardly, "take it easy, buddy." Christmas widened an eye.

"Are you a doctor of medicine?"

"Me?"

Christmas didn't reply. He was noting the man's T-shirt. It said 'Bethesda, Maryland'.

"Soooo," said the woman brightly, trying to reclaim the moment, "you here on vacation?"

"No."

"You work here?"

"No."

"You live—?"

"No. I am an inventor," he said bitterly. He couldn't even be bothered to lie well. "I have come here ..." A bottle of rum and three glasses arrived on the table "... to invent." He opened the bottle. "You?"

"No thanks, not for—"

"Splendid."

"So – I'm sorry – you're here to invent something?"

Christmas paid no attention. He splashed his glass full and took a long draw on it, squeezing his eyes closed as all of his senses left their posts to join hands and dance in the sweet golden ford that now brooked his tongue. "The humidity," he gasped, "helps me think. Keeps the mind sticky; the synapses, you understand, more ... adhesive."

192

"Really? Well, isn't that interesting."

"What have you invented?" said the man, who was finding the whole situation rather less interesting than his girlfriend.

"I dunno. The self-cleaning teeth? Oh, I'm sure you've heard about those – and the chair that acts like a table."

"You invented stools?"

"Condoms for dogs!" Christmas toasted himself. "That was the big one, but I suffered terrible reprisals at the hands of the animal liberation front, Catholic wing. They hounded me out of the country," Christmas held up the moment with his eyebrows.

"Hounded," said the man.

"So I moved to Ruritania where I became famous for – shall we say – my psychic speed-reading events."

"Speed-reading?"

"I'm at a table, they're in a queue: 'Teacher – sock fetish – mother died of boredom. Next!' It was so successful they gave me my own television programme, from which I had a string of hits culminating in the ratings-buster 'Is Your Daughter A Virgin?' where parents stood to earn ten thousand Ruritanian yen if they guessed correctly. Extra bonuses depending on how accurately they guessed the sexual acts she had accomplished. Lie detectors. Crying. All the usual humiliation. Great success. Unfortunately some parents took the avalanche of information rather badly and one poor girl was shot. End of commission. But what do you do? You move on. Then I became head of the Texas Communist Party. I know what you're thinking: you're thinking, but he's British, and that shows just how bad things are down there. Then I became a dentist, just like my father, only rather better than him as I was only drunk in the afternoons." Christmas stopped abruptly. There was an uncomfortable silence. "I say," he said, pouring another rum, "would you permit me a modicum of unwarranted levity?"

"I'm sorry?"

Christmas laughed in their faces. It was a coarse, false laugh, of the kind one might make on learning that one's worst enemy has contracted a venereal disease. They were stunned. "Do you know," he said, "the thing I've noticed about you Americans is that you're rather young in the eye. It's as if the reincarnation department had to release a whole raft of first generation souls just to fulfil your rapacious expansion. What's it like living over there? I mean, really? Sleepwalking through hell?"

"OK, buddy, now you wait there just a minute—" Christmas eyed the man's T-shirt while draining his glass.

"You know, I think I've just realised what the real difference is between our two nations."

"I think you'd better stop right there—"

"English idiots wear T-shirts of where they've been. American idiots wear T-shirts of where they're from."

"Are you calling me an idiot?"

Christmas poured another drink while the man came to his own conclusion. "Now here's an important question," Christmas looked straight at the woman: "Would you like to have sex?" The man grabbed Christmas by the lapels.

"I meant with each other—"

"You watch your goddamn mouth!"

"It's a little bit too close to the nose for that."

"Asshole!"

"The word," he said, "is *arse*-hole."

"You're goddamned lucky I'm on vacation," snarled the man, leaning further into Christmas' face, "or I would rip your fucking neck off, you hear me, asshole?"

"*Arse*-hole! I'm an arsehole, the devil take you!"

The man released Christmas in disgust.

"Come on, honey," said the woman, standing up. "Let's go."

194

"Is he honey?" smiled Christmas, "looks more like a bit of a jam to me."

"You've been warned, pal!" spat the man, stabbing the air with his finger. Christmas watched them storm out of the bar and upstairs to their room. At the top of the stairs, the woman turned round to give him a look. This convinced Christmas she was secretly attracted to him. He toasted their backs. Then he turned to the rest of the room, silenced and agape, and toasted them too.

"We closed," announced the woman behind the bar, looking straight at him.

Christmas went to his room with the rest of the bottle. He sat on the edge of the bed. Then he lay down. Then he sat up again. He opened the wallet and looked at the photograph. He turned on the television. Numbers whizzed and flew, financial data ticker-taping at different speeds. *Why were they always showing this rubbish?* he thought, sliding once more down the flume of rum into the comfortable baths of complaint: The Rot. Those digits were meaningless code, unless you were a professional financier, in which case it was available on your computer screen at work. Why all these channels of the stuff? Why the updates after every news programme, the insistence, the ubiquity? Christmas was certain that the answer lay in its unintelligibility: it was something people didn't understand, something else to make them feel there was a vast world of inscrutable mystery run by people cleverer than they, so it was best just to shut up and toe the line.

He took out the money from Bridget's wallet. Twenty dollars, 110 bolívares. He counted them, fingered them, held them to the light. They were relics just as he was. Modern transactions now were pieces of digital information flying back and forth through the godforsaken wires that were strangling the earth. Money itself had to make money. It had to contain information about where it had been and whom it was going to, information that could be sold. These banknotes were too finite. They had no potential beyond themselves. In the world he was from, things just were – contained, understandable. They didn't need to be connected. They weren't part of this obscene archipelago. Christmas sighed. He lay back on the bed. The Rot was here too. The Rot was everywhere.

These days it seemed as if everyone was talking from the same bad script – practised, learnt, regurgitated: a never-ending re-en-actment. Walking past the tube stations at rush hour as the crowd streamed to get under the ground, he felt as if he were walking between the lines of some terracotta army. They creaked and groaned and protested but in the clamour he could see only obedi-ence. Obedience and the glorification of suffering – religion, then, but what new kind of God was this, brewing for thirty years in the mulch and mucous of The Rot? What age was rising, suckled by the glossy swamp? Switching, sniffing blindly over its own eggshell, retching, an idiot grin stretched across its damp face? Whatever its character, there would be no place for old Harry. Between the death of old Rome and the reign of the new messiah, when all is turmoil and cultish frenzy, here he was on the edge of his own Black Sea, a drunk and talentless Ovid, poet to no one but himself.

He turned off the television. *The devil take the lot of it!* He picked up the bottle. Slade. He still couldn't believe it. He took a drink and sat on the edge of the bed as if waiting for something. He had nothing to wait for, nothing but morning and its cold burial of the stars.

By four a.m. he was naked, unable to sleep and seriously drunk. His hands grasped nothing, legs entwined with sheet. He got up. He opened the door of his room and there was the American woman. She was smoking, looking out at the night and scratching a bite on her foot. He watched her puffing angrily at the moon, all the more convinced that she hated her boyfriend. She was bored, he decided, bored and trapped in a loveless union with a brainless bully to whom she felt obliged after he had delivered her family from financial ruin. Her life was empty. All she had to look forward to were secrets. Christmas suddenly knew he was going to kiss her. The conviction came upon him as suggestion, but, its origins quickly forgotten, was left in his mind as fact. He took a step forward, then another. The woman turned and froze in shock at the sight of this moonlit behemoth shifting towards her. She looked down at his penis. Christmas remembered he was naked. He dismissed it as a trifle. As she was about to make a noise, he kissed her – a deep, pressing kiss. Then he pulled back, retreating through the shadows, leaving those eyes without answer. Christmas shut his door and lay down on the bed. He felt he had completed some perfect moment, the elegance of its execution finally unleashing sleep across his frame.

Christmas dreamed he was on an island. He had been shipwrecked with some schoolgirls and all the teachers were dead. The schoolgirls were from the future. They wore earrings that were miniature holograms of waterfalls and sunsets, and ate packets of tiny swollen food that you lit from the bottom and inhaled like heroin. They wore ties round their heads. One girl had contact lenses that made it look as if there was a tiny bird trapped in each eyeball. They hated Christmas and were deciding between various cruel fates for him at some vile council. All their gadgets were running out of power and somehow he was to blame.

The girls became women he'd slept with. Diana wanted him tarred and feathered. Another suggested making toys out of his bones. A third wanted to throw him off the cliff onto the rocks. Christmas was on his knees in the dirt. His hands and feet were bound. He looked about for Emily but he couldn't see her. The women walked round him in a circle of menace, frothing themselves into an angry mob. He was put in a cage and sunk into crashing waves. He felt something at his feet, he looked down into the water, the salt attacking his eyes and saw Emily chained to the bedrock, inhaling sea, clawing at his feet in panic ... Christmas woke up. He was being punched in the face.

35

"Fucking pervert! Think you can make a move on my fucking woman, huh, old man? Do you? Do you?" It wasn't the first time Christmas had been woken in this way; the mysterious echo of pain that brings a sudden dawn, hands to the face, the taste of blood and a consciousness struggling to stand. "If I ever see you, or you ever fucking come near us again, you're dead. You hear me you fucking pervert? Dead!" Then he was gone.

Christmas opened his eyes to the ceiling. He wiped the blood from his nose with his fingers then, with an arm dangling over the side of the bed, he laughed in an empty, put-on way, as if some concealed person was listening.

He lay there for a long time. He may even have slept. At some point in the morning he heard the American couple leaving, banging their luggage along the corridor. "Asshole!" the man shouted. Christmas winced at the diction. He was alone again.

It was early. His brain felt like cold mud. He roused himself upright in bed and took a swig from the rum bottle. It was warm and vicious and almost done. He checked his hands; they were shaking. Christmas went to the bathroom and washed his face. He had a black eye. He checked the stitches in his head and examined the mosaic of bruises, noting how the new were mating with the old, admitting to himself that his ribs were probably broken. He could only move his right arm a few inches before his shoulder screeched. Opening the door he looked up at a scaled, reptilian sky. The posada was still. He felt as if he were the last man on earth.

An hour later the rain started. New guests arrived. He ate breakfast with the women of the posada staring at his eye. There was a bus to Guiria, he discovered, later that afternoon. He drank several cups of coffee and then sat in the hammock on the verandah outside his room. He stayed there all morning. He bought another bottle of Cacique. He went back to his room.

There, in the dark, he drank. He sat on the edge of the bed and drank. He read Emily's Montejo book and drank. He sat by the fan and drank. He stood in the doorway and drank. He drank in front of the mirror. He drank in front of the open wallet. He drank from the bottle. He drank from the glass.

Swinging in the hammock, he thought about his dream. He hadn't thought about these women in years. The one who wanted to turn his bones into toys. Vanessa, the yoga teacher ... must have been four or five years before he met Emily. What was her last name? He remembered they went on a yoga retreat together and he got the giggles in every class. The sterner the looks she gave him, head bent beneath a knee, the more he laughed. Eventually some sinewy hippy with a lisp asked him to 'pleath leave'. The subsequent conversation was the end of their relationship:

"I'm really disappointed in you, Harry. Really, really disappointed. Why can't you take anything seriously? Why can't you honour yourself?"

"Oh, come on now, Vanessa—"

"No, Harry, I mean it. We have this beautiful connection, yet you are constantly trying to sabotage it. Us. You are constantly trying to sabotage our union."

"Oh, Vanessa, do try and lighten up a little. I mean, come on, it was pretty funny ... Ommmm ..."

"It's not funny, Harry, actually; it's not funny at all. Why do you have to be like this?"

"Like what?"

"Like *this*."

"Like *what*?"

"You know, if you could only just change this one ... *thing* that you have, then—"

"Change?"

"Don't pull that face, Harry – we all need to change things about ourselves. That's *growth*, Harry, that's a *relationship*. If there's something you want *me* to change, then fine, I'll do it."

"OK," he shrugged, "shave off your moustache."

Then there was Lisa, the high-powered businesswoman. He had met her while he was pretending to be a travel journalist, enjoying the free delights of a country house health spa he was supposedly covering for the *Sunday Times*. Lisa was also spending the weekend there. She turned up pissed for her vegetable enema and ended up in a fight with the therapist. Christmas was getting a massage in the room across the corridor when he heard the commotion. As soon as he opened the door, a therapist ran past him, crying, with bits of carrot all over her face and there was Lisa, shouting abuse and wearing a plastic robe the wrong way round.

Lisa. Orgasmed like she was having an exorcism. They used to go out drinking together for days and then sit in the bath, unable to get out, weeing and laughing. What happened there? She started talking about children. That was it. One day he went out for cigarettes and never came back.

Who came next? Stephanie Oodles, conceptual artist. Then that married woman with her husband downstairs in a wheelchair. And then Debbie the pianist. He'd helped her get rid of her flatmate by sitting too close to him on the sofa and whispering, "Things from hell are after me ..." Everything was fine, until she mentioned settling down.

"Now look here, Debbie, it can't be helped," he had said, rounding off his announcement. She was in the middle of a piano lesson with a little boy. "We've had a good run. Run's over. We'll just have to get on with it." Debbie had burst into tears. The little boy had played a low key.

Clumsily grasping the bottle with his armpit, Christmas took out the wallet and looked at the photograph again. Yes, Judith was a fruitcake, but she was a brave old girl really. Just lonely like everyone else. Didn't deserve the old dip-the-shoulder-and-out. A mosquito settled on his ankle. He wondered if this was the only living thing on earth that wanted to be near him. He tried to kill it. After a swig he inspected the bottle. *Are you drinking to forget?* Bridget was asking him again. He would miss Bridget. "No, young lady, no," he said out loud. He was drinking to remember, that the sting of spirits on his tongue might remind him he was alive. "Alive!" he cried, and pushed off against the wall. He burst out laughing.

Thick ribs of cloud were binding the earth. The afternoon was darkening. A family came out of their room and Christmas pretended he was asleep. With his eyes closed he listened to their music, their bickering song of family love; the high voices of children, the tinkling chime of the mother, the low warm tone of the father, scrapes of bags and flip-flops slapping against the floor. They went downstairs. He heard bare feet pad across the floorboards towards him. He recognised the step. It was Emily.

He could feel her stop just behind his head. She was in her pyjamas, her hair all awry. She was cross because he hadn't woken her up for lunch. "But you looked too happy, Em," he murmured, smiling, "I didn't want to – well, OK, what do you want? I'll get them to make it and bring it up ... of course they will ... Just toast and jam? Nothing else? You'll waste away ... oh, har har, very funny ... Snoring? What about you? Thought there was a train going by ... yes, you were, oh yes, you were ... Now why don't you come and give Pops a kiss, eh?" Christmas lifted his hand in the air and waited for it to be filled. He waited and waited. When he let it drop it was to wipe the tears from his face.

The sky heaved and fell; Christmas watched rain chatter with the ground. He slipped into sleep. When he woke it was evening. He felt he should eat before his journey to Guiria. Christmas inspected his black eye in the bathroom mirror. He put on his jacket. He showed himself his teeth.

Christmas went downstairs. The man at reception told him he'd missed the bus to Guiria but if he went into the village he'd find a taxi. Christmas paid his bill with the remaining dollars and began to ask him how much it cost to set up a posada, what the logistics were, the bureaucracy and so on, but the man walked away from him while they were in the middle of talking.

Christmas left the posada and walked along the road to Chacaracuar. He came across an empty restaurant, four plastic tables under a palm frond roof. The weather had cleared and the sun was setting. The waiter got up from watching television and took his order of fried *pargo* fish with rice, plantain, coleslaw and another bottle of Cacique. Christmas folded a paper towel in his hands. He folded it over and over until it was too small to fold it again. He aimed it at the ashtray and missed.

A group of teenage girls came in, half talking to the waiter, half watching the soap opera on television. Christmas floated them a crooked smile; how womanly they were! He condemned Europe and its haunchless daughters, then bent his head, an apology to Bridget. "Not you, not you," he said out loud. He poured another glass of rum. "You're a fine young woman. The best."

"*Si, Señor?*" The waiter was above him. "*Algo mas?*"

"Ah, dear heart," sighed Christmas, helpless with emotion, "I beg only for such rustic viands as I see before me now."

"*Que?*"

"*Nada, gracias, amigo. Nada mas.*" Another mosquito was biting his ankle. He examined it. A vein in his foot was visibly pulsating.

When Christmas had finished the meal, he felt like smoking a cigarette for the first time in years. He had given it up when he started coughing up bits of his lungs and discovered he had pulmonary embolism. Somehow, at this moment, it seemed appropriate. He rested his chin in his hand and watched the crimson evening turn black. The girls shot looks at him and whispered. Finally he asked for the bill, leaving an enormous tip in defiance. He stood up, general of a deserted army, and snatched up the Cacique. It was time to leave this outpost. It was time for Guiria.

36

Christmas walked into Chacaracuar with the aggressive loose-ness of the drunk. He flagged down a passing taxi, a 1970's Chevrolet that looked as if it had been driven straight off the scrapheap. Christmas eased himself in, took off his jacket and opened the window. They pulled out onto the road and, sipping at the rum, he let the breeze cool his face. The village became dark countryside. He rolled up his jacket as a pillow and fell asleep.

They crossed the Paria Peninsula and arrived in Guiria three hours later. It was the middle of the night. Christmas paid the driver, got out of the car and watched it drive away all before he was fully awake. He'd left his bottle of Cacique on the floor of the taxi. He looked at the money in his hand. Forty bolívares. It was less than a ticket to Caracas. Where had the dollars gone? He looked around. He was in the town's main square, a Plaza Bolivar, geometric red tiling inlaid with quadrants of trees and scraps of grass. It was deserted. Christmas had no idea what he was going to do. He put his jacket on, lay down on a stone bench and fell back to sleep. He awoke to the atrocities of dawn.

A madman was going through his pockets. Christmas pushed him away. The man giggled and cursed, his face cast in a Kabuki pose of suffering. Christmas sat up. A woman walked past trying to hold five children by the wrist. There was a dog underneath him. It had bits missing from its scalp, the wounds still raw. It panted. Christmas inspected his clothes. They were filthy. His mouth cried out for water. His brain wriggled with distress.

Guiria was starting its day. He was here, finally, in Guiria, the Caribbean outpost where Emily's grandmother had grown up. But this was no beach paradise. It was a concrete port town, half-built and hellish. He gripped Emily's book against his heart. He could not perform his ritual here, not in a place like this. He wasn't ready. He must rest, get his bearings, get himself straight. He must ... Panic was overtaking him.

He could see queues for buses, *empanada* and coffee stands crowded with workers, people crossing the plaza in every direction. On the other side of the square there was a tall blue and white church. Beside it, on the corner, he thought he could make out the word 'posada'. He got to his feet. His legs trembled. His bones snapped. Everyone he walked past looked at him and whispered.

At the posada he asked for a room. The man was opening shutters that revealed a *licorería*, the metal clatter some dread applause to the vision of bottles, rows and rows and rows, dark brown and deep in promises of magic. The man took Christmas through the back, into a small restaurant with a television on full volume hanging from the ceiling like a head. On the far wall there was a row of rough wooden doors with painted numbers one to seven. They were padlocked shut. The man opened number one. It was a blue cell, not much wider than Christmas, with a fan missing its front guard and the mattress covered in a slightly burnt sheet. Christmas sat down, the black mandrake of the hangover now unfurling a new, even more savage character in his guts. The man told him it was forty bolívares for a night. Forty bolívares was all he had left. Forty bolívares for this pen in which to thrash. They walked back out front. Christmas bought a cold beer. Then he spent twenty-five bolívares on a bottle of Cacique and left.

The temperature rose. He walked to a seafront lapped with rubbish. Had he crossed the world for this? He walked back into the streets of Guiria, looking for a place in which to dissolve. He walked past nervous and forgotten buildings, market traders setting up their stalls, pavements piled with shoes. Children and beggars asked him for money. One made a grab for his bottle. Christmas was a specimen, pale and alien, wandering past pharmacies and banks, shelves of bootleg music, stiff mannequins in bras and track-suits. "I want to go home," he whispered.

In some streets he was warned to turn back with the sign language of guns and robbery. In others, people beckoned him into their restaurants, into the shops, into their internet cafés. Eventually he turned a corner and found himself back in the Plaza Bolivar. He sought the shade of a tree, cracking open the seal on his Cacique. To his lips he held his last idea.

All morning he drank as the sun wrought shadows from the earth, splayed and half-mad from the heat. His shirt was open, his belly loose, his jacket folded neatly beside him. Every so often he picked it up, shook it, felt for the book, folded it again, and placed it beside him once more, neatly and with great care. He watched the women of Guiria go about their day.

Like all desperate people, he was hungry for omens. A little girl with a dog on a lead stopped in front of him. The dog crapped in the middle of the street. The girl left the crap but took out a tissue and wiped the dog's backside. Then she left the tissue on the crap.

Hunger came and went. He acquired drinking companions, boz-eyed alkys with faces of bark and dirt for shoes. They wittered and argued, grabbing him by the shoulder in friendship, in confrontation, in sympathy, in plea. He drank anis.

By the afternoon he couldn't hear anything. He was aware of noises, of people talking but as if through water. There was only the pressing of lips to glass, patting his jacket and his hat, sweat and the sun and broken pieces of thought. Policemen were talking to him. Then a group of youth on mopeds. He understood there were warnings. He laughed at the idiot logic. In the afternoon he saw the town was scorched and yellow, the clouds dark and wet. It was as if some northern continent had made off with the sky, swapping it for its own. He understood it was raining. He laughed at the idiot logic.

Christmas fell in and out of sleep. It grew dark. He got to his feet, the cause of great drama amongst his drinking companions, who held his arms and face. The world pitched like a boat. Christmas lurched and straightened. He picked up his jacket, walking away to piss messily against a tree. In his pocket he found his last banknote. He did up his shirt. He put on his jacket. He saw a sign for a karaoke bar.

At the bar he ordered beer. The barman asked him several times if he was OK. People watched the screen as song lyrics were highlighted in sequence, hopeful mimics droning along in tandem. The man next to him at the bar was almost as drunk as he was. They began to talk to themselves in the posture of talking to each other. Christmas argued with his own spirit. The song changed. The microphone was passed to a young woman sitting with a large group at the central table. Her voice was soft and ruthless. She sang of loss, of the unspeakable sadness of life, of all lives. Christmas felt what little was left of himself corrode. The man at the bar was explaining how to eat an iguana. "I have pieces of coal," Christmas agreed, "in my heart." He got off his stool to congratulate the singer, but someone passed him the microphone. He was in the middle of the bar. Everyone was cheering. The video started, couples on bridges and visions of rural paradise. He tried to give the microphone away but his hand was pushed back. He couldn't follow the words. The tables were laughing. He heard his own voice behind him, cracked and low. "Emily," he said. Then he began to weep.

Someone took the microphone. He was led to a chair and sat down. He wiped his eyes. "Em ... Emily?" She wasn't there. "Disgusting!" he cried out loud. Someone patted his shoulder. A man at the bar began another song. Christmas pulled a sneer across his face then slammed both hands on the table.

"So that's it? That's? You people, eh? That's it!" He stood up. "You? Eh? You people that's?" He was shouting. The barman had his hand on his neck. The next thing he knew he was out on the street, cast back into night, stumbling across the Plaza Bolivar. The church reared up beside him and sent him reeling against a tree. He flung his arms round it. He couldn't breathe. He sensed people around him and growled. He sank down to the base of the tree and looked up to the branches. *But soon you'll be dead*, they seemed to say, *and all you will taste is the earth.* He turned from their snickering leaves to a rock that jumped forward and hit him in the head. His face fell into the soil, then he rolled onto his back. His mind began to vomit; song lyrics, memories of his dead wife, Bridget's voice: *don't you want to be good?* He coughed and coughed, his face washed in rheum and muck. He felt thieves were grabbing at him, but perhaps they were demons. Then someone was picking him up, helping him to his feet. Christmas pushed them away. He looked up at the church. Emily jumped from its roof. He yelled out but she turned into a seagull.

He stumbled off into the dark. He passed a children's playground padlocked shut, heading down a road of shadows to the sea. Mosquitoes whined in his ear. Through cars and trees he could see the lights of a dock, cranes and derricks. There were oil drums and rusted gas canisters lined up along the water's edge, upturned boats rotting without masters. He could smell gasoline. He fought his way under a tree, into the mud and rubbish and bog-shrubs, towards the nothing of the black ocean. He fell forward between two boats and tried to steady himself on their sides but one hand missed, so he swung down into the bilge, the slum of the land, plastic bags and bottles texturing the mire. Wetness spread through clothes to skin, his face raised but then defeated as it fell against the ooze with a smack.

The mud stank, stewed and shitty. He heard himself laugh inside his chest. He began to whisper, "Em ... Emily ..." mouth caked and foul tastes leaking onto his tongue. He began to shout, to splutter, making noises of explosion, "Psccchhewwww ... Boom!" Then he was silent. Harry Christmas pushed his face into the sop. He was still.

Someone was rolling him round. There was a commotion. He was being yanked and raised. He glimpsed a policeman's uniform and the ragged dress of his drinking companions. Sounds veered closer to his ear. He was being hooked by his armpits, lifted up, a half-dead seal, squinting with marine eyes at the mouths and their sounds. There were arguments, hands in his pockets, more arms around him. He was being helped into a boat. Someone was wiping his face. There was cheering and music and the yearning of an engine. There was a bottle of rum at his mouth. Christmas' lips were moving but he spoke no human language. It was a dialect of the dead. He went into the oceans of the night.

37

When Christmas came to, something was wrong. He was upside down. So this was hell: simple, cruel, upside down. Some kind of parched territory see-sawed in front of him. He was swinging by one leg from a tree. He was drunk. So – they let people stay drunk in hell. He might have laughed, but his entire body felt as if it was trying to cram itself into his face. Sweat ran off his neck over his chin. There were raised voices. He thought he must be in the courtyard of some kind of factory until he identified the pounding noise as his own heart. He struggled. He spun even faster. The voices stopped. He understood there was someone before him holding a machete.

"What you doing, stupid gringo?"

"I am not a gringo," Christmas croaked, "I am an Englishman." He heard a chopping sound. Then he was on the floor. He passed out.

He woke in a bed. He could hear trumpets. There were people standing about him, talking too fast. He realised he was no longer in his clothes. Christmas dared not open his eyes. Different species of headache were warring over his skull and spirits raced across his eyeballs. Someone was near him. Others were laughing; judges, jesters, torturer-generals. There were chair-scrapes. He could hear a television and the rasping choke of beasts at feed. Christmas turned further into the pillow, praying that it would destroy him. He fell asleep and dreamed of mud in his throat. When he woke again it was the middle of the night. He was on a camp bed under a corrugated roof set high on thin beams. Raising himself onto his elbows, he realised was in the middle of a living room. He could hear snoring. He was naked except for a pair of Bermuda shorts. Behind him was a kitchen area.

Christmas staggered to the sink and drank mouthful after mouthful of water. His insides clenched and shook. He vomited. He needed to shit but didn't know where to go. The shit almost came out of him. He held himself, shuffling across the kitchen, and came out into a yard and the violent noise of crickets. In the middle there was a toilet with no door, next to an upturned skiff. Christmas sat on the toilet and released a torrent of black sand. The flush didn't work. He was sweating but his bones were cold. He went back to bed, one thousand years old.

Christmas dreamed in broken fury: eating a chicken sandwich then shitting out a live chicken; being alone in a wood; some problem with buying an electric fan. He dreamed a tortoise doctor was inspecting him while a boy prayed at the end of his bed. When he finally opened his eyes, head hanging from the mattress, there was the tortoise. The skin on its neck was like an old sock. It staggered forward and raised its powerful jaw to clamp at Christmas' chin. A woman's hand gripped his cheeks. They were calloused and smelt of coconut oil, and turned his head in firm inspection. Then the woman's face was in front of him. Her eyes were the colour of morning light through leaves.

212

She walked off to a chair by the front door letting in a blare of day. Christmas pulled his cheeks to his forehead, watching her huge thighs in a tight pink tracksuit turn and sit down. The woman crossed her legs, picking her T-shirt from her belly. She was wearing big hooped earrings, hair cocked up to one side. She was drinking a beer. She was Lola Rosa.

"*Idiota!*" she spat. Christmas didn't understand what was happening. Yet he knew it was no dream. The hangover made every cell in his body wretched with consciousness. Never had he felt so bad after drinking. It was punishment. It was revenge. Memories of Guiria revealed themselves all at once. Then Judith at her wheel. Being introduced to Slade's mother. Emily's funeral. His whole rotten life.

"*Habla pues!*" Christmas blinked and looked about. The room was turquoise. There were diplomas on the wall, photographs of dead relatives, a clock made out of a ship's wheel and a thickly painted scene of a beach at sunset. The boy from his dream was still kneeling at the end of his bed. The tortoise snapped its jaw. Lola stared at him with eyebrows raised. He tried to say her name. His throat made a high-pitched squeak.

Lola Rosa was from the village of San Cristóbal, thirty kilometres from Guiria along the southern coast of the Paria peninsula. Lola told all her friends about the preening gringo she had picked up on her last trip to Caracas, enjoying many laughs at his expense, so it had been no small surprise to go out one night into her own village and find him hanging from a tree.

News spread quickly about the foreigner who had arrived on a boat full of drunk fishermen, initially unconscious, then springing into a fit of dangerous activity. Raving and gabbling, he had fought walls and bushes and other more invisible foes until his companions caught his foot, wrapped it in rope, and winched him to safety.

213

Lola went to check on the commotion with everyone else, only to be engulfed in double-takes. That she not only knew this foreigner, but had slept with him, was the kind of electric gossip that lights up any village. He had obviously remembered where she lived and tracked her down.

"What you do in my village? Why you in San Cristóbal?"

"Lola ...?"

"What happen to you? Why you drunk like crazy man? Look at your face – why they hit your face? And the rest of you! Someone hit you with a car? What happened? What you doing here?"

"Where ...?"

"You come from Guiria. You in San Cristóbal. You in Estado Sucre, *coño,* you in Venezuela!"

"You ..."

"Me! Why you come here, gringo? Why you come to this village? Why you here? You come to see me, like this, like a drunk? Because I don't want to see you! *Idiota! Hijo de puta!*" The boy at the end of the bed glared at his mother in reprimand. "You shut up!" she said to him in Spanish.

"How did I get here?"

"That is what I want to know! Why you here? *Verga!*" and with that she drained her beer and threw it out the door.

"Where is you hotel? Where you bags? You money? You stay in Guiria?"

"I don't have anything" wheezed Christmas, more fragments of Guiria returning, "I had ... some bad luck."

"It's me with the bad luck, gringo, *oíste?* You don't have no money?"

"I ... was robbed."

"Of course you was robbed! You gringo. You can not to drink like that, the people will see you and they will take everything."

"I was robbed before I got drunk."

"And you think drink like that going to help you? *Verga!*"

"I was trying to get to Guiria ..."

"By drinking rum? You try to go to Guiria by drinking rum? Rum don't take you Guiria, gringo. Boat take you Guiria!"

"But you ... Caracas ..."

"That was the house of my sister. This is my house. This is my son. He don't speak no English." The boy stretched forward to shake Christmas by the hand. He had an oval face and a teenage moustache.

"Aldo," said the boy, "Peace be with you." There was a curious silence.

"I – I don't understand ... " Christmas began, "It's too ... how did you find me?"

"*Verga, coño!* I didn't find you, *oíste?* I didn't find you. You come here on a boat with *borrachos* and you so drunk they tie you to tree and then I see you. I don't want to see you again! You come here drunk and without shame. Everybody see you! Like crazy man! Why you here!" She stood up. "I can't to believe it! *En todo Venezuela ¿estás aquí? En San Cristóbal?* You tell me you not come to find me?"

"I had no idea ... I don't even know where I am."

"You lie!"

"It's a miracle," said the boy in Spanish.

"It's a bad miracle!" she replied.

"There are no such things as bad miracles."

"We're all bad miracles. He," she pointed at Christmas, "is just bad."

"You didn't – we were going to have dinner ..." started Christmas.

"Are you joking?" Lola folded her arms. "Eeeee," she groaned, "You deaf, gringo? I said 'no' because I don't want to see you again. And now I must to see you again! In a tree! *Verga*, look at your face! Someone hit your face! Why are you here? Why are you in my house?"

"But you ... you must have brought me here." Lola blew a note of disagreement through tight lips.

"That was the idea of *him*!" Christmas followed her finger to the other side of the room. "He don't speak no English." There, on a sofa, lay an old man the colour of cigars. He was grinning.

"I'm very sick," said the old man in Spanish, "my legs don't work."

"Your legs stopped working because you smoke crack!" thundered Lola, "Last week your legs were fine!" The old man looked as if he had been poured onto the sofa. His head was too big for his body. He had a long face with brown teeth that fanned out like monkey toes, except for the front two which were gold. He smiled at Christmas, twirling a finger next to his ear in a 'she's crazy' gesture.

"Now he's awake, he can go back to Caracas!"

"He can stay as long as he likes."

"No! He goes!"

"I am her father," he confided to Christmas, pushing out his lips towards her, "and she shows me no respect."

"You show yourself no respect!"

"You're just in a bad mood because everyone's laughing at you."

"Shut up!"

"You shut up, woman! This is my house! If I say he stays – he stays!"

"Wait, wait, wait," said Christmas, sitting up and shaking his hands before him, "I've got to – I can't stay here; I have no money—" There was his jacket beside him on a chair. He clenched it. The book was there, thank God – but his passport ...Where was his passport? Christmas lay down. "Jesus fucking Christ," he whispered. His passport was at Judith's.

216

"Look at your face. You are still sick," said the old man. "You are my friend. If you have no money, no problem. You get money later."

"I've got to ... I have to—" whispered Christmas as a wave of shame broke over him. How had he ended up like this? What was happening to him? Something was very wrong. Something terrible was on it's way. He could feel the last ray of alcohol disappear from his system and the approaching storm of suffering.

"God has brought you into this house for a purpose," said Aldo.

"Pah!" Lola stormed off into the kitchen, clipping her son round the ear as she went.

"I agree," said the old man.

"Eeeeee!" Lola shouted back. "See, gringo, only an idiot could make these two idiots agree."

"Do you read the Bible?" said the boy.

Christmas closed his eyes. *I am still dreaming*, he thought, *or I have died.* "I ... No."

"Are you a member of the Evangelical church?" the boy tried again. The old man started to cackle.

Christmas sighed. "Are you?"

"Yes. How long have you been an alcoholic?"

"How long have you been an Evangelical?"

"Five days," shouted Lola from the kitchen, "Last week he wanted to be a computer engineer." The tortoise was biting the boy's flip-flops.

"Before that he wanted to be a tattooist," said the old man. "But his mother only let him give tattoos to the pigs." The boy, affecting serenity, picked up the tortoise and took it out into the yard.

"Peace be with you."

"Bleeurrgh," replied the old man, "So friend – your name is Arri?" He lit a cigarette.

"Harry."

"Arri," he nodded. "My name is Luis, but you can call me Papa." Christmas looked over.

"No thanks."

"You are from the United States?"

"England."

"English ... really. Tell me, is it true?"

"What?"

"Is it true that you have carpet in your bathrooms?"

"Could I get a glass of water?"

"Have you been to Trinidad? It's only an hour from here by boat. They speak English in Trinidad." The old man reached for the remote control on the floor beside him and turned on the television to an incredible volume.

"So Lola tells me you make movies – you make any famous ones?" he shouted.

"No."

"What kind of movies do you like?"

"I don't like movies," Christmas shouted back. Then, thinking it left an odd moment between them, he said, "What kind of movies do you like?"

"I like the type of movies that start with Stallone having a bad day," shouted the old man. Then, "You want some rum?" and produced a bottle of Cacique from under the sofa. The old man took a swig and passed it over, but Christmas' stretched, shaking fingers were denied the touch of glass. Lola snatched the bottle.

"You," she said, taking a swig, "come here," The old man raised his eyebrows at Christmas, pushing his lips out towards her. Such pouting was a popular gesture in the village of San Cristóbal. It replaced pointing, but with an added dash of mockery. Christmas got to his feet. He followed her through the kitchen, supporting

218

himself where he could, a headache thumping him again and again in the back of the face.

Out in the yard, Lola took the lid off the back of the toilet, pulled up a length of wire and showed him how it flushed. Suddenly in the sun, Christmas thought he was going to vomit. "We have other toilet inside, but you use this one to make poo-poo, Ok, poo-poo man? I don't want to clean up your poo-poo again, *oíste*, gringo? And no more drinking!"

The enclosed yard was full of junk and crisscrossed with washing lines. There were holes in the wall. It sloped to one side and at the far end was a concrete shower room, its blue metal door swinging loose. Christmas followed her back inside and caught himself in a mirror: belly hanging over the ill-fitting shorts, hair awry, a boiled face. His black eye was now a grim yellow, the whole right side of his upper body an ugly rainbow of harm. *Repulsive*, he thought.

As he re-entered the kitchen she told him to sit down at a round white plastic table. His knee joints cracked. On one side of the room there was a row of bedroom doors. On the other, an old cooker attached to a rusting gas cylinder, the sink, wooden cupboards with a rack for plates, a sideboard, a shelf stacked with some glasses, well-used pans and a fridge. Lola took out a griddle and put it on the cooker. Then she poured corn flour into a bowl with some water, kneading it until it was dough, pinching off a piece, rolling it into a ball, squeezing the ball into a disc, patting the disc between her hands until it was a flat, round *arepa*. She put the *arepa* on the griddle and turned on the hob. She repeated the process several times. When the griddle was full, she covered it with a saucepan lid, took a coffeepot from another hob and poured out two cups of coffee. Aldo stretched out on the camp bed to watch television with his grandfather. Christmas felt his face. He was struggling to come to terms with his situation. He knew he must lie down again. His mind prickled with the onset of a terrible sickness.

She put the cup down in front of him. Christmas' hands were shaking so much he could barely lift it. The smell of coffee yanked him further into the world. Some magic had taken place, some stout movement of fate. He was with Lola Rosa. He was in her kitchen, sharing her coffee. Christmas took a sip. It hit his stomach. He only just made it to the toilet.

38

For four days Christmas lay there, churned by fever and withdrawal. Lola became less angry but only because she pitied him. He would wake, knowing he had been crying out, to find her holding his hand against fading horrors. He felt as if he was on a laboratory slab, exposed, observed, the subject of an undefined experiment. The television fused with his dreams and hallucinations; game shows and war. Sometimes he woke into darkness, trembling and fearful, a galaxy of bugs surrounding the naked bulb above him, thick shadows masking the roof while the pulsing screech of crickets raged at the moon. Sometimes he thought Slade was attacking him and he would shriek out for help, the family holding him down, calming him, before the tempest sleep of withdrawal pulled him back under. It rolled him and cast him out into a world where Emily was still alive, struggling from his bed to hold her before the vision receded into a horizon, erupting, a tidal wave of energy crackling with electrical charge which bulldozed desert towns. He saw a tiger about to attack suddenly lying down in defeat, conscious of its own extinction. He saw Emily with blisters around her neck as if strangled by a rope wet with acid. He saw a well full of chicken heads and Slade standing alone in an airfield, all the planes and terminal buildings burnt out and rained on. Then there was an awful howl, as if the earth itself was a beast, curved and folded in like a sleeping cat with a mouth at its core. He covered himself with the pillow as poison gas descended – thick, green and fast moving. It was dawn and everybody was dying. Christmas was by a low brick wall watching a crow that had a CCTV camera for a face. Then he was with Emily, walking by a canal full of oil. He dreamed he was in a room full of sculptors. They were on ladders. He watched one drive his chisel into the shoulder blades of a statue and take out something bloody and slippery. The sculptor dropped it into a bucket and it made a slapping sound. The bucket was full. He was in a field on bonfire night, eating a toffee apple and smelling the sparklers. The smell changed. It became sickening. It was a bonfire of wigs. Dark shapes danced through the flames. An unseen hand began throwing open beer cans at him. He was bellowing at a field of cows. He was walking to the end of a pier, only to turn round and see the mainland break off and float away. He woke. He was eating roast swan. He woke again. He was suffocating, his face wrapped in caul. There was Aldo. There was the old man. He was on the floor in the shower room. They were washing him.

Lola fed him broth. Christmas began to feel a little stronger but he did not leave the house. He could not. He had chronic diarrhoea. A steady stream of observers came in to discuss him, most often an old woman with hardly any hair and a teenage mother with a baby attached to her hip. Christmas was too weak to respond. With the diarrhoea came a shivering fever. He could only drift and groan and perspire, his spirit as rankled as the sheet.

It rained often. He stared at it through the door. He listened to it against the roof. He felt the character of rain, its changing moods, as if it were alive and he but a season of pressure. He reviewed his life and found nothing but reasons for misery and regret. Mosquitoes whined and fed.

Privacy was out of the question: he was on a camp bed in the middle of the living room. From this bedroom without walls he struggled to his toilet without door, helpless to hide himself should anyone walk past. Nor could he mask the noises, the parp and splutter, which provoked laughter from the house, even the occasional '*Epale!*' Once, he sat down to see the old lady on a stool in the yard sewing up a plastic bucket with string and a hot needle. She was staring straight at him. It was too late for either to move. Christmas could only close his eyes, clothing himself in invisible dignities.

He watched Lola cook, sweep, dust, take out buckets of clothes, drink beers in the evening sun, argue with her father. She cajoled and insulted him. She wiped the invalid's face with a cold cloth. In the evening she watched her favourite soap opera '*Sin Tetas No Hay Paraíso*' – 'Without Tits There is No Paradise' – about a Colombian girl prostituting herself to afford breast implants which are then filled with drugs by an unscrupulous plastic surgeon. Christmas watched Lola bathed in the cathode light of Colombian nightclubs and pictured himself in her eyes. It was not a pleasant reproduction. What was he? Nothing more than a creature to be pitied, helped, made room for?

In the shower room's cracked mirror he looked down at the protuberance of his body without flinching, without sucking in or tensing up. He was old, saggy, beaten. He looked at his head wound. Lola had removed the stitches that morning.

There was no pretending here, no Harry Strong.

There was no money to borrow, no city of dens in which to evaporate. He had nothing but this chance shipwrecking on Lola's shore. He leant towards his reflection, pulling his cheek from his eye, examining it swivel in the socket. What would have happened to him if he had not landed here? Alcohol withdrawals could kill a man, he knew that. How close had he come to revealing the rest of his own skeleton? Christmas released the skin.

During the day Lola and Aldo left the house to work in their cacao plantation. It was clear that the old man had insisted Christmas stay with them so that, eventually, he could ask the foreigner for money.

"So with the movies you make good money?"

"Sometimes."

"You have money in the bank?"

"Sometimes."

"So later you can help me? Like I helped you?" nodded the old man, "Yes? But don't say nothing to Lola."

"I won't," said Christmas.

The old man was his constant companion. He found almost anything on the television hysterically funny, as if still marvelling at the invention. Below the television there was a hi-fi system, all the plugs of which were hanging from a socket half way up the wall, crowded into an adapter and held in place by an arrangement of rubber bands. When the afternoon children's cartoons were over, the old man turned off the television and turned on *Vallenato*, cowboy accordion music from Colombia. He played one particular song over and over again. It was the most popular song in the village. When the old man wasn't playing it, Christmas could still hear the tune in the distance. The old man liked to sing along, pointing at the foreigner: "*Que se acabe la plata / pero que goce yo / que se acabe el dinero / pero mi vida no.*" – "*All my money's gone / but look how I have fun / All my money's gone / but I'm still alive*". He offered the gringo rum. Christmas refused. He knew he must give the drinking a break.

Sometimes the old man would shuffle outside to talk to neighbours dropping by, and if there were no neighbours he would talk to his chicken. This was a fighting cock, winner of several bouts, and thus kept on his own and fed a special diet of corn, fish and the odd cooked egg. The feathers had been removed from its legs and back. The old man liked to discuss tactics with it, and then pick it up by the tail and toss it around so as to exercise the wing muscles. He tossed it at Christmas. He found this very funny.

39

After he raped Bridget, Slade drove for a couple of hours until he thought he was far enough away. He spent the night at a roadside posada – four small, low rooms at the back of a restaurant. His had a brand new fan, a lean bed and walls made of earth. There was a shared bathroom. He showered. As soon as he stepped out of the water, legions of mosquitoes began to attack his wet skin. He went back to his room and sat in front of the fan. Then he lay down and covered himself with the sheet so only his face could be bitten. The roof was bamboo. It had traces of paint on it.

In the morning, he told them he was heading to Caracas and then back to England. Instead he drove to the city of Cumana. There he bought new clothes. He went into a barber's and had his hair and beard shaved off. He bought some round, mirrored sunglasses and a baseball cap. He found the Thrifty Car Rental office and parked his car there, leaving the keys on the roof. The seats were torn and ravaged. Pulling his rucksack onto his shoulder, he came out of the lot and saw an old fort overlooking the town, the Castillo de San Antonio. He walked up to it and came to a deserted

226

roundabout at the top of the mount beside the fort. There was the sea. He stared out at the horizon and its false promise of an edge.

A man approached him on a motorbike. He was honking his horn. "Hola? Hello?" said the man. "Moto-taxi?" The man drove up beside him. "Hey, amigo, you want I can take you somewhere? Let's go, no problem."

"Fuck off," said Slade.

"Yes, yes, English, no problem." The man was wearing a motor-bike helmet. His face was auburn with the sun. He was tall with a broad, fixed smile and was offering his hand. Slade stopped. They were alone. He examined the motorbike. He had an idea.

"Oscar," said the man, "I am friend of tourists."

"Slade," he replied, taking his hand.

"No problem. I have moto-taxi. You want go some place, I take you no problem."

"Where is the bank?"

"Not far. Look, I take you bank, I bring you back here, no charge, OK? Then if you want me take you some place, I take you, OK?"

Slade took his rucksack and got onto the back of Oscar's motorbike. They wound down into the town, past the Guaiqueri Park and down Calle Marino to Banesco Bank. There Slade took out the photo of Harry Christmas. He told Oscar that Christmas was his father and that he was looking for him. His father was in the Rio Caribe area. He needed someone to check all the posadas and find him.

Slade went into the bank with Oscar and took out his bor-rowing limit on his Visa card, three thousand dollars in cash. He let Oscar see the money. He told him he would pay one hundred dollars a day to look for his father. If he found him, he'd give Oscar a bonus: one thousand dollars.

"If he knows I am looking for him he will run away, understand? You've got to be —" Slade tapped his forehead, "— undercover." Oscar nodded.

"So what happened? Why he here?"

"He has gone crazy. My mother wants me to find him and bring him back to England. That is why there is a big problem if he sees me or even knows that I am looking for him, so you tell no one, OK?" Oscar nodded. "Secret mission. Black Ops."

"*Discreto*," he said. "No problem. *Entendio*. I will say just a gringo owes me money."

"When you find him you come back here, you get me, we go there, I pay you. Operation terminated." Slade stuck out his hand. Oscar shook it. Slade looked up at the sun.

"So where you stay?" Slade didn't respond. "My family have one room. Very cheap. Very nice. Better than hotel."

"Barracks," said Slade. "Perfect."

Oscar took Slade through Cumana to his house. It was in a quiet street on the outskirts of town. The yard was enclosed by a blue wall and a sturdy metal gate decorated with barbed wire. Oscar lived with his wife, his children, his brother's family and his elderly parents who slept in separate rooms and didn't talk to each other.

Slade's room was built onto the roof of the house, a makeshift first floor of naked breezeblocks and tin. Oscar charged him thirty bolívares a night. His door was a bed sheet. A fan faced his bed, a mattress on the floor, with a cane shelf in one corner that was empty but for a gold plastic Japanese cat, forever smiling and waving. Open concrete steps led up to it from the yard, a small ledge outside just big enough for the woven plastic chair that stood there.

Slade sat down. It was hot. He took off his shirt. He looked over the other rooftops of the street. Down below he watched Oscar push his moto-taxi back out of the gate and onto the road. He waved at Slade, revved his engine and headed off into Rio Caribe. His wife closed and locked the gate. She started talking to the little girl and boy who were hanging off her legs. Her name was Milagro. She looked up at Slade. The sun was caught in his glasses.

40

Christmas woke late. No one was there. His clothes, washed and folded, had appeared on a chair. He found a cold *arepa* in a basket, ate half, and fed half to the tortoise. For the first time in a long while, he stepped outside.

Lola's house was set on the outskirts of San Cristóbal. Surrounded by a grove of *cambur*, there were flowers everywhere, the porch flooded with plant pots made from plastic bottles and paint tins. Tyres hung from the beams, cut and painted to look like parrots, their bodies stuffed with earth and spider plants. A serene *flamboyan* tree with orange and white flowers cast serried light onto the dirt and grass. Beside the house there was an adobe hut with a palm frond roof and next to that a pigpen. The fighting chicken was tied to a post, squawking and stamping about in a puddle of rice as if complaining about its lack of arms.

Christmas stood on the porch inhaling animal waste and blossom and soil baked in sun. Hands behind his back, he walked over to inspect the pigs, one black and one pale, both agitated by his presence. Christmas pulled a face; the pale one had tattoos. They were bad tattoos: wonky gothic lettering; a Virgin Mary with a Mr Man face; a patterned band round one leg like a suspender belt. Christmas wondered if this pig had been to prison.

In the hut, Christmas found the tattoo gun on a workbench amongst tools and old buckets. There were curled newspaper cuttings above it, tattoos of the famous, and a plastic water bottle full of ink. The gun itself was a home-made marvel: a transformer connected to a three-volt motor from a cassette player and strapped to a bent strip of aluminium. This was taped to the shell of a propelling pencil which had a wire soldered to a pin inside it. The wire ran up to a cog attached to the motor. As the motor and the cog turned, the pin was lifted up and down in rapid motion. Mystified as to how Aldo got the pig to stay still, Christmas went back inside the house, put on his shoes and then took them off again. It was too hot for shoes. It was too hot for anything but shorts and a hat. He found a red baseball cap and so, belly-led and barefoot, Christmas set off into the village.

He followed the path through the *cambur*, the small green bananas bunched as yet unripe beneath wide drooping leaves, and came out onto another path, following it alongside a stream strewn with rubbish. He crossed it at a ford and came up through a narrowing of bushes into a wide street with one-storey homes set on either side, each one a different colour. The street looked deserted but was full of noise – mothers shouting at children, a steady hammering.

Christmas walked down the road, his bare feet registering the change to weeds and sand. Villagers lounging in front of their houses noticed him. They waved and smiled. They shouted greetings. He had felt uneasy in just shorts but all the men were dressed the same. Even if they wore a T-shirt, it was rolled up over the paunch. Some were drinking beer. It was whistling to him, at a frequency only drunks can hear. He shut his ears to it. Kids cycled past. A group of young men clapped their hands, running out from under a tree to pass on incomprehensible information. He walked past a medical centre then an evangelical meeting room on one side of the street, and the cockfighting rink on the other. "*Epalé!*" said the people as he passed, "*Como va, gringo?*"

"*No gringo,*" he corrected, "*Yo soy Ingles.*"

A small Plaza Bolivar opened out on his right and beyond it a concrete stage with a mural of Christ and Columbus as its permanent set. Here the road was cobbled. The houses were older and larger, pitted and weather-worn, remnants of posters hanging ghostly in the paint. He turned left towards the noise of a turbine and past a group of little girls beholding this pink man in wonder. A car rumbled past. A donkey brayed. There was moss on the electricity lines and children asleep in the road. The buildings exhaled like the plants, the whole village sagging from heat. '*Si! Con Chávez*' said the graffiti. *Maybe after lunch* said the birds.

He walked on towards the electricity generator, thundering in a grand shed. On one side there was the village jail, on the other a boat yard, upturned ribs in a ruined warehouse of some former purpose. Opposite, a jetty ran out into the sea, boats rocking on tin-foil waves, while above them a great ridge stooped down to the headland that made up the eastern limit of San Cristóbal's bay. Men were seated on a low wall, smoking and looking to the horizon. They greeted Christmas with a cheer. He noted with satisfaction that in San Cristóbal the moustache still reigned on faces of experience. They spoke in Spanish.

"*Verga!*" said one, "You drink too much that night."

"Yes," said Christmas, "I know."

"*Verga!*" said another, "We had to tie you to a tree. You were going crazy, brother."

"Yes," said Christmas, "I know."

"*Verga!*" said a third, "In Caracas you boom-boom with Lola!"

"Yes," said Christmas, "I did."

"We've all been trying to do that for years. She didn't let anyone, not anyone, and that's the truth, brother."

"Really?"

"The truth."

"*Verga,*" said Christmas. He sat down, and tried to apologise for his behaviour. They wouldn't let him. He told them he had been robbed and was drinking out of sadness. They offered him cigarettes and patted his back. Then they asked him what sex with Lola was like. Every few seconds, everybody spat.

"So how long will you stay in San Cristóbal? *Hoch-tooo.*"

"End of the month is the festival – *hoch-tooo* – the festival of San Cristóbal. Six days of pure fiesta. The music never stops, there are women everywhere, drinking all day and all night. It's superfine, brother. *Hoch-too.*"

One of the men stood up and started salsa dancing with a deeply-loved and invisible partner. Everyone cheered. They started singing, "*Que se acabe la plata / pero que goce yo / que se acabe el dinero/ pero mi vida noooooo ...*" A drunken man staggered towards them, attempting to join in with slurred and broken notes. The men winked at Christmas, pushing their lips out at the new arrival. The drunken man embraced Christmas.

"Anything you want," he insisted with disconnected eyes, "Me. Everyone. San Cristóbal. Me. Here." Christmas thanked him. "I've been everywhere," said the man, "I know everything."

"Well," Christmas replied, "that is impressive."

The man bit down on the world with his face then, opening it again, said "Colombians!" and wandered off.

With handshakes and smiles, Christmas left the fishermen and continued on by the shore, his mind full of the quarrels and longings of alcohol, past a small library and *infocentro*, back up the other main street. He walked to the end of the village, to the far curve of its bay, beyond structures storm-whipped and rusting; an abandoned cement plant, gutted workshops, a cemetery overgrown. He walked over a beach of stones, rounded yet square, as if ten thousand animals had discarded their hooves before transforming in the swell. He sat by the sea and eased his feet from the land. The sun pressed against his neck. His ribs and shoulder still hurt. He examined his bites, rubbing them, plotting their course into the water. Was this the right place for Emily? That beach over on the other side of the bay? Or just further along the coast here? Or round that next headland? Christmas watched the waves. He tried to follow the minute patterns that existed within their rhythm. *Oh Emily, what have I become?*

The first few months after Emily and their baby's death, Harry had barely left the house. He drank. After a year he moved back to London, back to his old ways. He started two businesses that failed, made bad investments, spent their savings. He borrowed money. He ran up credit card debts, pushing his friends away with unpaid loans and cruel remarks brewed in misery and the mash tun. He lived off the women he slept with. The drink took over. He doubled in size. Then the credit crisis came. He had trouble making his mortgage payments. The lender ended the period of leniency, he fell further into arrears and his flat was repossessed. When he met Diana he was squatting in his own home.

Something caught his eye. It was a coin. He picked it up, a fifty cent piece from Trinidad and Tobago. His first thought was if he could buy a drink with it, but that would not do. The whole Harry Christmas show – none of that would work here. It wasn't the right currency. He threw the coin into the sea.

Further along the beach, Christmas could see a group of teenagers jumping and splashing with infants. He followed the horizon to the grey smudge that was Trinidad. Fishing boats careered across the bay, bouncing with speed. These were fishermen. What was he? He was a parasite. He was a broke, out-of-work parasite. He had not the worth of one of these stones. He thought of Judith and Bridget, wondering if they knew by now that he wasn't Harry Strong. Christmas heard bird calls. He felt grain between his toes. A sudden claw gripped his heart. Pain.

It held his chest, compressing. He inhaled to fortify himself. He looked about, but everyone he could see was far away. He took short breaths. He lay down, grabbing at his chest, and felt the full intensity of the sun, a shimmering disc dancing above him that winked and glinted and teased him with death. He closed his eyes. Was this a heart attack? He was frightened, his ankles digging into the sand and water, but the pain ebbed away. When he sat up again there was a shining blue butterfly on his knee. He had never seen such colour in nature. It applauded his surprise with its wings and rose into the air, instantly camouflaged.

Christmas walked slowly back towards the house, testing if the pain had really gone with breaths of irregular size. He recognised the teenage mother on her stoop. Young children crowded round older brothers working on a motorbike. Others splashed about in a paddling pool in the street.

"So you're feeling better?"

"Getting there."

"Do all the people in your country have yellow teeth?"

"Yes. It's extremely fashionable."

"Why are you sweating so much?"

"I'm an Aquarius."

"You and Lola are about as fat as each other." The girl shifted her baby. "How old are you?"

"Fifty-eight." At that moment two little boys ran past with spinning tops.

"Will you look at that?" whispered Christmas to himself. "Unbelievable."

"They don't have those in your country?"

"Not any more."

"What games do the children in England play?"

"It's called 'Stabbing each other to death'."

"You have beautiful eyes."

"Thank you."

"Will you take me to England?"

The motorbike roared into life. The younger kids backed away as it was revved and inspected. "So you're up, gringo," somebody shouted.

It was Lola. She walked into the middle of the street, a machete over one shoulder, her baseball cap pulled down low against the sun. A thrill of children buzzed around her legs, tugging and giggling. She batted insults and greetings with every stoop she passed. Aldo pulled the donkey behind her, laden with sacks of cacao. When she got to the motorbike she gave her machete to a tiny child who ran back and handed it to Aldo. She was talking to the young owner, nodding with interest, until she suddenly pushed him off and into the paddling pool. She hopped onto the bike and zoomed away, her backside gripping the seat like a mitten, laughing as the boy scooped water at her, chasing her, round and round in circles, trailed by the kids and cheers from the stoops. Christmas realised he was chuckling. *This mighty woman*, he promised himself, *will see a new Harold Christmas*.

Lola jumped off the motorbike and chased the boy who had been chasing her. Once she had pushed him back into the paddling pool, she jogged off to the house, following Aldo and the donkey, shouting things over her shoulder and peeling off kids from her legs.

Christmas set off after them. He picked some flowers. When he came through the *cambur* into the yard, Lola and Aldo were heaving the sacks off the donkey.

"Lola—" he began.

"So you stopped shitting all over my house?"

"I wanted to say thank you. For everything. I know you didn't want to see me again and – but I promise you I wasn't following you, I – my – it was just—" Christmas produced the bunch from behind his back. Aldo laughed through his nose. Lola smiled. She patted Christmas' face, took the flowers and fed them to the donkey.

"Hey," cheered the old man as he went inside, "He's up and he's lost some weight! The fat gringo has lost some weight!"

"I am not a gringo. I am not an American."

Lola came in holding two plant pots, both containing the dried and shrivelled remains of cacti. "In Venezuela the people say that Aloe Vera is a special plant. If you have enemies, if someone hate you, the Aloe Vera absorb the bad energy. Since you come these two have died." She dropped the plant pots on the floor. She had a plastic bag hanging from her fingers. It contained a yellowtail tuna. She laid it down on the porch. Then she took a sturdy knife from the kitchen and hacked off its fins. She stabbed it through the top of its head, pulling downwards to cleave the skull in half. She cut into the jaw, loosening it, then returned to the body, sawing a line along its belly. The fish was split. She scraped out the viscera and the eggs. She dug out a worm burrowed in its flesh. Then she cut out each side into steaks. She ordered Aldo to fetch her a bowl, and piled it high with fish, the head saved for soup.

While Aldo hosed clean the porch, Lola cooked some of the steaks with crispy fried *arepas*. She made onion and tomato salad with slices of avocado picked from the tree. Everyone sat down together at the plastic table in the kitchen. They cut open the *arepas* and smeared them with butter. They stuffed them with salad, mixing bites with the fish, fingers smeared and licked.

"Everyone," Christmas started, not sure how to proceed. "I just wanted to well, thank you, all of you, for looking after me and especially you, Lola – I – well, I am more than a little ashamed of myself – and – I am not making excuses here but I have behaved in a very bad – awful – I – things have not been – I just wanted to say that your kindness has helped me, I—"

"What's he saying?" the old man asked Aldo. Aldo shrugged.

"I am going to be a better man," said Christmas, finally. Everyone carried on eating. Christmas considered continuing with his speech, but decided to get back to his food.

"So," said Lola through a mouthful, "Who's Emily?" Christmas stopped. His chin tightened. "You said her name many times when you were sick." The family looked at him. He fought it, but the surprise of hearing her name out loud had caught him off guard. He blinked furiously. The more he fought it, cursing himself, the worse it became. He pushed back his chair and tried to leave the house but he only got as far as the porch. He couldn't hold it back any longer. Christmas wept.

Lola followed him out. Aldo bent his head around the door and disappeared.

"Why is he crying like a woman?" he heard the old man say. Lola was beside him. Christmas hid his face.

"Emily was my wife," he said, pinching his eyes and trying to get himself together. "She died. With my daughter. They both died."

"*Si, Señor*," Lola sighed, "people do that a lot."

41

Christmas dreamed he was torturing a contortionist. He demanded answers, but as he bent the man's limbs, the man laughed and bent them further. He woke to the battle drone of mosquitoes in his ear. He scratched. He swore. He thrashed and lashed out and turned like a broken handle in his bed. The old man's snoring rang through the house. He heard a door open and spied the old man shuffle to the toilet, but the snoring continued. The snoring was Lola.

Some time before dawn, the cocks crowed to signal another night stolen. He fell asleep. Lola woke him with a shake. "Up," she said. "You come with us today." He stared up at the corrugated roof. *Today I will find Emily's beach.*

Christmas got up and went out across the yard into the shower room, a cold tap six foot off the ground. He pulled back the plastic curtain to find the old man stuffing white crumbs into a home-made cigar. "I'm very sick," he said. "My legs don't work."

"Papi! Are you in there?" Lola was banging on the door.

"Yes," said Christmas.

"No," said the old man. Lola burst in.

"Are you smoking crack with him?" she bawled in Christmas' face.

"I am naked," he protested in despair, "I am trying to take a shower." Lola looked him up and down, grunted, grabbed the cigar off the old man, took his wrist and led him jog-hobbling into the yard. The door slammed shut.

After coffee, scrambled eggs with onion and *arepas*, Christmas, in shorts and a blue T-shirt that inexplicably said 'Kazakhstan', pulled his red baseball cap down against the sun and followed Aldo, Lola and the donkey out through the village. They took a pathway that ran along the shore to the eastern ridge. There it rose steeply over headland where Christmas had to rest against a large rock before following the others down into jungle, cutting past mango trees and a giant bristling of bamboo. Bushes rustled with unknown creatures, insects clicked and trilled.

Aldo rode the donkey. When the boy was almost out of sight, Lola said, "You know, when my husband died he was already living with another woman in Carúpano. He got very drunk and tried to dance with a truck. Actually, I hated him, but I cried – *si, Señor*." She tugged free a long blade of grass. "I lost a girl before she was three. I lost another child in the womb."

"I'm – I'm very sorry to hear that," mustered Christmas, unsure of what to say, cursing himself for being unable to think of more. "How did your little girl die?" he said at last.

"She got sick."

They turned off the path over a stream and into the cacao trees. Wandering Jew plant covered the ground. The sun left footprints of light. A narrow track took them through the orchards of other families until they crossed a rough hedgerow and came out into a clearing.

Two heaps of old and blackened cacao pods were divided by two logs that made a passageway between them. They unpacked the donkey, Christmas swatting mosquitoes from his ankles. "OK, gringo?" Lola said. "You go with Aldo." The boy was crouched on the ground, sharpening a billhook against a stone. He affixed it to the end of a long bamboo pole and then they toured the trees together, one lancing the cacao pods from the branches, the other collecting them in a sack.

When it was full they delivered it to Lola, now joined by the old woman with hardly any hair. The two women sat on the logs between the piles of old pods, the ground between them covered by plastic sheeting. They split the pods open with a hatchet, gouged out the white slimy seeds with pieces of wood flattened at one end and tossed the empty husks over their shoulders onto the piles. The seeds smelled of sweet vinegar.

Flying ants and mosquitoes hovered and crawled everywhere despite the low fire of leaves crossing the workers with smoke. They fed on the foreigner, they made him dance and grunt, but Christmas felt Lola's eyes upon him and was determined to endure. He kept his mind on the smooth, heavy pods that crashed to earth with a thud, making sure he wasn't hit on the head. He didn't want to be the patient any more.

At lunchtime they rested against tree trunks and ate fish and *arepas* and drank cold water from the brook. Smoke performed in the light shafts. Christmas closed his eyes. He felt Emily's presence. Then she was gone. Things were crawling up his ankles.

While the family ate and talked, he considered his situation. As soon as he felt strong in his heart he must take a proper walk, explore the coastline and find the right spot for Emily. But what then? He had no money so he could not leave; he could not afford the bus fare to Caracas. He could not leave because he had no money; he could not repay Lola and her family. Only this work, the act of contributing, was doing something to loosen the hot tar of shame that cladded his ribs.

He hadn't had a drink in several days, but his mind felt no clearer for it. There was only a rush of Emily. The noise she made when she turned over in her sleep. In that suit that showed off her hips. How she laughed. Her political opinions. Her funeral. The way her big toe lifted when she brushed her teeth. How belligerent and spiteful she could be when she drank white wine. Her dead body in the hospital bed. That superstition about magpies. The way she threaded her hair under her nose when she was concentrating. Preparing dinner. He was chopping carrots, and there was Ella Fitzgerald coming in from the living room. Emily was stuffing rosemary under the skin of a chicken. He cut himself. She ran his finger under the cold tap. She was wearing the apron they bought from the Chatsworth shop. She kissed his finger then his lips. They fell back against the wall map of Venezuela. His finger dragged blood across her shirt. She got cross.

The old woman was gabbling without pause. He understood it was for his benefit, though she only looked at her food.

"When I was a little girl, the people were happier. They worked hard but they were happy. My mother washed and ironed clothes every day of her life, but when she went to bed she went to sleep. Not like now. Now people go to bed to worry in peace. In my day the electricity went off at nine. People closed up their shops by putting a chair against the door – no locks! Oh no! You could go to Guiria and you knew someone would be looking after your children; you didn't have to ask. Now there are all these drugs. *Dios mio*! Everybody wants to destroy themselves ..."

Christmas finished his plate and held out his hands as Aldo poured water over them. He returned the favour, holding out the

242

bottle for the old woman and then Lola. Sweat and dirt brushed her cheeks. Her gold crucifix rested between her breasts. Crouching, she washed her hands, filled her mouth, spat, washed her face then her green eyes looked up at him from under her baseball cap. She laughed.

"What?" he said, but she only shook her head and stood up.

At the end of the day Lola stood over the pile of seeds and filled up two hessian sacks using an old metal plate. They packed up the containers and plastic bottles from lunch. Aldo pulled the billhook off the end of the bamboo pole while Christmas and the old woman folded up the plastic sheeting. Lola hacked off a young branch and laid the thick end of it against a log. She beat it with the end of the machete until the bark loosened and could be stripped to use as binding for the sacks. Once tied shut, Christmas and Aldo hauled them onto the wooden cross frame trussed to the donkey's saddle, Aldo tying and retying until the two sides were balanced. Then they followed the donkey home, machetes swinging.

Christmas' wrists, cheeks and ankles were red maps of attack. The next day he woke again determined to search the beaches for the right spot and was there, in the doorway with Montejo in his hand, but Aldo appeared with some gumboots and told him to put trousers on. Before he knew it they were walking together through the cacao, Aldo carrying an old paint tin stuffed with dry leaves and embers to drive off the worst of the mosquitoes.

Christmas' sweat-sodden shirt cloyed on his back. There was silence but for birdsong and their trampling of the brake. A sea breeze blew through the grove. Perhaps this was what they meant by the nobility of labour, thought Christmas, nobly. Yes, it felt good to be doing something. It gave his mind a break from the torrent of memories that sobriety was pouring through him. For the first time in almost a week, he was in the mood for conversation.

"So Aldo, you are an Evangelical, correct?"

"Yes."

"So you believe in hell?"

"Of course."

"But if Christ died for our sins, shouldn't hell be closed?"

"Closed?"

"Like a shop."

"Gringo, you should come to a meeting and ask Christ for forgiveness and for his blessing."

"The problem, Aldo, is that if Christ was alive now, the last thing he'd be is a Christian."

"Have you sold your soul to the devil?" asked the boy.

"Everybody has sold their soul to the devil," sighed Christmas. "That's why you can't get a decent bloody price."

Every day he promised himself he would look for Emily's beach, either before work or after it or at sundown, or at night, but the rhythm of their days took over. Sometimes Christmas chopped open the pods and scooped out the seeds, but mostly he and the boy wandered the boles, staring up into the leaves and the sun, trailing sack cloths and ash. They cut back the overgrowth. They cleaned the trees with the brunt of the bill-hook, chivvying at the ants' nests that warted their groins. They peeled away the green veins of parasite weeds. They broke off dead limbs.

One afternoon he was sitting on a tree stump, rubbing the billhook against the flat sharpening stone, pouring water on it to cool the metal while Lola sewed up a hole in one of the sacks. They had been talking about her family when she rearranged herself and said, "So what was she like, your wife?" Christmas hacked the billhook into some rotten wood.

"You know, I remember one time when we were invited to these people's house for dinner. We didn't know them really. They lived in our town and I had this business deal I was going to do with the husband. That's what you do in England – you go round to other people's houses for dinner, apparently for the company, but really it's just so you can have a nose about, and then bitch about their bad taste in the car home afterwards. Anyway, Emily had a bad stomach. I didn't want to go to the dinner much. It was a weekend and I was much better off in the pub – which is like a bar here but with carpet and more than one type of beer. So I said, you know, let's just call it off, darling, let's just not go, but no – we'd said we'd do something, so we'd do it. That was Emily. No messing.

"So we were in the car on the way there and her stomach just got worse and worse, so we pull into this petrol station, which in England are pretty much like hotels, with shops and restaurants and that sort of thing – massive – so Ems can use the toilet. While we are there she bumps into this friend of hers, a great friend, one of her oldest, Claire her name was, and she takes one look at Emily and says, what do you mean you're going to dinner, look at the state of you, you've got to cancel, you've got to get yourself into bed, but Emily wouldn't hear of cancelling. What about the poor hostess who's cooked all the food and cleaned her house and everything? We're meant to be there in ten minutes, we can't cancel now. That was Emily. Would never let anyone down, even if she didn't know them. But then she got this wicked look in her eye and that's what I miss really, this wicked, fun look, and she says to Claire, if you aren't doing anything tonight, why don't you go? You pretend to be me.

"Well, I was desperate for Emily to go home and look after herself, so I thought it was a brilliant idea and Claire was always up for anything, so off we went, you know? I introduced her as Emily and we start having dinner. After the first course, I skip upstairs to ring the real Emily, see if she was all right, and she was asking me how Claire was performing and I told her what fun we were having, how delicious the food was, how good the wine was – basically that her plan was working perfectly.

"Well, Emily had driven home in Claire's car and on the way back her stomach trouble had cleared up completely. So now she was at home, bored, and do you know what she did? We were eating dinner, the doorbell went, and there she was. She introduced herself as Claire, said she was my second wife, that we all lived together in a *ménage a trois*, which she didn't think was anything to be ashamed of and could she come in."

"*De verdad?*"

"I swear it. The look on those people's faces ... Jesus Christ. That was the thing about Emily. Didn't give a damn."

"And how was the dinner?"

"They let her sit down, gave her some food. We all had a great time."

"And how the business deal go?"

"Never heard from him again. Didn't even answer my phone calls!"

"Wow. I like the sound of her."

"Yes, yes. She was quite something. Her grandmother was Venezuelan, you know. From Guiria, actually. Before she got pregnant we – that's why I was ... you know ..." he fell silent.

"Seven years ago is a long time, Harry."

"I know, I know."

"Another hour and we go home, OK?" She tugged on the sack. It was mended. "Well, it is good that you're here." She slung it over her shoulder. "Less work for me," and off she went to find Aldo.

246

Christmas watched her go, smiling to himself. *It's good that you're here.* She had just said that, hadn't she?

42

It was night. Slade was in his room, drinking whisky and masturbating. He was thinking about Bridget, reimagining his crime, her head pressed down against the sink. Now she was goading him, daring him to attack her. Now the noises she made were of grudging pleasure. He came into some toilet paper.

Slade had been there eight days. Some evenings Oscar came back to give him a report of where he had been and which villages he was going to try the following day. Some evenings he didn't come back at all. Slade stayed in his room drinking or he sat in the plastic chair watching Oscar's wife Milagro doing chores down there in the yard, her small, tight body in small, tight shorts.

Slade turned to the wall. He could hear Oscar's estranged grandfather listen to the radio. He tried to follow the Spanish words. He could smell something cooking. It was burning. He was walking into the kitchen. He could hear his father beating Diana and she'd left carrots frying and they were spitting and blackened and flaring smoke. He turned the gas off and went into the corridor and Diana was on the floor and he went up to her hair and pulled it away from her ear and whispered, "The carrots are ready."

Slade woke up. He was curled up against the wall. The house was silent. The bed sheet that was his door moved. He looked over. There was Oscar's daughter. Next to her, in the corner of the room, was The General. The General opened its mouth and Milagro's voice came out of it, calling her daughter downstairs.

Slade got to his feet. He parted the sheet and watched her take one step at a time down to her mother. Milagro glanced up at him and hurried her daughter inside.

"I want him gone!" she hissed, "I don't like him!"

"Don't be ridiculous and lower your voice!" said Oscar through a mouthful.

"Why? He can't even speak Spanish."

"We are making good money and soon he'll be gone, OK?"

"I don't like the way he looks at me! He is crazy!"

"We find his father and we make one thousand dollars. You want me to kick him out because you don't like him?"

"I can hear him talking to himself."

"Look, when I am not around, I'll tell Alejandro to come by, OK? Make sure everything is all right and—"

"Shush!" Milagro and Oscar looked up at the ceiling. They could hear the rumble of Slade's English.

"Why are you here?" Slade asked the cat again. "Where's my father?"

"Boo-hoo," The General replied. "You haven't got the fat man. Boo-hoo. You can't see him. Boo-hoo, boo-hoo."

43

San Cristóbal was a nest of factions. The Evangelicals didn't like the Jehovah's Witnesses. The Catholics cared for neither. The drinkers disapproved of the crackheads, except for that subsection that were crackheads themselves. Everyone smoked marijuana and agreed it was good for the health, except for the old people who broadly disapproved of the young people and new ideas in general. Countless familial and inter-generational rivalries bubbled away and yet even the most spiteful, back-stabbing neighbour was proud of how much nicer the people were here than in Caracas. The village greeting was to act as if you hadn't seen that person in years: an '*Epalé*!' cried out with open palms and an expression of surprise. As there were only six streets in San Cristóbal, they greeted each other like this continuously, perhaps only minutes passing since their last meeting, perhaps their twentieth that day. '*Epalé*!' – it was like a big family of amnesiacs.

Striding through the village, his strength restored and the bruising much reduced, Christmas thought the whole thing was wonderful. '*Epalé*!' cried the people from their stoops. '*Epalé*!' he cried back. Christmas excelled at the cheerful insults that often followed and was buoyed by the feeling that, on the whole, the villagers had taken to him: "Hey gringo! You have sex with my donkey again last night? You wake me up with the noise, man!"

"I'd rather have sex with your donkey than your wife, Gustavo – she looks like a knee in a wig."

Some asked for money, the refusal process infinitely eased by the truth: he was potless. The men asking him were always the same – members of the small but highly visible fraternity of serious crack smokers. They looked like Old Testament prophets, weather-beaten and bearded, with eyes like fire behind burnt glass. Robbed of the ability to steal – the village was far too small and remote – they were the hardest working men in the population. They ferried goods around in wheelbarrows. They collected the rubbish. They cleaned the streets, delivered beer crates, unloaded cargo boats, painted houses. Then, at night, they smoked their daily fortunes and forgot to wash.

Christmas entered into a routine with one of these men. He was known as *El Perro*, 'the Dog'. He wore two baseball caps, one on top of the other, the visors parting left and right. His torso looked like a woven tree root.

"Give me ten bolívares," said El Perro, putting down his wheel-barrow as Christmas walked by.

"No," said Christmas.

So it continued, several times a day, with no animosity on either side. Christmas couldn't help wondering if there was not some lesson here with these industrious addicts, some wider truth for the nation. Perhaps Chávez could employ all the crackheads in Caracas on community service projects, pay them one crack rock an hour, call it *Misión Crack*. Perhaps the mayors of Britain should do the same. Perhaps crime would plummet, perhaps cities would be clean, perhaps junkies would be taken care of. Had not these men just slipped as he had, though down a different mountain? Christmas resolved to think about it some more, wondering once again if he had not missed his vocation as a politician.

There was one basic shop in the village that sold *ocumo*, yucca, *pan de año*, onions, garlic, eggs, oil, rice, curry powder, salt, pepper, tinned sardines, corn flour, fizzy pop, soap, detergent, shampoo, toilet roll, razors and Alka Seltzer, but he soon learnt behind which doors mothers made freshly baked bread, home-made sorbet, pastries and cakes of every type, hamburgers and hotdogs, sweetbread, yoghurts, cheese and ice-cold fruit juices. For a village surrounded by cacao, there didn't seem to be much chocolate. "The people don't have the machines here," the old man explained. "We do it all by hand. It's too much work. But we'll make some for the festival. Arri, it's going to taste like whooompf! You mix it with rum and whaboooof!"

"Whooompf *and* whaboooof? In the same glass?"

"That's right, gringo man!"

"I am not a—"

"Bleurrgh," said the old man, changing channel.

When Saturday came the fishermen got paid. As Christmas walked through the village, men with bottles of Cacique stuffed into their belts cornered him and demanded he take a swig. He declined.

The night was hot. The sea was the colour of wine. Music hammered out the dents in their lives and everyone wanted to talk to the foreigner. There was a great deal of interest in England amongst the men, largely because of football, and Christmas secured impact by describing the country as a ghost story: "It is dark. Fierce winds howl through the streets. Everybody is angry. Then suddenly the snow arrives and everything turns pure white, everything you can see, and the people are happy. For one morning. Then they are angry again for six months until the sun arrives. You wake up one morning and there it is. Everybody goes crazy and strips naked. They get drunk in the sun and they are happy. Until they get too drunk. Then they are angry again."

"Is it true," asked a woman, "that men in your country ..." and she made a V-shape with her fingers and began to simulate oral sex. The other women with her cackled uncontrollably.

"I'll tell you this," he replied, putting one foot on their stoop and pushing up the brim of his baseball cap, "whatever you ladies think, there are plenty of husbands here who do it. Only they make their wives not tell anyone." The women hooted. "You, for example," he pointed to the youngest, who was covering her mouth. "Definitely you." Stifling giggles, she raised a finger in denial as the others pushed and poked her. Christmas straightened up. He saw Lola walking down the street eating a mango. He readied himself to greet her. She threw the mango stone at his head.

Lola, undeniably, had a growing affection for Harry Christmas. In San Cristóbal, even this clumsy pink bear counted as exotic. His behaviour was certainly unusual. What other man in this village always offered up his seat if she was lacking? Who else rushed to open doors for her, or thanked her for everything she did, however small? And he was funny. That morning he had been in the kitchen, a ventriloquist singing English songs with fish heads for puppets. Even the old man had joined in, clapping and banging on the floor.

Lola was wearing a brightly-coloured wrap-around dress, hair pulled back against her head, face sparkling with make-up. All the women dressed up on Saturday night. The village had three bars and they were all open, people crowding them inside and out, drinking rum and beer, playing cards and pool on uneven tables. As he watched Lola saunter off into a group of friends, he was beckoned to a stoop where the fishermen from his first walk around San

Cristóbal were drinking Cuba Libres from plastic cups, *Vallenato* shaking the house behind.

"*Epalé*! Hey, brother!" they welcomed him. "Sit down, sit down." Orlando, Gabriel and Ricardo shook his hand, pulled him down and they all sat there, spitting, drinking and watching the village alive.

"So," asked Gabriel, "have you—" and he made an obscene gesture with his fingers, "with Lola again yet? *Hoch-too*."

"No."

"*Verga*! Why not, brother? *Hoch-too*."

"For some reason, women don't think hanging from a tree covered in vomit is very romantic." The men collapsed over each other with laughter. "But you're working on it, right?" Christmas smiled. They all slapped him on the back.

"Good luck, brother. And if nothing happen, no problem. Plenty of women here, and they all like you. We hear them talking. *Hoch-too*."

"Yes, man – don't worry. We support the English team, *oíste*?"

"Roo-ney," said Ricardo, pointing at him.

"Beck-ham," said Orlando.

"George Best, more like," said Christmas. They gave him a blank look.

"Can you dance salsa?"

"No."

"Oooo," they crowed in a low tone of disapproval, biting on tongues and shaking their heads. "If you want a Venezuelan woman, brother – *hoch-too* – you must learn salsa. If you can't dance with her, what's she going to do? She's going to dance with someone else."

"Tonight we go to the disco. It's just over there. Everybody goes. You coming, brother?"

"No," replied Christmas, "Absolutely not."

254

The disco was a youth club that had once been a basketball court. Roofed above the bar but otherwise open to the night, couples with expressionless faces simulated sex to calypso music. Men and women of all ages crowded the tables, lined the walls and filled the street outside. They danced through the steam of cigarette smoke, bright ends blinking in the dark. The music was so loud Christmas felt as if the beat was trying to take over his heart.

He sat with his companions a little way off from the dance floor. They had a bucket of Cuba Libre bobbing with ice and lime, from which they scooped full their plastic glasses. Christmas watched them drink. He was given a glass of Coca-Cola. Again and again giggling women of all ages tried to pull Christmas onto the dance floor but he refused. He watched his friends dance. The steps were simple but there was something too unfamiliar in the rhythm. He thought he'd look like a fool.

The music changed from calypso to soca and then to salsa. The younger ones sat down and the older generation stood up. Christmas felt some ice hit him in the chest. Lola had arrived with her girls.

"*Verga* – why aren't you dancing, gringo?"

"Because I have already suffered enough embarrassment in this village for one lifetime."

She blew a note of disagreement through tightened lips. "Rubbish," she said, scooping her glass into the bucket while his friends nudged him in the ribs.

"Christ alive, it's like being a fucking teenager," he mumbled in English. Lola and her group sat down on a nearby bench. Man after drunken man asked her to dance. She waved her finger, tutting 'no'. Ricardo asked her and he watched her pout towards him. The man returned slapping him on the shoulder. "OK, brother. Now you have to help me."

"What did she say?"

"She said she would dance with me, OK? But only if you dance. *Hoch-too.*"

"With her?"

"She said she doesn't want to dance with you." Christmas deflated. "Anyway she says you won't because you're a coward."

"What!" Christmas looked over. Lola bared her teeth at him with a smile. He tightened his lips and blew a note of disbelief. "Dammit," he grumbled, "Dammit all to hell." Christmas stood up. His friends cheered. He walked over to Lola's bench and bent his face down close to hers.

"Hello, gringo."

"Good evening."

"Do you want to say something?"

"Yes. Would you –" and he turned to the women next to her "– like to dance with me?" Lola sucked her teeth. "What's your name?" he continued.

"Beatriz," said the woman.

"Harry," he replied and he lead her off to the middle of the dance floor, followed by Lola and Ricardo. He felt very pleased with himself, but his moment of victory soon dissolved. Everyone was looking at him. They were laughing. He had no idea how to dance salsa. He held Beatriz's hip. He held her hand. He wobbled about a bit. Beatriz was biting her lip, giggling, trying to guide him. He looked at Lola, and she cocked her eyebrow. "It's like a nightmare," he whispered to himself, "a waking bloody nightmare."

"*Como?*" said Beatriz. Christmas didn't reply. He carried on tottering unevenly to the trumpets and drums as best he could, praying for the end of the song. He closed his eyes. When he opened them again, a child was dancing beside him, doing an impression of his efforts. Overcome with this excuse to stop dancing, Christmas let go of Beatriz and chased the kid around the dance floor to the whoops of the crowd. He caught the kid and tickled him without mercy. Sheeting with sweat, Christmas returned to his bench. He fanned himself with his hat and ran ice cubes across his face and neck. With the confidence of having accepted her challenge, he tried to talk to Lola. She sucked her teeth and turned away.

"Hey, brother," nudged Ricardo, "why didn't you ask Lola to dance?"

"But she told you she didn't want to dance with me."

"Gringo," he said, pouring Christmas another Coke, "you don't know nothing about women."

At that moment a scream went up beside them. A fight had broken out and a group of women were running out the way. Two men had each other by the T-shirt, throwing wide punches. They fell onto the floor. Others tried to pull them apart. One wrestled free from the pack, picked up a length of wood and dodged around the side, swinging it into the other man's face. It cracked into him with a sound so sickening it stopped the fight. The unconscious man was lying in the dirt, surrounded, while the other was pinned up against the fence, men shouting into his face. Christmas watched the loose body be picked up and carried away as other scuffles started, calmed, then started again. The music stopped. Everyone was shouting.

"Always the same," said Lola beside him. "I'm going home." He followed her out into the quiet of the village, people buzzing past them to get in on the action. The night creaked with crickets.

"So," he started, "you don't have a boyfriend?" He couldn't believe the stupidity of his question.

"Do you know," she said, "the last boyfriend I had said he wanted to marry me – si, Señor – and he proposed to me, and when he proposed to me, he got my name wrong. Not just a little bit wrong. Completely wrong."

"Ah."

"Yes. 'Ah'."

When they arrived home, Lola stopped at the doorway. The old man was on the sofa, stuffing white crumbs of crack into the end of his rough cigar. His hands were shaking. He hadn't noticed them.

Christmas expected Lola to start shouting and explode into the room, but she didn't. She watched him hold a flame to it, inhale, hold the smoke, let it out through his nostrils, his face licked with pleasure. Then he began to cough, an ugly cough that chipped and tore things out of him. Tears were running down her cheeks.

44

Christmas dreamed he was at an old friend's house that was somehow also a pub. Emily was there but she was different. She was taller, with long blond hair. She was in a glamorous dress and came out of a room with another man whom he didn't recognise but then later in the dream became Simon, his business partner when he ran a travel agency. Simon, his staunch friend and drinking companion, whom he had finally driven away by insulting his wife and children. Simon, who no longer accepted his calls, to whom he still owed several thousand pounds, was smiling with forgiveness. Christmas was overjoyed. He rushed over to greet them.

"Simon and I are getting married," she told him as his guts screwed into a jealous ball. "He's good for me."

On Sunday there was a storm. The mountains disappeared and the horizon came forward onto the quayside. Out of the haze, rain littered the ground before it beat the roofs, silencing everything. They gathered at the doors to watch it rearrange the earth and bring that brewed stench of regions in the sky that filter black space. They monitored the water level in the yard. They rescued clothes and machines.

The electricity still worked so, beneath the clatter, they watched television with the volume up high. Some senior officials in the state-run *Mercal*, the distribution network for free and cut-price food for the poor, had been arrested on corruption charges.

"Always corruption!" said Lola picking her T-shirt off her belly. "Now we're teaching the children something different, but my generation is used to another mentality: you want something done, you pay for it. They criticize Chávez for wanting to stay longer as president, but these problems take a generation to solve. Maybe two."

"So," ventured Christmas, passing the old man a lighter for his cigarette, "everyone in San Cristóbal supports Chávez?"

"She loves Chávez," he replied. "She is one hundred per cent *chávista*."

"Chávez is a great man! For one hundred years Venezuela was ruled by thieves who cared nothing for the people, who robbed the people, so the people were poor. Now, with Chávez, poverty is twenty per cent less." She bent back the points on her fingers. "Now, with Chávez, we have education. He built our school here in San Cristóbal. He built the *infocentro* so we have computers and we can educate ourselves about the world. He started *Misión Ribas* to teach reading and writing, especially to the indigenous people who did not have the schools before. He started *Misión Robinson* for the adults who never had the opportunity to get a high-school degree. He has changed what we teach to the children. They used to teach us your history, European history, but we didn't know about our own history. They taught us about the Christian martyrs in Rome, but we didn't know about the history of the indigenous people, of black people. Chávez has changed all that.

"Before Chávez almost half of the people didn't have clean drinking water. Now almost everyone does. He start *Misión Barrio Dentro* for when the people are sick – twenty thousand doctors in poor communities. There used to be one hospital miles away; now there are three places in this area where the people can get treatment for free. And you!" she pouted towards the old man, "When are you going to let them take a look at you?"

"Bleurrgh."

"Did you know that Chávez came here, to San Cristóbal?" Lola shifted to the edge of her seat, "and he came on his own! Driving a jeep, like one of us. The people were looking and they say, '*Verga*! It's Chávez!' And everyone ran out and they see – look, it's Chávez. Like this he came to our village. Not hanging by his foot and covered in vomit." Christmas bared his teeth at her with a smile. "Before Chávez all the big companies, the electricity, the petrol, the cement, the phone – they were all were owned by foreigners and they took all the money out of Venezuela. Chávez took them back for us. He is freeing the people, like Bolívar before him."

"He's not afraid of the gringos," smiled the old man, smoke curling out from behind his gold teeth.

"Are you *chávista* too?" Christmas asked him.

"Well, I used to be, yes of course, but now I listen to him, the state must own all the companies, the state must own all the land and I think 'Bleurrgh. He is just another man who wants to be in charge of everything.'"

"You are a stupid old man! The state must be strong to fight against the international companies. What about you, Harry? Are you for Chávez?" Lola was glaring.

"Well ... anything that helps people out of poverty or gives them more freedom, I'm for, but I'm not *for* anyone. I don't think its people's job to be *for* leaders. It's the people's job to criticize, and—"

"Typical!" she snorted with disgust. "Latinos are for everyone. Gringos are always for themselves."

"That's not what—"

"Why don't you make a movie about Chávez? So people can learn the truth."

"Me?"

"You are a movie producer, no?" It was what he had told her when they first met. Now he could admit he was lying. Now he could admit that he'd just said it to impress her.

"Documentaries aren't my genre."

"What about a movie about an old crack addict? Killing himself! In front of his family!"

"All my life I worked," exclaimed the old man, one finger raised, "now I can do what I want!" His nose was running. A shouting match ensued. Then a news item appeared about Iraq – scenes of wreckage after a suicide bomber blew himself up in a queue of police recruits.

"May Christ help them," said Aldo.

"They're Muslims," said Christmas, "Christ is the last person they want to see." Aldo knelt in front of the television and began praying. "May the love of Christ help them to stop this violence."

"*Verga!*" shouted the old man, throwing the cigarette packet at his head. "Get out of the way, boy!"

"May the love of Christ help Grandpa," he continued, "and the gringo."

"What's wrong with us?"

"You are wicked men."

"Lucky for you," said Christmas.

"For me?"

"Where's Christ without the wicked men? Without us he'd be a nobody." Tanks rolled across a wall and into someone's front room.

"Don't tease my son. Aldo is right," Lola puffed, "This violence ... they will not win their war with violence. Wars are not won with violence."

"I am afraid they are," said Christmas. He wanted to keep quiet, but could not. "We won the Second World War with violence. Quite a lot of it, actually."

"You won that war because the Americans helped you. You won it with friendship."

"Yes, but they helped us win it by dropping a great big bomb on the Japanese. Which was pretty violent."

"Men!" she cried, "*Verga!* Always you want to make everything about fighting!" Christmas looked at her father. A weary look advised silence. Then the old man started coughing.

"We must persuade," said Aldo, "with faith and reason, just as the Christian martyrs converted the pagan Roman emperors, with the force of good deeds and God's love."

"And horse racing," said Christmas.

"'Horse racing'?"

"There was this early Christian saint called Hilarion, lived out in the desert, did a lot of miracles, cured a lot of illnesses – that sort of thing. Anyway, a Christian racehorse owner in Gaza asked him to bless his horses because there was a rival pagan who was winning all the races with the help of a sorcerer. Hilarion blessed the horses and the next race they won, and they kept on winning, and this so impressed the crowd that they all started converting."

"You see!" the old man shouted, lifting himself onto his elbows, "I am no sinner!"

"Shut up! And you!" Lola turned to Christmas, "You would be a different person if you really were as intelligent as you think you are." Christmas didn't understand what she had just said. He filed it away for postponed consideration. Lola left the room.

"Hey, don't worry," said the old man, "she's like that all the time. What does she know? She's just a woman. But we are men! Can you lend me five dollars?"

"I don't have any money."

The old man took a deep drag of his cigarette and wiped his nose with his fingers.

"But your money is coming soon, right? To the bank in Guiria?" It was what he had told him when they first met. Now he could admit he was lying. Now he could admit he was just embarrassed by his circumstances.

"Yes."

"When do you think it will get here? Before the festival?"

"I hope so."

The old man lowered his voice. "Then you can help me, OK? Like I helped you. Lola didn't want you here, you know."

"I know."

"It was me that said, 'Cut him down from that tree and bring him to my house. He is our friend.'"

"I know, and I am very—"

"So you can help—" Lola came back in the room and the old man stopped talking. He gave Christmas a wink and then pouted at his daughter behind her back. "Anyway today is a special day. Today is God's day," he started up again in a loud voice. Aldo turned round from the television screen, scowling. "And gringo man, I need your help."

"With church?"

"*Verga*!" cursed the old man. "Don't be stupid! With the cock-fight."

45

Under an avuncular *saman* tree dripping with Spanish moss, the cockpit was a circular wooden fence surrounded by benches. At the weekend the villagers brought their roosters down to square off against each other and, if the conditions were mutually agreed on, to fight. What these conditions were, Christmas never found out. Young men wandered round shouting at each other. Eventually there was calm, two chickens were chucked in the middle and the shouting started again. Betting was done on a double-or-quits basis only.

While the old man spat, swore and haggled until he got himself a contest, Christmas held the chicken under his arm. Others swooped their birds close to test its reaction. They squawked and fluttered and provoked an urgent memory of Slade running at him with a knife. Running down back alleys in Rio Caribe. Being trapped in that bus – Christmas tried to push those thoughts away. What was he going to do about his passport that was still at Judith's? And why wasn't he busy trying to find a good place for Emily, for Montejo? Something was stopping him? What was it?

He saw Aldo ignore him and file into the evangelical meeting room across the street.

"What's the matter with Aldo?"

"They complain about the noise when they are trying to sing. We complain about the singing when we are trying to shout. They only built that place a few years ago. This cockpit has been here since before I was me!"

Organ music piped up from the evangelicals as the first two cocks were dropped into the circle. Their legs and bodies were shaved. Their spurs were supported by tape wrapped around the legs. A man with a cowboy hat and a seedy moustache spat water over each animal to cool them down. Then, as the crowd raved and hooted, they pecked each other to death.

The whole thing lasted five minutes. Eventually one was left, hopping about its opponent on the ground and jabbing it in the head with its beak. The one on the ground stopped moving. Half the crowd erupted. The old man had won some money and he shook his cane in the air while others ran round the ring, high-fiving and embracing each other. The evangelicals sang on.

Christmas, still holding the old man's bird under his arm and rather tired of being barged about by this rowdy mob, tried to translate the event into future profit. He needed to make some money. Could he get his own chicken and feed it some of the old man's crack? Or coffee – perhaps he could feed it coffee? How long did chickens take to grow in any case? Ideally he would need one that went from egg to warrior in about a week. Betting was a way forward perhaps. But to bet, he needed money.

The old man pushed through to Christmas and took the cock, whispering encouragements as he passed it on to the man in the cowboy hat to have its spurs taped. Christmas wandered around the crowd as they waited. He looked across at the evangelicals. Theirs was a simple room. A man with a microphone was talking to the congregation as they sang, rows of different coloured plastic chairs facing an electric organist and an arrangement of flowers. The women covered their heads with scarves. "*Dios esta aquí*," they sang, "*tan cierto come el aire que respiro*". They got to their feet, applauding, swaying, crying 'Hallelujah'.

"Hey," someone nudged him, "your girlfriend." Lola was walking down the street with a group of friends. Her head was covered with a scarf. She was coming to join her son. Could he be making a grievous *faux-pas* by being with the cockfighters? Panicked by this thought he skipped over the road and into the church, stepping next to Aldo who looked at him with surprise and then enormous pleasure. Christmas mumbled along to the words, "*Lo puedo ver en el hermano que tengo a mi lado / lo puedo sentir en el fondo de mi corazón ...*" planning out the casualness with which he would greet Lola when their eyes met. He even started to sway. "Hallelujah!" he shouted, joining in with the throng, "*Gracias a Dios!*" Suddenly Christmas was on his knees. There were tears in his eyes.

"Have you felt it?" said Aldo, grabbing Christmas by the shoulder. "Have you felt the love of Jesus Christ?"

"I felt the love of that woman's elbow," he grouched, "when she decided to embrace the Holy Ghost." Bleary-eyed, Christmas got to his feet to see Lola outside. Standing in the shade of the *saman* tree, she took the scarf off her head and wrapped it around her shoulders. Then she went into the cockfight. What was she up to? Was she about to admonish the old man? No, goddamit – she was placing a bet. Christmas made to leave, but some more worshippers had filled up the aisle and were in such rapture that it was impossible to get past. He heard the shouts of the fight starting up. The congregation increased their volume in response. Then they joined hands, trapping Christmas in a fleshy chain as he strained his neck to see the cockfight crowd cramming in around the action. Barely a minute had passed when a roar went up. Christmas was determined to see what was going on, but the congregation were now hugging each other; at every step forward he was clutched to the breast of another Christian. When he got to the door, there was Lola.

She had been watching him pull faces at each embrace as if they were flavours of vinegar. She was laughing so hard she had to bend over and rest on her knees.

"What you doing in there, gringo?"

"I ..."

"*Verga! Eres un corrupto!* Too late for you! Here –" she said wiping her eyes and recovering, "somebody gave this to me. It's yours, right?" She had Bridget's wallet. It must have fallen out when he was hanging upside down from the tree.

"Yes," said Harry, regretting his reply as he watched her open it.

"So this is your wife?"

"Yes," he said slowly. She was examining the photograph of Judith and Bridget.

"You didn't tell me you had a daughter."

"That's ... my niece. Her niece. That was my wife's favourite niece." Lola handed it to him.

"She was skinny, your wife," she said. "Like a stick," and then she walked off into the people collecting their winnings. The crowd fading away from the cockpit revealed the old man leaning over the wall, hugging and kissing his chicken as the dead one was picked up by its neck.

46

It was one in the morning. Slade's light was off. He lay on the bed, his face gauzed in sweat. He heard the unlocking of the door, got to his feet and looked down through the curtain. Milagro was walking across the yard. Oscar had not come home. Slade had been there for two weeks. The time didn't bother him. He knew Oscar would take him to Christmas eventually because Oscar, he was now certain, worked for Christmas. Milagro unlocked the gate and turned right into the dark street.

Slade left his room, went down the steps and into the house. He walked around the kitchen. He went into Oscar's bedroom. There, asleep on the bed, were his son and his daughter.

He left the room, crossed the yard and went out. Around the corner there was a small crowd of people buying ices from a vendor beneath a streetlight.

He stayed in the shadows for a moment then walked into the light. People noticed him and Milagro turned round. She had just paid for a red ice cone on a stick. Once he got there she forced out '*Hola*' then walked quickly back towards home.

Slade bought an ice. He followed her out of the circle of electric light into the darkness. The night was hot.

"Can't sleep?" he asked her. She didn't turn round but said something in Spanish. He was two steps behind her. She was wearing tight shorts. She flicked her long, curled hair. He watched it settle against her back. He glimpsed side alleys full of rubbish and saw The General was there, trotting beside him.

"Where's my father?" Slade hissed.

"*Que?*" said Milagro, turning round, seeing he was talking to the ground. She jumped through the gates and ran across the yard, shutting and locking her door as Slade watched her go. He sucked on his ice. The General was gone.

47

Lola, Aldo and Harry were laying out cacao in the yard. They spread it out on plastic sheets to darken and shrivel in the sun. As Aldo emptied the sacks, Lola and Harry evened out the seeds. She was silent. The old man hadn't come home since Sunday's cockfight.

"No, he won't have eaten," she said suddenly, as if in answer to a question. The winning chicken stomped and clucked in a spill of corn. "I should cut that thing's throat and turn it into soup. See if he can buy crack with soup!"

"I'll say a prayer for—"

"Shut up, Aldo."

"Why don't we just go and look for him?" said Christmas.

"Because – because he's stupid!"

"Aldo can stay here and finish this off so there's someone here if he comes back. We can go and look for him. We—" Lola was crouching with her head in her hands. "We'll find him. Come on." He crouched beside her, put his hands round her shoulders and squeezed her a little. "He'll be all right. This is a tiny village. It won't take us long."

For hours they walked across San Cristóbal. They went down paths Christmas hadn't even realised were there. They appealed to everyone, Christmas entering many houses for the first time; simple, immaculate. *If this is where Columbus first arrived*, he thought, *if it was from here that the plundered riches poured for centuries, then these people have certainly been denied their share.* Their wealth was of a different order.

They searched the edges of the village and saw the two men that had fought in the nightclub – one with a badly bruised face – sharing a cigarette under a tree. They looked in abandoned corners, behind rocks, in rooms half-roofed and overgrown. They searched the old cement plant, then houses destroyed by flood and given back to the forest. They wrenched open doors fat with damp that stammered at the frame before giving way with a squeal. Huts of ragged people who shouted at Lola were peered into and rejected. The hunt went on.

Calling the old man's name, they walked into the trees and followed the river to shaded banks where the stones made seats in the water.

"Before he started smoking crack we never argued. He was a very peaceful man. Now we argue all the time. And the lying! *Verga!* Always he is lying to me!"

"Perhaps," sighed Christmas, "he just got used to it and now it's some kind of damned reflex, and even though he can see, even though he can hear himself doing it, he just can't stop and—" She crouched by the cool water to splash herself. Sunlight reached through the trees and touched her face. "My God," he whispered to himself.

They found the old man by the sea under an upturned boat, surrounded by empty bottles of Cacique, lighters and tobacco leaves. He looked like driftwood. Another man lay next to him, passed out in the shade, with a bald, pink scar that ran the length of his belly and a face so thick with drink and hardship he could no longer feel the sun. Lola's father had spent all his winnings on rum and crack and was gibbering in a half-dream about things that had been stolen from him. He wasn't surprised to see Lola. He only widened then narrowed his eyes, his gold teeth winking, weaving her presence into his mumbles. Christmas picked him up. He was as light as a child. Lola was crying.

Christmas pulled the old man's wrist around his shoulder where, once upright, he fell asleep. They took him home. People came from their stoops, inspecting, throwing jokes, shaking their heads. He slept for eighteen hours. When he woke, Lola was primed.

Christmas couldn't understand what they were shouting at each other – the Spanish was too garbled, too high-pitched – but the volume that came from such a gnarled, shrunken frame as the old man's was certainly impressive. As Lola and her father warred, Christmas took Emily's book and stepped out through the kitchen and into the yard, intending to read it in the sun. He bent himself through the hole in the wall and stood listening. He heard something be knocked over and stood there for a moment, chewing at a finger. He decided it was better to leave them alone.

He sat down on a log, opened the book and closed it again. He didn't feel like reading it. Why wasn't he searching for her beach? *I don't want to say goodbye again.* Christmas put his head in his hands. Lola was screaming.

After a moment, he got up and went inside the adobe hut. It smelt of dust and rot. Aldo was at his workbench, bent over a piece of paper.

"So," started Christmas, "how goes the tattooing?"

"Do you want a tattoo?"

"No."

"Have you come to talk about Jesus Christ?"

"What's that you're doing there?" Christmas leant over his shoulder. It was a drawing of one of the pigs. The boy was trying to unite all its previous tattoos into some kind of nativity scene. New shouts came from the house.

"You know," said the boy, "there are many problems in this village."

"There are many problems in every village."

"Corruption. Drugs. There are many drugs here. People smoking crack. Grandpa. The Jehovah's Witnesses."

"Smoking crack?"

"They don't believe in hell," Aldo sniffed.

"Very interesting design," said Christmas, tapping the paper. "Been working on it long?"

"My pastor says I must use my talent to spread God's message."

"On the pig?"

"Everything," said the boy solemnly, "belongs to God."

"How do you get it to stay still?"

"Rum and sleeping pills."

"And you think drugging a pig is part of God's message?"

"Have you come to talk about Jesus Christ?"

"Why? – Do you have some news?"

"Jesus is helping me turn my back on my wicked life."

"Oh, you're fifteen, Aldo," Christmas scoffed, "What can you have possibly done that is so bad?"

"I have told lies."

"Come on. The occasional lie isn't so—"

"I have smoked marijuana."

"And the odd joint doesn't do—"

"I have masturbated."

"Let's talk about Jesus, shall we?"

After the argument was stopped by a coughing fit, Christmas was put in charge of the old man while Aldo and Lola went to Guiria to sell their sacks of dried cacao. Christmas was not allowed to let the old man leave the house. The old man was irritable. He insulted Christmas, then begged him for money, moaned with shame, drank some hidden Cacique and fell asleep.

Christmas spent the afternoon on the porch. He made a pot of coffee. He took out Montejo again.

He must find the right beach. There were plenty about but yet ... *You came here to say goodbye.* Something didn't feel right. Was it because of his feelings for Lola? Was it because a farewell to Emily in this place now seemed wrong? Or was this Emily's final gift to him? Had her spirit led him here to find Lola? Pushing her book into the sand – that really would be it, a last goodbye. Was he ready for Emily to leave him again? To free up his heart for another?

"Just listen to yourself," he said out loud. "'*Free up your heart*'. Listen to how you're talking, you bloody fool!" He stared out into the day and realised with a tiny laugh that even though Lola had been gone only a few hours, he missed her.

He stood up and took his coffee over to the pigs. They honked and scrabbled in their pen. He laughed at himself again. He looked back at the house. Heat waves were belly-dancing off the roof. England. He didn't want to go back to England. He didn't want to go anywhere. He wanted to be with Lola. "Bloody hell, boys," he said to the pigs, "I think I'm falling in love!"

Christmas went onto the porch and finished his coffee, the extra heat swelling sweat across his back and brow. He saw the tortoise approach, jaws ready to clamp on his toe. "You scaly rogue!" he cheered. As if in answer, there was a thunder roll. A new wind thrashed the trees. The sky quickly turned dark blue and then there was rain; sudden and furious. The mountains disappeared. The rain came crashing down in volumes he had never seen before, tipped from the sky as if from a pail. The pigs squealed. Christmas went back into the house, wind slamming doors. He stood in the kitchen and watched the harrying of the yard; the bent, corrugated roof sluicing in the water. The whole area was filling like a pool, especially on the sloped side where the washing machine leant against the wall. *The motor*, he thought, *the motor is going to get flooded.*

He took off his shirt and dashed through the rain. He stood in a plastic bucket to earth himself and disconnected the plug. He pulled out the intake hose that ran from a tap and then wrestled free the outtake tube and flung it away. Grunting and swearing, he scraped the unit to the back door. He rocked one end up onto the step, straightened himself, let out a breath, spat on each hand even though they were already wet, and bent over. The water from the roof sloshed down his back. Christmas grabbed the machine and prepared to lift.

Lola was on the boat, the cash from her cacao folded and thick in her pocket. Everyone was listening to the married couple opposite. The man looked embarrassed but he was smiling. The woman was laughing so hard she could only hoot out the story in chunks.

"– and then – and then my brother – my brother left his phone in our house and – and I say to him look, my brother's left his phone and he says to me – he says –" The man folded his arms. "– he says don't worry I'll call him so –" The man was laughing too now. "so I watch him call my brother's phone, the phone that is in his hand, and he looks down at it ringing, ringing in his hand and – and I think now – now he's going to realise how stupid he's being but – but no he – he – he passes me the phone and says, 'Here baby can you answer that?'" Everyone was laughing, his wife doubled up beside him, the man shaking his head.

Lola put her fingers over the side of the boat. She looked at Aldo lying on the prow with his eyes closed. She felt the sun on her skin, the light spray of water. She picked her T-shirt off her belly, adjusted her baseball cap.

The couple were embracing now and the conversation turned to a gringo woman raped in Rio Caribe, the forthcoming elections, an actor who had just died, yet more drugs murders in Guiria. Aldo shifted his position, covering his face with his arms. Lola thought of Aldo's father, a slow-moving, tall man. A liar. Just like her father. Would Aldo follow their example, or be more like Harry? Would he offer up his seat for women, work without complaining, always ask if there was anything he could do to help? Would he make his wife laugh like this couple in front of her?

Thunder boomed. The sky changed. The captain gave control of the rudder to his son, then went underneath one of the hull's slats, pulling out a roll of plastic sheeting. The rain started. The passengers unfurled the plastic over their heads and tucked it into the sides. The boat bounced over the waves as the rain hammered the sheet, the passengers all looking at each other in their sudden blue room. It was cold. Lola winked at Aldo who had slid from the prow and was now crouched beside others on the deck.

"*Dios Mio!*" exclaimed Lola when she ran into the house with an umbrella. "The—" but she saw the washing machine, safe and in the dry. Christmas sat at the kitchen table.

"You got that?" she asked.

"Yes."

"By yourself?"

"Yes." Lola blew a long note of approval.

"*Verga* – OK, you come outside. The pigs need—"

"That won't be possible."

"What?"

"I cannot get out of this seat."

48

For the next few days Christmas was confined to the house with a bad back. He couldn't have cared less. When he was close to Lola it was as if all the points of her face were points in his mind, the configuration to a forgotten safe, something unlocking. He found himself enslaved by a constant analysis of how she was acting, if she was playful or grumpy, and whether that meant he was more or less in favour. Neither back pain nor mosquitoes meant anything to him, as long as he could dimple that face with a smile.

She fed him plates of *guayaba* fruit, toasted sweetbread with butter and eggs, fried chicken with small, sweet peppers, rice with fish and carrots and fried *cambur*. He watched her flick her hair over her shoulder. He watched her buttocks barge each other forward, her green eyes shimmer and her brown skin shine.

One evening she cooked a *cunaro* fish with rice and fried *okuma* that was stuffed with mango chutney. The smells were irresistible, full of sweetness and spice. "I think I can make it to the table for this one," called Christmas as the others sat down to eat, but his back wasn't quite ready and it trapped him halfway through the rise.

Suddenly Lola had her arms around him, squeezing him against her, the old man shouting "*Epalé!*" as his daughter picked up the Englishman and danced him to the table. Their eyes were almost touching. She plonked Christmas down. The contact was too wonderful, too unexpected. He blushed.

Christmas felt the glow overpower his face. The more he fought it the hotter it got. He stared down at his plate, inspecting its contents with the greatest interest he had shown any meal since a winter's night in Cumbria in nineteen seventy-eight had forced him and his companions to rustle and butcher a sheep. *The devil take you*, Christmas cursed himself, *are you fifty-eight or four-fucking-teen?* After a few moments, feeling the flush subside, Christmas looked up to check whether his brief new colour had gone unnoticed. Lola was staring straight at him. A skew-whiff half-smile made its début appearance on Christmas' face.

The days were clear and hot. Festival preparations were underway, the Old Testament crackheads working even harder than usual. The grass that grew in the middle of the main street was cut, the earth raked, the rubbish cleared. Bunting was strung up across the streets. A building Christmas had never seen open before was now full of children stacking palettes of beer from the back of a pick-up truck. People gathered in bigger groups, there was more playfulness, more laughter. Tents appeared on the beach, families swollen with returning sons and daughters, cousins, friends; economic exiles back from Caracas. They arrived by boat, bright suitcases wrapped in plastic, baseball caps and bikini tops, bellies, guts and make-up.

"You can't sleep," the old woman with hardly any hair warned Christmas; "there's too much noise and too many people."

"Bleurrgh," said the old man from his sofa, "It's six days of partying! Six days of drinking! Six days of dancing!"

"Not for you, old man!" the woman cackled. "You can dance with your *pipi*! That's it!"

"When the disco arrives – boooof! – all day, all night, bom-bom-bom – you better learn salsa quick, gringo." The old man leant forward and turned on the CD player for the village anthem: "*Que se acabe la plata / pero que goce yo / que se acabe el dinero/ pero mi vida noooo ...*"

"Are you from Colombia?" shouted Christmas over the music.

"What?"

"Exactly. You are not from Colombia, so I do not refer to you as Colombian. I am not from the United States, so will you please stop calling me gringo!"

"Maybe if you dance good, like a Venezuelan, the people will stop calling you gringo."

"I have a personal style, developed over a lifetime of attending awkward events. I am not about to chuck it all away because of your fascist insistence on salsa ..."

But the old man was not listening. He was clapping, "Hep! Hep! Hep! Hep!" and she was on her feet dancing, albeit in a rather minimal way.

Christmas couldn't wait for the festival. He had great hopes he could get Lola drunk. On the Sunday, with his back improved, he went for a walk and found a twenty bolívar note screwed up in the mud. It wasn't much, but Christmas took it as a definite wink from the gods. He went to the cockpit, bet the twenty and turned it into forty, then into eighty, then into one hundred and sixty.

He took his winnings and sat on the jetty wall looking out to sea. He turned the notes over and over. He had enough money to get back to Caracas, to get back to England. "The devil take you,

England!" Christmas shouted. He bought two bottles of rum for Lola, a carton of Belmont cigarettes for the old man, vegetables, chicken, pork, a dusty and forgotten bottle of ketchup, coffee, eggs, chocolate bread, frozen yoghurts, ice cream and with great pleasure he hired his crackhead friend El Perro to wheelbarrow the whole lot to Lola's house.

Aldo was in the yard, lying on a sedated pig. An extension cord ran from the house and he was holding the homemade tattoo gun with one hand, the ink pot in the other, carefully following the new nativity design that was sketched onto the animal's skin. The contraption hummed and clicked. The other pig snorted uncomfortably from its pen. The original Virgin Mary had been joined by some other figures, one of which was an enormous kidney bean baby Jesus. The wonky gothic lettering was now a shed, or perhaps a mountain. El Perro seemed disgusted by the whole project.

"So," asked Christmas, "that's the Virgin Mary, that's Christ, who's—?"

"That isn't the Virgin Mary, that's Mama. That's Grandpa, that's me."

"Who's that?"

"That's you."

49

Oscar discovered that Christmas had spent a night in Hacienda Macuro. His name was in the guest register and the owner recognised the photo. It took a few more days to locate the taxi driver who had taken him to Guiria. There the trail went cold, but it was enough information for Oscar to get Slade out of his house and away from his wife and family. He too had come to loathe and distrust the foreigner. Slade never took off those round, mirrored sunglasses. He didn't wash. He didn't have a toothbrush. He was grinning all the time. It wasn't a human grin. It was animal.

Oscar took Slade on the back of his moto-taxi to Guiria. They stopped to eat at a roadside restaurant. "Get me a beer," Slade ordered when they sat down. "A cold one."

"You paying for a guide. You want slave, it cost more *oíste, cabrón?*"

Slade didn't reply for a while, then, smirking, he said, "How much more?" The waiter arrived. They ate in silence.

"So," said Slade, "How much is he paying you?"

"Who?"

"You know. How much more are you getting for this *thing* you're doing?"

"What 'thing'?"

"Oh. Oscar. I think we both know."

"No. I do not know."

"OK, OK. I understand," said Slade, patting Oscar's shoulder then squeezing it. "This is how it's got to be, right?" Slade was grinning. "This is how he wants it."

By the time they arrived in Guiria, it was already getting dark. They found a posada up some steps above a shoe shop. While Oscar negotiated with the owner, a black cat wound figures-of-eight between Slade's ankles. There were cats everywhere.

Beyond the reception area the posada was a corridor lined with rooms. Once he had given Slade his room key and had been paid for the day, Oscar disappeared into town, desperate to get away from him. Slade went into his room and put his rucksack on his bed. He took his mobile phone out of his bag and rang Diana. His number had been blocked. He turned on the television and watched a news channel he couldn't understand.

For three days they crawled about in the heat and dust of Guiria. They went to every posada, every hotel. They showed Christmas' photo to waitresses, to *licorería* owners, to *empanada* sellers, but all they got was a crazed barefoot drunk, the hundredth person to ask Slade for money that day, who saw the photo and hopped about, biting his lip and shrieking, "He is my friend! He is my friend!"

On the fourth day Oscar rose early. He opened the door of Slade's room and told him he was going back to Cumana to check on his wife. He saw the photograph of Christmas was tacked to the ceiling above his bed. Slade raised his head from the pillow.

The next evening Oscar was back. He parked and locked up his motorbike. He walked up the stairs, shooing kids out of his way. When he got to Slade's room, he could hear talking.

Oscar opened the door. Slade didn't notice. He was alone but he had captured one of the cats. He was kneeling on the cat's body, pushing its jaw against the cement floor with the flat of his hand. With his other hand, he pressed a teaspoon to its cheek. In one move he dug in and flicked out the cat's eye. The cat made a retching sound with its throat. Oscar whispered a short prayer. Slade turned round. His knee came off the cat's chest just enough for it to squirm its body free and scrabble out of the open window, screaming, its eye hanging by the optic nerve.

"What are you?" said Oscar

"What are you?" repeated Slade, grinning widely. "What are you?"

50

On Tuesday, the first day of the festival, a huge troupe of Lola's friends came round to do their hair and nails. The crowd of adaptors hanging onto the socket in the front room doubled in size; straighteners, curlers, hair-dryers, tongs. The old man disappeared out the back but Christmas was determined to brave this dragoon, knowing that if a man can get along with a woman's friends, his stock is up.

They were all over the house, on the porch, underneath the trees, silver foil twisted into their hair, shoulders covered with towels beside brushes and paint and combs and jugs of hot water. The stereo was on full blast: "*Que se acabe la plata / pero que goce yo / que se acabe el dinero/ pero mi vida no.*" Christmas bounced between the groups, keeping the Cuba Libres flowing, sipping only Coke himself, summoning all his charm; he complimented, he joked, he took impromptu salsa classes, he let himself be laughed at. Lola began to get tipsy. Then, as night fell and Christmas was arguing with two women who were determined to paint his nails, a great cry went up.

A man appeared through the *cambur*, a bit younger than Christmas, wearing a silk shirt and pressed cotton trousers. He looked as if he had spent his youth in a band. He was tanned and groomed, with broad shoulders and a big smile. He did not have a moustache. Lola got up and flung her arms around him. Christmas felt something hot slithering around in his stomach. The women readjusted themselves in the newcomer's presence. They bade him sit and gave him a drink. Lola was acting like a little girl, giggling, rolling her eyes, making high-pitched noises. They beckoned Christmas over. He shook the hand of the man, who immediately said something Christmas didn't understand. Everybody laughed. The man went on talking as if Christmas wasn't there. Christmas looked around but there were no free seats. He stepped back from the group and leant against the tree, listening. The man was back from Caracas. The man was working as such-and-such. The man was doing so-and-so. *Ponce* thought Christmas, *Bloody spic ponce.* Unwilling to count himself as part of this man's fan club, he sauntered off to the house.

"Hey, gringo!" Lola shouted. "Get some more ice!" She watched him go. Her friends started elbowing her, and telling the man the whole Harry Christmas story. She laughed and pushed back. Wasn't the gringo handsome now that he had a tan? Those blue eyes? Couldn't she tell how crazy he was about her? It was festival time – wasn't she going to do anything about it? Lola stood up and winked at her friends. They gave back a cheer.

Inside Christmas paced about, snatching glimpses through the door, listening to the jollity. Who the devil was this man? Why the devil was he here? He opened the fridge door, breathed, shut it again, opened it, shut it.

"Is there a problem with the door?" Lola was standing right by him.

"Yes. Fixed now." He opened it again. "See?"

"*Gracias*," she said, and kissed him on the cheek. Christmas was stunned. Lola was smiling. It was a drunken, full-beam, lazy-eyed smile.

"Who's that?" said Christmas, pouting toward the man.

"Old friend," she said. "His daughter is my god-daughter. He is from—" She pouted upwards. Guiria.

"Ah." There was silence. Her green eyes were getting lazier, her hair newly-curled, flecks of potato chip on her chin.

"Are you jealous?" Lola raised her eyebrows. She looked cheeky as the devil. She put her hand on his arm.

In every cell of his being, in every body and anti-body, in all the streams of plasma and in every worm hole of his wooden heart, Christmas recognised this moment. This was the kiss that he had been waiting for. But he was panicking. *Emily?* he called out, *Can I do this? Is this OK?*

Lola waited.

Still he did nothing, blinking, reddening, paralyzed as in dreams.

Aldo walked in. Lola folded her arms. Her eyes no longer looked lazy. Now she looked cross.

"Hey gringo, when are you going to let us do your hair?" another woman came in from outside. Lola sucked her teeth and took some ice from the fridge. Then she was gone.

What the fuck was that? Christmas railed at himself. *What the fuck is wrong with you, you bloody moron!*

Shaking with self-disgust, Christmas stumbled out the back door and into the yard. If it was any other woman, he thought, any of the ones he didn't really care about, he would be kissing her by the fridge right now. There was the old man. Christmas needed to smoke a cigarette.

"What's the matter with you?" said the old man.

"Do you have a cigarette?"

"I have a Russian."

"Fine." The old man passed him a hand-rolled cigarette made out of exercise book paper. It was about as far from a Sobrani as you could get, but Christmas didn't care. He lit it, inhaled, noted its strange odour, felt a numbing of the lips, a spangled exhilaration, thought *this isn't a cigarette*, and exhaled as Lola filled the doorway. She sniffed.

"*Mama guevo!*" she bayed, "You smoking crack! You smoking crack with my father!"

"Wait – no – Lola, I thought it was a cigarette. You said it was a cigarette!"

"I said it was a Russian," shrugged the old man, "marijuana and crack. Here it's called 'a Russian'."

"But—"

Lola stormed over and cuffed Christmas across the head. The old man started shouting but it was no good. She grabbed Christmas by the collar and pulled him towards the house.

"Get off me, woman! This is a mistake, will you just let me—"

"Get out of my house! *Hijo de puta*! Out!" She shoved him through the house, sending the tortoise spinning off into a corner, out into the group of silenced friends, past the man, to the dark edge of the *cambur*, shouting and struggling all the way.

"Go, gringo, enough! *Hijo de puta!*"

"Will you shut up and listen!"

"Go! Get away from me!"

"But—"

"Go!" She picked up an axe handle.

"Bleurrgh," said Christmas finally, and off he maundered into the village, swearing and shaking his head.

51

"UN-FUCKING-BELIEVABLE!" Christmas shouted up at the night and then sat down on a tree stump in despair. Men wandered about gripping bottles of Cacique, *Vallenato* music blaring from every house. People tried to talk to him but he waved them away. He walked down to the sea. He walked into the boat-yard, lay down in the hull of an unfinished boat and thought about his life. He got up and walked to the end of the jetty. He sat down on the jetty for a while. He got up and walked towards the village. He walked past the library. The door was open. It was a small room being cleaned by two women. There was a hole in the roof and the books were being taken from the shelves and piled up on the floor. Some were rotten, others curtseying from the damp.

Christmas wandered through into the *infocentro*. This room was pristine and air-conditioned, with rows of white computers. Christmas nodded at the people he recognised and sat down at an available screen. He typed 'Harry Strong' into Google. Up came a list of reviews for *When the Naa Tree Sings* and *Peabody's Boat*. He clicked on a thumbnail. The real Harry Strong looked like a celebrity plastic surgeon. He had a long, tanned face and floppy, perfect hair. Then he typed in 'What am I going to do?' The search engine referred him to an article subdivided into headings: 'What does success mean to me?' 'What are my non-negotiable needs?' and 'What are my non-negotiable boundaries?'

Outside, Christmas sought somewhere to lie down. He found a section of quayside wall hidden behind a tree. He filled his nose with the soft vegetable smell of the sea and closed his eyes to its lapping. The wall was only just wide enough. He crossed his ankles. *I could turn round and fall in,* he thought, *just roll off and away.*

"Gringo!" Lola Rosa was standing by his feet. She had some of the food he had bought, including the last bottle of rum, and his jacket. Christmas sat up. Lola dumped everything onto the ground, eyes wide with anger. "This is all your things. I don't want them in my house! Now you can leave San Cristóbal! Now you can go!" Christmas said nothing. He was the most tired he'd ever felt. He picked up the rum and thought *fuck it.* He opened the bottle.

"Huh!" snorted Lola and off she stormed into the darkness. Christmas took a long deep swig. He gasped, wiping his mouth. "*Verga!*" he cursed. Then he ran after her.

"Now listen here!" he said, grabbing Lola by the arm and swinging her round. She raised her hand to hit him.

"Let go of me, gringo!"

"If you listen! Jesus Christ, woman! You've done all the talking and all the shouting as per usual but now it's my turn so will you just listen? I never asked to come here. It was a mistake, OK? I just ended up here and you were here and that was a great bloody surprise and you and your father took me in and looked after me and I am very, very, *very* grateful for that. I was sticking around just until I could make a contribution and I know you didn't want me here and I've tried to do my bit while I sorted myself out – in a small way, I know – but I've tried. And don't worry, don't you worry –

you will never have to see me again, OK? And, as that's the case, I'll tell you this, and damn you, woman, you better listen because it's the last thing you will ever hear me say, but I just wanted you to know that – that—"

"That what?"

"That ..." he looked at the rum bottle "... that when I finally had one bloody bolívar in my pocket, all I wanted to do was buy something for you; all I wanted to do was give you something," and he shoved the bottle at her like a dare, "and the truth is, in the kitchen just then, I thought we were going to, you know – but – but I didn't and I don't know why, but – OK – I'm a *coward*, that's why – and so I went outside feeling bloody awful and I asked your father for a cigarette because I felt so bloody stupid and he gave me one with crack in it and I had no idea, OK? No idea at all. So you're kicking me out and that's fine. I know I have been hanging around like a fat old baboon and well, I deserve it, in general that is, but though you are absolutely right about me – I *am* an *hijo de puta* – you are wrong about that, OK? You are not right about that. I didn't know. You ask him. That's the fucking truth!" Lola yanked free her arm. "One drink, we'll say goodbye, that's it. I'm leaving." He shoved the bottle at her again. She snatched it, took a swig and shoved it back. "I'm telling the truth. I did not know that cigarette had crack it it," he repeated, taking a swig, returning the rum. She drank again, thrust it back. So it went on for several exchanges.

"It's the truth," he said again, towards the end of the bottle.

"OK," said Lola, gasping and wiping her chin. "I believe you."

"And there's something else."

"What?"

"I—" They heard shouts a little way off. Lola started walking towards them. Christmas finished the bottle, left it on the wall, picked up his jacket and followed her into a stampede running back towards the jetty.

The sound system for the fiesta had arrived. Lola and Harry were borne along by the crowd, the boat coming out of the night as if carrying a slain giant, a great form wrapped in plastic. The crowd leant over the quayside. Lola put a hand on his shoulder so she could see better. Once the engines were cut and the boat was pulled into position, the plastic was pulled back and men lifted boxes of wires and speakers onto their shoulders, through the water and onto the back of a pick-up truck. By the time the boat was empty, the Cacique had taken effect: Harry and Lola were plastered.

They meandered towards home up and then off the main streets, into the narrow pathways and the dark. Lola walked in front. He reached out and touched her fingers. She did not flinch but stopped and turned round. They were facing each other. There were crickets and moon shadow and the spinning mischief of the earth.

"Can I kiss you?"

"Stupid," she said, "Well. Yes."

He kissed her. She was full in his arms. They went back to the house, stopping and kissing all the way. She led him into her room and they made fierce, sweltering love. He was astonished throughout. They fell asleep. She started snoring.

52

It was an ugly music. Trolls in angry congress. Someone trying to drive pigs over a bridge. Christmas tried whispering, talking, shouting, rolling her over. Nothing worked for long. He woke up with his arm on her face, his finger and thumb resting either side of her nose ready for the pinch. It was early, the disco already booming *Vallenato* across the village. Even though it was a ten-minute walk to the Plaza Bolivar from Lola's house the music arrived loud and clear through the wall: "*Que se acabe la plata / pero que goce yo / que se acabe el dinero/ pero mi vida no ...*"

Christmas got up and walked into the kitchen. There was a man sparked out on his bed in the front room. The man woke up, looked about him, said "*Verrrrrga ...*" and then wandered out the door. The old man was asleep in a chair on the porch. Christmas inhaled. The morning burst across his soul. He released a bottle of Cacique from the old man's fingers and battled his hangover, fire with fire.

Harry, in the most tremendous of moods, spent the day with Lola drinking, eating and making love. The streets smelt of barbeque and marijuana. The disco never stopped. As afternoons became evening, crowds moved onto the plaza, couples in flip-flops dancing almost motionless salsa, then soca, then *Vallenato*, then calypso.

Everyone knew what had happened between Lola and Harry. They had to field nudges, slaps on the back, winks, jiggling eyebrows and even outright applause. The '*Epalé*' count broke all previous records. The camp bed was put away. Aldo affected indifference. The old man was overjoyed.

On a trip back to the house, Christmas came across him sitting with a couple of ancient comrades underneath a *neem* tree. Both these men were without teeth. One wore a red T-shirt '*Con Chávez Podemos!*' and the other a battered Arsenal top. He could tell by their deranged sparkly faces that they were also geriatric crackheads.

"*Epalé!* Here he is! *Verga* – my gringo son-in-law! Now you can call me Papa!"

"No thanks."

"So now you are –" the old man made a circle with one hand and an obscene gesture with his finger, "– you don't tell her about our agreement, OK? What are they saying, your bank? You get money after the festival?"

"After the festival. Exactly."

"Promise?"

"Promise."

"Very good! Very good!"

The festivities rolled on. They went to another beach with a group of Lola's friends, waking early and making love before opening their eyes. They walked down to the jetty holding hands, pink popcorn clouds exploding in the dawn sky. They climbed into the boat full of people and supplies, the waves black beneath the sun, scudding past cliffs sunk to their brows in jungle, cloud-cast shadow moving in slow fleet across the mountains. They found a beach fringed by palm trees and grass, unloaded their picnic and drank cold beers, splashing and pushing each other in the water.

Christmas, lying in the shade, watched Lola in her swimming costume trot into the waves. *What a wobbly bottom*, he thought, *I love that wobbly bottom*. Yet there was something too bright in the sunlight, a film of unreality over everything. He couldn't accept it. He didn't deserve it.

Then she was again beside him on the towel; wet, black, covered in sea-diamonds. One of the men came over from the icebox and handed them new beers. Lola twisted the cap off and closed her eyes against the cold on her tongue.

"By the way," she said, "you don't have to use the outside toilet any more. You can come inside."

"Oh, thank you, your majesty. Permission to—" he grabbed her as she squealed, rolling in the sand, cheers ringing out from the rest of their party, fallen beer turning to slugs. They stayed all day, grilling fish on the fire and waiting for sunset. When it came, they sang songs. They drank Cacique and lay beneath the darkening sky. On the way back the shoreline glittered with fireflies.

As they rounded the headland, they heard the disco resounding across the bay, a soca version of 'Hotel California'. Christmas held Lola to his chest.

"Where do your eyes come from? Did your mother have green eyes?"

"No. Maybe the Indian side. Or maybe my great-grandfather."

"Who was he?"

"He was French."

"French!"

"Yes. Why are you looking at me like that?"

"*Vive La France!*" cheered Christmas, before breaking into 'La Marseillaise' as the boat bounced across the waves and a triumphant ocean spat in his face.

On Friday the *Vallenato* band from Colombia arrived. The women of the village seemed very excited by the presence of its tubby young singer and, once again Lola's house became a beauty parlour. Aldo had finished tattooing the pig, and he brought it out of the sty to be admired. Christmas was in the front room. Lola and a friend were holding up a hand mirror and insulting him.

"Rubbish!" he said, smoothing down his kelp. "I've got a fine head of hair." It looked as if someone had dumped a child's wig on him the wrong way round.

"Then what about we cut your moustache – chop – or your eyebrows, baby, mnnn? They look like rats. If we don't cut them maybe they are going to shit in your eyes."

"Keep your blades away from my locks—" There was a crack from the other side of the room. The wall socket, overloaded with plugs, burst into flames and fizzled with electrical charge. The women leapt back. Christmas grabbed a broom handle and attempted to knock the socket off the wall. The plugs fell but it refused to budge. The flames rose higher. He pushed past the children who had run in when others ran out, looking outside to see where the wire left the building and looped through the trees to a small pylon. When he went back inside he saw Aldo about to stab into the socket with a carving knife. "No!" he bellowed, lunging through the crowd and snatching at his wrist just before the blade made contact. Christmas grabbed a chair, took it outside and stood on it, stretching for the cable first with his fingers, then, once in his hand, yanking it free of the mains supply. He could hear the crackle of electricity stop instantly. He went back inside.

Lola was holding Aldo in one hand and the knife in the other, her face a blend of terror and relief. "You don't stick something metal into a socket," Christmas told the boy, "or you will turn into a hotdog."

"You saved his life," Lola whispered. She had tears in her eyes. She covered Aldo in kisses. "He could have died."

"Well," replied Christmas, savouring his new hero status, "I have had some experience with electrics." Lola pulled Christmas towards her, embracing him with her son, muttering a prayer before taking off the gold chain she was wearing. She put it around Christmas' neck.

"Wait, no – no, Lola."

"You saved my son's life."

"This is ridiculous, I only—"

"You saved his life. Keep it."

"No, Lola, this is gold—"

"Take it. I want you to have it."

"Lola, for God's sake, I'm the one who should be giving you necklaces to repay you for all the—"

"Please, Harry. I want you to have it."

"Lola, listen to me, this is worth a lot of money. There is absolutely no way I can, or will, accept it. You've already done too much for me." He tried to take if off but she stopped him.

"I don't care how much it is worth. You saved Aldo's life. I want you to have it, Harry."

"No, Lola, please, it's too much—" She held his face and kissed him. He could taste the salt of her tears.

"Lola—"

"Thank you," she whispered, her eyes closed. "Thank you, Oh God, for sending this man into my life to save my son."

The plaza was crammed full for the band. There was a hamburger trolley, a blue wooden popcorn cart, racks of handicraft jewellery

297

and inflatable toys. Rockets screamed into the night sky, strings of bangers popped and smoked. Adults drank beer, rum and whisky. Teenagers drank anis.

Christmas and Lola were seated on plastic chairs beside the dance floor, eating *empanadas* from the teenage mother's stall; a pot of oil bubbling on top of a gas burner, the semi-circles of corn dough filled with fish or meat fizzing golden. They ate one after another, squeezing *guasacaca* sauce all over them – puréed avocado mixed with onion and coriander – chomping and wiping their chins. Lola was all in white, heels, tight trousers, tight top, nails painted, hair done up high. Christmas, in a clean shirt with his hair cut, fiddled with the chain. It felt like a medal. A line of men walked past, shook Christmas' hand and gave him the thumbs up.

"Who were they?"

"The ones who tied you upside down to a tree."

"When are you two going to dance?" asked the teenage mother. A bottle smashed. The ingredients of a fight dissolved into nothing.

"He can't dance."

"How do you know?"

"He tried before and he can't do it."

"Lies!"

"You can't dance to this music. If you could dance, we would be dancing, no?" *The devil take this woman*, he thought. *She knows just how to manipulate me.* For the first time that day, Christmas thought of Emily. He sat up, shocked. Never had he gone a day without thinking about her. He looked at Lola. She smiled, and her Caribbean beauty hit him almost like pain.

"Look at you – too frightened to dance, old man. *Verga!* You're chick-en-shit."

"Oh, really?"

"*Si, Señor,*" Lola leant back on her chair and gave a little burp. "Chickenshit." Christmas looked at the band. "He won't do it," she said to the teenage mother. "He's a pussyman."

"Oh, I am, am I?"

"Pussyman."

"You're sure about that?"

"Chick-en-shit-puss-y-man." Christmas got to his feet. The teenage mother burst out laughing. He was off. He had no idea what he was going to do. Even before he got to the dance floor people were watching. Couples on the perimeter saw him approach and made a gap. The gap became a space. The singer noticed what was happening and sang with arms outstretched in special welcome for the foreigner. The entire village was looking on.

Stepping over the edge of the dance floor his dread was so basic, so complete, that it permitted only one thought: whatever was about to happen was best done with his eyes closed. So, like someone searching for a light switch, Harry entered the circle. He felt the music and the crowd around him. He put his hands on his hips, tapped a foot and then ... he felt a hand on his, an arm at his waist and he opened his eyes. "I thought I better save you," Lola said, and there they were, swaying together in a tiny, crooked circle.

"You know, Lola," he whispered, "I badly want to make love to you."

"Badly?" she pouted. "I would prefer if you did it well."

53

With Oscar gone, Slade was alone in Guiria. It was the middle of the night. He lay on the bed of his hotel room, listening to laughter outside. He couldn't understand the voices but he was sure they were talking about him. A door closed. The voices stopped.

Slade went back to concentrating on the filaments of light shed by the curtain. He had been that way for hours.

"Can I book an appointment?" someone said. Slade sat up. "Our office wants to go paintballing." There was no one else in the room. He peered over the side of the bed. There was The General, sitting on its back legs with its eye hanging out.

"You're fucked. I know you. Oh boo-hoo," said The General, "I hate you too. *Be quiet, William.*"

Slade turned around in his bed. His heart was beating so hard his pillow sounded like a drum.

He stayed in his room all the next day. He left when it was dark. It was Friday. Across the other side of the plaza were neon lights he hadn't seen before. The karaoke bar was open for the weekend.

The barman recognised the photo of Harry Christmas though he spoke no English. Slade tapped the image until another man was brought forward who could muster a hesitant pidgin. Christmas had been here. He was very drunk. He was singing, then they threw him out. He went to San Cristóbal and the villagers tied him to a tree by his leg. Yes, he was still in San Cristóbal. He was living with a woman there.

Slade went back to his hotel room. He stuck the photograph onto the wall. He lay down on the bed and looked over at Christmas. Slade held the dive knife with both hands, the blade flat against his chest, a Saxon funeral pose. With a cry, he lept up and stabbed the photograph. Then he took the knife in one hand and pushed the point of it against his forearm. It quivered against the skin before splitting it, Slade holding up his arm so the blood ran to his armpit.

He lurked in his room until dawn. When the sun came up he had an uncontrollable fit of crying. He checked out of the posada and was directed to the pier. The boat left at three in the afternoon. He sat down in a café and tried to eat but he could not.

The Saturday boat was already full when Slade eventually picked his way over luggage and loud families, and settled himself against the prow. Everyone was in fiesta mood, bottles of Cacique passing back and forth, people greeting the foreigner with a cheer. Two ladies shifted to make a place for him and then pulled faces at each other when Slade ignored their kindness. He stared straight down into the hull. It was a deep, open boat with slats for benches that covered the bags and supplies crammed in below. A child started the engine while his father let loose the rope. They pushed off from Guiria's quayside. It was two hours to San Cristóbal.

Slade felt sick from the motion. The smell of gasoline was intense. He looked around the boat. They were all talking about him.

"Boo-hoo," said a voice. He looked down. The General was curled up on some luggage, staring up at him between the slats, his eye hanging out. Slade slipped off his seat to boot him but The General was gone. He sat back. People were saying things to him in Spanish.

That morning Christmas woke with a hangover. It was still dark. His body felt like someone else's, his mouth a dead fire. The last thing he could remember was Lola sitting on his lap, boxes of expensive whisky being passed around, and him saying, "This stuff doesn't affect me." He put an arm round Lola. She took it, kissed it, then wore his elbow as a beard. Christmas fell back to sleep.

When he woke again she was gone. It was dawn. He slaked his thirst at the sink, his legs weak, a podgy colt staggering out into the yard's early light. Lola was wearing an apron. There was a table set out in the front of the porch with a cast-iron hand-operated mill clamped to one end. Lola dropped in handfuls of toasted cacao seeds, turning the handle. The rifled screw cracked and demolished them against a circular plate. Its rim oozed rich chocolate paste into a container below.

"*Epalé! Cariño!*" she said, "How do you feel?"

"I feel like my stomach is trying to process a square shit – why are you laughing?"

"Let me see, let me see," Aldo pushed past him in the doorway, examining his face.

"Turn around, turn around," ordered the old man, shuffling across the yard. Christmas turned round. "*Verga!*" The old man started laughing too. Christmas went to check himself in the bathroom mirror. His moustache was gone.

"The devil take you, woman!" he thundered, stomping back outside, "You've shaved off my – my – my –"

"Harry—"

"Butcher! Delilah!"

"What's he saying?" asked Aldo.

"He's very happy."

Christmas frantically exercised his naked lip. "How dare you!"

Lola wiped her hands of chocolate, grabbed his face and kissed him. "You look much better, *Papi*. Much younger."

"Younger?"

"Try this."

"What is it?"

"Rum with cacao."

"But dammit, woman, there's a principle here and that principle is, 'Thou shalt not bloody shave a man's whiskers when—'"

"But you look *much* more handsome."

"That's not the issue! Do I?"

"Much. Drink that."

"You can't just assault me and then wind me round your little finger just by saying – oh, that's good. That *is* good. That is very good indeed." The taste made his eyes water; dark oils, forest butters, hidden wells of rum.

"Now you do this and I'll cook you breakfast." She put the apron on him and went inside.

"Helpless," Christmas muttered to himself. "Putty in her hands."

There had been a storm during the night and all the talk was of the damage done. After breakfast Lola and Harry walked round to see metal roofs torn open or tossed out into the street. Some trees were down, fencing blown over.

People in red T-shirts and red caps were taking measurements and discussing repairs with the villagers. They were from PDVSA, the state petrol company, and they had come to rebuild the roofs and survey the village to see what else it needed.

"See?" said Lola, pushing him. "This is Chávez. The storm was yesterday and they come today to help us."

There was also a policeman, who observed the foreigner with distaste. He was a short man with a pronounced double chin who considered it his professional duty to harass gringos. Overseeing the PDVSA officials was a rather boring job, so it was with great relish that he stepped in Christmas' path and folded his arms.

"Who are you? Why are you here? What is your name?" Christmas squinted at this new event.

"I am Christmas," he answered in English, "thy boon companion," and delivered the policeman a courtly bow. The policeman asserted his authority with a single word: "*Pasaporte.*"

"Leave him alone," said Lola.

"Where are you staying?"

"With me." Lola squared up to the policeman. She looked him up and down. He wasn't from San Cristóbal.

"Do you have a licence to run a posada?"

"He is not my guest. He is ... my lover!"

"This gringo?"

"That's right."

"You don't like Venezuelan men?"

"Me? Yes – why, do you?"

"Where is his passport? Where is your passport, gringo?"

"Why don't you leave us alone? It's festival time!" The policeman cast a look out to sea.

"If your gringo lover cannot produce his passport, I will arrest him."

When they rounded the bay Slade heard the deep thump of reggaeton. He saw the quayside and jetty thick with revellers. His

304

vision was pulsating. He took off his sunglasses, cleaned them, put them back on. The other passengers started waving. He stood up and scanned for a white man. Crackheads and children waited on the jetty with wheelbarrows to carry luggage and supplies. Slade stepped off the boat and up the concrete steps into a plague of offers. He kept his eyes on the village. It was five in the afternoon.

Slade took out the photograph. A shout went up and a crowd formed. "*Amigo*?" they asked him. Slade tapped his chest.

"Me. *Amigo*. Where? Where is he? This man?" The crowd assigned him a small boy. Slade, his rucksack slung over his shoulder, followed the child off the jetty and into San Cristóbal. Music pounded the village with his heartbeat. Unbearable smells flew into his nose. Everything had an echo.

Slade scanned every doorway, every face. Gangs of people cheered and toasted him as he walked past. The little boy shouted things and Slade understood the words *gringo* and *amigo*. People patted him on the back and offered him rum. Slade walked through a football match. He walked past a great mass of dancers. He followed the boy down a quieter street, then through some bushes to a stream strewn with rubbish. They followed the stream for a while until they came out through a grove of cambur and into Lola's yard.

"He's here? In here?"

"This woman's—" the boy replied, and he made an obscene gesture with his fingers. The boy ran inside. Slade followed. He was sweating.

Lola wiped her hands on a dishcloth. "You friend of Harry?" Slade felt for his knife.

"Where is he?"

"He back soon." Lola looked at the clock. It was quarter past five. She said something to the boy and he ran out. Slade looked at her tits.

"So you're his girlfriend?"

"Yes," she shrugged, smiling, "I guess." Slade dropped his rucksack.

"Good."

54

Though terrified by the overtaking, there was something magical about swooshing from curve to curve on the back of a motorbike, moisture leaking sideways from his eyes as if he were crying in space. Yet his enjoyment of the ride was only momentary. Christmas was heading back to Judith and Bridget's. He didn't expect they would be pleased to see him.

Christmas told the policeman that his passport was in Rio Caribe. After a long argument, he was given until the end of the day to produce it. Should he disappear, he was assured, the consequences for Lola would be severe.

Gabriel, one of his fisherman friends, offered to take him there on the back of a motorbike that he kept in Guiria. Christmas had no choice. If he was arrested, only money could free him, and he had no money. It was still early in the morning.

"If I leave now," he told Lola, kissing her, "I should be back by four – five at the latest."

With Bridget's wallet in his pocket, they took Gabriel's high-speed boat and were in Guiria by ten o'clock. They crossed the peninsula on a Yamaha. Christmas' mind raced with scenarios. If Judith and Bridget still thought he was Harry Strong he veered towards elaborate lies, stories of misfortune – kidnap? – no – ridiculous – it was best to confess everything, to unmask himself, ask for the passport and weather yet another of life's ugly confrontations. He simply had to get through it, however furious they were.

Cacti raised their stumps in supplication. Boys cut bundles of grass for donkey feed. Perhaps he'd be lucky – perhaps they'd be out. He could break in, nip upstairs, grab his passport from behind the wardrobe and disappear.

They zoomed through Rio Caribe. It was midday. Christmas' arms ached from holding onto the rear grill. They arrived at the turning to Judith's and, just in case he might witness something that was difficult to explain, he told Gabriel to wait there on the side of the road. Christmas began to climb the winding drive.

As he reached the top, nervous and panting, Christmas saw Judith's car. He hesitated. He ran his fingers over the chain around his neck. *Up on two legs, man!* he ordered himself. *In you go. Just got to take it on the chin.*

He advanced towards the house. There was something different about the garden. He moved further round. It was untended. The grass had been allowed to grow long. It was hot but the sprinklers weren't on. There were weeds in the flowerbeds.

Christmas went closer to the house and looked in through the window. The shelves were empty. There were packing boxes everywhere. He continued along the wall until he got to the kitchen. There were black smoke stains around the window. He cupped his hands and peered in. There had been a fire.

"Hello?" he said. "Hello?" He walked right the way around the house, looking in, seeing more boxes, empty walls, furniture stacked up. "Judith? Bridget?"

He turned a corner and saw a black girl, nine or ten years old. She was barefoot, wearing an oversized jacket and covering her mouth with her hand.

"Judith? Bridget?" he asked her. "The English women? Where are they? Are they home? Are they moving out?" She didn't say anything. He moved towards her but she ran off into the trees.

Christmas had come right the way around the house. He knocked on the front door. Nothing. His heart leapt at the possibility of getting his passport before they appeared. He tried the door. Locked. What about the kitchen door? He went back into the garden to check and there was Judith, wandering back from the ocean.

She saw him. She stopped. Then she bent down to inspect some pink orchids.

"Judith," he called but she didn't respond. He walked over to her, saying her name, but she didn't move. When he was in front of her, she stood up and walked past him as if he wasn't there. She looked terrible, pale and aged, her hair unwashed. *I've broken her heart*, thought Christmas.

"I know I ran off," he said, standing behind her now as she pulled down the blossom of a tree towards her, "and I'm not the person you thought I was but – and I know you will find this very hard to believe – there is an explanation for all of it and, well, I really don't know where to begin with this most profound of apologies—"

"I'm saying goodbye to my garden," she said quietly, turning to face him. "Do you know what he said?"

"Who?"

"He said, '*So he's a friend of yours.*'"

"I'm sorry, what?"

"'*So he's a friend of yours.*' Those were his exact words."

"Whose?"

"Before he raped her. That's what he said. Right before he raped Bridget."

Christmas took in the words, and as he began to comprehend them, his hands moved up to his face.

"He came here looking for you," she continued. "He came to our house and he raped my daughter, there, in my kitchen, on my birthday, while I was upstairs crying about you." Judith looked him over as he reacted.

"She's in London now," she said after a long silence, "She's only just started talking again. She's in a place where they help people who have been through … She's got her own room." Christmas tried to speak. He failed. "I have come back to shut the house. Who is he?" Christmas felt as if he were watching all this from afar, as if it were being told to another him. "Who is he?" she said again. Her eyes were blank.

"William Slade, he's – Judith, I—"

"No," she said. "Don't."

They stood apart from each other for a few moments.

"You have come back for your passport," she said. "I just found it. It's inside, on the kitchen table. There's a pad and pen there, on the windowsill. Write down his name and everything for the police and then just get out, whatever you are, just go away." Judith turned back towards the ocean. He watched her go. He watched her until she disappeared, then he went into the house. His hands were in his hair. His hands were on his face.

Inside he saw his passport on the kitchen table. He put it in his pocket and, finding Bridget's wallet there, he took it out and put it down on the windowsill. It fell open. There was the photograph of Judith and Bridget, their arms round each other, creased, behind plastic. He scribbled down Slade's name and Diana's name and her telephone number and he left the house, heading down the drive until the hacienda was no longer visible and his knees gave way

310

and he sat down in the dirt. He ground his fists together against his forehead and made a tight, low sound. *Bridget …*

How had Slade found Judith's? Easy. Of course it was easy! He'd just asked someone, anyone in Rio Caribe where the fat gringo was staying. How could he not have foreseen that? Why hadn't he come back here and protected them? Why hadn't he just let himself get caught – his mind rolled: if Slade could track him to Judith's, he could track him to San Cristóbal.

Lola.

55

Gabriel had no phone. They borrowed one from a man selling bananas on the roadside.

"What's her number?"

"I don't know," shrugged Gabriel. "Don't you?"

"No! Give me someone else's number then – anyone's!"

"I told you, brother. I don't have a phone. I don't know no numbers."

When they arrived at the jetty in Guiria, Christmas leapt from the bike before it had stopped and he ran amongst the men there, asking them if they had seen a gringo get on any of the boats to San Cristóbal? They said they had. What did he look like? One man hunched his shoulders and blew out his cheeks.

They jumped into Gabriel's boat and zoomed out across the sea. Christmas, unable to sit still, looked out over the waves, fidgeting with the chain as the boat hurdled the spume and birds flew overhead. Gabriel asked him many times what was wrong but Christmas could hardly speak, only able to repeat that Lola was in danger. He bit his knuckles, swearing continuously. The journey was endless.

When, at last, the boat thudded around the headland and San Cristóbal came into view, Christmas got to his feet, clambering to the front.

He vaulted the gap onto the concrete steps before the line had been thrown and ran into the festival, Gabriel close beside him.

Something terrible had happened.

People, their eyes wide in shock, were running up to him, gabbling, throwing their arms towards the house.

He was down the street. Over the stream. Through the *cambur*.

Christmas broke out into the clearing.

A crowd in front of the house.

He pushed through into the doorway. Pictures lay broken, furniture pushed into awkward angles. Smashed pots littered the kitchen floor, plates and pans scattered everywhere.

Emily's book, torn to pieces, and by the door to Lola's room – a hatchet covered in blood.

"Lola—" he cried, dashing out into the yard where he could see more people: the policeman, the old lady, and more neighbours standing around something on the floor.

Christmas pulled away the shoulders and looked down.

Once Slade had put his rucksack down he began to wander around the room, sizing it up as if he were to buy it. Lola knew right away that his intentions were bad.

"Christmas!" he called out. He saw Christmas' jacket hanging on the nail. "This is his," he said, searching it. "Stole my mother's money." He found the Montejo book. "Where is he?"

She didn't answer. Slade was grinning. He ripped the book in half, then tore out fistfuls of pages and threw them into the air. Slade took out the knife. He pointed it at her, watching the fear widen her face.

He came closer. He stopped.

He looked down and said something to the floor.

Just by looking at his face, those mirrored sunglasses, Lola knew he was insane. She saw this moment as something she had seen many times before: sudden, unpredictable – a moment of violence. It would end as quickly as it started, with only the outcome undecided. But she, Lola Rosa, had decided.

No one came into her house and threatened her with a knife. Not the biggest gangster in Caracas. Not God himself.

As this man talked to whatever evil spirit was by his feet, Lola took a step backwards into the kitchen and wrapped her hand around a heavy carving knife sticking out of its wooden stand.

"*Mama guevo!*" she cried, lunging at him, swinging the knife down in a great arc. Slade had only time to raise his right forearm in defence, the blade slicing into it, chipping bone.

He screamed. His right hand dropped the knife. He drove his left fist into Lola's face. She fell backwards, letting go of her weapon while Slade glanced at his arm – blood – but Lola was coming at him again, with her whole body this time, charging him against the chairs and the television.

They hit the wall.

Slade kneed her in the stomach. She grabbed his face, screaming, gripping his eye and cheek, digging in her long nails.

He punched her again in the head but the blow didn't shift her and she hung onto him as they swung and crashed forward, bouncing and rolling off the walls, dislodging pictures and ornaments, staggering back into the kitchen, Lola squeezing him close so he couldn't hit her. They slammed against kitchen shelves, glasses and pans clattering and smashing on the floor as she sank her teeth into his neck and bit down like a wolf. Slade let out the howl.

He grabbed her hair, wrenching her off him, and he elbowed her in the face. Her grip loosened.

He pinned her to the wall by her throat, breathing heavily.

He ripped at her T-shirt, exposing her breasts. She was concussed. He spun her round, bent her over the sideboard, and ripped down the velour tracksuit bottoms she was wearing. He looked down at her backside. She was moaning, semi-conscious. His blood was dripping on her buttocks.

The little boy that had shown Slade to the house was sitting under a tree, unwrapping a sweet. It was a present from the old man for delivering a message: they had a new guest and Lola wanted him to come home. The old man patted him on the head, bidding goodbye to his friends and shuffled off down the path.

Moving carefully down the bank, muttering to himself, the old man thought about crack. His friend El Mono owed him a rock and he intended to go round there later and reclaim the debt. It was easier to smoke there. No Lola swearing in his face and interrupting his high with her bullshit.

He shuffled along the stream, through the *cambur* and out into the clearing. There was his fighting cock. As ever, he smiled at the animal with pride. He bent down, undid the tethering and held the bird to his chest, whispering messages of love and encouragement. Then he heard a loud noise from inside. Then another. Then he heard his daughter scream.

Still with the bird under his arm, the old man picked up a hatchet sticking out of a lump of wood. He hobbled quickly up the steps. When he got to the doorway he saw his house turned over and a white man about to rape his daughter.

Slade, taking out his penis, heard something behind him. He turned. A cockerel was flung into his face. He was batting away this squawking mass of feathers when he felt the deep bite of a hatchet as it split open the top of his arm.

The old man had swung it into him with all his strength, sinking the blade into the muscles of Slade's left shoulder. Slade cried out and punched the old man in the face. He flew back with such force he hit his head against the wall and crumpled to the floor. But Lola was recovered. Finding herself prostrate over her kitchen sideboard, she gripped a heavy cast iron frying pan and with a mighty cry stood up and spun round, swinging its edge in front of her, axing Slade full in the face.

The sound was like two stones hitting each other.

His knees went.

He staggered forward. His smashed sunglasses fell off.

Lola looked down at her father. She raised the pan again and hit Slade in the shoulder, propelling him into the main room. He turned round. His face was burst apart.

Slade saw Lola had the head of a cat. He fled.

She went after him, but her tracksuit bottoms were around her knees. She pulled them up, got to the doorway and saw him disappear into the forest. She looked back at her father, a puddle of blood expanding over the floor by his head.

Everyone turned as Christmas burst into the centre of the circle. "Lola!" he cried out. "Oh God, what's happened? What's happened?" Her T-shirt was half torn off. The left side of her face was swollen with bruising. She was breathing with short, stabbing breaths, her father's face in her lap, his body limp, his eyes closed. He was moaning. His nose was a bloody mess. She looked into Christmas' eyes.

"He said you stole money! Why has this man come here? What have you done, *mama guevo*?" Christmas could not answer but she saw the guilt. He stepped towards her.

"Get him away from me!" she screamed out, then began to sob, cradling and kissing her father's head.

Christmas tried to get closer but Ricardo and Gabriel caught him and pushed him back inside, into the kitchen, into the main room and against a wall as he struggled against them.

Ricardo, his hands on Christmas' shoulders, told him what had happened, every detail pulling another groan from him, as his head rolled and the sound system pounded across the village.

The policeman came inside and tried to question him. "You know this man responsible? He's a friend of yours?"

"No, he's not a friend of mine! He is my *enemy*!" and then, in English, "Do you understand, do you fucking understand?" and Christmas started towards him but Ricardo held him fast.

"Listen to me," Christmas said to the policeman, "This man raped a gringo woman in Rio Caribe, OK?"

"Are you sure? This is the man?"

"Yes, I'm fucking sure! I know that woman. That's where I left my passport, in Rio Caribe; that's where I've just been to get –" and he dug into his pocket and threw his passport at him "– there!" The policeman blinked, absorbing this information. There was the possibility of a high profile arrest here.

"Well?" shouted Christmas. Ricardo and Gabriel had let go of him, all three men facing the officer, others on the porch looking in, with still more that had come into the kitchen from the yard. "Well?" Christmas repeated, "Are we going to get him?" The policeman put his hand on his gun. He nodded.

Christmas picked up the hatchet.

56

It seemed as if the whole village had emptied into the forest. Once the word got out that there was a manhunt, all the men, most of whom were drunk, had arrived carrying machetes and knives, some with ancient rifles used for hunting.

With the sound of salsa pounding the air above them, the policeman tried in vain to keep order; a rough line from Lola's house to the foot of the mountains where it was judged too steep for an injured man to make headway.

Lola had seen Slade running eastwards so they swept the forest in that direction, picking up the blood trail, then losing it, the policeman somewhere in the middle, bellowing orders everyone ignored. Some moved east but others spread north or wandered back into the village. Some fell over and fell asleep. There were kids everywhere.

Those that were close to Lola's family, or had seen the damage done, or were sober, maintained the line. They thrashed the over-growth with their weapons. They made catcalls and threats.

Christmas said nothing.

He scanned the territory in front of him. The men on his left and right disappeared and reappeared.

For the first time in his life he was experiencing the will to murder.

They hacked through the brake, seethed through cacao plantations, into close forests of bamboo and coffee, Christmas puddled in sweat, wiping his face again and again, trying to keep his eyes clear.

San Cristóbal was ringed by cloud forest. From Lola's house on the outskirts of its western end, they advanced between the village and the mountains until they had covered all the ground north of the village up to the ridge that defined the eastern side of the bay. There the men reconvened, coming out of the trees, squabbling about where Slade had gone. Some said he was hiding, others that he had pressed north into the mountains, the policeman trying to shout above all the other voices and maintain his authority.

Christmas looked around him. The path he often took to Lola's cacao trees traversed the ridge, went over the headland and then down into the fields and forest of the northern side of the peninsula. That path went on to connect the tiny villages there – Uquire, Don Pedro, San Francisco – and if an injured man could make it beyond them, eventually he would come to the start of the road and perhaps secure transport.

The policeman was dividing the party into three groups. One to go back over the ground they had covered and continue west to search the old cement factory in case Slade had doubled back, a second to head north, the third to go over the ridge. The policeman selected the gringo to go with him in the third group. Christmas only nodded.

The groups separated. Christmas, at the end of the line, began the familiar climb up the headland path and over the ridge. He looked west over the village, the festival still continuing, as the policeman fired questions at him. Soon all the Venezuelans, far fitter and stronger than he, were leaving him behind. There was the sea.

At the path's apex, Christmas rested for a few breaths against his usual rock. From here the path doglegged down the other side into jungle and cacao. He saw the policeman's back already disappearing around the next corner. Christmas was panting. He inhaled the smell of dust and sea and put his hands against the rock, hanging his head. He heard someone talking.

Christmas froze.

Where was it coming from? It was faint, carried on the sea breeze.

He stood with his back to the sea and stared up at the ridge.

He couldn't hear the voice any more. He closed his eyes – there it was again. Christmas turned round. It was coming from the sea.

With his hatchet ready, he edged around the rock. There was a tiny path that went down the face of the headland to the waves below.

He leaned over the edge.

He couldn't see anyone, couldn't hear anything – but there – again – definitely the cadence of English. Christmas couldn't make out what was being said but he could tell it was a conversation. *He must be on the phone*, thought Christmas.

His fury redoubled and, grasping at sprigs while keeping hold of the hatchet, Christmas struggled downwards.

"Boo-hoo," said The General. "You're dying." Slade was slumped into a cranny. He was soaked in his own blood; some dried, some fresh. The sun baked him, the smallest movement kneading liquid from his clefts and cracks and ruptures. He could only see out of one eye, the left side of his face ripped and mushroomed by the force of the pan, his cheekbone and jaw both shattered.

He had lost a great deal of blood and was falling in and out of consciousness.

"Where's my father?" Slade asked the cat again as dislodged earth began to rain onto the rocks in front of him. The General looked up.

"Boo-hoo," he said. "He's coming."

Slade tried to pull himself up, to be presentable, squinting with his remaining eye against the blood and the sweat and the sun and suddenly there he was, his father, with a hatchet.

"Daddy?"

Never before had Christmas seen a man in such a condition. Slade looked like some mangled sea-creature, torn apart by a harpoon. His face was unrecognisable. His chest jerked up and down.

"*What?*"

"Daddy—" and Slade tried to raise himself further, gasping, crying out, his body quivering with the effort as Christmas stood there, unsure of what to do. The animal in front of him was so terrified it sucked the vengeance out of him. He was left with so strange a fusion of disgust and sadness that he just stood there, disbelieving.

"Twenty-six thousand pounds?" he hissed, and then, yelling, "You've done all this for *twenty-six thousand pounds?*"

Slade, his hands struggling against the rock, almost standing, spitting with the strain, saw heaven open up in the sky behind his father and in that same moment understood that it was not for him. The sun was different, grey, massive. It was expanding. It grew bigger and bigger. It was charging towards him.

Slade threw himself out to his father for protection.

The next thing Christmas knew he had banged his head against rock, Slade's weight on top of him.

He looked up into that one mad eye: a child's eye.

Slade pushed himself up from Christmas' chest. He picked up the hatchet to examine it and the policeman shot him through the neck from the path above. He was aiming for his hand.

A slingshot of blood splattered over Christmas' face, pumping fast all over him as Slade fell forward.

Crying out in horror, Christmas pushed the body away and wriggled out from beneath it.

Slade was still alive. He made a gargling noise as he tried to speak. His eye was wild with death. Then it turned into cold jelly. Christmas looked up at the men above, shouting things, making their way down.

He turned back to the corpse of Diana's murdered stepson and thought *I did this*.

57

Christmas would never remember with clarity the moments following, only that he was walked into the sea to wash away the blood, his hands held, his head dunked; a baptism.

They carried Slade's body down to the village, wrapped it in plastic and left it on a table in the medical centre, surrounded by children. The festival was stopped, the music turned off. Christmas was only aware of crowds and questions and being in several rooms with the policeman, unable to speak except to ask after Lola and the old man.

Many more policemen of every stripe arrived by boat. He was questioned over and over. His photograph was taken. He spoke to British embassy officials on the phone, answering yes and no. He was taken into the small prison that stood next to the electricity turbine and left in a cell. It was dark, with graffiti chiselled into the wall. They brought in two chairs. Sometimes police officers sat with him. Sometimes he was alone, listening to conversations and phone calls outside.

The door opened. An officer came in.

"Can I see Lola? Is she there?"

"Who's Lola?" the man said. He took out some handcuffs and arrested Christmas for defrauding the Gran Melía hotel in Caracas.

"The old man – the one who was injured – is he OK?" The officer shrugged. "Can you get me some rum?" begged the prisoner. He bought Christmas a glass of water and, as he left, Lola came in.

Her face was swollen and gashed. Christmas groaned and whispered his congratulations to the devil. She went towards him then changed her mind and sat down on the chair opposite.

"How is your father?"

"He's OK—" but she fell quiet. Tears ran down her bruising. "He's OK, he's OK," she said, as if trying to convince herself of its certainty. She was looking at his handcuffs. "You are a liar," she said. "You are a criminal."

"I'm not a criminal, it's just – I should've told you – I was going to tell you everything, I swear it but – but—"

"So tell me! Tell it to me!" Christmas bit down on his lip.

"There was a woman – in England—"

"Is your wife really dead? Did you even have a wife?"

"Yes I did – and after she died, I just went bad. I went crazy. And I lost all my money and I ended up with this woman and I took some of her money and it was the biggest mistake I've ever made in my life – these debts and – and there was – I barely had the money to eat, the bank had taken my home, Lola ..." but he could see the disgust in her face. "I know how it sounds, but she was trying to get my money too, and—"

"Your money? You just said you had no money."

"Yes, but—"

"So you lied to her? Like you have lied to me!"

"Lola—"

"Who was this man?"

"Lola, please—"

"Who was he?"

"Her son."

"*Dios* ..." she gasped, holding herself.

"Her stepson, an evil fucking monster I didn't know about – she never told me about him and he followed me to Venezuela ... Lola, I have made such a mistake but I never knew, I never thought for one moment – how – exploded into this and ..." Lola was on her feet. "Don't go, please—"

"Stop it!"

"Lola, you have to let me explain the full story – I can't just – here – like this – I love you, don't you understand?"

"Understand?" she shouted. "Look at my face! You did this! Do you even make movies?" Christmas was silent. "Fuck you, gringo," she said in English.

Then she was gone.

The next thing Christmas knew he was holding a mobile phone to his ear and talking to someone else from the British embassy. The man was explaining that he would be brought back to Caracas.

"If you agree with the police officer's version of events, that this man Slade was about to strike you with the implement and therefore most probably kill you, then this whole unfortunate business will be concluded relatively quickly and you will only have the hotel fraud charges to face. If, however, you disagree with his report and there is any doubt, any doubt whatsoever, as to the legitimacy of the killing as far as the British government is concerned, well that could mean weeks, months – even longer to be honest – of delay. There will be inquiry, legal proceedings, court etcetera – are you following me, Mr Christmas?"

"Do the Lambs know?"

"What?"

"Bridget Lamb, the woman he raped – do they know?"

"Yes, I believe they have been informed."

"I—"

"Yes, Mr Christmas?"

"I ... I don't have any money."

"Really. Well, I can tell you, especially in that case, that it would be better for everyone all round if you agree with the officer's version of events. You do agree, is that correct? He was about to strike you with a – what was it now – an axe? A hatchet? Correct?" Christmas didn't reply. The official coughed. "Mr Christmas? Is that correct?"

58

Just before Christmas was escorted to the boat, the policeman who had killed William Slade came into the cell. He had bought Christmas' passport for the custody officers. "I saved your life, gringo," he said. He spat on the floor, raised his eyebrows and walked out into the sun.

Christmas was taken outside. The whole village was there. He searched desperately for Lola but couldn't see her. They all watched him, some silent, some murmuring. Ricardo and Gabriel were there. They nodded their heads in consolation and patted him as he was led past.

"Take care of yourself," said Ricardo.

"Tell Lola—" said Christmas but he had seen Aldo. They stared at each other. The prisoner was pushed on.

He was taken onto the jetty and into a small boat filled with policemen. He sat down and looked up at all the faces. *Lola*. Would he ever see her again?

He saw a movement, people shoved to one side, the crowd parting.

Somebody was coming through.

Lola ...! But no. A policeman appeared, then another. They were carrying Slade's body, wrapped and bound. They lifted it carefully down the concrete steps and then into the boat. The corpse was placed on the wooden slats in front of him.

The rope was untied. The motor sputtered and started, the boat see-sawing on the waves until it was clear of the jetty.

Christmas searched the crowd. *Please God, let her come. Just let me see her* ... The boat revved. Some people were waving. She was not coming. The boat began to cut through the sea towards Guiria and suddenly there was a disruption in the line of bodies and Lola was there, standing on the low wall.

He stood up. "Lola!" he shouted.

"Sit down," ordered one of the police officers.

"Lola!" he shouted again, "Lola!" She was getting smaller, she was moving down the wall, looking out at him.

"Sit down, now!" ordered the policeman again, yanking at his handcuffs, but Christmas yanked back and kept standing.

"I love you, Lola, I love you!" he shouted as loud as he could and the officer pulled out his gun and stuck it against his head. Christmas heard a cry.

Was that her? Did she still care?

He sat down, other officers shouting at him as he watched the coastline, her form already indistinct, blending into other villagers, blending into the village itself, now just a collection of shapes beneath the green mountains. Then San Cristóbal was gone, eclipsed by rock. Christmas was alone with policemen and the body of William Slade.

The boat was silent. There was only the noise of the outboard and the prow slamming against the waves that littered spray onto Slade's black plastic shroud. The sun was going down. Christmas stared at the body. There were white patches of drying salt water.

When they arrived in Guiria it was dusk. He watched the body be lifted out of the boat and into the back of a police van. Slade was gone.

The officers got Christmas to his feet and helped him out. He was put into the back of a car and taken to Guiria's police station for further processing. He was given a plain *arepa* with some water. Then they put him into the back of a police van and told him they would be driving through the night to Caracas.

The engine started. Christmas lurched. It was dark, the occasional streetlight illuminating the van so that he could make out the dirt and stones rolling around by his feet. He stared at them as if they were runes, thrown and re-thrown with every bounce. They told him he had lost Lola, completely. He felt her chain against his chest, tucked beneath his shirt. He had saved her son. Would she remember that? He felt afraid of what might happen in Caracas. He felt afraid of a life without her. He searched his heart for Emily but she was gone. Montejo lay ripped to pieces on Lola's floor. What did it matter? It was just a book.

They drove westward along the coast between the soughing of the sea and the heave of the land. The jerking movements of the van pulled him about. His buttocks were numb. The policemen listened to the radio. They smoked constantly. Other men were picked up along the way, but they weren't prisoners and were let out again. When the policemen stopped to eat, Christmas was not allowed to get out of the van. They gave him water but he wasn't fed.

Christmas did not sleep. There was only Bridget and Judith and Lola and Slade and his soul's pleading for alcohol. After many hours, with dawn breaking, Caracas enfolded them.

The engine slowed, then stopped. The back doors opened. Christmas was in front of Cotiza police station, headquarters for the *Metropolitana* police district.

They took him inside. It smelt of urine and dried screaming. He was led past ancient computers and walls of chipped paint to an interview room. After three hours he was visited by someone from the British Embassy, a tall, balding man in shorts who asked him exactly the same questions as everyone else had, scribbling down notes as he did so.

"Have you told his stepmother he's dead?"

"She has been notified, yes. We are flying the body back today, so I expect she'll be there to pick it up from the airport. Can you sign this please?" Christmas signed several documents.

"What happens now? I've got to—" but he stopped himself.

"A bloody enormous amount of paperwork, that's what happens now. You are going to have to stay here and find out what they plan to throw at you over this hotel thing."

"You don't know?"

"Me?" he said, collecting his papers. "No."

"But I don't have any money – don't I need a lawyer or something? I mean aren't you meant to provide—"

"We can provide an interpreter to make sure that you and your lawyer can communicate. Other than that we can make contact with your family and ensure that any money they send gets to you, but the embassy will not get involved with actual judicial proceedings. Have you got anyone you wish us to contact?"

"No, but—"

"I'm sure there's no need to be overly concerned. Goodbye, Mr Christmas." He knocked on the door and was let out.

Christmas was left in the room for another couple of hours. Then he was taken back through the building and sat down in front of the sergeant's desk. He was a stooped man with a moustache and pointed cheekbones. He was smoking. He detailed the charges of theft and fraud against him – charges that were, he emphasized, a different matter to what had happened in Sucre where he had no jurisdiction and about which he had no interest. The sergeant then proceeded to lay out the prisoner's options.

"Two thousand dollars. Two thousand dollars or you go to prison."

"I don't have two thousand dollars. Could I please have some food?"

"Perhaps you do not know about prisons in Venezuela. The cells we have in this station, *Señor*, are bad enough, but prison? This would be very bad for you. Very bad."

"I'm telling you, I do not have any money."

"If you do not get me two thousand dollars, then we take you to prison. It is probable that you will be raped."

"I don't think anyone is going to want to rape me."

"Even when the meat is rotten, *Señor*, the hungry dog will eat."

"I wish to call the British Government."

"If you do not have any money, how will you call them?"

"There's a phone right there."

"Yes there is."

"Can I use it?"

"For two thousand dollars."

"You can't deny my right as a British citizen to—"

"Are you telling me what I can do?" he bawled. Christmas looked up at the ceiling.

"Wait – I have a friend – a *Metropolitana* police officer ..."

"What is his name?"

"His name is ..." *What was his fucking name?* The taxi driver, the first man he met, the man who took him to the club where he met Lola. "His name is ... his brother owns a bar, and his name is ..." The custody sergeant raised his eyebrows, then called in another policeman to take him away.

"It is no use lying to me, *Señor*. You are a gringo. You have money. Now you will be taken to a cell while arrangements are made. You will be there for three or four days. If you have no money, you will not eat. There will be many men in there and they will hate you because you are a gringo. When things start to happen to you then maybe, if one of my officers hears you, you can send me a message that you are ready to pay. Or why not we make it simple? You can pay now." Christmas didn't reply. "You *look* like an intelligent man," the sergeant added, "but this is not true. You are stupid."

For an hour, Christmas was left handcuffed to a bench. He tried to stretch out his brain that it might give up the forgotten name, but the harder he tried the tighter it shrank.

Eventually he was taken to *Calabazo Para Detenidos Mientras Esperando Translados* – the detention block. It was a narrow, noisy corridor that reeked of sewage. There were rows of numbers written along the wall and Christmas could see people pissing out of the bars. As soon as they saw the policeman they started jeering and insulting, directing their piss towards him. When they saw the gringo, their tone lowered.

The policeman pulled his gun. The men backed away from the bars. The policeman unlocked the door and pushed Christmas in.

The cell was four metres squared with a low ceiling. It contained fifteen other men. The smell was suffocating. Graffiti covered the blue waterproof paint, flaking and pitted, and everyone was wearing their clothes inside out to protect them against the filth.

No sooner had the policeman disappeared than Christmas found himself crammed into a corner by a jury of faces, blackened gums and scars. "Why are you here?" came the question, once, twice, again and again. "Why you here? Why you here, you gringo son of a bitch?"

"Can't talk?" Someone pushed him.

"You're a fucking dead man, gringo."

"I am here ..." he began, fighting the panic. He knew his survival relied on one thing: an impressive lie. "... because I stabbed a policeman."

"What?"

"Eh?"

"What did he say?"

"You stabbed one of them?"

"I was drunk. We got into a fight. I stabbed him." Applause rang out round the cell. Some of the men introduced themselves. As the crowd moved back and he fielded more questions about the fight and who he was, Christmas was better able to survey the human wreckage. In one corner a man was crying. His clothes were awry and he was bleeding from the ear. In another someone was taking a shit on a newspaper. When he was done he rolled it up and threw it out into the corridor. Some were crouching against the walls, trying to sleep with their eyes open. People were looking at Christmas and whispering to each other.

Loud jeering started up again. The police officer was outside. Christmas looked down at the floor and tried yet again to summon the name. It began with a 'P' ... Pablo? Perry?

"Hey, gringo," said the policeman. "So what you going to do? You like it here?"

"I told your boss—"

"You see those numbers on the wall? We like to make bets on all the men here. Odds. Those numbers are odds. About what happens to these sons of bitches. And to you too. We agree the odds, then we bet. If you pay the money to the sergeant, then you get out of here. And everybody thinks that's what you do. I am betting that's what you don't do."

"Why?"

"I don't think you have any money. If you don't have money, I win money from them. Do you have any money?"

"What are the odds?"

"Five to one you don't have any money. Do you have any money?"

"So you're betting I go to prison?"

"No. Prison is a separate bet. Then there are bets about what happen to you in prison, which depend on the prison you go to. Like that."

"What do you mean?"

"If you get raped, if you get killed. Like that."

"You're betting on whether I will be killed?"

"Of course," he shrugged.

"What are the odds I will be killed?"

"If you don't have money, so you can't pay for protection, it's around eight to one. It's an OK bet."

"And being raped?"

"Much shorter."

"Who's setting these odds?"

"Him. This guy. Gonzalo!" Christmas strained his head against the bars to see another man doing the same in the cell further down. "He's a bookmaker for gangsters."

"Well, what are the odds on me getting out of here?"

"No money? No prison?"

"That's right."

"Ha – you mean, what the odds on you escape? You dig a tunnel?"

"I didn't say escape; I said what are the odds for me not paying the sergeant, and not going to prison, just walking out of here."

"Are you saying you don't have any money?"

"Could you just ask that man what the odds are?"

"OK?" he shrugged, "Hey, Gonzalo! This gringo wants to know what the odds are he gets out of here with no money and he doesn't go to prison!" Everybody started laughing.

"I give him five hundred to one!"

"Five hundred to one!" shouted the policeman to the officers at the other end of the corridor. They nodded their agreement. The policeman took out a pen and wrote it up on the wall.

"OK, now it's on the wall, it's official. You are a funny man."

"Why don't you put some money on me? You could win."

"Ha, ha, yes, but it cannot happen. So I lose."

"Not if you let me out."

"What?"

"You put all your money on me, then let me out. So you win the bet, I go free and you're rich. Everybody wins."

"You know, that is a very good idea. But there is one problem: the sergeant does not win. The sergeant wants two thousand dollars and if I let you out and he does not get his money, maybe he will shoot me."

"But listen, you could bet ten dollars, let me out, ten dollars at five hundred to one is five thousand dollars, give the sergeant his two thousand, you've got three thousand, I'm free. Everyone is happy."

"You think of everything, gringo. You are a very clever man!"

"OK, then!"

"But we are just poor *policia*, betting on misfortune. These men do not have five thousand dollars to give me if I win. If they had five thousand dollars, they would not be *policia*."

"Could you lend me two thousand dollars?"

"You're going to prison, *Señor*."

"Right."

"I can sell you a knife. For protection."

"I don't have any money. How about a fork?"

With the policeman gone, Christmas returned to eyeing his cell mates. He imagined the taste of Cacique. As he hung onto the bars, a man stepped beside him and started taking a piss into the corridor.

Slade had tried to rape Lola. Christmas had a moment of vicious happiness that the bastard was dead before his thoughts gave way to Bridget and because he could not bear these thoughts he looked around the cell. How was he going to get back to Lola? Was it really her who had cried out? Might she still love him? Was there hope?

He kept his back against the wall near the bars. He had just about got used to the stench when someone else took a shit. The man was ill, the violent-smelling silage of his intestines poisoning the air. Everyone covered their noses. Christmas retched. The man threw the newspaper full of shit out into the corridor. Later a fight started in the opposite corner. All the men crowded round to watch something unspeakable happen that Christmas couldn't see. He heard crying, and when he could bear to look over he saw somebody on the floor shaking uncontrollably. Various people tried to talk to him. One man said he had been tortured by the police. He showed Christmas the burn marks from electric shocks and a charred divot in his shoulder where he had been touched by the hot iron.

Christmas could not risk sleep. Instead, he let his eyes shut down and lose focus, snapping back when he sensed movement nearby. In this way he had a smeared dream of being in a public toilet and trying to dry his hands, but the machine just made them wetter. Then some female prisoners were taken past and there was a rush to the bars. The women snarled and fired out insults. The men made ugly promises.

Christmas, stunned by hunger, fear and fatigue, stared vacantly at the floor. He was at the reception after Emily's funeral. They served beef sandwiches. She hated cold beef. He picked up a sandwich and started laughing. Everyone was staring at him, the widower laughing at his wife's funeral, and he thought how funny she would find it, him laughing and everyone thinking he had lost his mind, all because of a beef sandwich. He laughed even louder. Then he drank to blackout.

It was the day she died. He was in Waitrose. He was looking for Robinson's Lemon Barley Water. It was her favourite drink. He had driven to the supermarket from the hospital. She was resting. She was fine. The baby was fine. He had left his mobile phone on the windowsill. Standing in the aisles, he couldn't find the barley water. A girl with braces showed him where it was. She told him it was her first day on the job. He congratulated her. He told her his wife was in the hospital having their first baby. She congratulated him. He paid for the barley water. He got back into the car and turned on the radio. The station was playing 'Hotel California'.

When he walked onto the maternity ward he was told undiagnosed eclampsia meant Emily had started having massive convulsions. She had gone into a coma. They had taken out their child, a daughter, by emergency caesarean section but due to acute foetal distress her heart had already stopped. Then Emily suffered an intracranial haemorrhage. She died moments later.

He was led into Emily's room still holding the bottle of barley water. There was a bag of flesh in her bed, wearing the mask of her face.

Christmas was watching a line of ants cross the cell floor. They carried bits of a bigger ant. Lola. He wanted Lola, massy with life. The smell of coconut oil on her skin, the heat of her, the peel of her laughter. His arms around her belly, kissing her neck as she leant her head towards him. On the porch with Aldo and the old man. Cooked fish and the evening wind. He didn't even have her telephone number.

The door slammed. *Lola.*

But it was three new men.

As soon as they set eyes on him, Christmas could feel their greedy hatred. One wore a baseball cap. One was bare-chested with faded tattoos and a strangely distended stomach. One had a swollen eye and was cut around the mouth. All three had scrappy beards. Their eyes glittered with narcotics. They said things to him that he didn't understand. Christmas didn't respond. He felt too tired, too broken. Then one of them spat on him.

It hit his shoulder. Those next to Christmas inched away.

He looked down at the spit. He looked up at his enemies. Their glare was crushing him. He breathed deeply, trying to control his terror and then, suddenly, he felt a familiar pain in his chest.

The tightness knuckled his heart. It tugged at his breathing. *Not now*, he pleaded to himself, *Not now* ... The pain increased.

"This is ..." he whispered to the deadly men, "this ..."

"What? What'd you say, you gringo piece of shit? I am going to cut out your fucking heart." The gang fanned a little and moved on him. He saw one had something rough and metal in his hand. *Pepito*, he thought, *Pepito Rodriguez Silvas*. Christmas closed his eyes. He gave up.

"Motherfuckers to the wall!" The policeman, holding a new prisoner by the neck with one hand and his gun in the other, appeared the other side of the bars. The gang cursed at the interruption but backed away. Everyone else did the same except for Christmas. The policeman put his gun through the bars and into his face.

"Move, gringo."

"Pepito ... Rodriguez ... Silvas," Christmas whispered, squeezing his chest.

"What?"

"Pepito ... Rodriguez ... Silvas."

"Pepito?"

338

"The policeman. He is my very ... good ... friend." At this a great wave of insults exploded over Christmas. He felt spit hit various parts of his body. He was kicked. The policeman cocked his gun and the inmates receded.

"Pepito knows you?"

"I go ... to his brother's bar in Sabana ... Grande and we ... became friends he ... picked me up from ... the airport ... in his taxi." The policeman scrutinized Christmas for a moment, opened the door, shoved in the prisoner and beckoned the foreigner out. Christmas staggered out of the gate, wiping spit off his face, avoiding the screwed-up bundles of newspaper and puddles of urine, breathing in quick shallow stabs.

"What's wrong with you?"

"I'm old," said Christmas, the pain disappearing as his respiratory system rediscovered its stride. He turned round for the scowls, but his eyes were drawn instead to the man who had been on the floor shaking. He was crouched at the back, hugging himself. He looked at Christmas.

Christmas was taken back through the corridors and left in an interrogation room for four hours. He watched the door, hoping like a child that Lola would appear, but when it finally opened there was Pepito, holding a small bottle of water, tracksuit bottoms and a plain blue T-shirt.

"*Señor* Christmas!" he cried, "My English friend! You really fucked up." Christmas let out a long sigh and hung his head. "Look at you – nobody kills you – you survive the night! Drink this and change you clothes, OK? You dirty. But why don't you tell my name to the people before?" Christmas took the water and drained it. Pepito put the clothes down on the bench beside him.

"They don't let me – they didn't understand – Pepito – I – I have to eat."

"Hey, no problem, I get you an *arepa*, OK?"

"Yes. Yes, please."

"Cost you two thousand dollars."

"What?"

"Two thousand dollars."

"I don't—"

"Only joking!" He opened the door and shouted some instructions. In a few minutes, Christmas was devouring the tastiest thing he could ever remember eating and telling Pepito what had happened in Sucre.

"So, what's going to happen to me?"

"Why do you do that? You crazy man. Why do you leave Gran Melía hotel and not to pay? This is very stupid, *Señor* Christmas. Why you do these things?"

"I didn't mean to do it! I lost my wallet with all my fucking money in it! In fact it was in your brother's bar – I went to your brother's bar—"

"I know this. I was there, remember?"

"You were there?"

"*Dios mio* – you don't remember? Me and my brother and you, we drink very much."

"I – no. I don't remember."

"And you left your wallet there. Next day I went to your hotel but they say you ran away."

"But I ran away because you – you have it? You've got it now?"

"Well. No."

"But—"

"This is weeks ago, *amigo*. I don't think I see you again. The money is gone. The wallet I give to my brother. I can ask to my brother if you want the wallet ..."

"But I need that money."

"I told you. It has gone."

340

"Then you owe me! You've got to get me out of here!"

"The only way you get out of here is if the sergeant is paid, and the money in the wallet is gone, *Señor*. I do not have it to pay the sergeant. If I had it, I would pay, but I do not have it."

"But – but you have to do something, damn you!"

"Hey! You calm, OK? If it was not for me you still be in the cell, and you will not last long in there, OK? Now put on those clothes! You fucking stink, gringo." Christmas put his head in his hands. "Just call someone in you country to give you the money."

"There is no one I can call," Christmas replied, holding the new T-shirt out in front of him. He began pulling off the one he was wearing.

"No one? A brother? A sister?"

"No one, I told you! Jesus fucking Christ!" Christmas threw his old T-shirt onto the floor.

"What is that?"

"What is what?" Christmas looked down at his belly.

"Around your neck. Is it gold?" Christmas covered his neck. "*Señor* Christmas—"

"No."

"Or it is prison, the real prison. To be honest, I am not even sure the sergeant will accept, but you lucky. I try, because I am your friend. You will lose the chain in prison. You will also lose much more than the chain. Understand yourself. There is nothing else you can do, *Señor* Christmas."

59

Christmas, his passport returned, was released into Pepito's custody. He was given new clothes. He arranged his flight. They went to a sex hotel that rented rooms by the hour and Christmas took one to shower and change in.

He stepped under the faucet. There was warm water, controlled and plentiful, but when he pushed the door, it did not open into Lola's yard. He squeezed out a luxurious dollop of shower gel onto his hand and wished that it was the fading lozenge of pink soap, picked off the concrete and covered in hair. The mirror wasn't cracked. The towels were not bald.

After he had washed, Christmas sat on the bed and dressed himself beneath his own reflection. He was alone in a sex hotel. He held his head in his hands. He looked at the phone from between his fingers. He didn't have her number. He didn't have her chain.

Pepito was waiting for him in the lobby. The owner waived the bill. They went to a restaurant that had the flags of the world strung from the ceiling. They sat in a booth. The waiter brought *perico* eggs and beer. Christmas clasped his bottle, filling his hand with cold relief. He downed it. He asked for another. He asked for a glass of rum.

While they chewed, coughed, bare scrapes of cutlery against plate, Christmas looked out through his ghost in the window and watched the night grow thick. Their meal was over. Pepito lit up a cigarette. Christmas asked for another glass of rum.

"So you have problems about what happened in Sucre?"

"A girl was raped. It is my fault."

"You raped a girl?"

"No! The man who was killed. He did it."

"So it is good he was killed."

"I watched a man *die*. I had his blood on my face."

"You have never seen that before. It is troubling you."

"Of course it's fucking troubling me!"

"Whoever he was, whatever he did, he is in a better place now."

"You're a Christian. What a surprise."

"No. I am just saying: this world is hell. It is better to be dead than alive."

"If you believe that then why haven't you killed yourself?"

"I like to be around people," he said, exhaling through his nostrils. "Hey – you ever see that woman again? The fat one from the bar?"

"Lola."

"I don't know her name."

"Her name is Lola Rosa."

"OK," he shrugged, "you see her again?"

"I've been living with her. She gave me that chain."

"Then maybe she save your life."

"She did save my life. She did, she did ..." Christmas put his elbows on the table and covered his face.

"This woman is still there. She is still alive. You are still alive. The other man is dead." He extinguished his cigarette. "These are the facts."

"Will you do one thing?"

"What?"

"If the chain is sold, will you keep a record of who buys it, where it goes?"

"You want to buy it back?"

"Yes."

"Forget the chain. The chain is gone."

"I have to see her again!" Christmas shifted suddenly to the edge of their booth. Pepito made the same movement.

"Don't do any more stupid things, *Señor*," he said.

Christmas looked out of the window. He looked at the rum and cursed it. He pushed it away. Then he downed it and cursed it again from the edge of his teeth. He could write Lola a letter. Surely it would find its way, though he didn't know her address, or if she had one, or even if there was a postal system – he had never seen any letters arrive. But the *infocentro* – some villagers must have email addresses. If he could just find one out – on the internet somewhere – that's what it was for, wasn't it? That kind of thing ...

Pepito said something to the waiter. There was no bill. The two men got up to leave. He would write some kind of letter and explain himself, apologise, hope that somehow it would get to her, that she would read it and understand, that she would forgive him. Surely it was her that had cried out. Surely there was hope. They walked out of the restaurant into the warm night. His lies had destroyed everything.

They climbed into Pepito's taxi and set off towards the airport. The streets were full. How would he get back to San Cristóbal, to Venezuela? He must face Diana. He owed her that. He owed her his version of her son's last moments. And Judith? And Bridget? How could he ever make amends? That, at least, was simple. He could not.

A motorcycle carrying three people sped past his elbow. England. He was flying back to England. The smell of wet tarmac and chewed leaves. He was broke. He should try and face the scope and detail of his debts, sit down with someone professional and unpick the web. He must find a job. He must take control of his drinking. *Oh God, give me a drink.*

Either side of the highway thousands of naked bulbs illuminated the deprivation of the barrios. Pepito turned on the radio and lit another cigarette.

He would visit Emily's grave. He would make a doctor's appointment about his chest pains.

A sign for the airport rushed overhead.

He would get older. He would die alone.

He was hovering in the air, a tiny figure above the dark volcano.

Oh, Lola. Soon he would drop.

They pulled up in front of the terminal building. She wasn't going to be there. She wasn't going to appear. Pepito took him inside, watched him check in, and led him as far as the metal detectors.

Pepito shook his hand. "Goodbye, *amigo*. I hope you take it more easy." Christmas started to say something, then shook his head. He stepped through the frame.

In the departure lounge, Christmas sat down on a row of empty plastic chairs. He stared at his hands. The airport felt empty. He watched a man mop the floor. He examined a family asleep. He went to the bathroom. He saw that he had a tan. His face was covered in lines. He had no moustache. He was an old man in a tracksuit. She had come to the jetty to see him leave. She had cried out – hadn't she? Would she remember he had saved her son from being electrocuted?

Christmas sat down in front of a monitor and watched the capitals of the world move upwards, blink and disappear. His flight was boarding. He walked down the hall to his gate and joined the queue. The woman who took his boarding pass didn't look at him. She was beautiful. Then he was behind her with his stub, facing a plastic tunnel.

Christmas boarded the plane. A steward welcomed him. He took his seat by the window and looked out at the moon, listening to the people settling around him, the security announcements, the ping and click of the machine readying itself.

An old Indian woman sat beside him. She had sunglasses in her hair and wore a warm jacket over her sari. She stowed her book and took out the in-flight magazine. She rifled through it, put it away and took out her book. She snapped back the pages, sighing and shifting in her seat.

The plane began to move. She muttered a prayer. Christmas turned to her from the window. She forced a smile, her neck iron with fear. The plane rolled into position. She seized the armrests. It accelerated. It roared and rose.

Bridget. He had the rape of a girl on his conscience now, burnt on like a slave brand, something he could not remove or disguise except with drink and he must stay away from drink. He was an agent for evil. How could he live? How could he still be walking through the world with all that he had caused? There was nothing to fix, nothing to do but accept. He must go and see Diana. He must at least present himself, and then, whatever she said, work and earn and repay her. What was the price of a dead stepson? Christmas curled in his seat. There was pressure in his ears. He was being cast out from the human race. *Oh, the drink.* How it would hide his heart. But there must be no drink. The only offering he had left for the dead and the maimed was his torment held pristine. He saw a road open up in front of him beneath this low moon that offered no rest, no end except death. He must meet this road with a clear mind, with courage. He must conduct himself from here on without the easy deceits of the past. Emily was gone. Bridget and Judith were destroyed. Slade was murdered. Diana was alive. *Lola.* He must find a way to get back to her. He thought of her injuries. *Let me drink,* said a voice, and he caught the eyes of a passing stewardess. She smiled. He turned to the window. The moon. The plane was levelling. Christmas looked down.

Venezuela. It was already just a dwindling constellation, one of many that cover the earth: sparks of mankind in stubborn struggle against the night.

ACKNOWLEDGEMENTS

Sarai Rodriguez

Marie-Elisa and Billy Barker
Seorais Graham
Christoph Hargreaves-Allen, king of readers.

Al pueblo de Macuro, Estado Sucre, especialmente a la Señora Beatriz, a la Señora Luisa, Juriana Martínez, su hija Daisy mi ahijada y su padre Pinpon Kezama, Laurie y su familia, Alve Medina, Jose 'Nango' Medina, Adolfo 'El Pargo', Reina, Milagro, Caridad, Thomas, Modesto Jose, mi jefe Pedro Pablo y su familia, Luis, Roberto y a toda la gente de esta comunidad de tal fuerza, dignidad y generosidad.

Frances and Hugh Gibson, Effie and Phiz Phizackalea, Amelia and Paddy Lyndon-Stanford, Patrick Gibson, Bea Gibson, Nick Gordon, Orlando Hermandez, Aldo Centeno, Salvador, Tael and Laura, Rosie Flint, Dom Minns, Peta Kennedy, Bill Curtis, Shauneen Lambe, Will Goodlad, Anne-Marie and Mathew Court, Matthew Clark, Ellie Wyatt, Kam and Lloyd Hudson, Richard 'Speedy' Byrne, Farah and Miles Cleret, Rachel and Roland Marks, Jane and Ben Maschler, Rachel Oakes, Mr and Mrs Squat Boy, Pawna and Mike Spencer-Nairn, Toby Tripp, Becky and James 'the

Baptist' Razzal, Chris Milton, Niall Griffiths, Tracey Rogers, Nat Turner, Lulu and Mick Sadler, Laurence and David Ambrose, Chloe Aridjis, Cath and James Herring, Lee Bramley, Lana Henry, James Haddon, Nick Fuller-Sessions, Buster Turner, Carla Rodamilans Castillo, Ed Maklouf, Max Bayer, Claudia Zimmerman, Elizabeth Carrillo, Pablo and Virginia Silberschmidt, Bing Taylor, Pam Rose.

The people of Barceloneta, Catalonia. Jose-Maria and his family at La Cova Fumada. Margarita, Susanna and everyone who works at the New Orleans Café, Plaza Poeta Bosca.

Everyone who works at Le Chien Qui Fume, Boulevard Montparnasse.

Natalie Bennett, Nick Gillett.

Lewis Heriz, Zissou Limpkin, Olivia Wood, Scott Pack, Caroline Gorham, Laura Kincaid, Jenny Todd, Sian Gibson, Alan Jessop, Payhembury Marbled Papers, Genoveva De La Peña, Bookcunt, India Waters, Jamie Byng, Sam Hart, Peter Ho, Jeremy Wood, Raffaella De Angelis, Claire Harris, Nick Marshal, Mark Ollard, Jo Dickinson, Matt Bates, Ruth Killick.

In particular I would like to thank Crispin and Rowan Somerville for their belief and energy, without which this book would not exist.

Finally, for all her support and insight, I would like to thank Daisy Sadler, whom I love so very much.

BADDENDUM

Thanks for reading my debut novel. After several failed attempts at starting a short story, and then starting a nap, I've decided I'm going to tell you a true story instead, not about writing this book, but about writing one of the others that many other publishers failed to publish; about how I came to hear a screech of tyres behind me, turn around, and see two Armed Response Unit vehicles emptying their guts of policemen with machine guns. They were screaming orders. The guns were all facing in my direction. Then I was on the floor being arrested under the Prevention of Terrorism Act.

Most ideas writers have are bad. I'd recently had one of my very worst ideas: a novel about modern-day pirates on the Thames, set in a world where everyone has removable genitalia. Stage one of my research was buying a plastic vagina and leaving it in a bowl on the kitchen table. How I wish I'd remembered to remove it before my mother came round. Stage two was meeting T–.

T– was a captain for hire who bought boats to London from other European ports. We arranged to meet in one of the capital's greatest drinking establishments: the Wibbly Wobbly, a floating pub moored in Surrey Quays. After a boozy evening of me asking questions about how the Thames was policed, we said our goodbyes and within a couple of minutes I was in handcuffs, and assuming this was an unfortunate case of mistaken identity. I was wrong.

*

Counting white tiles in a police cell is difficult. You lose your place. You get back to the top corner and start again. You lose your place. You become discouraged and look around for inspiration. I found mine in a message scratched on the gurney frame. Fuck the Shit, said the nameless philosopher. Yes, I thought, fuck the shit! But I was too thirsty to maintain such impressive levels of rebellion. I was sobering up. It was three in the morning.

I rang the bell and asked for water. When it came the officer told me that T– had been arrested and was in the cell block. "T–!" I shouted through the hatch once he had gone. "T–!" someone shouted back in a girlie way.

I lay back on the plastic mattress. Unsettling thoughts began to creep across the hour. I'd only just met T–, what did I really know about him? Maybe I'd been arrested because of him. He'd just bought a boat back from Amsterdam – perhaps it was stuffed full of drugs. Perhaps he was an arms smuggler. Perhaps he was one of those Nazis they still ask you about on your way into America.

At midday, I was visited by two CID detectives. At last! Now this whole mess would be sorted out. I stood up.

"So," said Detective P., "are you going to tell us about the weapons-grade plutonium?"

I sat down. "If you can tell me what weapons grade plutonium looks like," I sighed, "I'll tell you if I've got any." The two detectives looked at each other. Somewhere, somehow, there had been one enormous cock-up.

They took me to search my flat. The atmosphere had relaxed and, as we drove across town, Detective S. was telling me about his love of real ale. The relaxed atmosphere, however, had not extended to a third officer in the car, who looked just like the singer Tricky, and insisted on saying everything very close to my face. We pulled up at traffic lights. My mother's cousin was loading shopping into her car.

"That's my mother's cousin," I said.

"Do you want us to stop and say hello?" said Detective P.

"Yeah," said Tricky, who was sitting next to me in the back. He leant close to my face. "And give you a slap?"

"No thanks." I said. We drove off.

Outside my flat I made a request. "I've just moved into the building. Any chance you can take these cuffs off?"

"Yeah, no problem," said Detectives S. and P.

Tricky came up very close to my face. "If you try and run," he hissed, "I will personally knock you down."

"I'm wearing Timberlands," I replied, "and you've got my shoelaces." Tricky looked down and grunted with satisfaction.

Once inside the flat, they quickly satisfied themselves that I was what I purported to be: an untidy writer. Tricky sat me on a stool in the corner of the kitchen, folded his arms and stood watch. Ostensibly this was a search for weapons-grade plutonium, though I was still in the dark as to where the idea had come from that I was involved in black market nuclear arms dealing. My flat had a secret room behind the back of a cupboard. They failed to find it. They did, however, find some rather private photographs of my then-girlfriend Peta.

"Who's the brunette?" shouted Detective P. from the bedroom.

"Hey!" I shouted, standing up. "Leave those alone!" This was the moment Tricky had been waiting for. He shoved me back on the stool and started bawling threats into my face. The other detectives carried on floating around my flat, picking things up and having a bit of a chat. This wasn't how I imagined a counter-terrorism search would be. It felt more like an episode of Through the Keyhole.

"My name is Jasper Gibson," I said into the microphone several hours later. "And I'm writing a book about removable vaginas." The detectives were giggling. They were ready to start the interview. One left the room to fart. Then, finally, they were ready to tell me what had happened.

An off-duty traffic policeman from Leeds, who owned a boat in the marina, had been listening to our conversation in the Wibbly Wobbly. He was either half-deaf or a complete fantasist, and had so selectively handpicked individual words from what we were saying, that he had convinced himself he was in a Die Hard movie and I was Alan Rickman.

Where had the plutonium idea come from? Suddenly I remembered:

T–: "The other option is your characters could use a radar jammer, like they use in jet warfare."

Me: "Yeah, but that would make them more conspicuous, not less, right? If the radar was suddenly jammed."

T–: "True. Also they probably couldn't get their hands on a radar jammer."

Me: "That doesn't matter. This is fiction. They can get their hands on whatever they want; weapons-grade plutonium, light sabers, you name it. They've got removable penises. Sky's the limit."

But instead of calling Darth Vadar, this man had called the Met.

With the interview terminated and my shoelaces returned I was finally released. The door to another interview room opened. Tricky walked in and behind him was T–! Only it wasn't T– . They had managed to arrest the only other person in the pub that night who had a beard. I burst out laughing. Tricky didn't seem so keen to get close anymore.

The custody sergeant exhaled and shook his head. "Don't," he said, "please don't." The not-T– burst into a torrent of expletives.

When I returned to the Wibbly Wobbly the following week, more details emerged. The manager told me how the pub had suddenly flooded with fake couples who ordered gin and tonics and only drank the tonic. Despite such massive amounts of surveillance, when T– left the pub, they had somehow managed to lose him and, in a panic, had raided all the houseboats until they finally found someone with the right facial hair. A waitress trying to get home had found her car surrounded by machine-gun toting officers screaming at her to get out. She was so scared, she collapsed and hit her head.

The off-duty traffic policeman and boat-owner was known to the publican and they had barred him for life. Someone stuck a policeman's helmet on the bow of his boat and graffitied 'pig' along the side.

I didn't feel sorry for him, but I did feel sorry for the detectives – except for Tricky, of course. They were under an enormous amount of pressure and that call had put unstoppable wheels in motion. Plus, they never found my plutonium. If anyone wants some I'll be down the Wibbly Wobbly next Friday.

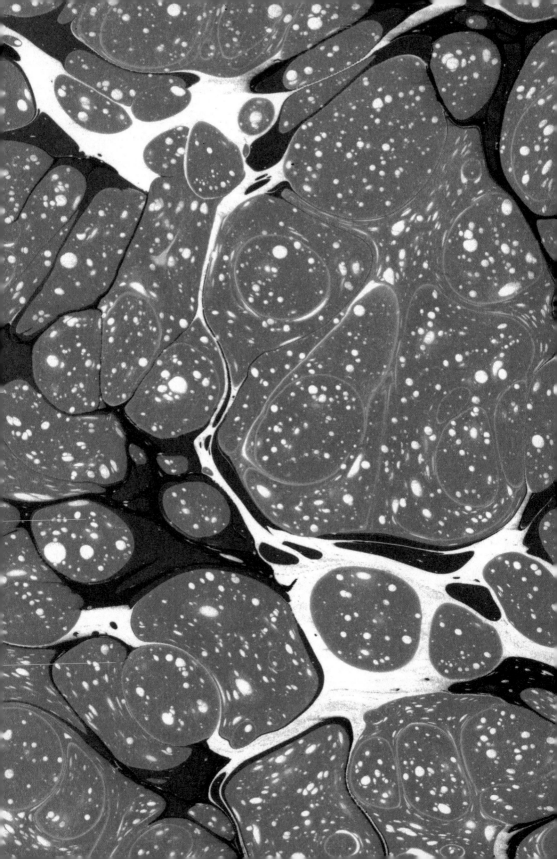